MIDNIGHT

Published by

Mesorah Publications, ltd

INTRUDERS

AVNER GOLD

FIRST EDITION
First Impression ... August 2009
Second Impression ... September 2012
Third Impression ... May 2020

Published and Distributed by
MESORAH PUBLICATIONS, LTD.
313 Regina Avenue / Rahway, N.J. 07065

Distributed in Europe by
LEHMANNS
Unit E, Viking Business Park
Rolling Mill Road
Jarow, Tyne & Wear, NE32 3DP
England

Distributed in Israel by
SIFRIATI / A. GITLER — BOOKS
POB 2351
Bnei Brak 51122

Distributed in Australia and New Zealand
by **GOLDS WORLDS OF JUDAICA**
3-13 William Street
Balaclava, Melbourne 3183
Victoria, Australia

Distributed in South Africa by
KOLLEL BOOKSHOP
Northfield Centre, 17 Northfield Avenue
Glenhazel 2192, Johannesburg, South Africa

Typography by CompuScribe at ArtScroll Studios, Ltd.
Printed in the United States of America
Bound by Sefercraft, Quality Bookbinders, Ltd., Rahway, N.J. 07065

CONTENTS

MIDNIGHT INTRUDERS

AUTHOR'S NOTE

TOWARD THE END OF THE seventeenth century, the European continent was in turmoil. In the west, the rise of French power and ambition was making England, Holland and the surrounding states jittery; a major war was brewing. In the Balkans, the Turkish Empire battled the confederation of Austria and numerous German principalities, otherwise known as the Holy Roman Empire.

The city of Budapest was the scene of a major battle in this conflict, and its Jewish community was destroyed. Half the people died, and the other half were either taken captive or driven into exile. One of the refugees was the young Rabbi Tzvi Ashkenazi, the future leading rabbi of his generation, the *gadol hador*, who would be known to history as Chacham Tzvi. This book, *Midnight Intruders*, traces the trajectory of his life.

Midnight Intruders is a groundbreaking step in the ongoing Strasbourg Saga. For the first time, the Saga comes up close to a *gadol* of such stature, but it is still a work of historical fiction; it blends the documented facts of Chacham Tzvi's life with the lives of fictional characters who interact with him and thereby bring his story to life.

The main fictional character in this book is Rabbi Amos Strasbourg, with whom readers are already familiar from the previous two books, *Scandal in Amsterdam* and *The*

Fur Traders. In this book, he forms a close friendship with Chacham Tzvi, a friendship that survives wars, wandering, separation and communal conflict in Hamburg and afterward in Amsterdam.

During this period, the massacres and expulsions were just a painful memory, and the frenzied movement of Shabbesai Tzvi, the false Messiah described in *The Impostor*, an earlier volume in the Saga, had come to an end with his conversion to Islam and his death a few years later. The Jewish communities now concentrated on strengthening their institutions and improving their economic conditions.

But the Sabbatean movement was not entirely dead. There would be periodic eruptions for many years. More than just promoting the personal acceptance of Shabbesai Tzvi as the Messiah, Sabbateanism was essentially a school of Kabbalistic thought that promulgated heretical concepts of the Almighty. It was, therefore, possible to be a Sabbatean even after Shabbesai Tzvi's death. One of these Sabbateans, Nechemiah Chiya Chayun, came to Amsterdam in the early part of the eighteenth century to publish a book of Sabbatean thought, and the result was one of the greatest communal uproars in the history of European Jewry.

Midnight Intruders follows the lives of Chacham Tzvi and Nechemiah Chayun both independently and when they cross paths until the harrowing climax of their clash in Amsterdam. It is a fast-moving book that features adventure, drama. mystery, conflict and, above all, an inspiring portrait of one of the greatest rabbis of modern Jewish history.

The information about the life of Chacham Tzvi is drawn almost entirely from *Megillas Sefer*, the autobiography of his son Rabbi Yaakov Emden, who will feature in some of the forthcoming books in the Saga. I have included many references to this work in the endnotes, especially in places that the story presents some historical people in a negative light.

The information about Chayun and other historical events is taken from general sources, which I have not enumerated. There seems to be some confusion about whether Chacham Tzvi and Chayun had met previously in Sarajevo and if they had a face-to-face confrontation in Amsterdam. For the purposes of this book, I have assumed that both events took place, and I have described them. I have also included a list of the historical characters mentioned in this book, arranged by category.

There are a number of Torah thoughts included in the story. I would not presume to put words into the mouth of Chacham Tzvi other than ordinary conversation, which I labored to portray in a manner suitable to a rabbi of such stellar stature. Chacham Tzvi's Torah opinions are drawn from *She'alos Uteshuvos Chacham Tzvi*. The Torah thoughts spoken by the fictional Rabbi Amos Strasbourg are drawn from my own *Abir Yosef* and other writings.

As always, I am exceedingly interested in the comments and criticism of my readers, who can reach me at avnergold@live.com. I make every effort to answer each person who communicates with me, but I must ask the indulgence of my correspondents if time constraints sometimes prevent a prompt response.

The challenge of writing *Midnight Intruders* was daunting but also exciting, and I feel a great sense of accomplishment. This book is especially meaningful to me on a personal level, because I am descended from Chacham Tzvi on my father's side. I ask Chacham Tzvi's forgiveness if I unintentionally wrote anything that impinges on his honor in the slightest degree, and I thank the Almighty for granting me the privilege of presenting his inspiring story to my readers.

A.G.
Lakewood, New Jersey
15 Av 5769 (2009)

★ Moscow

Baltic
Sea

TSARDOM OF
MUSCOVY

COMMONWEALTH OF
POLAND AND LITHUANIA

Poznan

Warsaw ★

Lublin

Wroclaw

Kiev

Lancut

Katowice

Krakow

Pulichev (fictional)

OTTOMAN EMPIRE

nna

Obuda

Budapest ★

MOLDAVIA

HUNGARY

Mohacs

Belgrade

WALLACHIA

Black Sea

CROATIA   SERBIA

Sarajevo ★

Danube River

BOSNIA

Dubrovnik

OTTOMAN EMPIRE

Istanbul ★

Salonika

Smyrna

Athens ★

Mediterranean Sea

PALESTINE

Yaffo

Jordan River

Yerushalayim ★
Chevron

EMPIRE

LIST OF
HISTORICAL CHARACTERS

CHACHAM TZVI'S FAMILY

Rabbi Tzvi (Chacham Tzvi) Ashkenazi
First wife and daughter (names unknown)
Rebbetzin Sarah Ashkenazi, his wife
Yaakov Ashkenazi, son (future Yavetz – Rabbi Yaakov Emden)
Rabbi Yaakov Zak Ashkenazi, father
Rebbetzin Nechamah Ashkenazi, mother
Rabbi Meshulem Zalman Mirels Neumark, father-in-law
Rabbi Zev Mirels Neumark, brother-in-law
Rabbi Binyamin Zak Ashkenazi, paternal grandfather
Rabbi Yaakov of Lublin, paternal great-grandfather
Rabbi Heschel of Krakow, paternal great-uncle
Rabbi Ephraim Hakohein of Vilna, maternal grandfather
Rabbi Eliahu Baal Shem, maternal ancestor

OTHER RABBIS

Rabbi Moshe Charif
Rabbi Shmuel Aboab
Rabbi David Oppenheim
Rabbi Naphtali Kohein
Rabbi Aharon Binyamin Wolff
Rabbi Meir Poperos
Rabbi Chaim Vital
Rabbi Shmuel Vital
Rabbi Yaakov Tzemach

Rabbi Tzvi Hirsch Chazzan
Rabbi Moshe Rothenberg
The rabbi of Smyrna
The rabbis of Yerushalayim

NECHEMIAH CHAYUN'S FAMILY

Nechemiah Chiya Chayun
Moshe Chayun, father
Rabbi Yaakov Chagiz, grandfather
Rabbi Moshe Chagiz, uncle

AMSTERDAM

Rabbi Yitzchak Aboab da Fonseca
Rabbi Yaakov Sasportas
Rabbi Shlomo Ayllon
Rabbi Aryeh Yehudah Kalisch
Leizer Shochet
Aharon de Pinto
Moshe Frankfurt
Moshe Diaz
Willem Surenhuis

OTHERS

Shmuel Oppenheim
Yosef Oppenheim
Moshe Leibushes
Ber Kohein
Furst family
Moshe Katz
Zalman ben Moshe Raphael
Chaim ben Yisrael
King Jan Sobieski of Poland
King Louis XIV of France

THE MALTESE DRAGON · 1

CAPTAIN MORTIMER MEACHAM, master of *The Maltese Dragon,* trained his spyglass on the distant horizon. The sun rode high in the cloudless sky, and the sea was awash in bright sunlight in every direction. Something caught the captain's attention. He scanned the western horizon with his spyglass, and he found what he was seeking. His back stiffened, and his breath came quickly. He examined the horizon for several long minutes. Then he turned to Amos Strasbourg, who was standing nearby and watching him with keen interest.

"You had better go below, rabbi," he said. "You'll be safer there."

Amos leaned against the ship's rail and strained to discover what the captain had seen, but he saw only the ripple and sparkle of gentle blue waves stretching off into the distance.

"What's happening, Captain Meacham?" he said. "There's nothing but water out there. Water, water and more water."

The captain shook his head and offered him the spyglass. "Here, rabbi. Take a look for yourself, and then tell me what you see."

Amos put the spyglass to his eye and pointed it in the direction the captain was indicating. At first, he saw nothing, but then he noticed a tiny black speck. As he watched, it grew perceptibly larger, and Amos thought he could see the outlines of a ship with black sails. He had never seen a ship with black sails before, and he found the sight disconcerting and even frightening.

"I see it," he said as he handed the spyglass back to the captain. "Who is it, and what do they want?"

"It's *The Black Widow.*"

Amos felt a shiver run down his spine. "The pirate ship? Mad Dog Kelly's pirate ship?"

"That's right."

"But what is he doing here? We're practically in Morocco. Doesn't Kelly usually stay close to his hideouts in Ireland?"

"That he does, old Mad Dog Kelly, may his black heart be eaten by sharks and may whatever the sharks miss rot at the bottom of the sea. Mad Dog fancies himself an Irish patriot protecting the Emerald Isle from the British, French and anyone else that might set foot there. But it's all a sham, mark my words. He's just a greedy scoundrel, and now he's coming after us."

Amos was about to ask another question, but the captain held up his hand for silence. He signaled to the first mate and issued his orders in rapid English that Amos did not catch. The first mate hurried off to execute the captain's orders, and the captain returned to his scrutiny of the western horizon. The black spot had grown larger as the speedy pirate ship closed the distance between them, and it was now recognizable as a seagoing vessel even without a spyglass. Finally, he put down the spyglass.

"Rabbi Strasbourg, I like you," he said. "You're an intelligent man, and I've enjoyed conversing with you and our occasional games of chess. But I have a crisis on my hands right now. What is your question? I'll answer one question and one question only, and then you have to go below."

"What's going on, captain?"

The captain chuckled. "Clever question. All right. There was a rumor going around the harbor of New York that our ship is carrying a vast treasure in gold and silver and that we're sailing without a naval escort. Mad Dog Kelly must have heard the rumor and decided to go after the treasure."

"Is there really such a treasure on this ship?"

"No, but Kelly thinks there is."

Amos caught his breath. "Then he'll attack us for sure. All we have is one cannon in the bow. We don't stand a chance against a fully armed pirate ship."

"We'll do our best, rabbi," said the captain. "Why don't you go below and do something useful? Say a few prayers. Maybe that will help."

Amos nodded to the captain and headed for the passage-way to the lower decks, but then he changed his mind and found an unobtrusive spot not far from the aft deckhouse from which to observe the activity.

On the main deck amidships, there were large mounds of cargo covered with canvas tarpaulins. As Amos watched, two dozen sailors armed with pistols, knives and cutlasses gathered around the tarpaulins and remained standing silently at attention while they awaited further instructions. The posture of the men indicated to Amos that they weren't ordinary sailors. They carried themselves with a military bearing that spoke of training and service in the Royal British Navy.

In fact, thought Amos, upon reflection Captain Meacham and the ship's officers all seemed to be naval people. Had they all left the navy and found new employment on merchant ships? Or were they actually naval people disguised as ordinary sailors? But why would they do such a thing?

Amos looked up and saw that *The Black Widow* was gaining rapidly on the port side of *The Maltese Dragon*. The black sails billowed out like evil demons, straining against the wind that drove them forward. There was a white insignia on one of the sails that Amos identified as the skull and crossbones favored by seagoing buccaneers. He could see lookouts high in the crow's nest training their spyglasses on *The Maltese Dragon*. Minutes later, he could make out pirates on the deck of their ship watching through their own spyglasses.

The pirate ship drew closer, and Amos could see very clearly the row of cannons bristling from its starboard side, and he had no doubt there was a similar row of cannons on the port side. He saw pirates milling about on their main deck, shouting and brandishing their weapons in the air. Amos could sense their excited bloodlust and greed across the narrowing expanse of open sea between the two ships, and he shivered.

"Now!" shouted the captain.

The sailors instantly sprang into action and scrambled over the mounds on the starboard side of the deck, which could not be easily seen by the pirate ship approaching on the port side. They snatched away the tarpaulins, revealing an array of huge cannons, piles of cannonballs and sacks of gunpowder. They wheeled the cannons to the edge of the starboard deck and secured them in place. Then they loaded and primed all the cannons.

The pirate ship loomed large on the port side, and blood-curdling screams of the eager pirates reverberated across the waves.

"Get ready, mates!" shouted the captain. "As soon as we come around, secure the cannons on the port side. There's not a moment to waste. They're smaller and faster, but we're bigger and meaner. All right, mates, now!"

The helmsman spun the wheel, and *The Maltese Dragon* turned into the wind. Amos could see the pirates on the deck of *The Black Widow* laughing at the clumsy merchant vessel trying to elude capture by turning around. As *The Maltese Dragon* went deeper into the turn, the sailors on the other side of the deck pulled away the rest of the tarpaulins and set up the second battery of cannons on the port side of the deck.

The ship came full turn until the starboard cannons were pointed almost directly at *The Black Widow*. The pirate captain, the notorious Mad Dog Kelly, stared at the huge cannons with alarm, then he screamed his orders to pull away.

"Fire!" shouted the captain of *The Maltese Dragon*.

Twenty cannons belched flame in unison, firing at the pirate ship at little more than point-blank range. The cannonballs flew across the open water with a horrible screeching noise and ripped mercilessly into the black ship. As Amos watched, one cannonball struck the forecastle of the pirate ship and instantly reduced it to a pile of splinters. Another cannonball ignited a magazine of gunpowder amidships, causing a massive explosion and setting the ship on fire. The torn and bleeding bodies of dead pirates littered the decks.

But Mad Dog Kelly was not ready to give up the fight. Amos could hear him shouting orders and encouragement to his men. "Bring her around, laddies. Their cannons are on the starboard side. We'll board them from the port side."

The burning pirate ship spun away and maneuvered to the other side of *The Maltese Dragon*, but to the horror of the surviving pirates, the port side was also bristling with cannons. The English captain gave the order, and a new barrage of cannonballs smashed into the blazing pirate ship. The sailors quickly reloaded and fired another salvo. The masts of the pirate ship came crashing down, and the raging flames licked at the deflated black sails.

The pirate ship was destroyed, writhing in its death throes amid the screams of the dying and the shouts of the desperate men lowering lifeboats into the water. But even as it lay mortally wounded, the pirates managed to fire off one salvo at *The Maltese Dragon*.

Most of the pirate cannonballs fell harmlessly into the water either in front of *The Maltese Dragon* or beyond it. But one of them struck the center of the aft deckhouse with devastating force, blowing it apart with such explosive energy that debris flew in all directions like small pieces of cannon shot.

Amos had been watching the engagement with the pirate ship from his vantage point near the deckhouse, and when it exploded, he was hurled across the deck. His body slammed against the ship's railing. A flying piece of planking struck him across the back of his neck, and he blacked out.

When he came to his senses, he saw everything in a red haze. He moved his limbs gingerly one by one to make sure they were all intact. They were painfully sore, but nothing seemed to be broken. He tried to stand up, but he was overcome by dizziness and fell back.

As his vision cleared and came into focus, he saw the pirate ship through the railing against which he lay. The ship was ablaze bow to stern. Two lifeboats had been lowered into the water, and twenty men, most of them blackened and bloodied, were crowded into each of them. The lifeboats pulled away from the burning ship and moved toward *The Maltese Dragon* several hundred feet away.

From his vantage point, lying in a heap on the deck, Amos saw the English captain standing ramrod straight against the railing amidships.

"Fire!" shouted the captain. "Blow them out of the water!"

The cannons roared, and after the sailors reloaded, the cannons roared again. Most of the cannonballs fell harmlessly into the water, spewing tall fountains of sparkling seawater, but a few of them found their mark. Both lifeboats were smashed to smithereens. Most of the pirates were killed instantly. The few that survived sustained grave injuries. They flailed about in the water, screaming for help. Captain Meacham watched impassively as their cries grew weaker and weaker until they slipped below the surface of the sea and disappeared from view.

The captain turned to his sailors with a tight smile on his lips. He touched the tips of his fingers to the brim of his cap in a casual salute.

"Well done, men," he said. "And good riddance. Carry on. We've got a ship to sail. You can leave the cannons where they are. There's no more need for deception."

Amos struggled to his feet, holding the railing for balance, but another wave of dizziness swept over him. As he staggered forward, he felt himself slipping into a pool of blackness, and he lost consciousness.

When he awoke, he was no longer on the deck. He lay on a narrow cot in a cabin redolent with strange smells. The fading light coming through the porthole told him that several hours had passed. The ship's doctor was looking down at him.

"Lie still, my good man," said the doctor. "Welcome to the sick bay. There don't seem to be any parts missing, so I expect you can go back to your cabin in a few hours."

The door opened, and the captain came in. He sat down on a chair, crossed his legs, pulled a pipe from his pocket and stuck it between his lips.

"So how are you doing, rabbi?"

"Could be better, but could be worse. The doctor says I'll be fine."

"Good," said the captain. "I'm in the mood for a game of chess."

"Right now?"

"I wouldn't mind that. It would increase my chances of winning. But I'll wait until tomorrow. So was this the first sea battle you ever saw?"

"It wasn't much of a battle, was it?" said Amos. "More like an execution."

The captain's eyes narrowed. "Mad Dog Kelly was a menace to sea travelers. We spread a rumor about treasure and lured him into following a defenseless merchant vessel, and then we blasted him out of the water. Do you have a problem with what we did?"

Amos shook his head. "No, I don't. I'm only sorry I stayed on deck to watch. If I'd listened to you and gone below, I wouldn't be lying here now."

"And if you'd been any closer to the deckhouse, you wouldn't be lying here now either. We'd be scraping what's left of you from the deck. There were two men inside the deckhouse, and you wouldn't have enjoyed the sight of them. We sewed up their remains in two bags and buried them at sea."

Amos shivered. "Those cannonballs are like black devils, screaming as they fly through the air until they smash into their targets."

"Aye, that they are, rabbi. That they are. Beautiful black devils with long tails of fire. I love the sight of them."

"Well, I hope never to see them again."

"Not much chance of avoiding it, rabbi. Not these days. Maybe if you'd stayed in New York, maybe you could have avoided battles and cannon fire. Maybe. But you're going back to Europe, and mark my words, rabbi, Europe will be in flames for many years. You're from Amsterdam, aren't you?"

"Yes, I am."

"So what are you doing on a ship headed for Venice?"

"It's a long story," said Amos.

The captain lit his pipe and leaned back. "We've got time."

"Well, we have a cousin in a small town in Poland called Pulichev. His name is Rabbi Shlomo Strasbourg. He is old and very wise, a great man and a famous scholar. My father wrote to me from Amsterdam that he heard our cousin was in poor health and that he was going to visit him, perhaps for the last time on this earth. He suggested I meet him in Poland and pay my respects as well. But he didn't want me to travel through Amsterdam and across Germany, because he was afraid that Germany was on the verge of becoming a battleground. He believed he could get to Poland before hostilities broke out, but he was afraid that by the time I got to Amsterdam, it would be too dangerous to travel across Germany to Poland."

"Your father is well-informed," said the captain. "King Louis XIV of France is way too powerful, and he's out to conquer as much of Europe as he possibly can. According to my information, Austria, the German states, the Netherlands, Sweden, Spain and Portugal are forming an alliance against France. And there's talk that England might join as well. It's going to be all of Europe against the French, and even so, it won't be easy to contain them. Europe is a powder keg, and it's about to explode."

"That's what my father wrote," said Amos. "Instead of traveling across Germany, he suggested I go north to Poland through the Balkans. My plan is to disembark when you stop in the port of Dubrovnik on the eastern coast of the Adriatic Sea and head overland through Bosnia, with perhaps a quick stop in the Jewish community of Sarajevo, to Belgrade in Serbia and then north to Budapest and on to Poland."

"You know, there's risk of war in the Balkans as well," said the captain. "The Turks have drawn back after their defeat at Vienna three years ago, and the Imperial armies haven't pursued them too far. But that could change any day. You could be heading directly into a war zone."

SHADOWS OF INDIFFERENCE · 2

Amos tried to ignore the jarring lurches of the wagon as it rumbled over the rutted road. Sitting on a makeshift bench nailed to the floor planks of the wagon, his feet outstretched, his back against the rough boards that formed the sides of the wagon, he reminisced about his experiences in the British colony of New York and speculated about what life held in store for him back in Amsterdam. But every few minutes, another violent movement of the wagon brought him back to the painful present.

That morning, after weeks of trekking through the rugged Balkan Mountains, he had finally reached Belgrade, the capital of the Turkish province of Serbia, situated at the point where the Danube River turned east. He was now less than two hundred miles downriver from Budapest, the capital of the Turkish province of Hungary. He had blessed his good fortune in quickly finding an opening in a wagon going north, but after two agonizing hours of heaving and pitching under the broiling summer sun, he suspected that he might have chosen too quickly and not too wisely. He couldn't decide which was worse, the pain in his back or the exhaustion.

He looked up at the back of the Turkish driver sitting high on his bench, a red fez clamped on his tightly curled hair, a wide green sash wrapped around his waist. The driver snapped the reins at the two gray mules that pulled the wagon and muttered at them in a language Amos did not understand.

As they left Belgrade behind, they entered a flat, verdant plain astride the Danube River. If all went well, Amos told himself, they could be in Budapest before Shabbos. There was a thriving Jewish community in Budapest, and he planned to rest there for a few days or perhaps a week before pushing on to Pulichev in Poland.

There were two other passengers in the wagon, a burly man in a raggedy shirt and patched trousers and a wizened old woman in a long black dress, her head wrapped in a white Muslim *hijab*.

The burly man stared at Amos. "We'll be traveling together for days, if not more," he said. "At least, we should know our companions. So let's make the introductions. I'm Zoran Miroslavic from Belgrade. Some people call me a peddler, but I like to call myself a traveling merchant. And what's your name?"

"I'm Amos Strasbourg from Amsterdam. I'm a . . . a rabbi."

"Thought you were Jewish," said the peddler. "What're you doing here? You're a long way from Amsterdam."

"I'm on my way to visit a sick relative in Poland."

"You picked a bad route, my friend. There's fighting up north. The Imperial armies are finally on the move. Two years ago, after the Poles and the Germans defeated the Turks outside Vienna back in 1683, Emperor Leopold tried to push the Turks out of Budapest as well. Didn't do him much good. He had to run back to Vienna with his tail between his legs. The exalted emperor is good at sitting back and letting others — like King Jan Sobieski of Poland — fight his battles for him. Now that Sobieski, there's a great general for you. If not for his victory at Vienna, the Turks would be at the gates of Paris by now."

"That's what they say," said Amos.

"And that's how it is. Trust me. I heard there were three hundred thousand Turks at the siege of Vienna, and Sobieski's cavalry just cut them to ribbons. But Sobieski's back in Poland, and old Leopold isn't much good on his own." The peddler shrugged his shoulders and made a doubtful face. "But now it's 1686. He's had three years to work up the courage to make another push against the Turks, and it looks as if he's going to try. I've heard people say that he dreams about driving the Turks clear out of the Balkans, all the way back to Istanbul. Pipe dreams, I say. Fat chance of that ever happening in our lifetime. But the brave emperor is trying. Last I heard, the Imperial army was about forty miles west of Budapest. Why do you think these roads are so torn up?"

"Why?" said Amos.

"Because the Turks have been lugging heavy cannons up to the front. Those black monsters will just chew up even the best roads." He turned to the old woman. "How about you, grandmother? Who are you?"

The old woman gave him a nasty look and looked down at her knuckles.

"What's your name, grandmother?" he persisted.

"I'm not your grandmother," she snapped. "If you must know, my name is Aygul Chughtai, and I'm a distant cousin of Sultan Mehmet. And that's about as much as I want to say to you. Leave me alone."

"Well, if you're the sultan's cousin," said the peddler, "maybe you can have him send us a royal carriage with real springs and some fine horses to take us the rest of the way to Budapest. And maybe you can give your two traveling companions a ride in comfort. Eh, grandmother, what do you say?"

He threw back his head and laughed until tears ran from his eyes. The old woman spat at him and turned away.

The traffic on the road was light, and for the next two hours, they made good headway. Amos conversed politely with the peddler when he wasn't looking into the small Chumash he carried with him at all times. For the most part, the peddler did the talking, regaling Amos with stories about his adventures and exploits. Amos gave hardly any credence to the peddler's boasts, but he did respond with polite comments and expressions of interest from time to time. The old woman, true to her word, remained absolutely silent, her eyes flashing disapproval, her lips pressed together as if she were sucking a lemon.

In the early afternoon, traffic came to a halt as a long column of Turkish soldiers and military equipment streamed into the road from a secondary road.

"Seems like we're in for a little wait," said Amos.

"That's for sure," said the peddler. "That road leads southwest across the mountains to Bosnia. The Turks are obviously stripping all their garrisons and sending them north to reinforce Budapest. We're headed into trouble, my friend. Do you want to turn back?"

Amos shook his head. "I have to get to Poland," he said. "My father is expecting me. And I want to see my kinsman as well. If it seems as if we're getting too close to the fighting, I can always turn east and come around through Walachia and the Ukraine."

The peddler shrugged. "Maybe I'll join you. And maybe not. It depends, you know, on whether I see an opportunity to make money off the army. Usually, there are plenty of opportunities, if you have the right merchandise to sell them."

After the army passed, the travelers pushed on for several hours until darkness forced them to stop at a roadside inn for the night. They left early the next morning, when the horizon was still tinged with pink, in order to make up for lost time.

The skies were overcast and the air warm with dampness as they got under way. A steady rain soon began to fall. The rutted road turned into a river of mud, and their pace slowed to a crawl. They wrapped themselves in coarse horse blankets and rode in exhausted silence, too miserable to sleep.

As the morning wore on, the skies cleared, and the hot sun reappeared. Looking back, Amos could see that it was still raining to the south, but they were past the rain. The condition of the road improved, and they began to make better time.

Amos hung his sodden blanket over the side of the wagon to dry. He closed his eyes and tried to fall asleep, but the relentless lurching of the wagon kept him awake. The peddler, however, had no such problems. He stretched out on his bench, and within moments, he was snoring loudly.

"Driver!" the old woman shouted.

The driver turned his head. "What do you want, Your Highness?" he said with a broad smile.

The old woman ignored his jibe. "Where are we stopping tonight?"

"Novi Zemlica, I hope. If the mules don't die on us before we get there."

She dismissed him with a wave of the hand. "Go back to your driving, and keep your eyes on the road."

The old woman turned to Amos and fixed him with a sinister stare.

"You seem like a good man, not like that snoring blowhard over there. Anyone could see that he was lying through his teeth yesterday when he was telling you all those stories about himself, but you didn't call him a liar. You seem to be kind, polite and respectful."

Amos smiled. "That's very nice of you."

The old woman snorted. "I'm not a nice person. Oh no, not me. I'm an old woman who is full of wind and fire. I'm a seeker, a traveler of long distances, a messenger of doom."

Amos was at a loss for a moment. "Well, I'm pleased to meet you," he said at last.

"I'm sure you are," she said, her voice cracked and rasping. "Are you really a rabbi?"

"I am."

"You didn't seem so sure yesterday."

"I'm an ordained rabbi," Amos explained, "but I'm not sure yet if I want to be a practicing rabbi. I think I do, but I haven't decided yet."

"Well, you're old enough to know your own mind, don't you think?"

"I suppose I am."

The old woman grunted. "Well, it's your life. I don't have to worry about your life. My own life keeps me busy." She lowered her voice and added in a conspiratorial whisper, "I'm in danger, you know."

Amos didn't know what to say, so he said nothing.

"What's the matter, rabbi?" the old woman snapped at him. She quickly looked up at the driver to see if he had heard her. Then she lowered her voice again. "Didn't you hear me? Are you deaf or something? Don't you have anything to say?"

"I beg your pardon. Did you want me to say something about your being in danger?"

"Well, you can't just ignore it, can you? And keep your voice down. You never know who's listening. Look here, rabbi. Someone tells you that she's in danger, and you just yawn and smile politely. What kind of a man are you?"

Amos fidgeted. "I'm really sorry. I didn't mean to make light of your situation. Would you like to talk about it?"

"I would. You see, I'm in danger."

"In danger?"

She leaned forward and whispered. "I'm being followed."

"Followed?"

"What are you, an echo? Say something of your own, rabbi. Don't just repeat what I say."

"I'm trying to think of the right thing to say. Um, do you know who's following you?"

"Now we're getting somewhere, rabbi. I have a pretty good idea of who's following me. You see, I know a dangerous secret."

"A secret?"

"There goes the echo again."

Amos squirmed. "What kind of secret?"

"Now you're asking good questions. Did you hear me say before that I'm a distant cousin of the sultan?"

"Yes, I did."

"Did you believe it?"

"Um, I suppose I had no reason not to believe it."

"Well, it wasn't true."

Amos arched his eyebrows. "Really? I'm surprised. You looked like you were telling the truth."

The old woman rubbed her hands together with glee. "Now this is getting better. Oh yes, much better. You thought I was telling the truth, even though I wasn't. Do you know why?"

"I'm completely mystified."

"Because it was partially true."

"Indeed? And which part was true?"

She leaned forward again. "I'm a relative of the sultan," she whispered, "but I'm not a distant cousin. I'm his older sister."

Amos opened his eyes wide in feigned amazement. The old woman was clearly demented, but there was no harm in humoring her.

"His older sister!" he exclaimed.

"I knew you'd be shocked," she said in a triumphant whisper. She put one gnarled finger to her lips. "Don't tell anyone. It would put you in danger, too. You see, I know a terrible secret about the sultan. After all, who would know about it if not his own sister? Oh, it's an awful secret. Your hair would stand on end if I told you the sultan's secret, but I won't tell it to you. At least not yet. The sultan knows that if I reveal his secret to the world he'll be deposed and probably assassinated. So that's why I'm in danger. My own brother is trying to kill me."

"Well, he has to find you first."

She smiled with delight and wagged her finger at him. "You're a smart one, rabbi. Oh yes, I was right about you. If he can't find me, he can't harm me. So I travel in disguise. I also use a false name. I told that windbag that my name is Aygul Chughtai. But that's not my real name. I don't tell anyone my name or that I'm the sultan's sister. Not a soul. If I would, I could be killed the next day. Who knows? Maybe even the next hour. I have to be careful."

"Yes, that's very important."

"How about you? Are you careful?"

"I ... think so."

The old woman cackled. "You think so? You think so? A careful person doesn't just think so. He makes sure he's careful. Are you always on your guard? Do you watch for midnight intruders?"

"Well, I mean ..."

"That's a yes or no question. Do you watch for midnight intruders?"

"I'm not sure."

"You're not sure? That means that you don't watch for them. You know something? I'll wager you don't even know about midnight intruders."

"All right. I admit it. I never heard about midnight intruders. Would you like to tell me what they are?"

"Fine," said the old woman. "I'll tell you. I know many things that other people don't know. I'm a wise old woman, can't you tell? Did you know I'm a thirty-third generation descendant from the prophet Mohammed?"

"No, I didn't know that."

"Oh yes, indeed. Well, it's not for nothing that I have so much wisdom. It's my heritage from my holy ancestors. I can see things that will happen in the future. I know things about people. I know that you've had trouble in your life. And I know that there's more trouble coming your way."

Amos smiled. "You can say that about anyone in the world."

"Don't mock me, rabbi," she snapped.

"I didn't mean any disrespect," Amos quickly added. "I was commenting on the irony of the human condition. Even the most fortunate of people are always dealing with troubles. And if they have no troubles, if everything is perfect, if their lives are empty of any kind of struggle, then that itself is very serious trouble."

The old woman gave him a sharp look, then she nodded sagely. "That is a very deep thought, rabbi. I see that you are truly a man of wisdom. Destiny has brought us together for a good reason. You deserve to know about the midnight intruders. Do you want to hear about it?"

"Of course."

"Do you really mean that or are you just humoring me?"

"I want to hear it. I really do."

The old woman spat over the side of the wagon and smiled at Amos. Her face crinkled up into a patchwork of furrows and wrinkles, and her lips retracted to reveal that she had no front teeth between her canines.

"Listen to me, rabbi," she said. "No matter where you are, beware of midnight intruders. That's my message to you. Beware of midnight intruders."

"You still haven't told me what these midnight intruders are. Are you talking about robbers? Assassins?"

The old woman shook her head. "Robbers? Assassins? No, midnight intruders are much worse. I spend my whole life running away from assassins. I don't really worry too much about robbers. I'm just a poor woman. What can they get from me? But I do worry about assassins every day, because my brother wants to kill me. So I'm on my guard, and they can't get to me. In a way, midnight intruders are more insidious than robbers or assassins. They come under cover of darkness, not the darkness of the night but the dark midnight of indifference. They put on friendly faces and warm smiles, and you think they're harmless, you think they're your friends, but they have evil intentions. They'll stab you in the back, and you'll never see it coming."

"Have you ever met any of these midnight intruders?"

"Oh yes, I have. I look for them, and I usually find them. But I can never be sure. Who knows? Maybe you're a midnight intruder, rabbi."

"You think I'm a midnight intruder?" said Amos.

"Are you?"

"I think you know the answer."

"And why would I know the answer, rabbi?"

"Because of your wisdom."

The old woman squinted at Amos, then she rocked back and forth, back and forth.

"You're not a midnight intruder," she said at last. "But you are wise. Use your wisdom to find the midnight intruders, the enemies that you think are your friends. And if you find one, don't relax your vigilance. Where there is one, there may be others lurking in the shadows."

"The shadows of indifference," said Amos.

"That's right, rabbi. The shadows of indifference. You catch on very quickly. So remember, beware of the midnight intruders."

The peddler stirred, and his eyes fluttered open. "Shadows? Intruders? What are you two discussing? What shadows? What intruders?"

The old woman clamped her mouth shut and turned away. She did not say another word until they stopped for the night in Novi Zemlica. The next morning, there was no sign of the old woman. She had not slept in her bed, and no one knew where she had gone. She had disappeared without a trace.

AN OFFER OF FRIENDSHIP · 3

Buda Castle, the medieval palace of the Hungarian kings, sat behind crumbling stone walls on a hill overlooking Budapest. One hundred and sixty years had passed since the Hungarian kingdom had fallen to the Ottoman Turks in 1526 after the Battle of Mohacs. Ever since, the Turks had used the castle sporadically as stables, barracks or warehouses, but for the most part, they allowed it to fall into disrepair and decay. It now loomed behind Amos like a gap-toothed derelict as he walked through the Jewish quarter in the ancient town of Obuda, just north of Budapest. It was already Thursday, and he would have to spend Shabbos in Obuda. Someone in the synagogue would undoubtedly invite him, and he would be on his way again by Sunday. In a week or two, he would be in Pulichev.

Finding the synagogue proved to be an easy task; Amos did not even have to ask directions. The day was fading fast, and he simply followed the Jewish men streaming out of their homes. The synagogue was in a modest building on a street paved with cobblestones. Its presence was identified by a small sign in the window. Amos found an empty seat at the end of a bench toward the back. He pushed the satchel with his personal belongings under the bench but kept his *tallis* bag clutched to his heart.

By the time Minchah started, there were about forty men in the synagogue. Most of them were dressed in the rough clothes and dusty caps of laborers. They held their Siddurim in calloused hands black with grime that only came off after intense scrubbing every Friday. A few prosperous-looking men dressed in pressed broadcloth suits, ruffled white cuffs and tall black hats took seats in the front. The rabbi was sitting against the east wall near the *aron kodesh* and surveying the congregation with gentle eyes as his lips moved with the words of the prayer. A tall young man in a long dark frock hovered near him. Amos could not get a good look at the young man, because he stood facing the rabbi with his back to the congregation.

Immediately after Minchah, the young man approached Amos with his hand extended and a warm smile on his face.

"*Shalom aleichem,*" he said, and he shook Amos' hand vigorously. "Welcome to Alt-Ofen; that's what we call the town of Obuda; it's the old German name for it. My name is Tzvi Ashkenazi. My father is the rabbi. His name is Rabbi Yaakov Zak Ashkenazi. He would like to meet you."

"*Aleichem shalom,*" said Amos as he grasped the young man's hand. "My name is Amos Strasbourg, and I would be honored to meet your father." He reached for the satchel under the bench.

"Don't be concerned about your satchel," said the young man. "It'll be safe right where it is."

Amos looked around the synagogue and cast a nervous glance at his satchel. The young man bent down and grabbed hold of the handles.

"If it makes you more comfortable," he said, "I'll hold it for you."

"No, I can hold it," Amos protested.

The young man grinned at him. "Absolutely not," he said. "You're our guest. I can't let you carry your own bags. I mean, what kind of a host would I be if I did that? Come, my father is expecting us."

He lifted the satchel easily and ran ahead to the waiting rabbi. Amos followed close behind. The people were settling down to wait for Maariv. Some were saying Tehillim, others gathered in groups to learn Mishnayos, and some just chatted amiably as they waited for complete darkness to fall.

"Father, this is Amos Strasburg," said the young man.

"Strasbourg?" said the rabbi. "From Pulichev?"

"My ancestors," said Amos. "Rabbi Shlomo Strasbourg is our cousin. In fact, I'm on way to Pulichev right now."

"He's a great man, an extraordinary person. We've only met two or three times, but he made a deep impression on me. And how about you? Where are you from?"

"Amsterdam."

"Ah, then you must be the son of Rabbi Mordechai Strasbourg."

"Indeed, I am," said Amos, pleased that the rabbi knew of his father, who was not nearly as famous and celebrated as Rabbi Shlomo Strasbourg.

"A fine man, your father. A fine man, a *talmid chacham.* The Strasbourgs are all *talmidei chachamim,* as I'm sure you are as well."

Amos colored. "I try not to be an embarrassment to my ancestors and my family, but I can't say that I measure up to their standards."

"A good answer," said the rabbi. "Spoken like a *talmid chacham.* And from now on, I will call you Rav Amos, as you deserve to be called." He stroked his beard thoughtfully. "So you're going to visit your cousin in Pulichev. "

"Yes, I am."

"And you've chosen to travel to Poland through Hungary? That is somewhat unusual."

"Well, I'm not actually coming directly from Amsterdam. I've been in New York for most of the past year. My father asked me to meet him in Pulichev on my way back home. He expects to be there for Rosh Hashanah."

The rabbi raised his eyebrows. "Oh? Is everything all right there? Is something amiss with Rabbi Shlomo Strasbourg?"

"I don't think it is anything immediate," said Rav Amos. "It's just that he's getting old, and he's not in the best of health. My father wants to spend some time with him while he is still in this world, and he suggested I do the same."

"I understand. But why are you here in Hungary?"

"My father heard that war clouds are gathering over the western part of Europe, what with France growing stronger and more aggressive all the time. He thought the southern route through the Balkans and Hungary would be safer, but it seems events have overtaken us."

"Yes, it does seem that way, doesn't it? The Imperial armies are approaching and threatening the city, and we're expecting the Turks to mount a counterattack any day now. There will probably be another battle not too far from Budapest in the coming days. I suggest you stay with us for a while, maybe a week or so. Rest your weary bones. By then the Turks will have driven off the Austrians. They usually do, may the Almighty be at their side."

"Are the Turks better for our people?" asked Rav Amos.

"Yes. In general, I would say yes. They let us worship as we wish and engage in commerce without interference, as long as we pay the taxes. The Austrians hate us. The Turks do not. Keep us company for a while, Rav Amos. In a week or so, the roads to Poland should be clear."

Rav Amos looked uncertain. "I wouldn't want to be a burden."

The rabbi waved his protest away. "You won't be a burden. You'll stay with my son. He has a large house and servants." He looked at his son. "Yes, Tzvi? Is he invited to you?"

"Of course, Father," said the young man. "You know my door is open."

The rabbi turned to Rav Amos and smiled. "Sure, I know. I wouldn't have offered if I didn't think he'd be eager to have you. It isn't often that he gets the opportunity to spend some serious time with a young *talmid chacham* his age. Just don't let him keep you up all hours of the night."

"I'm so tired from the journey that I think it'll be a while before I can keep my eyes open for any length of time." Rav Amos smiled at the young man. "I'm really grateful for your hospitality, Rav Tzvi."

"Think nothing of it," said the young man. "It is I who should be grateful to you. It will be a true pleasure to have you."

"You know, Rav Amos," said the rabbi. "Tzvi was standing here without saying a word, and you might have thought he was a simple fellow. Well, let me tell you, he is a very respectful son. He was just holding his peace out of respect for his father. He never contradicts me or even interrupts me.[1] When I'm talking he is usually quiet unless I ask him to speak, but he is the farthest you can imagine from a simple fellow, and we're proud of him. He's a brilliant young man, a genius, a sponge full of Torah. Wherever you touch him, Torah comes out. He has a phenomenal reputation although he is young. Everyone knows he's destined to be one of the great Torah leaders of the generation."

The rabbi's son blushed, and he looked down at his shoes.

"Tell me, Rav Amos," said the rabbi. "We have a few minutes before Maariv. Are you up to hearing a question of Halachah that came up today?"

"Yes, I am," said Rav Amos, "as long as I don't have to give the answer."

The rabbi laughed. "This is not a test, Rav Amos. What else should Jewish men discuss when they have a little time to talk? We've already said all that needs to be said about the

Austrians and the Turks. Enough darkness. It's time for some light. Let's talk in learning."

"I am eager to talk in learning with someone like you. I've been deprived of that pleasure for a long time. Too long. What was the question?"

"A man came to me last week," said the rabbi. "He had promised to give an amount of money to charity equal to the value of his home. So how do we determine the value of his home?"

"We ask three expert real estate appraisers," said Rav Amos. "That's what the Rambam says."[2]

"That's right," said the rabbi. "We got the house appraised. It's quite a nice house. It was valued at three hundred ducats."

Rav Amos knitted his brows. "So that's the amount he has to give to charity. What is the question?"

The rabbi chuckled. "Is anything ever so simple? A neighbor heard that the house was being appraised, and he thought it was for sale. The neighbor thought it would be perfect for his elderly parents, so he offered four hundred ducats for the house. So is the house worth three hundred ducats or four hundred? How much does its owner have to give to charity?"

"An interesting question," said Rav Amos. "A house is not like a loaf of bread that has an exact price. So is the value established by what most people will pay for it, which is the appraisal, or by even a single serious offer?"

The rabbi exchanged glances with his son and nodded. "You put it very well," he said. "That is exactly the question."

Rav Amos closed his eyes and rubbed his right temple. "I think … hmm, yes … I think there's an argument regarding guaranteed sales in the Gemara.[3] It involves a creditor who accepted a house worth five hundred *zuz* as payment for a loan of a thousand *zuz*, and the Gemara seems to rule that the real value is what most people will pay. Five hundred in that case."

The rabbi embraced Rav Amos and kissed him on his forehead. "Beautiful. Spoken like a true Strasbourg. That is exactly what my Tzvi said. And you are both exactly right. It's an honor to have you with us, Rav Amos. We'll talk some more later. Maariv is about to start."

That night, Rav Amos did not go to sleep immediately, as he had predicted he would. Instead, he sat up late talking with Rav Tzvi Ashkenazi in his study about the difficult topics in Gemara they had learned, and Rav Amos was dazzled by the brilliance of the rabbi's young son, the incredible scope of his knowledge, the sharpness of his mind, his amazing ability to explain complex and original ideas succinctly and with perfect clarity. He had no doubt that Rav Tzvi would fulfill and even surpass his father's predictions.

It was almost midnight when the lone candle sputtered. The flame was about to be submerged in the pool of liquid wax to which the candle had been reduced, and in its last flickering light, Rav Tzvi looked up at the pendulum clock on the wall. He gasped.

"I'm such a poor host," he said. "Here you are, exhausted from your travels, and I'm keeping you up. Please forgive me, but I don't often have the opportunity of spending a few hours talking in learning with someone like you. Alt-Ofen is not Vilna, you know."

"The pleasure is all mine," said Rav Amos. "You are an incredible *talmid chacham*. I've never met anyone quite like you."

Rav Tzvi smiled and stood up. "You're just being kind," he said. "Come into the kitchen. My wife left us a platter of honey cakes. I'll make us some tea, and you can tell me something about yourself."

In the kitchen, Rav Tzvi lit a fresh candle. He brewed some tea, and they sat down at a tiny table in the corner. Rav Amos looked around at the gleaming new kitchen. His eyes widened when he saw a pendulum clock on the wall that was identical to the one in the study.

"I see you've noticed my clocks," said Rav Tzvi.

"Well, you don't often see clocks of that quality," said Rav Amos. "In fact, these are the new kinds that have second hands. You hardly ever see such clocks at all. And you've got two of them."

Rav Tzvi laughed. "Actually, we have three. There is one more in the dining room. My wife comes from a wealthy family, and we can afford more than most people can. I don't really need many material things, but the clocks are important to me. I think a person should always be aware of the passage of time. As the Sages say, 'The day is short and the things that need to be accomplished are many.'[4] Here, have some tea before it cools off. We'll have to keep our voices down. My wife and my little girl are sleeping upstairs. They're both light sleepers."

Rav Amos nodded. He took a sip of the tea and put down his cup. "You know, I'm at a little disadvantage here. You're familiar with the Strasbourg family, but I really don't know anything about your family. You remarked before that Alt-Ofen isn't Vilna. Why did you mention Vilna? Is your family originally from there?"

"Yes, we are from Vilna. And I'll be glad to tell you anything you want to know. Have you ever heard of Rabbi Ephraim Hakohein of Vilna, the author of *She'alos Uteshuvos Shaar Ephraim*?"

"Of course," said Rav Amos. "Who hasn't? He was the head of the *beis din* of Vilna. I heard that he had a record of his lineage all the way back to Aharon Hakohein. Pretty amazing if it's true."[5]

Rav Tzvi nodded. "Oh, it's true. That was my mother's father."

"Really? Did you ever see the records?"

"Unfortunately, I didn't. My grandfather fled Vilna during the Cossack attacks about thirty-five years ago. The records were lost. They were lucky to get away with their lives. My father's father was also one of the great *talmidei chachamim* of Vilna. His name was Rabbi Binyamin Zak Ashkenazi."[6]

"Zak? An unusual name."

"It's a contraction of the words *zera kodesh*, holy descendants. My family originally came from Germany, that's why we're called Ashkenazi. Over the years and the generations, there was a tremendous amount of pressure on the Jews of Germany to turn away from the Almighty and His Torah. The name Zak testifies to the unwavering faithfulness of my ancestors throughout the generations. My grandfather was a *talmid* of Rabbi Yaakov, the head of the *beis din* of Lublin, and eventually married his daughter. Rabbi Yaakov's son, my great-uncle, was the famous Rabbi Heschel of Krakow."[7]

Rav Amos took another sip of his tea. "You come from quite an illustrious family. It's no wonder that you are who you are."

"You're embarrassing me," said Rav Tzvi. "Whatever little I've achieved has been through hard work under the tutelage of my father and grandfather, of my teachers and then on my own. From my illustrious ancestors I inherited a special responsibility to live up to their standards."

"Yes, that — and a good brain."

Rav Tzvi laughed. "Well, I don't know how good my brain is, but I try to give it a lot of exercise."

Rav Amos chuckled. "Tell me, Rav Tzvi, isn't —"

"Pardon me for interrupting you," said Rav Tzvi. "Please call me Tzvi, and I'll call you Amos. We're both young and close in age. Friends call each by their simple first names. How old are you, if I may ask?"

"Thirty-seven."

"And I'm thirty. There's not even ten years between us. Someday, when we're old men and hopefully worthy of a little respect for the Torah we accumulate, we can call each other Rav in public. How's that sound to you?"

Rav Amos bit his lip and swallowed hard, a little overwhelmed by the gracious expression of friendship from this extraordinary young man. In his heart, he had the feeling that this was a life-changing moment for him, that his future was being defined for him and that a whole new world of opportunity was opening up for him in many ways.

"It sounds really good," he said at last. "You do me a very great honor by considering me your friend, but how can we be friends if you're here in Budapest and I'm in Amsterdam?"

"Friendship," said Rav Tzvi, "is a profound bond between two people that cannot be broken by separation in time and distance. Sometimes, it takes months or years to develop. And sometimes, when there is an instinctive sense of connection, it can take only an hour or two of learning Torah together. And then you're friends for life, even if you see each other only once in a while or even never. You can communicate by letters, and you know, people often express their thoughts and feelings in letters better than they do in person."

"Yes, that's true."

"I don't offer my friendship lightly, but I'm offering it to you." Rav Tzvi extended his hand. "I'm doing it because it feels right."

Rav Amos grasped the extended hand and shook it warmly. He tried to speak, but the words choked in his throat. He felt moisture gather behind his eyelids, and he looked down into his teacup so that Rav Tzvi should not notice the intensity of his emotional reaction.

If Rav Tzvi noticed, he made no mention of it. Instead, he changed the subject.

"Did you ever hear of Rabbi Eliahu Baal Shem?"

"The head of the *beis din* of Chelm? The one who made a *golem*?"

"Yes, that's the one."

"He lived a long time ago," said Rav Amos. "What about him?"

"He passed away about two hundred years ago. My mother's father was a descendant of his."

"And you as well," said Rav Amos.

"Of course. And I as well. Did you ever hear the story of his *golem*?"

Rav Amos shook his head. "I'm afraid not."

"I don't know all the details," said Rav Tzvi. "I'll just tell you the parts that I know. I know that he molded a man out of clods of earth. He attached a paper with the Name of the Almighty to his forehead and brought him to life. This creature was unable to speak, but he understood everything my ancestor said and served him hand and foot with absolute obedience. As time went on, my grandfather noticed that the *golem* was steadily growing stronger and larger. My grandfather became concerned that the *golem* would become dangerous and beyond control. So he jumped onto the *golem* and tore the paper with the Name from his forehead. The *golem* struggled against his creator and master, and in the struggle, he scratched my grandfather across the cheek. My grandfather was right. The *golem* had developed a mind of his own. But my grandfather had managed to tear the holy paper from his forehead while it could still be done, and the golem was immediately reduced to the mound of earth from which he had been formed."[8]

"That's an amazing story," said Rav Amos. "Are you sure it's really true?"

"Absolutely. It's been told from father to son in my family for generations. Everyone the story passed through was a reliable *talmid chacham*. You know, I sometimes think about that *golem* and whether it could be considered a Jew or even a human being. You know, of course, that the Gemara mentions that Rava made a *golem*."[9]

Rav Amos nodded. "Yes, I do. But the Gemara doesn't clarify what the status of that *golem* was."

"True." Rav Tzvi took a sip of his tea. "So that's our story."

"Your family came straight to Hungary from Vilna?"

"No, they were refugees, and they wandered for a while. They found peace and safety in Trebic in Moravia where my grandfather and his family were guests in the home of a wealthy patron who wanted my grandfather to learn Torah with his son. Then my grandfather was accepted as the rabbi of Broda, also in Moravia. And then, he was invited to become the rabbi of Alt-Ofen."[10]

"And your father?"

"My father had a harrowing experience during those times, but let's save that story for a different time. My father came along with his father-in-law from Moravia here to Alt-Ofen. When my grandfather passed away eight years ago, my father became the rabbi."

"And you? Where do you fit into this picture?"

Rav Tzvi smiled. "I'll tell you my life story tomorrow. Now, I want to hear yours. Tell me about your journey until you arrived at the age of thirty-seven."

Rav Amos fidgeted, but he knew he could not avoid talking about himself after accepting Rav Tzvi's offer of friendship.

"Let's see, where should I begin?" Rav Amos began. "I was born in Amsterdam, where my father is one of the assistant rabbis. My father sent me to the Etz Chaim Yeshivah, which belonged to the Portuguese — you know, the Sephardic — community of Amsterdam. My father felt the Sephardic *yeshivah* was better than the Ashkenazic one at that time, and he wanted me to learn Torah at the highest level."

"I understand," said Rav Tzvi. "My father sent me to the Sephardic *yeshivah* in Salonika, because he felt I'd benefit from it. Besides, it's good to know something about the Jewish people outside your own little circle."[11]

"Exactly. My father said that to me many times. Broaden your horizons. Learn to have appreciation, respect and tolerance for religious Jews who have different customs and traditions. In Etz Chaim, my *rosh midrash* was Rabbi Yitzchak Aboab da Fonseca. About fifteen years ago, he became the chief rabbi of Amsterdam, which he is still today. When I was sixteen, my father sent me to study with Rabbi Shlomo Strasbourg in Pulichev for a year, and when I was seventeen I went to the *yeshivah* of Rabbi Moshe Charif in Krakow. I was there for four years. Then I went back to Amsterdam."

"That's a pretty solid background. So that means that the Shabbesai Tzvi business happened about the time you arrived in Krakow."

"Yes. Oh, there were plenty of rumblings before, but he declared himself to be Mashiach right after I came to Krakow. There was quite an uproar, but our rabbis were against him. We were not allowed to talk about it in *yeshivah*. How about you, Tzvi? You must have been about eight years old at the time."

"That's right, but I have vivid memories of it. And what was the reaction in Krakow after Shabbesai Tzvi became a Muslim?"

"People were disappointed, and I have to admit that I was disappointed as well. I mean, the rabbis had denounced him, and I accepted it. But in the back of my mind, I held out a little hope that maybe after all he was Mashiach. But once he became a Muslim it was all over. There was nothing more to talk about, and we all went on with our lives. Back to the yearning, the prayers and the hope that soon we would welcome the real Mashiach."

"Well, that's the way it was in Poland and Germany and most other places in northern Europe. But he didn't lose all his followers after he became a Muslim. A number of them explained his conversion as a deep mystery and still remained loyal to him. Many of these people live in Salonika in Greece, where I went to the *yeshivah*. They're called the Donmeh. Our rabbis made sure we stayed far away from them."

"It won't last for long," said Rav Amos. "People just find it hard to admit they made a mistake so they have to hang on to old errors. But twenty years have gone by already. And he's been dead for ten years. How much longer can the movement last?"

"I don't know, Amos. But I wouldn't be so sure that it's going to come to a quick end. I heard all kinds of myths in Salonika. They said that he didn't really die and that he's coming back, maybe as he was, maybe as a *gilgul*, a reincarnation in another man. His followers are developing a whole new theology around Shabbesai Tzvi. These things can take on a life of their own and grow and grow until they're out of control. They're very dangerous."

"A theology?"

"Yes. It's a new interpretation of Kabbalah. But let's not get into that now. We were talking about you. So tell me, are you married? Do you have any children?"

Rav Tzvi was taken aback by the reaction his question elicited. Rav Amos bit his lower lip, and a dark cloud seemed to settle over him.

"It seems I've touched a raw nerve," said Rav Tzvi. "I'm so sorry."

Rav Amos shook his head. "No, what happened was not so unusual. It's just very painful for me."

"Well, you don't have to talk about it if you don't want to."

Rav Amos took a deep breath. "I want to talk about it. I've kept these feelings bottled up inside me for such a long time without ever speaking about them. Perhaps it is better this way. I feel that we really are friends and that you can listen to me in the right way."

"I'll certainly try."

"When I came back to Amsterdam, I was not quite ready to get married yet. I was twenty-one years old, and I was spending just about all my time in the *beis midrash* learning on a very high level. I was covering hundreds of pages of Gemara during part of the day, and during the other part, I was learning difficult *sugyos* in great depth. There were many *talmidei chachamim* in Amsterdam with whom to talk in learning, and I felt myself really progressing in my learning. I also did a little business on the Exchange so that I was supporting myself. My needs were meager, and it took me very little time to earn what I needed. I lived inside the Gemara. I ate it, I drank it and I thought about it all the time. I had few friends, and I wasn't interested in people other than my family. My parents wanted me to get married already, but I insisted that there would be time for marriage and its inevitable distractions later. I was satisfied right where I was. I resisted until I was twenty-five years old. By then, I conceded that it was time to marry."

"I myself got married at a younger age," said Rav Tzvi, "but twenty-five is a good age. The only problem is that if you start at twenty-five, there's no guarantee that you'll be married within six months. Sometimes, it takes a little longer to find the right *shidduch*."

"That's true, but I was fortunate. My parents found me a wonderful girl from a good family in Hamburg. I was married at twenty-six. My father-in-law had a flourishing import business in Altona, near Hamburg, and we settled there. He gave us a substantial dowry, which we invested in his business. It was a good arrangement. And my wife was a ray of sunshine in my life. She was full of life and laughter. She made me happy, and I became friendlier and more sociable than I had ever been. I began to give serious thought to the future. I didn't think I wanted to become a rabbi of a congregation, but the idea of a position in a *yeshivah*, or even opening my own *yeshivah*, intrigued me."

"A worthy ambition," said Rav Tzvi.

"Well, yes. But I admit I also had my own interest in mind. I was married, and someday I would have sons. I liked the idea of building a good *yeshivah* and then passing it on to the next generation, you know?"

"I understand."

"But the sons didn't come so fast. The years went by, and the blessing of children was withheld from us. My wife was not a strong person, and she wasn't able to have children right away, but we never gave up hope. Over seven years we waited, and then finally, we were expecting our first child. I was so happy, I can't even tell you how happy I was. I'd never been so happy in my life."

Rav Amos fell silent and bit his lip again. Rav Tzvi waited patiently with a kind look on his face and without speaking a word.

"She died in childbirth," Rav Amos finally managed to choke out the words. "And I was left alone. Without a wife, without a child. One day, I was on top of the world, and the next day, I was destroyed."

Rav Tzvi touched Rav Amos on the hand. "I'm so sorry for your loss."

Rav Amos nodded and a single tear rolled down his cheek. "I've never gotten over it. I'm ashamed to say that I did not handle my tragedy well. A faithful Jew should be able to move on. But my heart was broken, and it's taking a long time for it to mend."

"There's no shame in sorrow," said Rav Tzvi. "In your situation, considering your character and personality, the hurt was unusually deep. But you'll rebuild your life. You'll be happy again." He paused. "Amos, I'm honored you spoke to me of these things. The Torah tells us that if you feel distress you should talk it out.[12] I'm your friend. You can unburden yourself to me any time."

"Thank you, Tzvi. You know, it's strange that this morning I didn't even know you existed, and now I can talk to you like this."

"It's a little strange, but not really. We're natural friends. We've only been friends for a few hours, and we will be friends for many years. For the rest of our lives." Rav Tzvi stood up. "And now, my dear friend, we should both go to sleep. It's almost time to get up for Shacharis."

As Rav Amos sank into the soft bed and rested his weary head on the large fluffy pillow stuffed with goose feathers, he felt a sense of profound connection he had never felt with anyone before. And as he drifted off to sleep, it occurred to him that he was truly at peace.

THE SHRIEKING SOUNDS · 4

A week later, the Turkish counterattack against the approaching Imperial armies had still not materialized. The Imperial armies were moving forward with discipline and confidence, drawing inexorably closer to Budapest, and the Turks, instead of mounting a counterattack, were fortifying the city against the expected attack. It was only a matter of time before the battle would be joined.

Sultan Mehmed IV knew that the Ottoman Empire's continued presence in the European lands hung in the balance. Three years earlier, in 1683, a vast Turkish army had stormed the gates of Vienna, on the verge of breaking through into the Christian heartland of Europe and bringing the banner of Islam in one sweeping thrust all the way to the North Sea. But King Jan Sobieski of Poland and his allies had broken the siege of Vienna and crushed the Turkish armies.

The fortunes of the Ottoman Empire were now in decline. Gone were the ambitions of glorious conquest. Now the sultan would be content just to secure his hold on the Balkan Peninsula, and even that was far from assured. The defense of Budapest, therefore, loomed large. Two years earlier, the Imperial armies had tried to capture Budapest, but the Turks had driven them off. Now the Imperial armies were approaching again, and the Turks were preparing to drive them off again. Budapest could not be allowed to fall.

On Friday morning, Rav Amos joined Rav Tzvi for a light breakfast in the home of his parents. Rav Tzvi's mother, a regal woman in her fifties, made sure they had everything they needed and then went off to take care of her household duties in preparation for Shabbos.

""It doesn't look so good, does it?" said Rabbi Ashkenazi, the nervous tremble in his voice barely concealed. "It looks as if the city is going to be attacked. I don't see how it can be avoided. Do you, Tzvi?"

Rav Tzvi shook his head.

"We're all in danger," the rabbi continued. "The whole community."

"Maybe we should all leave the city," said Rav Tzvi.

"Where would we go?" said the rabbi.

"Anywhere but here."

"We could manage that," said the rabbi. "But there are a thousand Jewish people in Budapest. Are they all going to leave? It would take us weeks to organize something like that, and it doesn't look as if we have weeks. Days, maybe. But you should go, Tzvi. Take your wife and daughter and go south to Sarajevo or Belgrade or anywhere else. I have to stay here with the people."

"I can't do it, Father," said Rav Tzvi. "I can't leave you and Mother here by yourselves in the middle of a battlefield."

"We'll be fine, Tzvi. When the battle starts, we'll go down into the cellar and wait for the fighting to end. In any case, the worst of the fighting will probably be centered on Buda Castle and the other Turkish points of fortification, not here in the Jewish neighborhood of Alt-Ofen. But you should take your family and go."

Rav Tzvi looked doubtful. "I don't know. I mean ..."

"Look," said the rabbi. "You probably have a few days before you have to make a decision. In the meantime, just prepare yourself for that possibility. Be ready to leave at a moment's notice."

"All right, Father. I'll get my family ready, and we'll make a decision later."

The rabbi was pleased. "Good. Your mother and I will feel better if we know that you and your family are out of harm's way." He turned to Rav Amos. "And how about you, my dear Rav Amos? There's no reason to stay here a moment longer than necessary. You should leave right away."

"Right now?" said Rav Amos.

"Well, you can finish your breakfast first," said the rabbi, and then he laughed. "I'm just joking, although this isn't exactly a joking matter. You should stay for Shabbos and leave early Sunday morning. Nothing is holding you here. You can't go north to Poland, but you can go south. When the fighting is over, you can come spend a few more days with us and then head north to Pulichev. You should get there in plenty of time to meet your father for Rosh Hashanah."

Rav Amos drummed his fingers on the tabletop. "I would prefer to stay here. I'm still young and strong, and I can help if help is needed."

"There's no reason to endanger yourself," said the rabbi. "We'll be fine."

"I don't think I'll be in any particular danger," Rav Amos protested. "I can hide in the cellars along with everyone else. It's one thing for Rav Tzvi to leave. He has a wife and little girl to protect. But I don't have any family here. I'm all by myself, and I can pretty well take care of myself."

"Look, Rav Amos, we have grown fond of you over this last week, and my son Tzvi considers you a close friend. We've enjoyed hearing your stories about your exploits in Amsterdam, on the high seas and in the forests of America. But this is different. This is a large, brutal army approaching, and you have the option of just leaving. You are only a traveler, my friend. This is not your home, and there is no reason for you to expose yourself to even the slightest risk of injury or worse, Heaven forbid. I really want you to leave on Sunday. Come back when it is all over, and we'll make a *seudah* to thank the Almighty for delivering us. Go, my son."

Rav Amos sighed and nodded. "Sunday it will be. And may the Almighty watch over you and protect you until we meet again."

"*Amein*," said the rabbi.

"*Amein*," Rav Tzvi repeated. "Go to Belgrade, Amos. I'll meet you there as soon as I can. I spent a little time in Belgrade on my way back from Salonika, and I know some people there. They'll take care of us."

The rabbi clapped his hands together. "In the meantime, Shabbos is coming, so let's put all these depressing thoughts out of our minds."

Late Friday afternoon, when the heat broke a little and the cool evening breezes began to rise, Rav Amos and Rav Tzvi took a short stroll before going off to the synagogue. They walked south along the eastern bank of the Danube River, absorbed in the discussion of a difficult *sugya*.

As they neared the lower outskirts of Alt-Ofen, they saw barges hitched to teams of horses on the riverbank and Turkish sailors steering them upriver. The hill on which the decrepit Buda Castle stood was aswarm with Turkish soldiers and artillerymen. Gangs of laborers were throwing up earth-works on the hill and digging trenches in the fields below. The streets were choked with wagons laden with munitions and provisions, and the air was thick with the shouts and smells of armies preparing for battle.

A Turkish officer directing traffic caught sight of them.

"Get away from here," he shouted in Hungarian.

"We're leaving," Rav Tzvi replied in perfect Turkish. "When and from where do you think this battle will begin?"

"That is none of your business," said the officer. "You think I have time now to stop and chat with a couple of Jews? Leave right now before I have you both arrested."

"With all due respect, *agha*," said Rav Tzvi, "my question is not idle. We are concerned for the women and children in our community."

The officer peered at him through squinted eyes. "I'll answer you, but only because your Turkish is so good. You've spent some time in Istanbul, right?"

"Right."

"That's what I thought. All right, I'll give you a minute of my time. When are the Austrians going to attack? Who knows? It could be tomorrow. It could be in a week. From where? They're northwest of the city now, so I imagine that's where the attack will come. It doesn't look like Obuda is in the path of the attack, but you should tell your people to take precautions anyway. The Austrians don't like you. Stay out of their way."

"Thank you, *agha*," said Rav Tzvi.

The office grunted and nodded. "Now get out of my sight," he said in a gruff but not unfriendly voice. "And take care of yourselves."

When they arrived at the synagogue, they told the rabbi what the officer had said. They talked no more about the situation for the entire Shabbos.

Sunday morning, Rav Amos said goodbye to the rabbi after Shacharis and went back to Rav Tzvi's house to pack his belongings. Rav Tzvi's wife prepared a substantial breakfast for him and gave him a package of fruit and biscuits for his journey to Belgrade. A driver named Moshke waited outside with a peddler's cart and an ancient horse to take Rav Amos to the marketplace where he would find transport to Belgrade. Rav Tzvi assured Rav Amos that he would also be leaving with his family for Belgrade in a day or two, and they would be reunited there. The two men embraced.

Rav Amos threw his belongings into the back of the cart. Clutching his *tallis* bag, he climbed into the cart and took his seat on the bench next to Moshke.

Moshke was careful not to tax his horse's meager reservoir of strength. He flicked the reins gently, and the horse plodded forward at a very leisurely pace. Rav Tzvi waved to him as they pulled away.

They turned into the next street and were halfway toward the river, when Rav Amos heard shrieking sounds in the distance behind him. His blood froze, and he spun around to find their source. Those sounds, he knew them, but he could not place them immediately. All he knew was that, for some reason, they struck terror into his heart. For a brief second, he thought they were the shrieks of birds of prey. But he knew they were not.

Just as he remembered what those shrieking sounds really were, he saw the flashes of fire and heard the explosive roar of cannonballs finding their targets. The assault on Budapest had begun, but the bombardment was not coming from the northwest as the Turkish officer had surmised. The cannonballs were raining fiery destruction onto Obuda to the north of Budapest. Instead of launching their attack from their positions to the northwest, the Imperial armies had veered east and were advancing from the north, and the Jewish community lay directly in their path. The memories of his own close encounter with a cannonball flooded into his mind, and the thought of his friends amidst a hailstorm of cannonballs filled him with horror.

As he watched in total shock, he saw another fusillade of cannonballs smash into the Jewish quarter, filling the air with the deafening sounds of death and destruction. He saw writhing tongues of flame licking at the sky, and he thought he heard shouts and screams above the din of bombardment, but then he realized that it must have been his imagination.

A pall of thick black smoke rose above the roofs along the streets from which he had just come.

The old horse suddenly found new vigor. It rolled its eyes and tried to shake itself loose from the cart, but Moshke, trembling with fear, held onto the reins with all his strength.

"Turn around, Moshke," Rav Amos yelled at the driver. "We have to go back."

"Go back? Into that furnace? Are you out of your mind?"

Rav Amos was frantic. "The rabbi's family," he managed to say. "We have to go back. Right away. There's not a minute to waste."

"Forget it," said Moshke. "Plenty of families are also in danger, but I'm not going back. I don't want to die along with them. I'm going to get away from here as fast as this old nag will take me."

Rav Amos climbed out of the cart. "No, you're right, Moshke. You have to save yourself, but I'm going back. Take care of yourself."

He gave Moshke a few small coins, grabbed his *tallis* bag and started back in the direction of the Jewish quarter. Moments later, he broke into a run.

"Wait a minute!" Moshke shouted after him. "Your bags!"

"Hold them for me," Rav Amos shouted back over his shoulder.

"But what if you ... you know ... don't come back."

"Then you can keep them," Rav Amos shouted just as he turned the corner and disappeared from sight.

There was a lull in the bombardment, and the cannonballs were no longer falling as he entered the ruined streets of the Jewish quarter of Alt-Ofen. Row after row of houses had been reduced to smoldering ruins. Dazed and wounded people wandered through the suddenly quiet street in search of other survivors. Rav Amos saw a woman sitting on the ground in front of a pile of rubble. As he drew closer, he saw that she was holding the lifeless body of her child in her arms. She was rocking her child back and forth and singing a lullaby, as if a mother's love could bring the child back to life. An old man with a blood-stained face held a child by the arm and staggered through the street, looking for a way out of the killing field that his neighborhood had become.

With his heart full of pity and pain, Rav Amos continued to run ahead in desperation. He passed the synagogue, which had taken a direct hit. One wall had completely disintegrated, and the building listed heavily on the verge of collapse. The synagogue and all the contiguous buildings were covered in what seemed like a single sheet of flame, and black smoke was pouring into the street. Rav Amos covered his face with his sleeve and ran on. Rav Tzvi's house was just ahead, around the next corner. Was it still standing? Were Rav Tzvi, his family and his parents safe? Rav Amos hoped they had gone down to the cellar at the first sign of bombardment.

As he turned the last corner, he breathed a sigh of relief. Rav Tzvi's house and the homes around it had escaped harm. People were beginning to peek out into the street to see if it was safe to emerge from hiding.

Rav Amos allowed himself a sigh of relief and slowed to a walk. Exhausted, he stopped altogether, put his hands on his thighs and took a few deep breaths. Somewhat refreshed, he stood up and continued toward Rav Tzvi's house. That was when the shrieking sounds returned with a vengeance. Houses all around him began to explode under the impact of the fiery projectiles, black devils as he had called them back on the ship.

"Tzvi!" Rav Amos screamed and he sprinted toward the house.

The cannonball struck Rav Tzvi's house just as Rav Amos reached for the door. The force of the explosion flung the door open. It struck Rav Amos in the chest and sent him sprawling to the ground amid a shower of shattered glass. He blacked out for a few minutes. When the black haze began to lift, he strained to return to consciousness. Then he lay there for a few minutes more until the ringing in his ears subsided and he was able to struggle to his feet.

He entered the house through the opening where the door had stood. The cannonball had struck one side of the house and demolished it completely. The other side of the house seemed practically untouched.

"Tzvi!" he shouted. "Where are you? Are you all right? Tzvi!"

"I'm here," his friend's voice was barely audible in reply.

"Where?"

"The parlor."

The parlor was in the part of the house that had taken a direct hit. Rav Amos had to clamber over a pile of steaming debris to enter the room. Rav Tzvi was sitting on an overturned cabinet. He held his head in his hands and wept quietly. Across the room lay the lifeless bodies of his wife and daughter.[13]

"Tzvi," said Rav Amos.

Rav Tzvi looked up with tear-filled eyes. "You're back," he said.

"I'm back."

"You see?"

"I see, Tzvi. I'm so sorry. So sorry."

"When did you leave? A half hour ago?"

"About."

"There was a different world a half hour ago. At least for me there was a different world."

"And for me, Tzvi. My heart breaks for you. And for your dear wife and daughter. I'm so sorry. I know there's nothing I can do or say that will ease the pain, but I wish there was."

"You've come back, and you're here. It is something."

"How about your parents, Tzvi? Are they all right?"

"I think they are. When the first bombs fell, I told my wife to go down to our cellar, and I ran to my parents' house to make sure they went down as well. Then the bombing stopped, and I went home. My daughter was frightened in the cellar, so my wife brought her up. We were just going to go back down when the … when the …"

He buried his face in his hands. His shoulders trembled, and he burst into tears once again. Rav Amos laid down his *tallis* bag, sat down beside him and put his arm around his shoulders. He said nothing. There was nothing to say. They sat that way for many minutes, Rav Tzvi weeping bitterly and Rav Amos a silent but comforting presence beside him.

A faint sound in the distance broke the sorrowful spell. Rav Amos jumped to his feet and cocked his head to one side.

"What's that sound?" he said.

Rav Tzvi wiped his eyes and looked up at him. "What sound?"

"Listen," he said, straining to hear. "It's gunfire!"

"The assault is coming through here?" said Rav Tzvi.

"It sounds like it," said Rav Amos. "Stay right here. I'll be right back. You know what, go down to the cellar, just to be safe. Take my *tallis* bag down with you. I'll see what's going on, and I'll come back to tell you."

Rav Tzvi nodded. He picked up Rav Amos' *tallis* bag and stood up.

"We do what we have to do," he said. "There'll be time for grieving later. If we survive, that is."

Rav Amos watched as Rav Tzvi made his way through his shattered home and disappeared into a back room. He returned momentarily with his own *tallis* bag. Then clutching the two bags under his arm, he opened the door to the cellar.

"Wait for me here," said Rav Amos. "I'll be back as soon as I can."

"Amos."

"What?"

"Saying that I thank you seems ..." said Rav Tzvi, his voice breaking, "it seems ... so completely inadequate. All I can say is that you are truly a good friend and that ... and that ..."

"I understand, Tzvi. I understand. We'll talk later."

He stepped out through the opening that the door had once occupied and headed in the direction of the main street. Many Turkish soldiers wearing olive green uniforms and red sashes were running north. They were carrying muskets across their chests, and their swords flapped against their legs as they ran. A number of wounded soldiers, their uniforms stained with blood, staggered back in the opposite direction. Rav Amos waited until the soldiers had passed. Then he followed close behind them.

He had not gone very far when a bullet whizzed by his face and struck a brick wall. Rav Amos flung himself to the ground and gingerly lifted his head. Up ahead, the Turkish soldiers had taken positions under cover and were returning the fire of the Austrian troops. In the distance, he could see the gray uniforms of the Imperial soldiers. As he watched, he saw the tide of battle go against the Turks. The Imperial soldiers charged, and the Turkish defenders fell back to new positions, just to the left of the rabbi's house.

A new sound suddenly caught his attention. It was the sound of hoofbeats. It was coming from the west. Rav Amos doubled back and turned into one of the streets leading to the northwest. He ran in a low crouch on the side of the street that lay in shadow until he reached the outskirts of Obuda. The sight that greeted him took his breath away.

German cavalry lancers were arrayed as far as his eyes could see. They sat on their big horses, waiting patiently for their officers to give the order to charge. The Turkish defenders of Obuda were surrounded. The attack could begin at any moment.

Running as fast as his exhausted legs would carry him, he returned to the ruin that had once been Rav Tzvi's home. He burst down into the cellar. Rav Tzvi leaped to his feet at the sight of his friend.

"What happened, Amos?" he said. "What's going on?"

"We're in a trap. I just saw German cavalry to the west. There must've been thousands of them, and they're lined up for a cavalry charge. The Austrian infantry is coming down from the north, the Germans are to the west, and the river is to the east. When the Germans charge, they'll probably seal off the south as well. We have to get out of here right away."

"My parents. What about my parents?"

"The fighting has reached their house. You can't get close without getting shot. Let's hope they stay in the cellar and get through this safely. They don't have much choice. But we do, Tzvi. We have to save ourselves. Who knows what those Germans and Austrians will do to us if they capture us?"

"And who knows what they will do to my parents."

Rav Amos nodded. "That's true, Tzvi," he said after a long moment of silence. "I won't pretend it isn't. I'm sorry. But you can't help by staying here and suffering the same fate. Doesn't the Torah require you to save yourself?"

Rav Tzvi sighed. "Yes, of course. And maybe if we save ourselves, we'll be able to do something for my parents."

"There's certainly a better chance." He picked up a burlap sack and emptied it of its contents. The he put both his and Rav Tzvi's *tallis* bags into the sack and flung it over his shoulder. "Let's go."

"Where are we going?"

"I don't know. All I know is that we have to go south, away from this terrible place."

The two men slipped through the streets, running past the ruins of the Jewish quarter. Straight ahead and to their right, they could see that Buda Castle was swarming with infantry and artillerymen like an anthill. Flashes of flame lit up the battlements as the Turkish cannons belched their own projectiles of death at the invading armies.

The roar of the cannons and the shouts of the Turkish soldiers were suddenly joined by the wild neighing of excited horses and the thunder of galloping hooves. The charge had begun. It was sweeping across the entire length of Obuda and threatened to engulf the castle on the hill as well.

Rav Amos grabbed Rav Tzvi by the arm and shouted, "Run! Harder than you ever have. Run for your life!"

The clamor of the charging cavalry bore down on the two men as they fled south past the castle on the hill. They ran alongside the river until they could run no more, then they collapsed panting on the ground. The battle raged behind them. They had reached safety, even if it was only temporary.

That afternoon, they passed beyond the outskirts of Budapest and into the Buda Hills. They had bought some vegetables from a vendor in the city, and now they shared a meager meal in a wooded spot overlooking the city. Beneath them, the entire city of Budapest crackled and burned. They could see the campfires of the invaders all around the city. They thought they could even hear the faint cries of men rejoicing and other men dying in agony, but then again, it might just have been their imaginations.

Far off in the distance, they saw Turkish barges on the river.

"Look at that," said Rav Tzvi. "Those barges are carrying away the Turkish dead. The Turks don't leave their dead on the battlefield. Muslim burial customs require them to wash the bodies and bury them right away. At least those dead Turks will be buried. But what will happen to the bodies of my wife and daughter, Amos? Will they find no rest?"

"They'll be buried, Tzvi. I'll see to it."

Rav Tzvi gave him a quizzical look. "How?"

"I don't know. I'll think of something."

"What can you do? You can't go back there."

"I'll go back into the city tomorrow. I'll see what I can find out about your parents, and I'll give your wife and daughter a proper burial."

Rav Tzvi allowed himself a crooked smile. "I don't know how you propose to do all that, Amos, but I'll come along with you."

"No, it's best you stay here. If the Austrians catch me, I stand a better chance than you would. Don't forget that I'm a full Dutch citizen, and Holland is an ally of the Austrians. You, my friend, are a Jewish supporter of the Turkish state. You are the enemy."

CHAINS AND SHACKLES · 5

R av Amos fingered the gold coins in his pocket as he
trudged down the road from the Buda Hills to the
ruined capital of Hungary. He did not have a specific plan
for discovering the fate and whereabouts of Rav Tzvi's parents. Nor did he know how he would manage to bury Rav
Tzvi's wife and daughter. But of one thing he was sure. A
well-placed gold ducat or two would go a long way toward
helping him achieve his goals.

The sun beat down on him as he walked down the narrow
lane. Soon his neck and back were bathed in perspiration,
but he did not allow himself to dwell on his growing discom-
fort; he had long since discovered that he could disassociate
himself from any irritation less than excruciating pain to the
point where it did not occupy his consciousness.

For the next hour, he focused all his energies on formulat-
ing a plan for getting through the Austrian lines and doing
what he had to do, but he could not come up with a feasible
plan. He sighed with disappointment and offered up a silent
prayer to the Almighty to lead him in the right direction,
not for his own sake but for the sake of the distinguished
Ashkenazi family who had been visited by so much tragedy
and misfortune.

"Hey, rabbi!"

Rav Amos turned to see who had called out to him. He saw an old horse harnessed to a cart following him down the road. The driver was waving to him. It was Moshke.

"Rabbi, I'm happy to see you," said Moshke as he pulled alongside. "I thought you were dead. Do you mind if I touch you?" He reached out and touched Rav Amos on the sleeve. "Yep, I wanted to make sure you're real."

"So, Moshke, are you convinced?"

"Pretty much. What happened to you?"

"It's a long story."

"Get in the cart, rabbi. I'll give you a ride. Where are you going?"

"To Alt-Ofen," said Rav Amos and climbed into the cart.

"You can't go there," Moshke protested. "The Austrians are all over the place, and I heard that all the people were killed in the bombardment. That's why I thought you were dead. It's at times like these that I'm thankful I have no family. But I'm happy you're alive, even though it's going to cost me."

"Why is it going to cost you?"

"Because I'm going to have to give you back the things you left in my cart. I looked through them last night. There's quite a bit of money there. But it's yours, and I don't want it. It's better that you're alive. If the Almighty wants to make me rich, I'm sure He can find a better way to do it."

"You're a good man, Moshke. Where are you coming from?"

"I have a cabin up in the hills. That's where your things are. It's not much at all, but I use it sometimes when I can't get back home before dark. I guess my cabin is my main home now, because it looks as if I don't have a home in the city any more."

"Probably not. Listen to me, Moshke. Rabbi Ashkenazi's son is back there in the woods up the hill. His wife and daughter were killed in yesterday's bombardment."

"Oy! How terrible! Is he wounded?"

"No, he escaped injury. But we don't know what happened to his parents. That's where I'm going now. To find out what happened to his parents and to bury his wife and daughter. Then I'm coming back to him. Can I take him to your cabin for a while? He has to sit Shivah somewhere."

"Rabbi! It would be such an honor for me. The young rabbi is one of the greatest people in the world, even though most of the world doesn't know it yet. But they will."

"I agree with you. Thank you, Moshke."

"So where am I taking you?"

"How far are you willing to come with me? All the way into Alt-Ofen?"

Moshke shook his head. "Too dangerous. I can drop you off near the city, and I'll wait for you there. All day if need be. And if you don't come back by dark, I'll come back and wait for you all day tomorrow."

"And if I'm not back by dark tomorrow?"

"Then I don't think you're coming back at all."

"I suppose you're right, Moshke. Can this horse go any faster?"

"If he could go any faster, someone else would own him, rabbi. So be happy that he is who he is."

Rav Amos pursed his lips and looked at Moshke with new respect. "That is a very good point, Moshke. A very good point. I have to think about it."

They turned into a road going in a northerly direction, and an hour later, they caught sight of the vast encampment of the Imperial forces. Just as Rav Amos got out of the cart, a squad of eight cavalrymen led by two officers came galloping down the road toward them. Rav Amos could readily identify the officers by their manner and because their uniforms were more elaborate than the simple gray tunics of the cavalrymen.

The cavalry squad stopped fifty paces away, and one of the officers came forward with his sword drawn.

"Sit still, Moshke," said Rav Amos. "Let me handle this."

"Identify yourselves," the officer commanded in Spanish. His powerful war steed was so large that it towered over Moshke's horse and cart combined. It was as if he was speaking down to them from a balcony.

"I'm a Dutch citizen," said Rav Amos, also in Spanish. "This is my driver."

"Are you a Jew?"

"Yes, I am. I live in Amsterdam"

"And you are a full citizen of the Netherlands?"

"Yes, sir."

"Let me see your documents."

Rav Amos handed him his identity papers. The Spaniard looked them over carefully and handed them back.

He looked back to his companions. "Maarten! This fellow is a countryman of yours. Come over here. You take care of this."

The Dutch officer spurred his horse forward and joined them.

"Good day," he said and tipped his hat. "I am Captain Maarten van den Groot. What is your name?"

"Amos Strasbourg, sir."

The Dutch officer's eyes widened, and he peered at Rav Amos with interest. "Amos Strasbourg, you say? I recognize the name. You're a friend of Sebastian Dominguez, aren't you?"

"Yes, sir, I am."

"A good man, that Dominguez."

"You know him, sir?"

"Sort of. You know, indirectly. I'm a good friend of Gonzalo Sanchez, and I've met your friend once or twice. But most of what I know about him is from Gonzalo. I'm a frequent visitor to The Toothless Beggar, Gonzalo's tavern back in Amsterdam. That's how I recognized your name."

"So why is a Dutch officer here in Hungary?"

"Because we've come to beat back the Muslim hordes who threaten to engulf all of Christendom. There are over seventy thousand Imperial troops here, mostly Austrian infantry and German cavalry, but also including Dutch, Englishmen, Spaniards, Croats, Italians, Frenchmen, Danes and Swedes. We're volunteers. We're Christians, and we're not interested in bowing down to Mecca five times a day. Believe me, the Christian people will never let the Muslims conquer us. We have to make a stand and fight."

"Then it's my good fortune that, of all the tens of thousands of soldiers in the Imperial army here in Hungary, I've met a Dutchman who knows me."

"You certainly are fortunate," said the Dutch captain. "The Almighty is watching over you. Who knows what my friends would have done to you if I hadn't been here." He laughed and slapped his knee. "But then again, maybe they would've been nice to you. Who knows? They're not barbarians, you know. But then again, one never knows, does one?" He laughed again. "I hope you don't mind, rabbi. I'm just having a little fun at your expense. But you needn't worry. Any friend of Sebastian Dominguez and Gonzalo Sanchez is a friend of mine. So what are you doing here? Where are you going?"

Having found a sympathetic ear, Rav Amos told him the entire story. The Dutch captain listened gravely until he had finished.

"I'm very sorry to hear that, rabbi," he said. "War is a dangerous game, and many innocent people get caught in the crossfire. But don't worry. I'll help you. Why don't you just wait here with your driver while I go investigate? I'll meet you back here in two hours."

"Thank you very much for your generous offer, Captain van den Groot. But I really do need to see for myself what happened. It has something to do with Jewish legalities for establishing evidence of death."

The Dutch captain looked doubtful.

"Please, captain," Rav Amos persisted. "If you could just assign a soldier to escort me, that would be a great help. I would pay him, of course."

"I ... I don't know."

"And when we get back to Amsterdam, captain, I'll treat you to as much as you can drink in one evening in Gonzalo's tavern."

The Dutch captain smiled broadly. "Now you're talking, rabbi. You know what, I'll escort you myself. And you don't have to pay me anything. But instead of one evening in Gonzalo's tavern, we'll make it two. How's that?"

"Done."

"Good. Let's shake on it."

The two men shook hands, and the deal was sealed.

The Dutch captain turned to his Spanish companion. "You see, Francisco? When two civilized gentlemen talk, solutions can always be found."

"Do you consider a Jew to be a civilized gentleman, Maarten?"

"Absolutely. You Spaniards are just harming yourselves by persecuting your Jews. We Dutch welcome them, and they're making us rich." He turned back to Rav Amos. "All right. Now, how are we going to do this?"

"Why don't I just follow you in the wagon?" said Rav Amos.

Maarten snickered. "With that old nag? We might as well walk. No, that's not going to work. Can you ride a horse, rabbi?"

"Yes."

"All right, this is what we're going to do. Francisco, you give the rabbi your horse. Then you get into the cart and head for the camp. By the time you get there, we should be back."

"Come on, Maarten," said the Spanish officer. "You can't be serious. I'll be a laughingstock if I come riding into camp in that … thing."

"Then get out and walk the last stretch, Francisco," said the Dutch captain. "Come on, be a sport. When you come visit me in Amsterdam, you'll join me for refreshing beverages in Gonzalo's tavern. It'll be the rabbi's treat for both of us." He looked at Rav Amos. "Do you agree, rabbi?"

"Absolutely."

"There you go, Francisco. Now give him the horse."

The Spanish officer got off his horse slowly. "I'm crazy for going along with this. But all right. And take the squad with you. I don't want anyone at all to see me in that … that … bucket."

A short while later, Rav Amos and the Dutch captain entered the Imperial encampment. Beyond it, the city was in flames, and a cloud of acrid smoke hung over the entire area. The Dutch captain led Rav Amos straight to the tent of the general of the cavalry. They dismounted, and the Dutch captain asked to see the general. After a wait of about five minutes, the general emerged. He was an exceedingly tall, heavyset German with a porcine face and a bushy blond mustache.

"Good morning, general," said the Dutch captain. "This gentleman is a distinguished rabbi from Amsterdam. He is concerned about the Jewish residents of Obuda. Do we have any information for him?"

The German general looked at Rav Amos through narrowed eyes. He thought for a moment, and then he shrugged his massive shoulders.

"Sure, why not?" he said. "It might even be helpful. About half of the Jews perished in the attack. The rest are in our custody. We have a few hundred of them. We're taking them back with us to Germany."

"If I may be so bold as to ask a question, Your Excellency," said Rav Amos. "For what purpose are they being taken to Germany?"

"You do take liberties, but I will answer your question anyway. The Jews of Obuda are allies of the Turks. That makes them enemy prisoners. We will deal with them as with any other prisoners of war."

"Will you allow them to be redeemed?" asked Rav Amos.

"Redeemed, you say?" said the German general. "Now that's an interesting idea. If some of the Jewish communities stepped forward to redeem our prisoners, perhaps we would consider their offer. We may also decide to execute them. Who knows what the future will bring? Only time will tell."

"Can I see the prisoners?"

"Yes, you can. Then you can tell your friends about it." He gave Rav Amos a sly look. "There may even be a little something in it for you if the negotiations go well. Wouldn't you like that, rabbi, eh?"

"I would like to help the prisoners gain their freedom, yes, I would."

"Then get to work, rabbi. Captain van den Groot, we keep a separate compound for the Jewish prisoners. It's all the way at the end of the encampment. You have to go past the compound for the Turkish prisoners and keep going. You'll find it."

Without another word, he turned and went back into the tent. The Dutch captain and Rav Amos remounted their horses and rode to the Jewish prisoners' compound at the other end of the enormous encampment. The Dutch captain spoke quietly to the sergeant in charge for a few minutes; then they were allowed to enter the compound.

The Dutch captain remained at the gate, chatting with the sergeant, and Rav Amos entered the compound by himself. The Jewish prisoners presented a sorry spectacle. Many of them were wounded. Some were bandaged and able to walk. Others lay on the ground and moaned. Even those who had escaped serious injury looked bedraggled, shocked and disoriented. All the prisoners wore leg chains and shackles.

Rabbi Ashkenazi, his head bandaged, was sitting on a stool. His wife dabbed at his forehead with a wet cloth. As soon as the rabbi saw Rav Amos, his eyes lit up, and he struggled to his feet.

"Rav Amos!" he cried out and wrapped the younger man in a tearful embrace. "Thank the Almighty that you're alive."

"How are the two of you?" asked Rav Amos.

The rabbi sighed deeply. "What can we say? We're alive, and we're thankful to the Almighty for that. But our family, unfortunately, has not been spared the bitter cup. My daughter-in-law and granddaughter have been killed, my son has disappeared, and we ourselves are barely hanging on."

"Your son is alive and well," said Rav Amos.

"Yes, I too trust and hope that he is well," said the rabbi. "Both of us do."

"Hope is good," said the rabbi's wife. "Who can live through such hard times without hope? But hope is only hope. My son has disappeared, and we don't know if he is alive or if he is one of those buried under piles of rubble."

"Your son is alive and well," Rav Amos repeated. "I was just with him a few hours ago. He managed to escape. Right now, he is up in the Buda Hills."

"It is true," breathed the rabbi. "Oh, thank you, Almighty, for sparing our son. There is no end to Your kindness."

The rabbi's wife tried to say something. Her lips moved, but no words emerged, only the soft sounds of her weeping with relief.

"Tzvi is very worried about both of you," said Rav Amos. "He knows that his wife and daughter were killed. He was in the house when the cannonball struck it. We had to leave them and flee, and he is concerned about their receiving a proper burial."

"You can tell him not to worry," said the rabbi. "After we were taken captive yesterday, they allowed us to bury all our dead, not out of the kindness of their hearts but because they did not want disease to spread. All our dead have been laid to rest according to Jewish law and custom. I specifically asked about Tzvi and his family. The men in the burial party told me they had buried his wife and daughter, who had been found together in the house in a room that had suffered a direct hit. But even though they searched for my son, they found no trace of him. I've been thinking that his body must be lying somewhere forgotten under a pile of rubble. Oh, thank you, Almighty, for letting him live and escape. Maybe someday I'll lay eyes on my beloved son once again."

"I'm sure you will," said Rav Amos. "And how about the two of you? How are you managing? What shall I tell Tzvi when I see him later today?"

"Tell him that we survived. We'll be fine, I suppose … I hope … I pray. We're not so young any more, but we're not so old either. They say they're taking us to Germany."

"Yes, they are."

The rabbi's eyes narrowed. "How do you know that?"

"The general told me. He implied that they are holding you as hostage until someone pays ransom money."[14]

The rabbi nodded. "Makes sense. They have a chance to squeeze a little money out of the Jewish communities, they take advantage of it. But that's good news, I suppose."

"Good news?"

"Yes. If they expect to collect ransom for us, they'll make sure to keep us in good condition. Those who step forward to pay the ransom will want to see us first. And the Germans won't want them to think we're all on the verge of death. They'll think it's just good business to give us back in good shape."

The Dutch captain ambled over.

"Time's up, rabbi," he said. "The sergeant wants you to leave, and I don't have any more time to escort you around the camp. Time to go. Say goodbye."

Rav Amos and the rabbi embraced again. The rabbi blessed him, and he hurried away without looking back. They mounted their horses, and minutes later, they were back in the open countryside. In the distance, they could see Moshke waiting in his cart.

"This is where you get off, rabbi," said the Dutch captain. "I'll take the horse back to Francisco. You can walk to your friend. And remember, if you see Gonzalo before I see him, send him my best regards. And tell him about our little arrangement."

"I certainly will, captain," said Rav Amos. "And thank you very much. I know that you did what you did because you have a kind heart, not because you need free drinks in Gonzalo's tavern."

The Dutch captain colored with embarrassment. "Maybe you're right, rabbi. There is too much suffering in the world, and it is a good feeling to alleviate some of it. But I insist that you honor our agreement. I want those free drinks."

"Absolutely," said Rav Amos. "And thank you again."

He dismounted and shook hands with the Dutch captain. Then he handed over the reins and started walking toward Moshke and his cart.

MOSHKE'S CABIN · 6

Rav Tzvi was waiting beside the same stream where Rav Amos had left him hours earlier. When he saw Rav Amos approaching in Moshke's cart, he ran forward, searching Rav Amos' face for a sign that his mission had been a success.

"Your parents are alive and well," Rav Amos called out as soon as he caught sight of Rav Tzvi. "And your family has been properly buried."

Rav Tzvi's shoulders sagged with relief. "Thank the Almighty," he breathed. "Oh, my dear parents. Alive and well. Oh, thank you, Almighty, for Your never-ending kindness. I was so worried. So worried …. And thank you, Amos. I don't know what to say. You, too, Moshke. Thank you. You obviously had a part in this."

"Not really, Rabbi Ashkenazi," said the wagon driver. "I just saved Rabbi Strasbourg some walking time, and considering the condition of my old horse, it wasn't that much of a savings."

"Don't be so modest, Moshke," said Rav Amos. "If not for you, we might never have met the cavalrymen, and I wouldn't have had the Spaniard's horse to take me to the camp."

Moshke shrugged. "Suit yourself." He filled a feedbag with oats, unhitched his horse from the cart and led him off to the stream.

"I want to hear all the details, Amos," said Rav Tzvi. "But first I want to thank you again. I know I thanked you already, but there is no end to my gratitude. You came back, right into the bombardment, when you had already left. You saved my life. And now you risked your life and freedom to find out what I needed to know. You're the best friend I've ever had in my whole life. I will be grateful to you forever."

"It was really not such a big thing, Tzvi," said Rav Amos. "Ask Moshke. We met a compassionate Dutch officer, a volunteer with the Imperial forces. I promised him a night in an Amsterdam tavern at my expense, which he accepted as if it were the greatest treasure. He took me into the camp and brought me to the prisoners. That's where I saw your father, and he told me about your family. It was really quite simple."

"I'm sure that another man in your position might not have been so successful." He sighed. "Tell it to me again, Amos. I want to hear all the details, but right now I need to know the essentials. What did my father say about my wife and daughter?"

"He said that the soldiers had given them permission to bury the dead because they were afraid of disease. They buried all the dead properly yesterday before nightfall."

"Did he just assume they buried my wife and daughter because the burial party said they'd buried all the dead?"

"No. He asked them specifically about your family. The burial party said they found them together in a room that had taken a direct hit."

Rav Tzvi nodded. "So it's true. They've been buried." He looked around for Moshke. The wagon driver had finished watering his horse and was attaching the feeding bag to its bridle. "Moshke! Do you have a small knife or something else sharp?"

Moshke found a rusty blade under the bench in the cart and handed it to him.

Rav Tzvi made a small cut in his clothes. Then he rent his clothing in mourning and sat down on the ground. Moshke looked at Rav Amos, and Rav Amos nodded. They both sat down near Rav Tzvi and remained there in silence for a long while. When the sun sank low in the western sky, they stood up and spoke the traditional words of consolation.

Rav Amos touched Rav Tzvi on the shoulder. "We have to go, Tzvi. It's time. We can't stay here."

"Where will we go?"

"Moshke has a cabin close by. He said we can stay there until we're ready to go. Is that all right with you?"

"Yes."

"We need to get going."

"Of course. Now that I know that my wife and daughter have been buried, I just need a few minutes to put on my *tallis* and *tefillin*."

Moshke's cabin turned out to be nothing more than a ramshackle one-room hut alongside a stream in the lower stretches of the Buda Hills. It was set in a tangle of trees and shrubbery with overgrown branches scraping against the loose-fitting shutters. The cabin could only be reached over a rutted forest trail barely wide enough to accommodate Moshke's little cart.

Moshke had built the cabin himself years before. His carpentry skills were poor to say the least, and the ravages of time and the elements had pushed the cabin to the brink of collapse. The timbers were rotted and full of gaps. The thatched roof had thinned out in a number of places so that it no longer protected the interior from the rain; it only slowed down its flow. Small forest animals lived in the thatch, and during hard rainfalls, they sometimes fell into the hut and eventually died there.

Whenever Moshke stopped by the cabin, he immediately removed the carcasses of the dead animals and opened the shutters to allow some fresh air to enter. But try as he might, he could not rid the hut of its dank and fetid smells. Nonetheless, it served his most basic needs. There were a table and chairs, a few mismatched dishes and eating utensils and a cellar-like hole in the ground in which he kept jars of pickled meats and vegetables. There was also an oven. He slept on top of the oven on a pallet that he kept covered with an oilskin to protect it from the rain.

The overpowering stench of the cabin billowed out at them as soon as Moshke flung open the door and ushered them in.

"It's usually worse," said Moshke. "I spent last night here, and I cleaned the place up and aired it out. Can you imagine what it would be like if I hadn't been here in days or even weeks?"

"I can't imagine, Moshke," said Rav Amos. "And even if I could I wouldn't want to imagine it. The way it is now is more than enough for me."

Moshke shrugged. "It's not very fancy, but it works for me."

"And for us," said Rav Tzvi. "It works for us. Right now this cabin of yours is like a gilded palace, because it's the best we have. It's a good place, Moshke."

Moshke was pleased. He began to bustle about, clearly enjoying his role as host to the young rabbis. He set the table as best he could and climbed down to the cellar to get some food.

Rav Tzvi sat on the dirt floor. He drew up his knees and wrapped his arms around them. Moshke brought Rav Tzvi a plate of food, while he and Rav Amos ate together at the table.

"Distinguished rabbis, it's almost dark," Moshke announced, "and I don't have any candles. Usually, when I'm here, I go to sleep when it gets dark and get up at first light, so I don't have to use candles very much. They're expensive.

Actually, I do the same — I mean, I used to do the same — in Alt-Ofen. So I suggest we all go to sleep. I'll be off early in the morning, and I'll come back with some candles and bread and other provisions."

"Let me give you some money," said Rav Amos.

"What do you think I am, rabbi?" said Moshke. "You are my honored guests. Do you think I would take money from you?"

"Forgive me."

"It's all right, rabbi. You meant well. There are piles of branches and heavy blankets in the corner. Make yourselves beds and go to sleep. If it were winter, I would offer you beds on top of the oven, but now the floor is just fine."

An hour later, Rav Amos lay awake on his bed of branches. A cool breeze came in through the open shutters and caressed his face. He could make out Rav Tzvi's sleeping form nearby in the dark and hear his soft and regular breathing. Moshke was asleep on the other side of the room, his snores reverberating from wall to wall, his lips fluttering noisily with every exhalation.

Life was so strange, thought Rav Amos. Less than two weeks earlier, he could never have imagined that he would be sleeping on the floor of a foul-smelling dilapidated hut in the woods above Budapest … and that it would bring him so much happiness. But it did.

During his thirty-seven years, he had not had too many close friends, but there had been a few. Most recently, he had formed a solid friendship with Sebastian Dominguez in Amsterdam, and circumstances had brought him into a bond of friendship with Immanuel Almeida. He had even traveled to America with the two of them out of friendship for both. But he had never felt anything like the powerful connection he felt to Rav Tzvi Ashkenazi, who was not only his friend on many different personal levels but also his equal and even superior as a *talmid chacham*. It was the most complete and deepest friendship he had ever experienced, even though it was less than two weeks old, and he could feel it growing stronger and more permanent every moment they spent together, especially in these circumstances of adversity.

When they woke up in the morning, Moshke was already gone. He had left a little food for them on the table and a reasonably clean pitcher of pure mountain water from the nearby stream.

After Shacharis and breakfast, Rav Tzvi was feeling faint from the closeness of the air in the cabin, and Rav Amos suggested that they sit outside where the air was fresh and clean. They found a spot under a spreading oak with a very thick trunk. Rav Tzvi sat on the ground with his back against the trunk, while Rav Amos sat on a chair he had taken from the cabin.

The sun shone brightly, and birds were twittering and singing in the branches. The morning air was warm and velvety but with a slightly chilly edge, a harbinger of the coming autumn.

Rav Amos sat silently, allowing Rav Tzvi to initiate the conversation. Rav Tzvi was also silent for a while. He bit his lower lip, and his eyes misted over again and again as a cavalcade of thoughts passed through his head.

"I'm glad you're here, Amos," he said at last. "It's a great comfort to me. I don't know what I'd have done without you. I'd probably be dead."

"Don't say that, Tzvi. The Almighty protected you. I was just His messenger. If it hadn't been me, it would have been someone else. The Almighty has an unlimited supply of messengers."

"Well, I'm glad He chose you as His messenger."

"So am I."

"And now, sitting Shivah here alone in the hills, I can't think of anyone else whom I'd rather have here with me."

"You're much too kind, Tzvi. Your father would certainly be a greater comfort to you than I am."

"In a way, that's true, I suppose. But it's different with someone from your own generation who's a very close friend. Especially someone who suffered a similar tragedy, as you did when you lost your own wife and child. I tell you, Amos, the pain is so deep it feels as if it'll never heal. But I know it will."

"It will."

"I close my eyes, and I see my wife, her face full of kindness and love for the whole world. I see her sitting at the Shabbos table listening with such pleasure to my father and me discussing a very complicated *sugya* from the Gemara, even though she really couldn't be expected to understand what we were saying. I think that her share in my Torah was so clean, so pure and so selfless that she was able to sense and appreciate its inner core even more than I did. She saw beyond the words into the holiness deep within, and that gave her a pleasure greater than mine."

He tried to say something else, but the words caught in his throat, submerged by gentle sobs.

"And then I close my eyes and see my sweet little girl," he said at last with a great effort. "I'm opening the door and coming into the house, and my little girl sees me, and she squeals with excitement and runs toward me and ..." He lowered his head and wept.

Rav Amos said nothing. He just lowered his eyes and waited for Rav Tzvi to speak.

"I accept what happened, you know," Rav Tzvi continued. "I believe with all my heart that everything the Almighty does is for the good, completely and without reservation. My wife and child did nothing to deserve a punishment, of that I'm sure. But there was a purpose in their life and a purpose in their death, although I don't understand it. Who knows? Perhaps someday I'll understand the justice of it. Perhaps it'll happen while I'm still here in this world, perhaps in the next, I don't know. But someday I'll understand. In the meantime, I grieve, not so much for them as for me. They've fulfilled their purpose. They're in Heaven with the Almighty, enjoying their well-earned rewards. I'm the one sitting here with a broken heart."

Rav Amos nodded. "No one dies without justice."

"Well, that's not exactly correct. It does happen sometimes. The Torah says so.[15] There are people who die unjustly."

"But you know what the Gemara says about that," said Rav Amos.

"Yes, I do. A very strange situation about the messenger of the Angel of Death making a mistake and taking the wrong person.[16] That's the example the Gemara gives."

"That's right," said Rav Amos. "The Gemara doesn't say that an innocent little child who dies has been the victim of injustice. No, that death was somehow just, because it fulfilled an important divine purpose. If the Almighty hadn't wanted it to happen, it wouldn't have happened."

"I know. But it hurts. Oh, it hurts."

"I don't think the hurt ever goes away. We just learn to live with it. I think that's what life is all about, learning to live with the pain of the inevitable tragedies we suffer, and growing from them."

Rav Tzvi nodded and fell silent. He leaned back, closed his eyes and breathed the scented air into his lungs. He sat that way, in a pensive pose, for a long time. When he finally opened his eyes, they were moist with tears.

"Things change so quickly," he said. "The day before yesterday, I was living in a different world. My life was comfortable, orderly and altogether wonderful. All my needs were provided so that I could sit and learn Torah with peace of mind. I had a beautiful family and a home large enough to have guests as often as I wanted. My parents were well and lived nearby. We enjoyed safety and security without any real persecution from the Turks. In another few years or so, I would have sought a position as a rabbi. I was also thinking of opening a *yeshivah* as well. Life was about as good as it could get for me. And now, in two days, everything is gone. Destroyed. And here I am sitting Shivah for my wife and daughter under a tree in the forest while my parents are being led off in chains to Germany."

"You'll rebuild your life, Tzvi," said Rav Amos. "Your Torah will illuminate all of Klal Yisrael for this generation and all future generations. You'll have your position and your *yeshivah*. This is not the end for you. It is the end of one life and the beginning of a new one."

"I accept whatever the Almighty has in store for me, Amos. I really do."

Rav Amos stood up. "I'm going to get water," he said. "Do you want some?"

"Yes, please. My throat is parched."

Rav Amos brought out a pitcher and two glasses from the cabin. He filled the pitcher from the stream and poured some water for both of them. They drank in silence.

"Back in Alt-Ofen," said Rav Amos, "you mentioned that your father had a harrowing experience during the Cossack attacks. You said you would save it for a different time. How about now? Is it a good time?"

"I suppose so," said Rav Tzvi. "Now is as good a time as any. As you know, those were horrible times in Poland and Lithuania. My parents got married not long before the Cossacks attacked Vilna. My father was a very young man, and his wife Nechamah, my mother, was little more than a child. There was pandemonium in Vilna in those tragic days. People were fleeing for their lives. My father described to me the fright, the brutal butchery, the panic, the chaos. I tell you, I don't know which was worse, what happened to us in Alt-Ofen or what happened in those days."

"You can't really understand unless you were there."

"Yes, that's true. Anyway, in the chaos and panic, many families lost contact with each other. No one knew who was alive and who was dead. My father was one of those who were separated from family. For days, he couldn't find his way back to their house, and by the time he did, my grandfather had taken his family, including my newlywed mother, and fled for Moravia. He left a message for my father to follow them, but he didn't even know if my father was alive."

He took a sip of the water and continued.

"That was the last they heard of my father for months. One day, two men from Vilna appeared in Trebic, the town in Moravia where my grandfather and his family had found refuge. As soon as he heard about them, my grandfather sought them out and asked them if they'd seen any sign of his son-in-law. As it turned out, they had news of my father."

A look of relief passed across Rav Amos' face.

"It's not what you think," said Rav Tzvi. "These men knew my father quite well. They were also among the people fleeing in panic before the attackers. They managed to find a hiding placed in the ruins of a house, and as they trembled in fear of being discovered, they peeked out at the killing field beyond the window. They saw my father captured by the Cossacks. They watched as a Cossack officer ordered my father to get down on his knees and stretch out his neck. They saw my father do as he had been ordered. They saw him prepare himself to die to sanctify the Name of the Almighty. To their horror, they saw the Cossack raise the sword high over his head and bring it down across my father's neck. They reported that they saw my father fall among a pile of corpses and that his head rolled away. Unable to watch any more, they turned away."

"How terrible."

"It was terrible news, but at least the uncertainty was put to rest. So many thousands of Jews had died to sanctify the Name, and now they had learned that my father was among them. They mourned and they grieved, and then it was time to move on. My mother was a lovely young woman in the bloom of her youth, and my grandfather wanted her to remarry. He sent a letter to Rabbi Heschel of Krakow, his brother-in-law, in which he gave the full detailed report of the two men from Vilna and asked him if my mother could remarry."

"I imagine he gave his permission."

"He did. The testimony of the witnesses was clear and reliable. But my mother refused to hear any talk of her remarrying. She felt in her heart that her husband was still alive, and she was determined to wait until she could be reunited with him. She was determined to bear his children. My grandfather pleaded with her. Why should she be an *agunah*? Two reliable witnesses had seen her husband die. They had watched it happen. The report had been sent to Rabbi Heschel, who had given her permission to remarry. Of course, it was difficult to accept that her young husband wasn't coming back. But that was the curse of the times. Why ruin her entire life by entertaining some unrealistic notion that her husband was coming back even though the evidence of his death was so strong and clear? But my mother absolutely refused to hear of it."

"Amazing. A heart feels a heart, my grandmother used to say."

"My mother was right, of course. The testimony of the witnesses was indeed strong, clear and well-intended. But it was mistaken. My father had not been killed. At the last moment, the Cossack took pity on my father and instead of bringing the edge of the sword down on his neck, he struck my father in the side with the butt of his sword and sent him sprawling. 'Run for your life, you young dog,' he said to my father. 'Save yourself.' My father ran for his life. He hid among the piles of corpses, covering himself with a sack during the day and venturing out under cover of darkness to scavenge for a bit of food to keep him alive. More often than not, he subsisted on blades of bitter grass. And then it was back among the corpses."

Rav Amos shuddered. "How long did this go on?"

"Eight days. Eight days that seemed like eight years. And then the blood frenzy was over, and the Cossacks withdrew. At last, my father was able to escape Vilna and get far away from the Cossack murderers. Like most of the refugees, he went west. He wandered from town to town, looking for some news about his wife and her family. My grandfather was a famous man, the head of the *beis din* of Vilna. Before long, my father learned that they had found refuge in Trebic in Moravia, and that was where he went."

"I can imagine the scene when he suddenly showed up in Trebic, back from the dead."

"Back from the dead for everyone except for my mother. She had never given him up for dead. Six months after they were separated by the tides of death, the young husband and wife were reunited in a joyous celebration."[17]

"There's something I don't understand," said Rav Amos. "You explained how the witnesses made the mistake of thinking your father had been killed."

"That's right. They saw the Cossack bring the sword down on my father, and they didn't realize that at the last second he turned the sword and, instead of striking him with the edge of the blade, struck him with the butt."

"I understand. But how do you explain that they saw your father's severed head roll away?"

Rav Tzvi shrugged. "Who knows? The mind can play tricks on people. They see what they expect to see. They expected him to decapitate my father, so when he fell onto the pile of corpses, they thought they saw his head roll."

"Both of them made the same mistake?"

"You're right. Two people don't usually make the same mistake. But both of these men were expecting my father's head to roll, and when one of them thought he saw it and mentioned it to his friend, the other one thought he saw it, too. That's what must have happened. They thought they saw it."

"That's an incredible story," said Rav Amos.

"There's one more part," said Rav Tzvi. "When they told Rabbi Heschel, my great-uncle, what had happened, he was shocked and mortified. He couldn't believe he'd given a married woman permission to remarry."

"But it wasn't his fault."

"It really wasn't his fault, but he blamed himself nonetheless. He felt that he should have understood that during such times of panic and hysteria even two witnesses are not fully reliable. And then and there he decided that he would never again consider any more *agunah* questions."[18]

"The humility of the great," commented Rav Amos. "A man of lesser stature would have absolved himself of blame."

The days crept along, one after the other, in the little cabin in the woods. Moshke was away most of the time, returning in the evenings with food and provisions. Rav Amos had his little Chumash with him, which he pored over several times a day, but otherwise, he and Rav Tzvi sat together and talked about anything and everything. Back in Alt-Ofen, he had told Rav Tzvi a few stories about his life in Amsterdam and about his exploits in America, but mostly, they had talked in learning, something they both found far more exciting and intriguing than chatting about their experiences. During his Shivah, however, Rav Tzvi was forbidden to learn Torah, which left plenty of time for histories and reminiscences.

By the time the Shivah was drawing to a close, the two men had explored the highways and byways of each other's lives, thoughts and dreams, and their bond of friendship had cemented and grown exceedingly deep.

Almost as an afterthought, Rav Amos told Rav Tzvi about the old lady with whom he had shared the wagon from Belgrade. Rav Tzvi laughed as Rav Amos repeated the conversation almost verbatim.

"It's funny now," said Rav Amos, "But at the time I didn't think it was so funny. In fact, I took it quite seriously."

"You felt the sultan's sister was delivering a divine message to you?"

"It sounds a little ridiculous now, doesn't it? But at the time, yes, that's what I thought. And by the way, I doubt she was the sultan's sister."

"Aha! You didn't say she wasn't the sultan's sister. You said you doubt it, which means that you also consider it a possibility."

"No, it's not a possibility," said Rav Amos. "She was just a crazy old woman."

"So you're sure she was not the sultan's sister."

Rav Amos threw up his hands. "I can't say that either. How could I tell?"

"I don't know."

"So what do you think, Tzvi? Was she the sultan's sister?"

"How should I know? I wasn't there. I don't think it's likely, but I don't know for sure. Just like you. Where does reality end, and where does fantasy begin? You never know for sure."

"So what about the message?" said Rav Amos. "What about the midnight intruders? What do you think?"

"You thought it was a divine message, right?" said Rav Tzvi. "It felt like a divine message?"

"I really didn't think so much about it at the time, only later when the old woman disappeared mysteriously. The answer is that, yes, I did think so."

"Then it's probably true," said Rav Tzvi. "We certainly need to consider it a real possibility. Hmm. Midnight intruders. I've never heard that expression, but we should beware of them anyway, whoever they may be."

"It seems it can be anyone. People you don't suspect. Anyone." Rav Amos smiled. "Do you think Moshke could be a midnight intruder?"

Rav Tzvi smiled. "I don't think so, but who knows? I can't be sure. All I can say for sure is that you and I are not midnight intruders."

UNEXPECTED ENCOUNTERS · 7

There was not much military traffic on the road as Moshke's cart with its three passengers headed south toward Belgrade. Nearly two weeks had passed since the Imperial army had conquered Budapest after having bombarded it into a pile of rubble. This round of the endless ebb and flow of the war between the Europeans and the Ottoman Turks had gone to the Europeans. The Turks now occupied defensive positions further south. Both sides needed a little time to lick their wounds and catch their breaths.

Moshke sat on the driver's bench with the reins held loosely in his hands, while Rav Amos and Rav Tzvi sat in the back of the little cart, their clothes worn, bedraggled and blackened by the smoke of battle. The horse, seeming even older and more tired than ever, clopped along at a glacial pace. They had been on the road for three days, and they had still not come halfway to Belgrade.

"At this rate," Rav Amos remarked in a low voice, "it'll take weeks to get to Belgrade."

"What can we do?" Rav Tzvi replied. "Walk? We'll get there when we get there." He leaned forward and tapped Moshke on the shoulder. "Moshke, could we stop sometime soon? It's time for Minchah."

"Sure, rabbi. There's a nice spot not too far ahead, a big flat rock with a nice view of the river and the mountains."

They rode on for a little while, then Moshke pulled the cart onto a flat slab of scrub-covered rock that gleamed in the afternoon sun. He tethered the horse, and the three men got out and walked a good distance from the noisy road. They turned to face in the direction of Yerushalayim, their backs to the road, took out their Siddurim and were soon absorbed in their prayers.

When they turned to go back to the cart, they noticed a large, beautiful carriage standing beside it. Four strong horses were hitched to the carriage, and a portly liveried driver sat high up on the bench. Two well-dressed gentlemen, one tall, lanky and youngish, the other round as a ball with grizzled hair, were leaning against the cart nonchalantly.

Moshke eyed them suspiciously. "Who are you, and what do you want?"

"Oh, you needn't worry about us," said the round man. "We're from the Jewish community of Sarajevo in Bosnia. We saw three Jews praying by the roadside, and we noticed that your ... ahem ... um ... mode of transportation ... was somewhat on the primitive side. So we stopped to see if you need any help. Is there anything we can do for you? We're on our way home to Sarajevo. Are you going in our direction? Can we offer you a ride?"

"That's very kind of you," said Rav Amos. "We're on our way to Belgrade, and we'll get there just fine. Thank you for the offer."

Rav Tzvi hung back and said nothing, and the two well-dressed gentlemen paid him no heed.

"Well, we're happy to hear that. My name is Ezra Benshushan, and this is my nephew Machlouf Murabia. We're on our way back from Budapest. Are you gentlemen aware of what happened there?"

"We are," said Rav Amos.

"There's nothing left. Nothing." Benshushan shook his head and sighed. "We were on our way from Istanbul .... You see, my nephew and I are in the diamond business together, and we were in Istanbul on business and … um … for other reasons …. Anyway, that's neither here nor there. So as I was saying, we were traveling from Istanbul to Budapest to see someone in Alt-Ofen … for the other reasons … but … never mind. So as we got closer, we heard that the Austrians had attacked and conquered the capital. We heard there'd been a bombardment, but we thought … you know … maybe …. But there's nothing left of the place. We never thought the community had been wiped out completely."

"It wasn't," said Rav Tzvi. "Some of the people were taken hostage and carried off to Germany."

Benshushan looked at Rav Tzvi for the first time. Something about the tall young man caught his attention. Even in his shabby condition, Rav Tzvi had an impressive presence. He tried to imagine him in better clothing, barbered and groomed.

"Pardon me, young man," he said. "You look familiar. I have a feeling I've seen you somewhere once before, but I can't recall the time and place. Could you help me out? I didn't catch your name or the names of your companions."

"Of course," said Rav Tzvi. "This is Moshke, our driver and our host for the last two weeks. This is Rabbi Amos Strasbourg from Amsterdam. And my name is Tzvi Ashkenazi, formerly of Alt-Ofen, now homeless."

Benshushan's mouth fell open. "Did you say Tzvi Ashkenazi?"
"Yes."
"Are you the son of Rabbi Yaakov Ashkenazi?"
"Yes."
"Then you're the one we were coming to see. Now I recognize you. Of course, how could I not have seen it right away? You look a little different now. You're older, your beard is fuller, and you've obviously been through a … difficult time … Er … your father …?"

"My father survived," said Rav Tzvi, "thank you for asking. He's been taken captive and is on his way to Germany."

"Oh, I'm sorry to hear that. I mean ... that came out wrong ... I'm sorry to hear that he's a captive ... but I'm so very happy that he's alive."

Rav Tzvi smiled at his discomfiture. "I understood what you meant the first time, Señor Benshushan. So how do you know me? When and where did you see me before?"

"It was in Belgrade seven years ago," said Benshushan. "I was at a feast of celebration, and there was a long table with many *chachamim* sitting around it. One of the *chachamim* was a messenger from the community of Chevron in Eretz Yisrael who was in Belgrade to raise funds. I remember him clearly. He was a *nazir*, you know, no wine and no haircuts. He had long gray hair down below his shoulders and the longest white beard I have ever seen. They honored him with the *zimun*, you know, leading the Birchat Hamazon. He asked someone else to hold the cup of wine, and he did the *zimun*."

Rav Tzvi nodded. "I remember that night."

"Well, so do I," said Benshushan. "So I saw this young man seated at the table with the other *chachamim*. He looked to be, I'd say, twenty or twenty-one years old."

"Twenty-three," said Rav Tzvi.

"Twenty-three, yes. Anyway, after Birchat Hamazon, this young man spoke up. He said that, in his humble opinion, a *nazir* should not be allowed to do the *zimun*, since it was inappropriate to have someone else hold the wine during the *zimun* and it was also inappropriate for him to hold the wine himself. He brought many proofs to his position.[19] There was a heated discussion, and in the end, all the *chachamim* agreed with you, didn't they?"

"They did."

"So I asked about this brilliant young man. Who was he? And I was told that he was Rabbi Tzvi Ashkenazi, the grandson of Rabbi Ephraim Hakohein of Vilna who had passed away in Alt-Ofen the year before. He had distinguished himself in Rabbi Eliahu Covo's *yeshivah* in Salonika, and afterward he spent some time in Istanbul, where the *chachamim* conferred the title *chacham* on him, even though he was an Ashkenazi, in recognition of his achievements. The young *chacham*, I was told, had stopped over in Belgrade on his way home to Alt-Ofen, where he intended to help his father who had become the new rabbi. Oh yes, I remember you well now. Do you remember me?"

"I'm afraid not. You must have looked somewhat different then."

"Well, it is true that I looked different then. Seven years ago, my hair was black as coal, and I was not as … um … prosperous-looking … if you know what I mean." He patted his protuberant waist. "But you are really being too kind. Why would you remember me? I was just another face in the crowd. I didn't do or say anything remarkable."

"Well, we meet again, Señor Benshushan," said Rav Tzvi. "And this time I will remember you. Unless you change your appearance again."

Benshushan patted his waist ruefully and shrugged. "My wife wants me to … um … you know … um …. But what can you do? I've tried to eat less, but a man has to keep up his strength, doesn't he?" He suddenly slapped his forehead. "What's the matter with me? Here I am, talking to you about this, that and the other, and I'm neglecting the main thing for which I came all the way to Budapest. I had to ask you a question."

"All right. What is your question?"

"This is awkward." He looked around. "It's not the kind of question you ask standing by the roadside with the wagons and the horses."

"Are you uncomfortable speaking in front of my friends?"

Benshushan shook his head. "No, it's not that. It's just ..."

"Would you like to go down by the river? Would that make you more comfortable?"

"No, no. I'm making a fool of myself, I know. I'm making it more complicated than it really is. It's just that I imagined it differently."

"It?"

"All right, I'll just blurt it out." He took a deep breath. "We've come to invite you to be the rabbi of Sarajevo.[20] We know that ours is a Sephardic community and you are an Ashkenazic rabbi, but you studied in Sephardic *batei midrash* with Sephardic rabbis, and you are a *chacham*. And we would be honored to have you as our rabbi. When we were looking for a new rabbi, I remembered the young man I had seen in Belgrade, and I thought that he would be perfect for the position. We made inquiries about you in Istanbul, and the information we received was even better than we expected. So we want to extend the invitation to you. May I call you Chacham Tzvi?"

Rav Tzvi blinked. "This is unexpected."

"You understand why I was reluctant to ask the question here and now under these circumstances, don't you? This invitation should have been presented to you with the honor and ceremony such a momentous occasion deserves, not while standing by the roadside in front of the horses. So what do you say, Chacham Tzvi? May I call you Chacham Tzvi?"

"Yes."

Benshushan's face beamed. "So you'll come? Oh, I'm so happy. You will love Sarajevo, I promise you. And from now on we'll call you Chacham Tzvi."

Chacham Tzvi held up his hand. "Wait a minute, wait a minute. All I meant was that you could call me Chacham Tzvi if you wish. As for your invitation, believe me, I'm deeply honored, very deeply honored —"

Benshushan groaned. "This doesn't sound so good."

"Look, if you'd come a month ago, I probably would have accepted, if my father approved. But things have changed. I am a man without a family and without a home. My parents are on their way to Germany in chains. My place is with them. I must travel to Germany and do what I can to gain their release."

"If I may add a thought, Chacham Tzvi," a deep voice interjected. It was Machlouf Murabia, Benshushan's nephew, who had been silent and practically invisible during the entire conversation.

"Please do," said Chacham Tzvi.

"Thank you." His voice was such a rumble that it seemed to be emanating from deep inside a cave, and coming from such a lanky fellow, it was exceedingly incongruous. "Your parents are probably in Germany already by now, while you are traveling in the opposite direction at a, shall we say, very slow pace. By the time you get to Germany, they may already have been redeemed and on their way back here. And where would they go? You have no home, and neither do they. Not anymore."

"All right," said Chacham Tzvi slowly.

"So wouldn't it be better," Murabia continued, "if you established yourself in Sarajevo first? You can send inquiries to Germany from Sarajevo, and we would help you. We would also help you with any arrangement you have to make for the release of your parents. And then they could join you in Sarajevo until they decide what to do with the rest of their lives."

Chacham Tzvi stroked his beard for a few long minutes as he considered Murabia's arguments. Finally, he turned to Rav Amos.

"What do you think, my friend?" he said at last. "What would you advise me to do?"

"There is merit to what Señor Murabia is saying," said Rav Amos. "But at the same time, if you make a commitment to the community of Sarajevo, you will restrict your options."

"It's no problem." This last comment had come from Moshke the Driver. "Do you mind if I explain, Rabbi Ashkenazi?"

"No, Moshke. Go right ahead."

"I really shouldn't speak up," said Moshke, "when two distinguished rabbis are having a discussion. I know my place. But I think I have a simple answer for you. Take the job temporarily."

"Moshke is right," said Rav Amos. "Don't make a full commitment. Take the position on the condition that you can leave for the sake of your parents if the need arises. If things work out, you can stay. If not, you'll be free to go."

"Makes sense," said Chacham Tzvi. "Thank you, Moshke. The simple answer is usually the best." He turned to the men from Sarajevo. "So you heard; this is how it is. Does your invitation stand if those are my conditions?"

Benshushan and Murabia exchanged glances.

"We will be pleased to accommodate your needs, Chacham Tzvi," said Benshushan. "Let's shake hands on it."

Rav Tzvi shook hands with both men. Rav Amos shook Chacham Tzvi's hand and embraced him. Then he shook hands with the others and complimented them on their wise choice. Benshushan broke into a dance, moving about with an agility unexpected for such a rotund man.

"Oh, what a great day this is for Sarajevo!" he crowed. "What an honor for our community to have such a bright star as our own rabbi! I'm beside myself with joy. Our mission is a great success, Machlouf. The Almighty guided our steps and brought us to this place. Thank the Almighty for His kindness."

"Uncle, we have to make plans," said Murabia. "We need to provide our new *chacham* with some fine garments before we present him to Sarajevo. I'd offer some of ours, but I think yours would be too large and mine too small."

"Don't worry, Machlouf. I'll take care of everything. We'll stop in Tuzla on the way back to Sarajevo. There's a good tailor there. We should be home for Shabbat."

Rav Amos and Chacham Tzvi bid a warm farewell to Moshke, transferred their meager belongings to Benshushan's carriage, and they were off.

The news of their arrival swept through Sarajevo like wildfire. Within minutes, most of the community was gathered in front of Benshushan's house, eager for a glimpse of the new rabbi.

Chacham Tzvi embraced his new congregants with love and devotion from the very beginning. He listened to their problems and issues and gave his advice and guidance. He spoke in the synagogue three times on Shabbat, addressing the people on every level. He went to visit the sick even though he had never met them when they were well. He interviewed the shochet and checked his slaughtering knives, and he checked the *mikveh*. And all this within the space of a few days.

The quarters the community provided for him were adequate, and he shared them comfortably with Rav Amos. Within days, he had settled into his new routine, which kept him busy from morning until night. Rav Amos helped with some of the tasks, but for the most part, his time was free, and he spent it in the *beis midrash*.

One morning over breakfast, Chacham Tzvi brought up the unspoken subject that was on both their minds.

"Rosh Hashanah is drawing near, Amos," he said. "I think you should be on your way to Pulichev as soon as possible. Your father is expecting you for Rosh Hashanah. I can manage here."

Rav Amos shook his head. "I've been giving the inevitable some thought, just as you have. I can't stay here with you forever, much as I'd like it. There's really nothing for me here. But I can't leave you just yet. Who knows what tomorrow may bring?"

"I'll be fine, Amos. I know you saved my life once. But you don't have to stay here with me just in case it may need saving again."

"I think I should stay until the situation with your parents is resolved. We've sent out letters of inquiry to different cities, and hopefully, we'll hear some good news. But don't forget that your acceptance of this position was conditional. What if you have to leave here and go to your parents' assistance? You'll need my help then, even if you think you can manage on your own. So I think I should stay here for a little while longer. Until we know what happened to your parents."

"Amos, my dearest friend, there's no question that your help would mean the world to me if I needed to leave here and go and rescue my parents. But who knows if that will happen? Everything may work out just fine. Meanwhile, your father is waiting for you in Pulichev, anxious and worried."

"I sent him a letter a few days ago. He won't be worried."

"But he'll be disappointed," said Chacham Tzvi. "He is expecting you, and he is looking forward to spending Rosh Hashanah with you and visiting with his cousin, the great Rav Shlomo Strasbourg, together with you, the son of whom he is so proud. You should not deny him this pleasure. He's your father."

"You make a good point, Tzvi. And I'm really saddened that I won't be there with him in Pulichev. But I know my father, and he would undoubtedly want me to stay here with you under the circumstances. I'll write him another letter, explaining the situation a little more clearly. More than meeting up with me in Pulichev, my father wants me to get Rav Shlomo's blessing and draw on his wisdom while there is still a chance to do so. I'll reassure my father that after your situation is resolved, I'll go on to Pulichev by myself."

Chacham Tzvi sighed. "You know that I have no friends or family here in Sarajevo. When the time comes for you to go, I will be lonely. So I'm very happy to have you stay here with me for as long as possible. But I feel that I shouldn't hold you back from going on with your own life."

"This is where my life is right now, Tzvi. The most important thing for me to do right now is to be a good friend to you in this difficult time, what with the tragedy you've suffered and the situation with your — "

A sharp knock on the door interrupted him. Chacham Tzvi got up and opened it. Ezra Benshushan came rushing into the house.

"Chacham Tzvi," he said, "we may have a slight problem."

"Come sit down at the table," said Chacham Tzvi. "Make yourself comfortable, and we'll talk."

Benshushan cast a sideways glance at Rav Amos, who was sitting at the table.

"You can talk in Rabbi Strasbourg's presence," said Chacham Tzvi. "He is my friend and my brother. I have no secrets from him. Unless it's private business that relates to you personally."

Benshushan took a seat at the table. He took off his hat and twisted it in his hands. Then he dropped it on an unoccupied chair. "No, it's nothing to do with me personally. It relates to you."

Chacham Tzvi raised his eyebrows. "To me? So what's the slight problem that relates to me? It seems to me by your agitation that it's more than slight."

"I'm so sorry I have to speak to you about this, Chacham Tzvi. I'm so embarrassed. But what can I do? You know Moshe Chayun, the one who lives around the corner from the synagogue?"

"Yes."

"Did you know that he's the son-in-law of Rabbi Yaakov Chagiz, may his memory be a blessing, one of the *chachamim* of Yerushalayim, the leading opponent to Shabbesai Tzvi?"

"No, I didn't know that. Rabbi Chagiz was a great man, and the entire Jewish world owes him a debt of gratitude."

"Indeed, it does. Well ... um ... speaking about Moshe Chayun ... um ... he has a son."

"All right."

"His son's name is Nechemiah. Nechemiah Chiya Chayun."

"All right."

"I think Moshe was hoping that his son would become the rabbi of Sarajevo. I think Moshe Chayun may try to organize opposition to you in favor of his son Nechemiah. I think .... Oh, Chacham Tzvi, I'm so humiliated and ashamed. I brought you here, and now they may want to remove you."

"All right, calm yourself, Señor Benshushan. I've met Moshe Chayun several times, and he seemed friendly enough. He never gave me the slightest hint that he wasn't happy with my coming here to be the rabbi. What makes you think otherwise?"

"His son was away. Until yesterday, that is."

"Oh."

"You see the problem?"

"Not really. Not yet."

"Señor Benshushan," said Rav Amos, "could you tell us something about this Nechemiah Chayun? Who is he? Where was he until now? Why do you think his father wants him to be the rabbi?"

Benshushan nodded rapidly. "Do you mind if I have a glass of water?"

Rav Amos poured him a glass, and he swallowed it in one gulp.

"Nechemiah Chayun," he began. "A very bright fellow. I would say he's about your age, Rabbi Strasbourg. Maybe a year or two younger. Very bright. As a young boy, his father sent him to learn in a *yeshivah* in Chevron. He came back here in 1668, when he was eighteen, and within a few months, he had secured a position as rabbi of Uskup, that's a small community near Salonika. He was rabbi there for three years, and then he left."

"Why did he leave?" asked Chacham Tzvi.

"I'm not sure. I think he didn't like the duties and responsibilities of being a rabbi." He shrugged. "In my opinion, he shouldn't have taken a position as a rabbi at such a young age. Eighteen! Why, he was little more than a child, and already he's a rabbi? Three years later, he was twenty-one years old, bored and restless. So he became a merchant for a while and traveled a lot in Palestine and Egypt. He came back to Sarajevo a few times, but that was many years ago. His father tells me that even though he was involved in business he always put his first emphasis on learning and that he has blossomed into a real *talmid chacham* of stature."

"So what's the problem?" said Rav Amos.

Benshushan studied his nails for a moment. "Well, here it is. Nechemiah arrived on his father's doorstep late last night. This morning, Moshe Chayun approached me. He said he wanted to talk to me. So we talked. He told me that his son had come home last night and that he was no longer the impetuous boy of his youth but a sober and mature *talmid chacham*. He said that he thinks Nechemiah is finally ready to marry and settle down. So I said, 'That's wonderful. I'm very happy for you and your wife.' So he said that his son was thinking of settling down right here in Sarajevo."

Benshushan paused to study his nails again.

"I haven't heard the problem yet," said Chacham Tzvi.

Benshushan gulped and plunged ahead. "Moshe Chayun wants his son to be the rabbi of Sarajevo. He feels Nechemiah is perfectly suited to the position. He was born and raised in this community and knows the people and their backgrounds, even though he's been away for a few years. He is a *talmid chacham* with a few years of experience as a practicing rabbi, so he has the qualifications for the position." He swallowed hard. "So Moshe wanted to know if we could still withdraw our invitation to you, especially since it is only conditional and since you haven't even been here a full week yet."

"I see," said Chacham Tzvi.

"Moshe feels very bad about this. He really likes you and was very happy that you agreed to come here, but … you know … his son … you know how it is … a father always thinks about his own children before anything else."

"I understand," said Chacham Tzvi. "And what do you want, Señor Benshushan?"

Benshushan squirmed. "I'm in a difficult and delicate position."

"But what is your own preference?"

"I want you to be our rabbi, Chacham Tzvi. I think that your arrival here is the most wonderful thing that's ever happened to our community. Now, I'm not particularly opposed to Nechemiah Chayun. He's all right. In fact, I think it's possible that he could make a fine rabbi, but he is not in your class, not even close. But on the other hand, I am concerned about a dispute breaking out and our close-knit little community being torn apart by dissension. It would be a disaster."

"So what would you like to see happen?"

"I don't know. I don't know. I'd like to see you continue as our rabbi, Chacham Tzvi, but I don't want a battle."

"No one does," said Chacham Tzvi.

"Something is not quite clear to me, Señor Benshushan," said Rav Amos. "All this you told us, is it coming from

Nechemiah Chayun? Did he ask his father to intercede with you and secure the position for him?"

"I'm not sure," said Benshushan. "Moshe said that Nechemiah arrived late last night, that he seemed different and that he said something to the effect that he was finally ready to settle down. He said that Nechemiah was exhausted from his journey and that he went to sleep soon after he arrived. I didn't ask him your question specifically, Rabbi Strasbourg, but it seems to me that Moshe was making his own assumptions based on what he had heard from Nechemiah. Not unreasonable assumptions, I would add."

"So why don't we wait," said Rav Amos, "until Nechemiah speaks his own mind. After all, he is a grown man, a scholar and a world traveler. He doesn't need his father to speak for him on this matter. Rest assured, if he wants the position, we will hear from him."

Benshushan turned to Chacham Tzvi. "So we should wait, Chacham Tzvi?"

"Rabbi Strasbourg has given us good advice," said Chacham Tzvi. "Let matters take their course. Why do anything when we don't even know which direction they will take? Does Moshe Chayun know that you've come to speak with me?"

Benshushan fidgeted. "He asked me to come, and I told him I would."

"It's all right, Señor Benshushan. You did the right thing, and I fully appreciate the difficult position in which you find yourself."

Chacham Tzvi stood up, signaling that the meeting was over. Benshushan jumped to his feet. He kissed Chacham Tzvi's hand and bowed slightly to Rav Amos. Then he grabbed his hat and was out the door.

"Well, what do you make of that, Amos?" said Chacham Tzvi after he had gone.

Rav Amos shrugged his shoulders. "Who knows? It may be much ado about nothing. Let's see what happens."

"Well, I'll tell you one thing. If it involves quarrels and conflicts, I'll step aside and leave. Benshushan is right. I'm only here conditionally. I never asked for this position, and if it becomes a problem, I'll just walk away from it."

"That's the wisest thing to do," said Rav Amos. "Look, even under the best of circumstances, this was only going to be a temporary position for you anyway until you could rebuild your life. Sarajevo is a small Sephardic community in a remote part of the Jewish world, and even though you're certainly qualified to serve as its rabbi, there's no doubt in my mind that you're destined for a position in a major Ashkenazic center, a position in your own ancestral traditions from which your influence can reach far and wide. If we have to leave here, then this too is for the best."

Chacham Tzvi laughed. "You have very high hopes for me, Amos. Unrealistic expectations can lead to disappointment, you know. And you really don't have to console me. Believe me, if I have to leave, I won't be heartbroken. The main thing on my mind right now is the fate of my parents."

"Mine, too. So what do you say we go to the *beis midrash* for a little while. You know that *sugya* we spoke about with your father back in Alt-Ofen about how to establish the value of a house?"

"I remember."

"I've been going through the Gemara and the Rambam, and I have many questions. You know, like what exactly is the role of *ilui damim*, putting it up for auction? Does it help establish the real value or is it just a way to generate more revenue to pay off the creditors? Maybe you can help me figure it out."

"Well, the Rambam learns that the Gemara isn't discussing a case of *ilui damim*."

"Then why does Rami bar Chama compare it to the Mishnah?"

"That's the problem, I know. I have some ideas, so let's go to the *beis midrash* and take a look inside. I think —."

A loud knock interrupted him, and he went to open the door.

"May I come in?" said the man standing on the doorstep.

Chacham Tzvi stepped aside. "Please do."

The man had olive skin and a large black beard and *peyos* flecked liberally with gray. His large brown eyes were intense but friendly, as if he had a harmless secret that brought him constant amusement. He wore a long robe trimmed in green and red, and a round multi-colored cap covered most of his closely shaven head.

He smiled at Chacham Tzvi and Rav Amos and shook hands with both of them. "*Shalom aleichem*," he said, his voice full of gusto and good humor. "You must be Chacham Tzvi, and you are Rabbi Amos Strasbourg. I'm Nechemiah Chayun."

"I'm pleased to meet you," said Chacham Tzvi.

"We've heard so much about you," Rav Amos added.

Chayun laughed and slapped his thigh. "Do you mind if we all sit down?"

The three took seats around the table.

"You say you heard about me," said Chayun. "From Ezra Benshushan no doubt. I saw him leaving here a few minutes ago."

"He was here," said Chacham Tzvi cautiously.

"And he no doubt told you that my father wants me to replace you as the rabbi of Sarajevo."

"He did mention something to that effect."

"My father means well. He wants me to settle down, marry and provide him with grandchildren. He thinks that installing me as the rabbi of Sarajevo would anchor me down here. But don't worry about me, Chacham Tzvi."

"Do I look worried?"

"Actually, you don't look worried at all. I suspect that you would not be too upset if you had to leave Sarajevo. And I suspect that no matter what happens, you will move on before too long. Isn't that true?"

"Perhaps."

"Yes, I have no doubt about it. Sarajevo is too small to contain you. But the position is yours for as long as you want it. First of all, I wouldn't dream of taking it from you after it was offered to you and you accepted it in good faith. But even if you were to leave tomorrow of your own accord, I wouldn't take the position as rabbi."

"Really?" said Rav Amos.

"Oh, absolutely. Sarajevo is not big enough to contain me either. My ambitions run in different directions. I want to publish my writings and give them to the world. I want to do something important, something that will make a lasting impression on the world, something that will be alive and thriving hundreds of years after I'm gone. I want to achieve immortality, don't you?"

Rav Amos chuckled. "I'd like to achieve immortality by not dying."

Chayun threw back his head and laughed. "A good idea, Rabbi Strasbourg. But I think my plan has a better chance of success. How about you, Chacham Tzvi? How do you propose to achieve immortality?"

"By living my life in this world as a good and honorable Jew. All of us achieve immortality in the next world."

"True, true. Spoken like a proper pious rabbi. But you know what I mean. I want to use my creativity to contribute to the constant blossoming of the Torah, as I'm sure you will someday as well."

Chacham Tzvi smiled. "With the help of the Almighty. What parts of the Torah do your writings address?"

"Many different parts," said Chayun. "Did you know that Rabbi Yaakov Chagiz, the author of *She'alot Uteshuvot Halachot Ketanot*, was my grandfather?"

"Yes, Señor Benshushan mentioned it. His rulings are excellent and widely accepted. Are you also writing on questions of Halachah?"

"A little bit," said Chayun. "But mostly, I study the holy Zohar and the works of Arizal. In the course of my travels, I've studied Kabbalah with many holy rabbis, and I've been initiated into some of its most esoteric concepts. It used to be that when I stood under the sky I felt like a little person dwarfed by the vastness of the universe. But with the secrets I've learned, my spirit has been unlocked, and it reaches out to every corner of the universe. Can you appreciate what I'm saying?"

"I think so," said Chacham Tzvi.

Chayun's eyes twinkled, and he winked at Chacham Tzvi. "You are too modest, Chacham Tzvi. I've heard about you. You probably know more Kabbalah than I do, but you're wise to keep your knowledge concealed. My destiny, however, is different. If my mission in life is to help the world discover the beauty of Kabbalah, I can't very well conceal my knowledge of it, can I?"

"I suppose not. So what are your plans?"

"Right now, I don't have any firm plans. I'd like to visit with my parents for a while. Maybe a few weeks, or even a few months. And then I'm off, footloose and fancy free, to wherever my heart and spirit will take me. New places, new people, new ideas, new opportunities for the mind and the heart and the spirit. I wasn't born to be tied down to one place."

Chacham Tzvi smiled and stood up, and the others rose as well. "Well, it was certainly … an experience … meeting you. I wish you success in all your endeavors."

"The same goes for me," said Rav Amos.

"I just want one thing from you, Chacham Tzvi," said Chayun. "And from you, Rabbi Strasbourg. I want the pleasure of having made your acquaintance and perhaps the honor of having found kindred spirits in you. It was worth coming back to Sarajevo at this time just for the special privilege of having met the both of you."

"Well, that is very kind of you," said Chacham Tzvi.

Chayun stopped at the door and flashed him a brilliant smile. "We'll be seeing something of each other in the coming weeks," he said. "I'm looking forward to a close relationship with you. In fact, I feel close to you already."

A DIFFICULT DECISION · 8

WITH EACH PASSING DAY, Chacham Tzvi became ever more popular with the people of Sarajevo. They flocked to hear his sermons, lectures and talks. They peppered him with questions regarding law and custom and delighted in the clarity of his quick and incisive responses. When they had no questions, they manufactured them. Men followed him in the streets wherever he went and kissed his hands. Mothers brought their babies to him for blessings. Old people stood up for him when he passed by. He was the crown jewel of their celebrations and the apple of their eye.

Travelers spread his fame far beyond the boundaries of Sarajevo, and many people from neighboring districts flooded into Sarajevo for Rosh Hashanah, Yom Kippur and Sukkos. Whoever had a spare room, alcove or attic rented it out to the excited visitors, and the local merchants did a booming business selling them food and all sorts of other provisions.

There were very wealthy merchants among the community, men with connections in every commercial center in Europe, and they all volunteered to help Chacham Tzvi find his captured parents. According to the information Rav Amos had received, the captives were being taken to Germany, but he had not been told where in Germany. Therefore, the merchants of Sarajevo sent instructions to their agents throughout Germany to make inquiries about the captives of Alt-Ofen in general and the parents of Chacham Tzvi in particular.

The first reports of Chacham Tzvi's parents arrived in Sarajevo right after Sukkos. As expected, the Jewish captives were considered valuable assets because of the ransom money they would command. Everyone wanted them, and a compromise had been reached. They were divided up among the German generals who had fought in Hungary. Chacham Tzvi's parents had fallen to the lot of the General of Freisen, and he had taken them to Berlin.

A week later, new reports from the European agents mentioned efforts being made by the Jewish communities of Prague and Hamburg to negotiate the release of the Jewish captives. The situation was tense, the agents reported, but there was hope and optimism that a satisfactory solution could be found.

During all this time, Chacham Tzvi and Rav Amos, as the people began calling him, had very little interaction with Nechemiah Chayun. He was often gone for long stretches of time, traveling to other communities in the Balkans, but he was in Sarajevo for the Yamim Tovim and almost every Shabbos. On those occasions, he came to synagogue in a flowing white robe tied at the waist by a sash of purple velvet embroidered with gold thread. Wrapped in his *tallis*, he stood in a corner in the back of the synagogue, flamboyantly unobtrusive, and prayed for hours at a time.

Often he lifted his hands to the heavens and sang mysterious songs that were barely audible to those around him while prancing and dancing in his place, his feet forming feathery steps to keep time with his songs.

On a few occasions, he asked Chacham Tzvi a question about the weekly Torah portion. This always led to a wide-ranging discussion of the approaches of the commentators. Afterward, Chayun usually offered a Kabbalistic interpretation, which usually led to new discussions and arguments. If the disagreement was not resolved, however, Chayun graciously and invariably conceded defeat.

Chacham Tzvi did not know what to make of the man. He was clearly a *talmid chacham*, and he also had a good grasp of Kabbalah. He was cheerful, friendly and always in a good mood. But he was also a bit of an eccentric, a scholarly vagabond too restless to marry and settle down or even stay in one place for very long. He was ambitious and opinionated, but at the same time, he was ingratiating and conciliatory. So what was he, a holy mystic or an adventurer?

A few weeks before Chanukah, Chacham Tzvi was walking back at a leisurely pace from the synagogue after Shacharis. His eyes were fixed on the ground in front of him, while his mind was absorbed by a difficult question regarding the proper distribution of the inheritance left behind by a recently deceased congregant. As was often the case with substantial inheritances, a bitter dispute had arisen among the heirs, and now it was up to him to untangle the mess. If only the deceased had sought rabbinical advice when he wrote his will, he thought ruefully, so much unnecessary heartache and acrimony could have been avoided.

A sudden eerie sound pulled him out of his reverie. What was that strange sound? Could he have been mistaken? He shrugged and continued on his way. The second time the sound was louder than the first. It arose as an ululating cry of pain and anguish, but as it grew in intensity, it became a cry of joy, even ecstasy. The cry sent a chill up his spine.

Chacham Tzvi looked around for the source of the cry. A freezing rain was falling, and the street was deserted. He saw no people or animals or even birds that could have made the sound he had heard. There was an orchard on the other side of the street, and beyond it, the rolling fields rose gently toward the mist-covered mountains in the distance. Curious and intrigued, Chacham Tzvi pulled his coat more tightly around him against the cold. He crossed the street and walked through the orchard into the fields.

Nechemiah Chayun was standing barefoot on the ground. He wore only a thin shirt and trousers and a voluminous pair of *tzitzis*. His arms were spread wide, and his face was upturned to the rain and the wind. He stood frozen for a long time as a marble statue, his eyes closed, his mouth open and his face immobile like a mask. Then his eyes opened, his whole body began to tremble, his mouth opened even wider, and the strange ululation rent the air once again.

Chacham Tzvi could see that Chayun was in some kind of a religious trance, and although it was unlike anything he had ever seen, he respected the man's right to serve the Almighty as he chose. There did not seem to be any harm in what he was doing, and he decided that he was intruding on another man's privacy. He turned to go.

"Chacham Tzvi!" Chayun called to him. "Wait! Don't go."

Chacham Tzvi turned and stopped. Chayun came running up to him. He had thrown a coat over his drenched body, and he carried a bag over his shoulder. His face was aglow with excitement.

"I saw you looking at me," he said.

"My apologies," said Chacham Tzvi. "I did not mean to intrude on your privacy. I heard a cry and went to investigate. Perhaps I stayed a moment longer than I should have."

"We were in the open fields," said Chayun, "under the vast expanses of the clouds and the mountains and a sea of grass and trees. That is a realm that belongs to all of us. No one can hold it private to himself."

Chacham Tzvi smiled, nodded politely and turned to go again.

"Wait," said Chayun. "Do you think what I was doing was odd?"

"It was unusual, but who am I to judge if it was odd? Every man has his way of reaching out to the Almighty, which is what I assume you were doing."

"It is exactly what I was doing. I was using a formula that was given to me by a blind master of the Kabbalah in Smyrna, Turkey, an unusual rearrangement of the Ten Spheres and the letters of .... No, I'm not supposed to talk about it, but if you insist ..."

"No, I don't insist," said Chacham Tzvi. "If you promised not to reveal your formulation to other people, you should honor that promise."

"You are right, of course. And besides, you don't need me, Nechemiah Chayun, to teach you about the Kabbalah. You can probably create your own Kabbalistic formulations with the best of them."

Chacham Tzvi did not respond.

"Are you going home?" said Chayun.

"Yes, I am."

"Do you mind if I walk with you?"

"Not at all."

They walked together in silence. When they reached the house, Chacham Tzvi invited Chayun in for a cup of tea.

"Chacham Tzvi, I wanted to walk with you," said Chayun, "because I am leaving tomorrow."

"Oh? Well, I wish you much success wherever you go."

"I wanted to give you something before I go." He reached into his bag and pulled out a large item wrapped in a soft cloth. He unwrapped the cloth to reveal an exquisitely ornate silver wine cup. "This is an extraordinary piece. It was designed and produced by Daoud ibn Daoud, the finest silversmith in Damascus, Syria. I found it in the marketplace of Dubrovnik. And I thought that this is truly a wine cup fit for a king. And then I immediately thought of you, because who are kings if not the rabbis?[21] So I bought the cup, and I'm presenting it to you."

"That is very kind of you," said Chacham Tzvi. "It really is a beautiful cup, but I can't take it."

"It's the cost, of course. You think the gift is too extravagant. Well, first of all, I got it for a very good price. You should see me in the marketplace. I am a very good bargainer. And I am not a poor man, *chacham*. I can afford to buy something like this once in a while. I knew I was leaving, and I wanted to buy you something special, something to show my respect and esteem for you, something by which you will remember me kindly. It would be the greatest honor for me if you'd accept this small token of my esteem. Please take it."

"I appreciate your sentiments, and I'm touched. But I cannot accept it. It's a personal resolution of mine never to accept gifts from anyone at all. I've never accepted gifts in the past, and I pray to the Almighty that I should never have to do so in the future."

Chayun started to speak, but then he thought better of it. He nodded, wrapped the silver wine cup and put it into his bag.

"I understand," he said, "and I respect your decision. It is an honor to have met you."

He stood up, and the two men shook hands.

"Until we meet again," said Chayun, and he walked out the door.

Five minutes later, Rav Amos returned from the synagogue, where he had been learning Mishnayos with a group of men. He found Chacham Tzvi sitting motionless at the table, his mind far away.

"Tzvi, are you all right?"

Chacham Tzvi shook his head, as if the motion would bring him back from where his thoughts had taken him.

"I'm just fine," he said. "Tell me, Amos, do you think that Nechemiah Chayun may be a midnight intruder?"

Rav Amos stroked his beard and thought for a few long moments. Then he shrugged his shoulders. "I don't know. Time will tell."

A week later, reports reached Sarajevo that the Imperial armies were making a concerted push to attack and capture the city before the onset of deep winter. Tens of thousands of infantry and cavalry were moving southward along with hundreds of pieces of artillery. The Turkish army had rushed reinforcements to Belgrade, the capital of the Turkish province of Serbia, which lay directly in the path of the invaders, but the invaders had veered west into Bosnia and were advancing toward Sarajevo. In a matter of days, they would be storming the gates of the city.

On Friday afternoon, Chacham Tzvi sought out Ezra Benshushan.

"I find myself in a very delicate position," he said. "We agreed that I'd serve as rabbi conditionally until the situation with my parents was resolved."

"That is correct."

"The situation is not yet resolved, but if I stay here, it will become more complicated."

Benshushan blinked. "You want to leave?"

"Yes."

"But why? I don't understand."

"You think I'm abandoning the people in their time of need?"

"I … um … I don't know what to say, Chacham Tzvi. I … mean …"

"Look, I'm not concerned for my own safety. In other circumstances, I would not leave the city with the enemy at the gates. But I can't abandon my parents. They need me. They have no one else to stand up for them. You know that I didn't want to come here if it jeopardized the safety of my parents. You know that my whole acceptance was conditional.

Well, the time has come to invoke my right of refusal. If the Austrians attack Sarajevo and I'm injured or taken captive, who'll fend for my parents?"[22]

Benshushan sighed. "The people will be disappointed. Look, Chacham Tzvi, I appreciate your position, because we did speak about it at length when we first met. And I agree that you're justified in leaving Sarajevo, considering the situation, and traveling to Germany to help your parents. Those were the conditions of your acceptance; there's no question about that. But I'm not sure the people will see it as clearly as I do. They'll be perplexed and disappointed, especially because you want to leave them in a time of crisis, at a time when they need you the most."

"Are you trying to make me feel guilty, Señor Benshushan?"

Benshushan looked shocked. "Heaven forbid! Why would I do a thing like that? I'm genuinely concerned. And I don't even know how I could break the news to them. I mean, what would I say?"

Chacham Tzvi patted him on the shoulder. "Don't be concerned, Señor Benshushan. I'm not leaving until Sunday, and the invasion is a week away. I'll speak to the people in the synagogue tomorrow. It will be all right."

Word of Chacham Tzvi's impending departure spread quickly throughout the city even before nightfall. As Benshushan had predicted, his decision was deeply disturbing to the people. They were already struggling with anxiety and fear, and the knowledge that their revered and beloved rabbi was leaving them in such a situation was a terrible blow to their morale. Benshushan defended Chacham Tzvi to the best of his ability, but the resentment still smoldered.

On Shabbos, the synagogue was packed to overflowing; there was not an empty seat to be found even in the women's gallery, which was usually sparsely populated except for festivals and special occasions.

Chacham Tzvi got up to speak before Mussaf.

"My dear brothers and sisters," he began. "I know that most of you have already heard of my decision to leave. Many of you are undoubtedly unhappy with me. Many of you undoubtedly feel that I should not be abandoning you at such a dangerous time. My main purpose in speaking to you now is not to defend myself, although that is also important. It would be wrong of me to let you think I'm guilty when I'm in fact innocent. So first I will explain my decision, and then I will get to the main purpose of my talk.

"Three months ago, I was living a quiet peaceful life in Alt-Ofen, the section of Budapest in which the Jewish community lived. My father was the rabbi, and I assisted him to a small degree and spent the rest of my time learning. And then the same Austrian armies that are approaching Sarajevo attacked Budapest and leveled the city. Alt-Ofen was destroyed. My wife and daughter were killed, as were more than half of the Jewish people living there. My parents and the rest of the survivors were taken captive and carried off to some undetermined place in Germany where they would be held for ransom. Only I managed to escape with the help of my dear friend Rav Amos Strasbourg, whom you've all come to know and respect.

"My first and only thought was that I had to find a way to save my parents, and I immediately set out to find and rescue them. And then I met Señor Ezra Benshushan and Señor Machlouf Murabia on the road to Belgrade, and they convinced me to come to Sarajevo and continue my efforts from here with the help of the community. I agreed on the condition that I would leave if it were no longer helpful to my parents for me to stay here. That is the situation now, and that is why I must leave. My parents need me, and I cannot abandon them.

"But what about you? What about the people of Sarajevo whom I have come to know and love over the last months?

How can I leave my flock without a shepherd? The question is a good one. It is one with which I struggled long and hard before I reached my decision.

"My dear beloved brothers and sisters, we face a terrible danger here in Sarajevo. The Austrians will be here, probably before next Shabbat, and you can expect them to do to Sarajevo what they did to Budapest. They are merciless. They do not care if they kill innocent people, even women, little children and defenseless old people. So what are we supposed to do? Should we organize groups to say Tehillim nonstop twenty-four hours a day? Should we increase the level of our prayers and our learning?

"These are certainly excellent and important things to do in times of distress. But what did the Almighty say to Moshe when the Jewish people stood at the edge of the sea and the Egyptian army was bearing down on them? He said, 'Why are you crying out to Me? Speak to the nation, and let them travel.'[23] And Rashi explains, 'Now is not the time to pray at length, because the Jewish people are in distress.' What do you do when the Egyptians are bearing down on you? The Almighty tells us that we should do something to save ourselves.

"The Egyptians are bearing down on us right now, the new Egyptians in the guise of Austrians, Germans, Spaniards, Croats, Italians, Frenchmen, Danes, Swedes and whoever else has joined up with the Imperial forces. At this time, we must flee if flight is possible. Nothing else matters right now, not our homes, not our businesses, not our valuables, nothing but the safety of our families. We cannot fool ourselves into thinking we will survive this if we stay in place. All we have to do is look at what happened in Budapest. That is what the Austrians have done, and this is what we have to expect from them.

"There is still time. Save yourselves and your families. Run to the next city, and if the Austrians approach that city as well, then run to the city after that. Your responsibility is to save your lives. If you lose your lives, then your stay in this world is over, but if you save your lives and lose your money, the Almighty can and will replenish your pocketbooks.

"Too many times in our history have Jewish people been reluctant to uproot themselves, because they did not want to give up their wealth and comforts, and the results have been tragic. Look what happened in Spain. If the Jews of Spain had liquidated their properties for whatever they could get and emigrated, there would have been no Inquisition, and the Jewish people would be in a much better position all over the world. I beg you, my dear brothers and sisters, do not make the same mistakes. Do not risk being killed or captured. Flee while you have the chance. The Almighty wants us to make a *hishtadlut*, an effort, in our own behalf, and then He blesses our pitiful efforts with success, which comes entirely from His kindness and not from our skill.

"I implore you, my dear brothers and sisters, make the effort to save yourselves, and the Almighty will bless your efforts and watch over you. He granted you prosperity here in the first place, and He will grant it to you again, but save yourselves and your families. And may the Almighty bless you and protect you from all harm.

"*Shabbat shalom.*"

THE MERCHANT OF VENICE · 9

THE GONDOLA SLIPPED through the waters of the lagoon as the sun settled slowly into the western sky. The gondolier stood in the back of the gondola. He thrust his pole into the water and steered the gondola into a canal that led to the Jewish ghetto in Canaregio, the northernmost of the six districts of Venice. Chacham Tzvi and Rav Amos sat together in the center of the gondola together with Signor Jacobo Tarantella, a merchant from Venice they had met on the crossing from Dubrovnik.

"We're almost there," said Tarantella. "I really cherish the time we've spent together these past few days in Dubrovnik and during our sea voyage. It's not often that I have the privilege of spending a little time with such distinguished rabbis."

Chacham Tzvi smiled. "From Dubrovnik to Venice is not such a major sea voyage." He glanced over at Rav Amos, but his friend was drowsing with his chin on his chest.

Tarantella shook his head. "A sea voyage is a sea voyage, I always say. I know your friend has crossed the ocean twice, so after hearing all his stories, a quick trip across the Adriatic Sea doesn't impress you much, but a person can drown in a puddle as well. I've been through some frightening storms on this crossing of the Adriatic, especially at this time of the year."

"I don't dispute that. Believe me, I'm no sea traveler. Crossing the Danube or the Bosporus is about as much nautical experience as I have. As for spending time in your company, the feeling is mutual. It was really a pleasure traveling with you, Signor Tarantella. You were a very gracious traveling companion and extremely helpful."

"Well, I have a lot of experience, and I'm always willing to share my knowledge with other Jews. As I always say, isn't that what brothers are for? Business takes me to Bosnia and Croatia quite often, although considering the situation there I think I'll give that area a wide berth for a while."

"A wise decision."

"As I said, we're almost there," said Tarantella. "We have to get into the ghetto before nightfall, because they close the gates and lock them. Every place has its positives and its negatives. We live locked up in a ghetto, but we don't have massacres as in other places. Anyway, we still have a couple of hours of daylight. When we get there, we'll go and see the rabbi before anything else. You'll leave your things in the gondola. Giuseppe will keep an eye on them."

"Can we trust him?" said Chacham Tzvi.

"Of course, he's been in my employ for seventeen years."

"A gondolier? How often can you use a gondolier?"

"This is my private gondola," said Tarantella. "Being my gondolier is only one of the many things Giuseppe does for me. I'm his sole source of income."

"I see," said Chacham Tzvi.

"So as I was saying, we're almost there. We'll first go see Rabbi Shmuel Aboab.²⁴ He's the rabbi of the Scuola Spagnola, the Sephardic synagogue of Venice. If he hears I brought you to Venice and didn't take you to him right away, he'll be annoyed with me. Is that all right with you?"

"Of course," said Chacham Tzvi. "He's a renowned *talmid chacham*. It's only right that we pay our respects as soon as we arrive."

"Yes, that's what I was saying," said Tarantella. "You know, we rarely pray at the Sephardic synagogue. My family prays at the Scuola Italiana, the Italian synagogue. My father-in-law — he's from Germany — he prays at the Scuola Tedesca, the Ashkenazic synagogue. By the way, did you know that the Italian tradition is older than the Sephardic tradition or the Ashkenazic tradition? It goes back about two thousand years."

"I'd heard something of the sort."

"Yes, our tradition is really ancient. So what was I saying? … Ah yes, I was going to say something about Rabbi Aboab. He's not our rabbi, you see, but we have a close relationship. He is a very great rabbi, and we often seek his advice and ask for his blessing." He furrowed his brow. "So what did I want? Why was I telling you this? …. I forget …. Oh yes, that's why I have to bring you to him straightaway. Otherwise, he'll be annoyed with me."

"All right."

"So this is what we do. If the rabbi invites you to stay in his house, then that is, of course, what you'll do. But if he doesn't, or if he asks you about your accommodations, tell him you have an invitation from me. I didn't mention it until now, because … well … I didn't want to be presumptuous. But now that we're almost there, I have to speak. It's now or never. You would do me a great honor if the two of you would be my guests during your stay in Venice."

"You're too kind," said Chacham Tzvi. "If the rabbi doesn't invite us, we can rent rooms somewhere. We don't intend to stay in Venice very long."

Tarantella was crestfallen. "But I'll be so disappointed. And my whole family will be disappointed. How often do we get the opportunity to host people such as the two of you?"

"You're being very kind."

"I'm not being kind, Chacham Tzvi. I mean it for my own honor. Can you imagine how my prestige would rise with my friends and neighbors if I have the honor of hosting the celebrated young rabbi of Sarajevo?"

"But you told us your daughter is getting married in a few days. Your household must be bustling with preparations. You don't need two travelers underfoot. A guest has to know when to accept and when to decline politely."

"I assure you, Chacham Tzvi, that your presence will be no imposition. We have plenty of servants to do all the work. On the contrary, your presence will enhance our celebration. I really can't believe that my little Racquel is getting married; it's incredible how time flies. It seems just like yesterday that she was sitting on my lap, playing with my beard, or dancing around the room — she's such a dancer — and now she's getting married, my little Racquel. Who can figure the ways of the world? So as I was saying, it would be a wonderful memory for our family if you were to stay with us during this celebration." He lowered his voice. "I'm not publicizing this bit of information, but I've hired Giovanni Antonio Burrini, the celebrated portrait painter from Bologna, to capture this memory for us in a picture. If you were in the picture and we hung it in our parlor, oh, I can't begin to tell you what it would mean to us."

Chacham Tzvi cleared his throat. "Well, we'll see."

The gondola passed into a thick winter fog that hung over the canal and both its banks. A covered footbridge loomed out of the mist and slipped back into the mist as soon as they had passed under it.

Rav Amos shivered, and his eyes fluttered open. He pulled his cloak more tightly around his shoulders.

"Are you cold, Rav Amos?" said Chacham Tzvi in a low voice.

"A little. This chilly wetness gets into my bones."

Chacham Tzvi turned to the gondolier. "*Prego, Giuseppe, avete di coperte nella barca?*"

The gondolier handed him a blanket, which he passed to Rav Amos.

Tarantella gaped. "How do you speak Italian, Chacham Tzvi?"

"Poorly."

"I have to respectfully disagree with that. It's actually quite good. Even the accent is fairly decent. How is it that you speak Italian?"

"Languages come easily to me.[25] When I was in the *yeshivah* in Salonika, there were some boys there from Italy, so I picked up a little Italian."

"Amazing. How many other languages do you speak?"

"Not many."

"Let's see. Probably Hungarian and Turkish, and I'd say Spanish and German as well. Any more?"

"It's not important." He pointed to his right. "Who are those people?"

Tarantella turned to follow his pointing finger. They were passing a broad plaza with a massive domed church in the background. People in bizarre masks and costumes were mingling all over the plaza. Most of their masks were a deathly white color with painted red lips and black-rimmed eyes. Others resembled large-eared animals or birds of prey with huge white beaks. All the people in masquerade wore colorful cloaks and elaborate headdresses with exotic plumages. The masked people appeared out of the fog like macabre apparitions and disappeared back into the fog as if they had never been there.

"What's going on here?" asked Chacham Tzvi.

"It's nothing," said Tarantella. "It's an old Venice custom during Carnival, which starts in a week or so. It's a public celebration. Quite harmless."

Minutes later, they were ushered into the presence of Rabbi Shmuel Aboab. The rabbi was in his late seventies, elderly and frail, but his eyes were sharp and lively. He thanked Tarantella for bringing him such illustrious visitors, and he immediately insisted they stay with him as long as they remained in Venice.

After Tarantella left, the old rabbi asked one of his attendant to serve his guests tea and refreshments and another to prepare rooms for them.

"You'll stay with us for Chanukah, of course," said the old rabbi. "You can't very well continue your travels until after Chanukah."[26]

"We are very grateful," said Chacham Tzvi.

"I'm the one who should be grateful," said the old rabbi. "How often do I have house guests with whom I can really talk in learning?

"So we have a little time to get acquainted," said the old rabbi, "before we have to go to the synagogue. I'd like to hear some interesting thoughts from you about the topics you've been learning in the Gemara. But if you indulge an old man, I have a question first. Pharaoh summons Yosef from the dungeon and asks him to interpret his dream. But then, after he finishes interpreting the dream, Yosef says, 'And now, Pharaoh should identify an intelligent and wise man and appoint him over the Land of Egypt.'[27] When exactly did Pharaoh ask him for his advice?"

"Rav Amos has an answer to that question," said Chacham Tzvi. "We discussed it on the ship from Dubrovnik."

The old rabbi peered at Rav Amos. "I'm eager to hear your thoughts."

"Well, the Torah seems to draw our attention to Pharaoh getting up between the dream about the cows and the dream about the stalks. We're told, 'And Pharaoh woke up, *vayikatz*, then he slept and dreamed a second time.'[28] And Pharaoh himself draws Yosef's attention to it when he says, 'And I awoke, *va'ikatz*, then I saw in my dream ....'[29] What's the importance of this awakening?"

"Good question," said the old rabbi. "Continue."

"Rashbam explains that a person caught up in his dream may sometimes come partially awake and then sink back into his dream. That's what happened here. Pharaoh didn't come fully awake until after the second dream, but between the first and the second dreams he had a partial awakening. In other words, this partial awakening was really part of his dream. When Yosef gave Pharaoh advice about how to deal with the coming years of famine, he was really interpreting this part of the dream."

"Interesting idea. Please explain it a little better."

"I can only speak about my own experiences with dreams. I don't know what others experience. In my dreams, I sometimes feel that I'm being swept along with no control over events, and sometimes the dreams become really frightening. But in the dream itself, I sometimes have a partial awakening, and I say to myself, 'Wait! This is only a dream. I don't have to go through this. I can turn it in a different direction.' And I do. And then my dream becomes serene and pleasant."

The old rabbi nodded. "I have the same experience."

"And I," said Chacham Tzvi.

"I think this is what Yosef saw in Pharaoh's partial awakening. Yes, a famine was coming. A nightmare was developing. But events were not necessarily beyond Pharaoh's control. It was only a dream, and he could do something to turn the dream in a positive direction. He could find an intelligent man who would prepare during the good times so that the people would not starve during the years of famine."

"Very good," said the old rabbi. "I like it. It is the same in our lives, you know. Life can be like that. Things happen, and one thing leads to another, and a person just gets swept along by the torrent of events. He think he's helpless. But he's not. He can pull himself awake from his dream. He can change the direction of his life and make it better."

Rav Amos chewed on his knuckle. "I feel that I've reached such a point in my life," he said. "Events beyond my control swept me along in an aimless direction, and for a while, I just went along helplessly." He paused and glanced at Chacham Tzvi, who was looking down at his shoes. "But these last few months, I feel that I've awakened from my slumber. I've had a *va'ikatz* moment, and now I can face the future with confidence and enthusiasm."

He stopped, suddenly embarrassed.

"I apologize," he said, "for bringing up my personal life."

"There's no need to be embarrassed," said the rabbi. "We're supposed to seek guidance in the Torah for our personal lives. It's not everyone who can look at himself critically and make changes. May the Almighty bless you and guide you along your new path."

They spoke in learning for another hour, and then the rabbi inquired about their personal situations.

"I know a little about what has happened to you, Chacham Tzvi," he said, "but I did not want that to be the first hello. It's not as if there's an urgent need for immediate action. So now that we've become acquainted with each other through Torah, we can talk about the sad state of affairs in which we find ourselves."

Then he insisted that Chacham Tzvi tell him everything that had transpired in Budapest and Sarajevo.

"Terrible, terrible," he said when Chacham Tzvi had finished. "Ay, when will all this end? When will it end? Why is there no end to our suffering? Your grandfather, Chacham Tzvi, was a famous *talmid chacham*. I never met him, but I knew about him. I was so pleased when I heard he'd become the rabbi of Alt-Ofen. After all the troubles with the Cossacks, it was time for a little relief. Well, your grandfather had some peaceful years before he passed away. At least that. And your father, I don't know so much about him, but I understand that he's also a great *talmid chacham*. And he's still so young. What is he? Sixty years old? I pray that the Almighty watch over him and bring him back safely to you."

The old rabbi took a sip of his tea. Then he turned his sharp eyes on Rav Amos.

"And you, Rav Amos, I met your father a few years ago. A wise and interesting man. So how are things in Amsterdam? How is my cousin Rabbi Yitzchak Aboab da Fonseca?"

"I've been away from Amsterdam for over a year," said Rav Amos, "but my father always mentions him in his letters. I believe the rabbi is well."

"I'm glad to hear that. He is a very old man, you know," he added with a twinkle in his eye.

That evening, Rav Amos could see that Chacham Tzvi was agitated.

"What's on your mind?" he asked. "Did something happen?"

"I'm worried about money."

"About money?" said Rav Amos. "What do you mean?"

"After we leave Venice, we'll be parting ways. You'll go on to Poland, and I'll go to Germany. You know that I lost everything I owned in Budapest. All the money I have is what I earned in Sarajevo. A good part of it has already gone to get me to Venice. I don't have enough to take me the rest of the way."

"I can lend you some money."

"I can't take money from you. You have a long and difficult journey ahead of you. You might need all the money you have."

"I'll gladly lend you some of my money. But if you don't want to take it, I'm sure Signor Tarantella would lend you some."

"He would give it me as a gift. Sure, he'd call it a loan, but he would forgive the loan right away. In essence, it would be a gift. And I never accept gifts. You know that."

"Yes, I do," said Rav Amos. "You made that very clear when we left Sarajevo. The people wanted to give you a parting gift, but you refused to take anything more than the salary that was coming to you."

"I can't take gifts," said Chacham Tzvi. "I just can't. It would compromise me, take away my independence. I don't want to be beholden to anyone but the Almighty. It is very important to me. So what shall I do?"

"If that is so important to you, the Almighty will help you."

A few days later, Chacham Tzvi and Rav Amos escorted the old rabbi to the wedding of Tarantella's daughter, Signorina Racquel Tarantella. They arrived after the festivities were already under way. They helped the old rabbi to a chair at one of the tables reserved for rabbis, scholars and other dignitaries, and they went off to stand closer to the dance floor.

It was a lavish affair attended by every wealthy merchant in Venice as well as many members of the Venetian government and an assortment of aristocrats who had dealings with Tarantella. The princely Francesco d'Este, Duke of Modena and Ferrara, the closest neighbors of Venice to the south, also stopped by to pay his respects.

The tables groaned under platters piled high with the most succulent and expensive foods. Wine and beer flowed like a river. Twenty musicians played for the entertainment of the guests while they danced, and a solo harpist played while they ate. Troupes of hired dancers in costumes frolicked among the dancing guests, and clowns juggled and pranced on the sidelines. In a corner, an Italian man in his thirties was sketching the event on a sheet of paper with a piece of charcoal. This must be the painter from Bologna, thought Rav Amos. He could not recall his name.

During a lull in the dancing, Tarantella brought over a very tall, very thin, very young man with jet black hair, luminous blue eyes and skin pink with the glow of health and happiness.

"Chacham Tzvi, Rav Amos," Tarantella declared. "I'd like you to meet Zebulun Nissan Zecupa, my new son-in-law."

Zecupa bowed slightly. "I'm honored," he said in a surprisingly mature voice. "Your presence crowns our joy."

"Why are you two standing here?" asked Tarantella. "Let me find you proper seats."

"We have seats near Rabbi Aboab," said Chacham Tzvi. "We just wanted to get a better view of the ... spectacle."

Tarantella laughed. "It is a spectacle, isn't it?" He leaned forward and lowered his voice. "Did you notice the painter?"

"We certainly did," said Rav Amos.

Tarantella put his finger to his lips. Then he took his new acquisition by the hand and led him away.

A few minutes later, Chacham Tzvi felt a tap on his shoulder. He turned around and saw a short heavy man with an enormous mustache and side whiskers. He was wearing a uniform covered with gold braid and decorations.

"Rabbi Ashkenazi?" said the man. "Is that you?"

"Yes, it is."

"Don't you remember me? I'm Count Ignatz Esterhazy."

Recognition dawned in Chacham Tzvi's eyes. "Count Esterhazy!" The count was one of the foremost aristocrats of Hungary.

"I can't believe you're here, Rabbi Ashkenazi," said the count. "I haven't seen you in two or three years, and I have to say that you've aged a bit. Actually, I never thought I'd see you alive again after what happened in Budapest, so I suppose a little gray at the temples is a small price to pay for remaining alive."

"Well, it's good to see you, count. How have you been?"

"Oh, fine. Just fine. Don't think I've forgotten you, Rabbi Ashkenazi. You loaned me a large sum of money when I needed it, and I always repay my debts. I was actually upset when I thought you had perished in Budapest, and now I'm happy to see that you're alive. Come around to my rooms tomorrow, and I'll pay you every ducat I owe you."[30]

Chacham Tzvi stared at him. "You are a prince among men, Your Excellency," he finally said.

The count slapped him on the back and walked away.

"I guess your prayers were answered," said Rav Amos.

THE RABBI OF PULICHEV · 10

PULICHEV HAD HARDLY changed since the last time Rav Amos had been there. Sleepy houses crowded together on the hillside down to the Grizdna River. The massive synagogue with its white stucco walls and red tile roof loomed above the town. In the apple orchards beyond the town, the branches of the trees were bare of leaves and laden with snow.

Rav Amos walked through the streets, carrying his *tallis* bag and his satchel. It was the worst part of the winter, yet people were out and about doing business and making minor repairs to their homes. He found the home of Rav Shlomo Strasbourg, the rabbi of Pulichev, and knocked on the door.

A gangly boy of about sixteen opened the door.

"Can I help you?" he said. "Are you a traveler passing through? Do you need a place to stay?"

"The answer is yes to all your questions. I'm also a cousin of the rabbi, and I'd like to see him."

"Oh, you must be Rav Amos Strasbourg."

"I am."

"Well, come in. Come in." He shook hands with Rav Amos. "I'm Gedaliah Strasbourg, the son of Rav Mendel. My grandfather is resting right now, but you can make yourself at home. Please leave your things right here near the door. You'll be staying at my house. We've been expecting you."

"I was delayed."

Gedaliah laughed. "That was some delay. Almost a year."

"A lot happened."

"My father and you are pretty much the same age, aren't you?"

"Yes, we are."

Gedaliah seemed on the verge of asking another question, but then he thought better of it. Without another word, he led Rav Amos to a small kitchen. Rebbetzin Brachah, the wife of Rav Shlomo, a spry old woman in a white kerchief, was standing over a frying pan.

"Grandmother, we have a visitor," said Gedaliah.

She turned, and her face broke into a broad smile. "Amos!" she exclaimed. "Or should I say Rav Amos? They say you know most of the Talmud."

"Don't believe everything they say, *rebbetzin*," he said. "It's good to see you. How is my cousin?"

"He's been better. Here, sit down, and I'll give you something to eat. You must be starving. We can talk later."

She bustled about and sent Gedaliah off on a few errands, and within minutes, a veritable feast materialized before him. She shooed the boy out of the room, and sat down on the other side of the table.

"Your father was here for Rosh Hashanah," she said. "We had a wonderful time together. We had hoped you could come as well, but ... what can you do? *A mentch tracht un der Aybershter lacht*, my grandmother used to say. A person plans, and the Almighty laughs. We do what we can. At least, you're here now. I understand you've spent these last few months with Rabbi Tzvi Ashkenazi."

"We've become friends."

"A good choice," she said. "They say he will be one of our greatest rabbis, if not the greatest. There is no limit to how much you can grow from an association with such a person."

"So what is going on with my cousin?" asked Rav Amos, eager to turn the conversation away from himself.

The *rebbetzin* sighed. "It's really very painful. He just gets weaker and weaker. He has his days, but …. He's only a shadow of himself."

"What do the doctors say?"

She made a dismissive gesture with her hand. "Doctors? What do they know? My husband has painful sores all over his body, and all the doctors do is talk about maintaining the balance of the body's four humors. They also give him strange powders and poultices. But nothing helps. I don't think these doctors even begin to understand what goes on under the skin in the human body. Maybe there are doctors who know a little more in Paris or Amsterdam. But not anywhere close to here …. Wait, I hear him calling. I'll tell him you're here. Please finish your food. I'll call you in when he's ready. I have to warn you, today's not one of his better days."

Nearly half an hour passed before she called him into Rav Shlomo's bedroom. The rabbi was lying on his bed, propped up by a pile of pillows, his coverlet pulled up to his chin. His face was emaciated, his skin translucent, but his eyes still burned with the old fire. He pulled a waxen hand out from under his coverlet and extended it to Rav Amos.

"Welcome," he said in a hoarse and labored whisper. "Welcome … how was … your journey?"

"It was fine. I'm happy to see you."

The rabbi's lips moved, but no sound emerged. Rav Amos looked to the *rebbetzin*, unsure of what he should do. She was standing near the door, holding a handkerchief in her hand and twisting it again and again, a look of anguish and sorrow on her face.

The rabbi coughed a few times, then he managed a few words. "We'll talk … tomorrow … tomorrow … glad you're here."

A few days passed before Rav Amos was called again to see the ailing Rav Shlomo. In the meantime, he renewed his relationship with Rav Mendel and got to know his family. Rav Mendel had taken over all his father's duties and was now the rabbi of Pulichev for all intents and purposes. He did not have a great deal of free time, but the two cousins did manage to learn together for an hour every day.

On Friday afternoon, Rav Shlomo was feeling better, and he asked for Rav Amos to come visit him. This time he was sitting in a chair with a woolen scarf around his neck and a cup of steaming tea in his hand.

"I've been neglecting you," he said, his voice weak but steady.

"I feel that I'm imposing," said Rav Amos. "Perhaps I should leave."

"No, stay. I'll tell you when to leave. Your father wanted you to come and spend some time with me. I'm not sure what he thought you could get from me that you couldn't get better elsewhere. Anyway, I'm at your disposal. Maybe your coming here will give me a new burst of strength. You know? I feel a little better already. We'll make time every day to learn and to talk about past generations and about what's important in life and what isn't."

Days turned into weeks and weeks into months. It was a time of peace and stability for the Jewish people in Poland. There were no marauding armies or bandits. The entire world in which Rav Amos found himself, tucked away in the southeastern corner of the country, moved according to the rhythms and contours of Jewish life. After living all his life in Amsterdam and Hamburg, he was not accustomed to spending much time in such isolated surroundings. In fact, it sometimes seemed as if the outside world didn't even exist. A rare serenity and harmony came into his life, and he realized that it was just a state of mind and that if he tried he could achieve it wherever he was and under whatever conditions he found himself.

Most days, he spent a little time with Rav Shlomo, sometimes an hour or even two and sometimes only a few minutes. They talked about different things he was learning, and they talked about the outlook on life that had been passed down in their family from father to son for so many generations. Sitting with Rav Shlomo, he felt a deeper connection to the long line of illustrious rabbis who had served continuously in Pulichev for hundreds of years.

This was his identity. This was who he was and who he was meant to be. It began with a passionate embrace of the Torah and a love for every word in it. It meant a desire to know it and understand it on the deepest levels. It meant to live by it with moderation and humility, never to consider himself superior to anyone else but to love, accept and embrace all Jews as brothers.

He thought a lot about the rabbi who caught a glimpse of the next world and found that it was inverted, with those who had been in the upper ranks sitting in the lower ranks and those who had been in the lower ranks sitting in the upper ranks.[31] A Strasbourg, Rav Shlomo explained to him, never considered himself better than other people or looked down at anyone, because who besides the Almighty can take the measure of a person? This was the attitude he saw in Rav Shlomo, in Rav Mendel and in his own father. It was the heritage of the Strasbourg family. And it was the spirit to which he aspired.

In the summer, a long letter arrived from Chacham Tzvi. Rav Amos had wanted to write to him a number of times, but he had no address at which to reach him.

In his letter, Chacham Tzvi told of his continued efforts to find his parents. His information had led him to Ansbach in Germany and then to Prague in Bohemia. These communities had welcomed him with open arms and great honor, he reported self-consciously. Several illustrious and wealthy matches had been suggested to him, but he had turned them down. He was prepared to marry again and rebuild his life, but his first responsibility was to his parents. And in any case, wealth was not a consideration for him, only family.

He had finally learned his parents were being held captive in Berlin, and he was doing his utmost to get them redeemed. He was lonely, he wrote, and sorely missed the companionship of his great friend, and he expressed great interest in how he was faring in Pulichev. Perhaps they would soon be together again with the help of the Almighty.

He concluded by suggesting that letters for him be sent to the address of Rabbi Meshulem Zalman Mirels Neumark, the Ashkenazic rabbi of the Three Communities – Altona, Hamburg and Wandsbeck.

Rav Amos read and reread the letter several times before he tucked it away. The final words of the letter puzzled him. Why did he want his letters directed to Hamburg if hadn't even mentioned being there? Apparently, he was planning to be in Hamburg, but why? His parents had apparently not yet been freed from captivity in Berlin, so why wasn't he staying there? Why was he going to Hamburg?

The news that Chacham Tzvi was already considering getting remarried was unexpected but not surprising. It made Rav Amos think about his own situation. Five years, more or less, was long enough to be alone. His life was finally coming together, stronger and more stable than it had ever been. It was time to look to the future.

Two months later, Sebastian Dominguez arrived in Pulichev unexpectedly. Rav Amos had last seen his friend in New York over a year earlier, and he had not heard from him since. And now, suddenly, he turned up in Pulichev.

The two men were different from each other in many ways, but they had formed a bond of friendship under adverse circumstances in Amsterdam, and they had cemented that friendship when they had gone together to America. Since that time, however, Rav Amos had formed a profound friendship with Chacham Tzvi, with whom he felt a kinship and a commonality of interests that he could never feel with Sebastian.

Sebastian's unexpected appearance awakened mixed feelings in Rav Amos' heart. He was afraid that by forming his friendship with Chacham Tzvi he had somehow been disloyal to Sebastian, because they could never share the kind of closeness he shared with his new friend. But then again, he thought, why couldn't he remain great friends with Sebastian regardless? He truly loved Sebastian as a brother, and if he could no longer consider him his closest friend, was that any reason the friendship itself should be diminished? No, a Strasbourg didn't measure people against each other. A Strasbourg valued each person for what he was, and Sebastian was his close and true friend. All these thoughts passed through his head the moment he saw Sebastian standing on the threshold, and they were resolved moments later as the two men embraced.

"I should have written," Sebastian told him, "but I didn't know how things would work out. I didn't want to disappoint you if I couldn't manage to get here. I went to see your parents before I left. They're both well and send you their best regards. I brought letters for you. And now, tell me what's happened with you this past year. I heard a little from your father, but I want details. Tell me all the details. I understand you've had a very eventful year."

"Not the last few months," said Rav Amos. "Budapest and Sarajevo were in a war zone, but things have been very quiet here in Pulichev. I'll fill you in a little, but first I want to hear abut you and Immanuel. What happened in New York after I left? When did you get back to Amsterdam, and what happened there? How is Immanuel doing?"

"We left maybe two or three months after you did," said Sebastian. "We made arrangements in the fur trade so that it would bring us a steady income after we returned home. The supply of furs will come to us in Amsterdam regularly without our having to be in New York."

"And what happens when they come to Amsterdam?"

"I take possession of them and sell them to distributors and merchants. A few shipments have come in already. The profits are substantial."

"And have you managed to settle your old accounts?"

"Every one of them. They're all paid off. My honor is restored."

"So now you've got wealth and honor. I'm very happy for you, Sebastian."

"You should be happy for yourself as well, my friend. Your share of the profits has been deposited in your name in the Bank of Amsterdam. Johannes Hoogaboom is still the director."

"My share of the profits?"

"Well, we all went to America to make our fortune, so we're all entitled to profit from the venture."

"But I no longer have anything to do with it."

"Neither does Immanuel," said Sebastian. "This is how I've set it up. Half the profits go to me, because I am receiving the furs and selling them. The other half is divided equally among the three of us. So you are getting a sixth of the profits. If you don't spend it all at once, you'll become a wealthy man."

"I don't know what to say. This is very generous of you."

Sebastian made a dismissive gesture. "It's not generosity at all. It's fairness. The two are not the same. We all went together to America. We all risked our lives in the land of the

Indians. In fact, you're probably more responsible than any of us for our special arrangement with Chief Ganchichtuk. I think a sixth of the profits as long as the supply lasts is the right number. It's not a gift. You earned it."

Rav Amos smiled with pleasure. "Then I accept it as a blessing from the Almighty. It will allow me to do what I want with my life without having to think about money. And the same is true for you, Sebastian."

"I know. That's the other reason I'm here in Pulichev. A few years ago, I began a conversation with Rav Shlomo, your cousin, about finding direction in my life. I was totally lost, a Marrano recently escaped from Spain, accustomed to the life of a grandee and serving in the cavalry. I believed in the Almighty and the holy Torah with all my heart, but I didn't know how to find happiness and inspiration in Jewish life. I met Rav Shlomo in Vienna, and he helped me. We were in the middle of a conversation, and then I was arrested. We never finished the conversation. I think I'm ready to finish the conversation now. I'm no longer the man I was when I escaped from Spain."

"You have certainly come a long way, my friend. By the way, why did you question if you could manage to get here? Did you go somewhere else first?"

"Indeed, I did. I went to Krakow and Warsaw to establish connections for the fur trade. Did you know that the Polish aristocrats have a voracious appetite for furs? It's a cold country, and they like to wear fur hats and line their cloaks with fur. Sometimes, I think they look like giant beavers."

Rav Amos laughed. "All right. Enough about furs for now. Tell me some news from Amsterdam. How are your mother and Felipe?"

"My mother is doing very well. She's involved in all kinds of services for the poor and the sick. It keeps her busy and happy. Felipe? Well, Felipe has become quite the rabbi. Rabbi

Sasportas has taken him under his wing and is grooming him for a position on the rabbinical court."

"That's very impressive. And how is Immanuel doing?"

"Immanuel is doing wonderfully. Here's a piece of great news. He's becoming a doctor, and … listen to this …. He's married."

Rav Amos gaped. "Are you serious?"

"Absolutely. And you'll never guess whom he married."

"I won't even try. Tell me."

"Shamai Cohen's niece."

"No!"

Sebastian laughed with delight. "I knew that would shock you. And here's another piece of news that may shock you. I'm engaged to be married."

"I'm stunned," said Rav Amos, "but I don't know why I should be. Who is the lucky young lady?"

"Dulce Castillo."

"Now I'm doubly stunned. Dulce Castillo? The one and the same?"

"The one and the same," said Sebastian. "When I returned from America she was still not engaged, and when I came to make restitution to her father, he suggested that we consider picking up where we had left off. So we did."

"I am so happy for you, Sebastian. You can't imagine. I always felt that she was perfect for you and that you had lost her because of your sense of honor. Well, the Almighty held her for you, and you should thank Him."

"I do. Every single day. And now the only one left unmarried and unengaged is you, my dear friend. We have ideas for you as soon as you get back to Amsterdam. We won't allow you to be the only one to remain free."

"Well, we'll see about that. By the way, how is this fur trade going to work? Are you going to have to go back to America from time to time to keep in touch with the Mahonekett nation?"

Sebastian shook his head. "No, not even once. I have an agent in New York who's completely loyal to me. You'll never guess who it is."

"Then you might as well tell me."

"Try to guess anyway."

"All right," said Rav Amos. He thought for a moment and then his eyes lit up. "No!"

"Oh, yes."

"Domino Stuart?"

"Absolutely."

Rav Amos shook his head in wonder. "I think it's a brilliant choice, Sebastian. He owes his life and his freedom to you. And as a free man, he's protected by all the laws of the colony. He's smart and hard-working. And he knows Chief Ganchichtuk."

"There's more."

"More?"

"Yes." Sebastian chuckled. "There's more to the Domino Stuart story. He's married."

Rav Amos slapped his forehead. "Don't tell me that you want me to guess whom he married."

"I do."

"Well, I suppose it wasn't either Georgia or Georgette. I'm sorry I don't recall their African names."

"It wasn't either of those two."

"Then who was it? I give up."

"Feather Wind."

"What! Chief Ganchichtuk's daughter?"

"That's right. You were his first choice, if you remember."

"Don't remind me."

"Well, Domino Stuart is now the son-in-law of Chief Ganchichtuk, our unlimited source of furs, and he's also our agent in New York. I think it's a satisfactory arrangement."

"Couldn't be better," said Rav Amos.

"So now that we've caught up a little bit, when can I see Rav Shlomo?"

"I don't know, Sebastian. I'll ask and let you know."

Sebastian was allowed in to Rav Shlomo the following day. The rabbi was sitting on a comfortable chair with his legs raised on an ottoman. He had a blanket wrapped around his shoulders and another across his legs. He extended his hand to Sebastian who shook it and then bent over it and kissed it.

"Sebastian Dominguez," declared the rabbi with genuine pleasure. "Please forgive me if I don't stand up for such an honored guest. As you can see, I'm more in the next world than in this one. We were in the middle of a conversation some three years ago when we were ... interrupted."

"Yes, rabbi. I've come to finish the conversation."

"Yes, we should. If I recall correctly, we were speaking about inspiration. But before we continue our conversation ...." He paused to gasp for air. "Tell me a little about your life these past three years."

The rabbi listened without comment as Sebastian related as completely but concisely as possible all that he had experienced during that time. His eyes widened a little when Sebastian told of their exploits in America, but he still refrained from saying anything at all.

"A very interesting story, my dear Sebastian," he said at last. "I asked you to tell me all of this for two reasons. First of all, I wanted to hear what happened to you and how it affected your life. Second, I wanted to listen to you talk, to hear what you felt and how you thought. You are a different man from the one with whom I spoke three years ago, not as lost, more mature. You've grown, Sebastian, and I'm pleased to see it."

"Thank you. I owe a lot of that growth to my friendship with your cousin here."

Rav Shlomo nodded. "Undoubtedly. Rav Amos here is a good man to have as a friend. Consider yourself fortunate."

He paused to clear his throat of phlegm, but his cough was too weak to bring it up. He leaned back to catch his breath. Then he spoke slowly and deliberately.

"I'm not feeling well, so pardon me if I'm brief. Every Jew has his share in Torah, and you have yours. But that doesn't mean you must force yourself to sit over the Gemara for many hours at a time if you find that difficult. Some people don't have the temperament for it, especially if they've grown up riding horses through the mountains of Spain. Set aside time every day to learn, and learn what appeals to you. And get involved with the community. If the main pillar of your life is not Torah, then build up the pillar of chessed, kindness to others. If you cannot learn the Torah every moment of the day, then live the Torah every moment of the day. Do what is right for you, and do it well. You will find the inspiration you seek."

The rabbi closed his eyes and fell back gasping. Rav Amos sprang to his side, but the rabbi held up his hand. He opened his eyes and nodded, indicating that he was not in any immediate danger.

"Come, Sebastian," said Rav Amos. "He gave you more than I thought he could. It's time to go."

Sebastian picked up the rabbi's limp hand and touched it to his lips.

"Be well, my son," the rabbi whispered. "May the Almighty bless you with long life, prosperity and many children. Always be a good friend to Rav Amos. Give me your word that you will."

"I give you my word."

The rabbi closed his eyes and dozed off. The two men quietly slipped out of the room and stepped outside into the cool afternoon breeze.

"It's a terrible thing to watch a man dying," said Sebastian as they strolled down toward the river. "Did you find what you were looking for here?"

"Yes, I think I did."

"I won't ask you to tell me what it was, because I probably wouldn't understand anyway."

Rav Amos glanced sharply at his friend. Had he detected an undercurrent of resentment, of a sense that they were growing apart? But there was no indication whatsoever on Sebastian's face that he had meant anything of the sort. Rav Amos suddenly realized that Sebastian had never had any illusions that the two of them could have the kind of friendship that he had found with Chacham Tzvi. He had taken the friendship for what it was, a bond between two people with different backgrounds, different temperaments, different interest, who could still love each other with all their hearts. It was a friendship without judgments, without valuations, and that was what made it so precious. Rav Amos reached out and embraced Sebastian.

"What was that all about?" Sebastian asked afterward.

"Nothing. I'm just glad to see you."

"Well, so am I. Glad to see you, that is. Listen, there's one thing more I need to tell you about Amsterdam. Something mysterious and disturbing is going on."

"I'm listening."

"I've heard that people have been asking questions about our community, both the Sephardic and the Ashkenazic."

"What kind of questions?"

"All sorts of questions. Who's in charge of this and who's in charge of that? And what's the relationship between these people and those people? And so on. Just information questions, and it seems quite harmless on the surface. But who is behind this, and what is its purpose? Somehow, I have a sense of foreboding about this, as do many of us. I have a feeling that someday this information will be used against us. But how?"

"Have you spoken to any of these questioners? Or has anyone? And to whom do they address these questions?"

"They're just people, merchants, traders, craftsmen. Not Jewish. Mostly Dutch. And it's always different people. They claim that their intentionas are innocent. They say they've been hired to study our community for business purposes. Who hired them? They don't know. They were all hired through agents, so they don't know the identity of their employer. When we confront them, they stop their activities. But sooner than later, other snoopers appear to take their places. Someone is gathering an awful lot of information about us."

"Do you think it's a threat to the Jewish community?"

"I don't know. Maybe it really is just about making money. You'll see for yourself when you come back. By the way, Gonzalo tells me that a Dutch captain, one of his frequent patrons, came to his tavern with a Spanish cavalry officer. The captain told Gonzalo the whole story of your meeting in Budapest. He said that you'd promised to pay for all they could drink in one night."

"Yes, that's true," said Rav Amos. "So what did Gonzalo do?"

"He honored your promise."

"Good. I'll pay him when I come back to Amsterdam."

"It's all right. I paid him already. You can pay me when you come back to Amsterdam. Are you planning to come back home soon?"

Rav Amos shook his head. "I'm going to stay through the winter. You heard Rav Shlomo say that he's more in the next world than in this one. I think I should stay until … well … until the end."

ELIAHU'S MANTLE · 11

ELEVEN PEOPLE WAITED in the sun-baked alleyway on the outskirts of the old city of Chevron. They leaned against the walls or sat on the dusty ground as they waited for the fat man to call their turn. The fat man sat on a chair before a small table in the shade of a balcony. An inkwell, a quill and two piles of paper, one of full sheets and one of small pieces, lay on the table. Behind him, a low wall separated the alley from the building beyond, forming a long trench that was filled with garbage and debris.

A street urchin played in the alley with a pile of pebbles, and a barefoot Arab beggar dressed in tattered rags and a soiled *kaffiyeh* sat at the entrance to the alleyway, his hand extended to all passersby. Every few minutes, the fat man shooed the beggar away, but he always returned.

"Raphael Malik!" called the fat man.

A short man talking to a woman holding a baby wrapped in a blanket turned at the sound of his name being called. He quickly kissed the baby and hurried over to the table where the fat man sat.

"You are the first in line to see the holy man," said the fat man.

"Oh, thank you, thank you," said Malik. "We've been waiting so long."

"The holy man does not see people before the noon hour. And he does not touch money. Whatever you intended to give him, you should give to me. I see to it that all his needs are met."

"Of course, of course. How much should I give?"

"I can't tell you that," said the fat man. "Give whatever you wish. But I have to tell you that the holy man senses if you've really made an effort, in other words, if you've given something that does not come easily, or if you've just thrown him a few spare pennies that you won't miss anyway."

"I understand."

Malik took a few large coins from his pocket. After looking at them longingly, he deposited them in the fat man's hand, from whence they immediately disappeared into the folds of his robe.

The fat man took a fresh sheet of paper from the pile and dipped his quill into the inkwell.

"Listen closely," said the fat man. "The holy man does not have the time or the patience to conduct long interviews with the people who come to see him. He needs them to get straight to the point, but most people are incapable of doing that. So this is what we will do. You will tell me about your problems and needs in as much detail as you wish, and I will write them down. Then I will study the paper and write your name and the essential points on a small piece of paper which you will take with you when go to see him."

"And what about the first piece of paper?" said Malik. "Should I take that with me as well?"

"No, that paper will be discarded. Paper is expensive, and so is ink, but that is what we must do. The holy man doesn't approve of preserving the records of people's misfortunes. After we are finished and I've prepared the second paper for you, I'll crumple this paper and toss it into the garbage trench behind me. No record will remain of what you've told me other than the paper you bring with you to the holy man. Do you understand?"

"Yes, I do. It seems a little complicated, but if that is what the holy man wishes, that is what we must do."

"All right," said the fat man. "Let's begin. You've given me your name. Now give me your mother's name, your wife's name and her mother's name and the name of your sick baby and his condition."

"I am Raphael ben Mazal. My wife is Chanah bat Peninah. My daughter is Nechamah. There is something wrong with her heart, and she is not able to breathe well. The doctors say that she'll die before her first birthday."

"What do they know?" said the fat man. "Let's hear what the holy man says before we give up hope. What do you do, Raphael?"

"I'm a bookbinder."

"What kind of books?"

"Holy books."

"No other kind?"

"Almost none."

"Where did you learn your craft?"

"In Alexandria."

"Did you live there?"

"Yes, my family is Egyptian."

The fat man dipped his quill into the inkwell and scribbled a few lines.

"And your wife?" he asked. "Is she also Egyptian?"

"No. She is from an Ashkenaz family."

"Which country?"

"Poland."

"How did you meet her?"

"Her family moved to Chevron."

"Why?"

"Her mother was ill. She was told that the merit of living in Chevron would bring her a complete recovery."

"And did it help?"

"She died on the journey. She never reached Eretz Yisrael."

The fat man scribbled some more. "Does your baby run a fever?"

"Yes. A high fever."

"Does she cough?"

"A little."

The fat man dipped his quill into the inkwell again and spent a few minutes covering the page with fine script.

"One last question," he said. "Do you get along with your wife?"

Malik's face turned red. "Of course," he blurted.

"Always?"

"Almost always."

"I see. Everything is almost."

The fat man put down his quill. He pursed his lips and stroked his chin as he reviewed all he had written. Finally, he nodded with satisfaction, took a small piece of paper and wrote a few lines on it. He folded the small piece of paper again and again into a tiny square. Then he took the larger sheet, crumpled it into a ball and tossed it over the wall into the garbage trench behind him.

He handed the tiny folded square to Malik. "Here you are," he said. "Give this to the holy man when he asks for it. Go in by yourself first. You'll bring your family in when the holy man asks for them."

The Arab beggar wandered over and tugged at Malik's sleeve.

"Get away from here, Ahmed," the fat man snapped, "or I'll throw a rock at your head."

The beggar ducked his head and scurried away.

"Saeb!" the fat man called out.

The street urchin dropped his pebbles and came running.

"Saeb," said the fat man. "Take this man and his family to the holy man right away."

The urchin nodded and trotted off down the alleyway without a word. Malik gathered his wife and baby and followed. They walked at a slow pace through a courtyard, which led to another courtyard. Then they entered a dank and dark hallway and climbed two flights of stairs to a narrow landing illuminated by a grimy skylight. The urchin pointed to a door and ran back down the stairs.

Malik lifted his hand tentatively and knocked on the door. Silence.

He knocked again.

From inside, he could hear the faint sounds of a man singing with great joy.

"Come in!" The words seemed to merge into the song.

Malik opened the door and entered. His wife and baby remained on the landing. A man was standing at the balcony with his back to him, looking out over the sunny courtyards below. He was wearing a heavy cloak of a strange iridescent material and a multi-colored cap on his shaven head. He lifted his hands high and away from his body and turned around. With the cloak draped over his arms, he looked like a giant bird.

"What is your name, my friend?" he said.

"Raphael Malik."

"You are troubled. Very troubled."

"Yes, I am." He held out the folded piece of paper. "My —"

"Stop, don't speak," said the holy man. "And don't show me the paper yet. There will be time for that. Before I listen to your mouth, I want to listen to your heart. Sit down, and be still."

Malik sat down.

"You are not alone," said the holy man. "I can sense that there are others with you. They are waiting on the landing. A woman and a baby. I am assuming that these are your wife and baby, is that so?"

"Yes."

"There is trouble with the baby. I can see that. It doesn't take much to see that, does it? If you and your wife brought a little baby with you, there must be trouble. But it is not ordinary trouble. No, it is not ordinary trouble at all. It is a little girl. Yes, I can see that. The baby is sick, but her spirit is very troubled. Her spirit wants to leave this world. Her spirit has been in this world before and has now returned as your little girl. Why did this spirit come to you and your wife?"

"I … I don't know."

The holy man touched his fingers to his forehead. "It is a relative," he said. "A grandmother, perhaps. Has any relative died within the last few years?"

"Yes. My wife's mother."

The holy man touched his forehead again. "I sense a tension between your wife and her mother. Is that so?"

"My wife's mother died before we were married," said Malik. "But I never heard about any tension."

"But it is clearly there. I see it. Yes, I can see that this tension is reflected in their names. Tell me their names."

"My wife's name is Chanah. Her mother was Peninah."

"Aha!" said the holy man. "The two wives of Elkanah, one with children, one without.[32] It becomes very interesting. And what is your position in this situation, eh? Raphael, the healer. Are you a healer?"

"I don't know what to say."

"I see that Peninah died tragically. She lived in a faraway land, and there was something she wanted very much, but she died before she could achieve it. Perhaps that's why she has come back. What did she want? Do you know?"

"I'm not sure. I never knew her. All I know is that she was ill and that she died on the journey to Eretz Yisrael."

"From where?"

"Poland."

"Yes, that is a faraway land. They thought that by coming to Eretz Yisrael she would be healed, but she died before she arrived here. And now that she has returned and breathed the holy air of the holy land, she is satisfied, and she is not sure that she wants to go through a whole life again." He touched his fingers to his forehead again and moved his lips soundlessly. "Very well, give me your paper, then bring in your wife and baby."

Malik gave the folded paper to the holy man. Then he opened the door and motioned to his wife to enter.

"Tell your wife to wait by the door," said the holy man, "and bring the baby to me."

Malik's wife eyed the holy man anxiously and handed over the baby. The holy man opened the paper and perused it carefully.

"Nechamah bat Chanah," he said to the baby, "my name is Nechemiah Chayun. I know who you are. I know why you are here. What do you want? What are your intentions?"

He touched the baby on the side of the neck, and she began to cry. Chayun cocked his head and listened closely to the sounds of the crying.

"Yes, I understand," he said. "But this cannot go on. By the power vested in me by the prophet Eliahu, I command you to forget your old life and start life anew as the daughter of your daughter and son-in-law."

He slid his fingers across the baby's face, and she stopped crying. Then he spread his cloak across the baby and mumbled some words under his breath.

"This cloak is my *aderet*, my mantle," he said. "It was given to me by the prophet Eliahu as a symbol of my power, just as his own *aderet* was the symbol of his power."[33] He extended the edge of the cloak to Malik. "Kiss the mantle. Have your wife kiss it as well."

Malik kissed the edge of the cloak, then he stepped aside and his wife came forward and kissed it.

"You may go," said Chayun.

"My baby," said Chanah Malik. "Will she recover?"

Chayun turned to the balcony and looked up at the sky.

"I have done all I can do," he said. "It is out of my hands. If your mother obeys my command, your child will recover. If not .... Time will tell. Come back to me in three months. You may go now."

A minute after the Maliks left, there was a quick series of knocks on the balcony door. Chayun opened it and saw the Arab beggar panting on the balcony. He laughed and handed him a small copper coin.

"It is only the beginning of the day, Ahmed," he said. "If you are already exhausted from climbing down into the trench and up over the balconies, how will you manage the rest of the day?"

The beggar handed Chayun a crumpled ball of paper. "Do not worry, *pasha*. I get stronger as the day goes on."

"Good. Now go. Saeb will be here any minute with the next people."

Word of Chayun's supernatural powers spread quickly, and soon, the wealthy and the powerful were streaming to his doorstep. Within days, he established that he only saw people between the hours of noon and two o'clock, and under no circumstances did he break this rule. The limitations on the time he made available to the public only made it more valuable. Large sums passed hands between troubled wealthy people and the fat man, and ordinary people were pushed aside.

As time went on, Chayun worked hard to promote his reputation as not only a powerful mystic but also as an extraordinary scholar and a man with a deep knowledge of world affairs. In a deliberately casual way, he insinuated to the people who came to see him that he often discussed the deepest secrets of the Talmud and the Zohar with the prophet Eliahu. And he made occasional casual references to developments in the worlds of statecraft and science.

One day, a Turkish general came directly to his door. Chayun was startled, but he recovered quickly.

"Please come in, *pasha*," he said, bowing deeply from the waist. "Why have I been granted the honor of this visit?"

The general sat himself in the most comfortable chair in the room. "They say you are a mystic," he said. "They say you can see into the future, that you can see into the souls of men. Is this true?"

"Only sometimes, *pasha*. I see nothing myself. I only see what the Almighty chooses to show me."

"Very convenient. So if I ask you to tell me what is in my soul, you can always say that the Almighty didn't tell you."

Chayun sighed. "I cannot see what the Almighty doesn't show me. But if you want to ask me something, I can try to give you an answer."

"My son is in the army," said the general. "I want to know if he will survive the wars with the Europeans."

"Do you have any special reason for concern?"

The general grimaced. "Here we are in April of 1689. Our forces have suffered disastrous defeats in Budapest in 1686, in Mohacs in 1687 and in Belgrade in 1688. What does 1689 hold in store for us?"

"Where is your son serving?"

"Crimea."

"The situation is very complicated, *pasha*," said Chayun. "Last year, as you know, William of Orange and his wife Mary Stuart of England sailed from the Netherlands to England and deposed James II, Mary's father. So now that England is again a Protestant nation, it will join the League of Augsburg and align itself against Louis XIV and the French, who are the biggest danger to the rest of Europe. The Austrians will probably shift a big portion of their forces in the Balkans to the alliance against France. There will be rivers of blood in Europe, but the Turkish Empire should be fairly quiet for a while."

"So my son will be safe?"

"In the Crimea? I'm not sure. The Russians will invade Crimea again this year. Two years ago their invasion failed. This year ... it will fail again."

"How do you know these things? Do you see them with a crystal ball?"

Chayun shook his head. "No, what I have just told you is based on hard information. I have people everywhere, from Amsterdam to Moscow, who feed me with information. What I have told you, I have on good authority."

"And my son? What about my son?"

"What is his name?" said Chayun. "And how old is he?"

"His name is Erdip. Erdip Edroyyan. He is thirty-four years old."

Chayun threw back his head and closed his eyes. He began to hum a soft song with a mystical flavor, rocking his head from side to side as he sang.

"I see your son," he said at last, with his head still thrown back, "but I do not see him very clearly. Wait, he is becoming a little clearer. Yes, I can see that he is a handsome man with a large mustache and an erect bearing. And yes, he is an officer, a leader of men. I'm looking into his future, and it appears to me that he has a long life ahead of him. It also appears to me that he will one day become a royal minister. The image is fading ... I see ... wait ... I'm afraid I see nothing more. I'm so sorry, general."

The general grunted and stood up. He took one last look around the room and walked out without another word. He went directly to the home of a middle-aged rabbi four court-yards away.

"It is as you suspected," he told the rabbi. "The man is a charlatan."

"I fully agree," said the rabbi. "I've watched the proceedings carefully for a few days, and I think I've figured out his scheme. The fat man crumples up the paper and throws it into the trench, and the beggar retrieves it and brings it to Chayun before the people show up at the door. But how did you discover so definitely and so quickly that he's a charlatan?"

"I asked him what would happen to my son who is stationed with the army in Crimea. He hemmed and hawed and protested that he couldn't see what the Almighty didn't show him. But when I pressed him, he claimed he could see my son, and he described him to me."

"Did he tell you what the future held for your son?"

"He said he would be well and that he would one day become a minister."

"And this can't be true?"

The general's face broke into a broad grin. "Perhaps it'd be true if I had a son, but I only have three daughters. We don't want trouble, but this cannot be allowed to go on. Tell him that if he doesn't leave I'll have to arrest him."

The rabbi wasted no time carrying the message to Chayun. He put on his coat and stepped into the afternoon heat. A strong sirocco wind was blowing hot dust and sand from the Sahara Desert in North Africa across the eastern part of the Mediterranean Sea and the lands along the shore. The rabbi put his sleeve across his mouth and his nostrils and held it there the rest of the way to Chayun's rooms.

"The game is up, my friend," he said to Chayun. "You've been found out."

"Found out? I don't begin to know what you're saying."

"Don't play the innocent," said the rabbi, "because you are not. We know about the trench and the beggar, and the general has told me to tell you that he has no son. Only three daughters."

"I see."

"The general also said to tell you that if you don't leave on your own he will have you arrested."

Chayun smiled and threw up his hands. "Then that's that. It was nice while it lasted. I'll be gone from Chevron by tomorrow. Will that be satisfactory?"

The rabbi shook his head. "Be gone by tonight."

THE FINAL DEPARTURE · 12

The hot and dry sirocco wind passed through the streets of Chevron and blew north across Eretz Yisrael, Lebanon, Syria and Turkey. It gathered moisture as it passed over the Balkans, and it came to an end, spent of its force and laden with humidity, in a gentle rainfall over the funeral procession that snaked through the streets of Pulichev.

As it was Rosh Chodesh Nissan, no eulogies were delivered either in the synagogue or at the cemetery. Rav Shlomo Strasbourg had on several occasions expressed his unwillingness to be eulogized, but he had never actually put his wishes in writing. At the funeral, the people accepted Rav Mendel Strasbourg by acclaim as the successor to his illustrious father and the new rabbi of Pulichev.

There was a pall of sadness over the town, but also an air of acceptance. The townspeople had found it difficult to observe the relentless deterioration of their beloved rabbi and the debility of the last months of his life. Such was the way of the world. One generation passed away, and the next generation rose in its place. This was the beginning of Rav Mendel's time. He was young and vigorous, a brilliant scholar and a man possessed of a rare spiritual purity. The people had loved him from the time he was a precocious child, and now they embraced him as their rabbi and leader. It was time to move on.

It was time to move on for Rav Amos as well. He accepted the family's invitation to stay with them for Pesach, but he made plans to leave immediately afterward. Even had he wanted to leave, he could not have gone elsewhere in time for Pesach, since there was not enough time after the funeral and the Shivah to travel any appreciable distance. But he would have wanted to stay on in any case, because Rebbetzin Brachah and Rav Mendel needed his support. He had been part of their lives for nearly two years, and he felt a responsibility to help them adjust to the new realities of their lives.

A week before Pesach, Rav Amos received a letter from Chacham Tzvi. "I get a *mazel tov*," he wrote. "I am engaged to be married. You heard, of course, of Rav Meshulem Zalman Mirels Neumark, the Ashkenazic rabbi of the Three Communities – Altona, Hamburg and Wandsbeck. I believe I mentioned him in my last letter. I am going to marry his daughter Sarah. She is a fine girl with many outstanding qualities. Above all, she is wise and intelligent, and she fears the Almighty. The Mirels family is among the most distinguished of old Vienna, and it is connected by marriage to all the great rabbinic families. The Almighty has been very kind to me, and I am eternally grateful. The match was suggested by her brother Rav Zev when we met in Berlin. The wedding will take place in Hamburg, with the help of the Almighty, after Shavuos. I'm hoping that you'll be able to attend and that my parents will have regained their freedom by then, and that we can all celebrate together." The letter went on to discuss a *halachic* problem that had been presented to him and his thoughts on the proper procedure.[34]

Three days before Pesach, Rav Shlomo's old friend Elisha Ringel arrived together with his son Tanchum's ten-year-old son Sheftil, who was as tiny as his grandfather. When the news of Rav Shlomo's passing reached him in Poznan, Elisha immediately arranged to come to Pulichev for Pesach, and he had decided to take his grandson along as a traveling companion; his days of traveling unaccompanied were over. He had enjoyed a friendship with Rav Shlomo for nearly fifty years, and he could not see himself saying his final good-byes from hundreds of miles away.

As long as Rav Shlomo was alive, the festive family meals were almost invariably enjoyed in his home, especially during the last period of his life, when he was too weak to leave his home. He would sit in his chair, speaking little but enjoying the boisterous chatter of his grandchildren. He saw in them the assurance of a strong future for the Strasbourg line of rabbis of Pulichev. His father, the first Rav Mendel Strasbourg of Pulichev, had only one child. But that one child, Rav Shlomo, had fathered three children, the oldest of whom — Rav Mendel — was the father of five healthy children. In fact, Rav Mendel's two oldest, eighteen-year-old Gedaliah and fifteen-year-old Sarah, were not far from marriageable age. Rav Shlomo's other children, Usher and Sura'le, both of whom lived far away, also had children of their own. It was a comforting thought.

But now the meals shifted to Rav Mendel's home. Rav Mendel sat at the head of the table. Rebbetzin Brachah, his mother, sat in a place of honor at the other end of the table, while Rav Mendel's wife Miriam sat between her two youngest children, four-year-old Froyim Fishel and two-year-old Batsheva. The new arrangement symbolized the changing of the guard. It awakened feelings of sadness and loss, but also of hope and renewal.

On the first morning of Pesach, as the meal was drawing to a close, the peaceful serenity of the day was disturbed by the thunder of hoofbeats. The children immediately rushed to the window.

"Soldiers!" they yelled.

Rebbetzin Brachah's hands flew to her mouth, and her eyes filled with tears. She instinctively turned to Elisha

Ringel, whose resourcefulness had extricated the family from many a difficult situation in the past.

He stood up. "Don't be alarmed," he told her. "I'll have a look."

"I'll come with you," said Rav Mendel. "There may be no cause for concern. In the meantime, sit down, children, and sing a song."

There was loud banging on the door. Rav Mendel swallowed hard and opened it. It was a captain of the royal guard. Behind him, in the center of the street, stood a sleek black carriage, and all around were several dozen cavalrymen astride their horses.

"Is this the home of Rabbi Mendel Strasbourg?" asked the captain.

"Yes, it is. I am Rabbi Strasbourg."

"His Majesty King Jan wishes to pay his respects to the Strasbourg family."

Rav Mendel looked from the captain to the carriage and back to the captain. "Is he here right now?"

"Yes, he is."

The captain turned on his heel and strode to the carriage. He opened the door and stood aside as the Polish king emerged from the carriage. Without another word, he marched into the house, the captain right behind him.

King Jan III Sobieski, the great general who had fought and won so many battles for Poland, was now a man of sixty. He was still sturdy and vigorous and he still walked with a bearing both military and regal. But the weight of a life driven by ceaseless struggle and ambition had taken its toll.

The king held up his hand as soon as he walked into the house. "Please, everyone stay where you are. I will only be here for a few minutes."

The excited flurry of activity instantly came to a stop. Rav Mendel showed the king to his seat at the head of the table and poured him a glass of red wine. He remained standing, as did everyone else in the room.

"Sit down, sit down," said the king with an expansive wave of the hand. He drank deeply of the wine and wiped his lips.

"Passover wine?" he said.

"Yes," said Rav Mendel.

"Very good." He took another drink. "Do you have any Passover bread? I believe you call it *matzah*."

Rav Mendel brought a stack of wafer-thin *matzos* and placed them before him. The king took several bites of a *matzah* and chewed thoughtfully.

"Quite good," he said. "What's in it?"

"Flour and water."

"Nothing else?"

"Nothing else."

"Hmm," said the king.

He took another bite, chewed for a while and swallowed it.

"Really good," he said. "I swear there is not a trace of the blood of Christian children in it." He burst into laughter and slapped his knee. "I know this is not a joking matter with the Jewish people, but I couldn't resist it. It's amazing the nonsense that people can be made to believe if you pound it into their heads long enough. Well, I can promise you one thing. As long as I'm king of Poland, there will be no blood libels."

"Your Majesty," said Elisha Ringel, "we all pray for your good health and that you may live for a very long time."

The king laughed. "You can rely on me as long as I live, and then you'll have to rely on the Almighty. Anyway, I've got to go in a minute or two. I was on my way to review the troops in the south, and I heard that Rabbi Strasbourg had passed away. So I made a little detour to stop by and pay my respects. After that, I'll be staying in the castle in Lancut for a few weeks. If you need anything, just send me a message."

"We are very honored and grateful," said Rav Mendel. "My father was a great admirer of Your Majesty."

"Your father was a good man," said the king. "He saved my life once, did you know that? And he was a holy man. He gave me a blessing over twenty years ago that I would be victorious against the Cossacks at Podhajce, and I won. Then he gave me another blessing six years ago that I'd be victorious against the Turks at Vienna, and I won again. I owed him my life and two great victories. So I thought the least I could do was stop by and pay my respects to the family. He was a good man, and he will be missed."

The king stood up.

"Please don't trouble to escort me. Good day, and a happy festival."

He bowed to Rebbetzin Brachah and strode from the house. The captain clicked his heels, bowed and followed him outside. Moments later, they could hear the royal carriage rattle away, followed by the hoofbeats of its escort.

"Well, that was something," said Elisha after the shock had worn off.

"Yes, it was," said Rav Mendel. "It was a great honor for my father."

"Can I ask a question, grandfather?" said a squeaky voice. It was Elisha's ten-year-old grandson Sheftil. The boy was tiny for his age, but his eyes danced with an intelligence well beyond his years.

Elisha looked to Rav Mendel, who smiled and nodded.

"Go ahead, Sheftil," he said.

"The king said he owes Rav Shlomo … um … a lot. Does that mean that he now owes it to Rav Mendel? I mean, if we … the Jewish people … need something, can Rav Mendel go to the king?"

Rav Mendel laughed. "I don't think so, Sheftil. I don't think it works that way."

"Oh," said Sheftil, disappointed.

"Did you have something particular in mind?" asked Elisha.

Sheftil shook his head. "Not right now. But there's always some kind of trouble, isn't there? There's always something that we need, isn't there?"

"Unfortunately, you're right, Sheftil," said Rav Amos. "There's always something, and we have to do everything we can to protect ourselves. But our ultimate protection comes from the Almighty. Our lives are in His hands, and nothing can happen to us if He doesn't let it happen."

"So you're saying we have to pray?" said Sheftil.

"Yes," said Rav Amos.

"I know that," said Sheftil. "But when do we stop trying and start praying?"

"We never stop trying," said Rav Mendel, "and we never stop praying."

The day after Pesach, Rav Amos left Pulichev together with Elisha and Sheftil in their carriage. The first leg of the journey took them to Krakow, where they spent Shabbos with Rav Amos' sister Baila Mindel, her husband and her three little children. Baila Mindel was ten years younger than Rav Amos. She was married to Moshe Felsenberg, a popular *shochet* and *mohel*.

On Friday night, Baila Mindel put the children to sleep and served tea.

"I'm so excited to have you here, Amos," she said, barely able to contain her excitement. "Why I haven't seen you since my wedding, and that was eight years ago. Can you imagine?"

"That's what happens these days," said Elisha. "It's not like the old times when the families used to stay together in one place, more or less. I live in Poznan, and so does my son Tanchum and his family. But the rest of my children are scattered in Jewish communities far and wide. When I used to travel on business I used to see them more often, but these days I hardly ever see them. Maybe once every few years if I'm lucky. Travel is so difficult and expensive that people only do it for business or major family celebrations or some special reason. No one travels for a friendly visit. It's just the way it is."

"It's a terrible thing," she said. "My father visited me two years ago on his way back from Pulichev, and now Amos is here, also coming back from Pulichev. And if Rav Shlomo hadn't been ill, who knows when I would have seen either of them? Families should be close. Brothers and sisters should share each other's lives, not just show up when there's a wedding or some special reason. Most of the time, the celebrations are long past anyway by the time we hear about them. And how much real time do you get to spend with brothers and sisters at a wedding? How much opportunity do you have to talk about important things?"

Rav Amos took a sip of his tea. "So that makes this Shabbos extra special, little sister, doesn't it?"

"It certainly does," she said.

"You know," said his brother-in-law Moshe, "Baila Mindel has told me often that she hardly knows Amos. He went away to learn in Pulichev and Krakow when she was six …. He was away … let me see … uh …. Why don't you tell it, Baila Mindel? I get mixed up with the numbers."

"All right," she said. "You see, Amos is ten years older than I am. He's turning forty soon, and I'm thirty. He was sixteen when he went away to learn Torah, and I was six. He was away five years, then he was in Amsterdam for four years, and he got married and moved to Hamburg. I didn't see him again until my wedding, and how much did I see of him then?"

"But let's not forget those four years in Amsterdam," said Rav Amos.

Baila Mindel colored. "It's true. Amos was always my favorite, and when he came back to Amsterdam, I followed him everywhere."

Elisha laughed. "And did he chase you away?"

"No, he was very kind to me. He answered my questions and told me stories. He bought me honey and other treats. He even bought me chocolates a few times."

"You haven't forgotten?" said Rav Amos.

"No, I'll never forget. And now you're here for Shabbos. I can't believe my good fortune. You'll get to know my children, even though they're very young. And they'll get to know you. I'll make sure they remember you until the next time we see each other." She gave him a friendly frown. "It's time you got married again, Amos. If you give me enough time, maybe I'll come to your wedding. Unless you get married in America."

"Not much chance of that," said Rav Amos.

"But it's so exciting." She shivered deliciously. "America! I've never met anyone who's been to America. You have to tell me all about it. Mother wrote me that you went into the land of the red men. Was it frightening?"

"It's late," said Rav Amos. "If we start talking about my travels, we'll be up all night."

"So forget about America. What about getting married?"

"I'm thinking about it seriously. I'm ready to get married again."

She clapped her hands with delight. "I'm so excited. Right after Shabbos, I'll start working on a new dress. Wait a minute. I'm not sure I'm supposed to say that. No, I'll start thinking about a new dress. How's that? Better?"

They stayed in Krakow for two days after Shabbos, giving Rav Amos the opportunity to spend a little more time with his sister's family and to visit his brother Rabbi Baruch Ber Strasbourg, who was a respected *dayan*.

The night before they were to leave, Elisha returned from the marketplace with disturbing news.

"I spoke to some of my old contacts in the spice trade," he reported at the dinner table. "There's trouble on the roads. Things seem to be quiet for the time being on the front with the Turks, so the Austrians are shifting tens of thousands of troops to the western front against the French. There are also thousands of volunteers coming back from the Balkans to join the fight against the French. Those fighters are under no one's control, and many of them are passing through Poland on their way to Germany. They take what they want, and if you stand in their way … well. It's not a very safe thing to do."

"So what are you saying?" said Rav Amos.

"We should stay in Krakow for a while longer, if our hosts will have us. Things should clear up in a few days."

"With the greatest pleasure," said Moshe.

"I prayed that the Almighty would keep you here awhile longer," said Baila Mindel. "And my prayers were answered. I guess I was being selfish, but I couldn't help it. I'm sorry if I've caused you inconvenience, but now you'll have time to tell me all about America."

But things did not clear up in a few days. Elisha made daily trips to the marketplace, accompanied by young Sheftil, and each time, he came back with reports of continued troop movements. Two weeks later, the roads were finally declared free and safe, and they were able to continue their journey.

The reports of foreign troop movements had kept a lot of traffic off the roads, and now that they were clear, the traffic was very heavy. Nonetheless, they managed to get through most of the hilly countryside west of Krakow and reach Katowice by the end of the second day.

By noon the following day, the traffic on the road had thinned out, and Elisha's carriage, drawn by a team of fresh horses, was flying though the low hills that descended toward the old city of Breslau, where they would part ways. Elisha and Sheftil would continue north to Poznan, while Rav Amos would catch a riverboat on the Oder River to Berlin and another from there to Hamburg further to the west.

They heard the approach of the horsemen before they saw them. Seven horsemen, all of them blond, bearded and bareheaded, came galloping from behind. Two of them came alongside the horses and grabbed the reins. They pulled the carriage off the road and brought it to a halt in a wheat field. The horsemen surrounded the carriage.

The leader dismounted and flung open the door. He had two pistols, a dagger and a sword jammed into his belt.

"Get out!" he commanded in German.

Rav Amos stepped out, followed by Elisha Ringel and young Sheftil.

"You, too," he shouted to the Polish driver sitting high on the bench. "Get down here right away."

The driver clambered down and stood cowering behind the travelers.

The leader looked at them and turned to his men. "Well, what do you know, boys?" he said. "We've got us three Jews, one full size and two little miniatures. I'll bet you the little one has the money. Who wants to take me up on the bet?"

"Come on, Bjorn," said one of the men. "Let's not waste time with these games. Let's just do our business and move on."

The leader pulled a flask from his pocket and took a long swig. "What's the rush, Sigvard? It's a beautiful day. The roads are clear. Why not have a little fun?" He turned to the travelers. "Don't you agree, my friends? Shouldn't we have a little fun before we conduct our business?"

"I can see by looking at you," said Elisha, "that you men aren't despicable highwaymen molesting innocent travelers. You're clearly men of honor."

The man named Bjorn beamed at him. He took a bow and turned to his men. "You hear that, boys?" He took another swig and turned back to Elisha. "Go on, short man. What else can you see about us?"

"I can see that you're returning from Serbia," said Elisha, "where you fought to defend Christendom against the Muslim hordes. You're on your way home to Sweden. Or maybe not. You may fight the French for a while before you return to Sweden."

"Not bad, not bad," said Bjorn. "Clever little fellow, aren't you? Well, we'll see how clever you are when we cut you down to size." He took another mouthful from the flask.

"It'll be hard to cut that one down any further," said Sigvard. "If you do, he'll disappear completely."

Bjorn doubled over with laughter, and all the liquor came squirting out of his mouth in a big cloud of spray.

"Good one, Sigvard," he said. "Good one. Very funny. All right, let's get serious. What do you say we do with these clever Jews?"

"You should let us continue our journey," said Rav Amos. "We will contribute some of our money voluntarily to help you continue your journey with honor while we continue ours, so that you should not be forced to behave as common thieves."

"Oho, listen to this, boys," said Bjorn. "The big one talks. You are right that you will contribute your money. But not some of it. All of it!" He pulled the sword from its scabbard and brandished it menacingly. "What do you say, Sigvard? Should we leave witnesses?"

Elisha stepped in front of Sheftil. "Run when I give you the signal," he whispered, "and don't look back."

"What are you whispering there?" snapped Bjorn.

"I'm just reassuring the boy that you mean him no harm," said Elisha.

"Well, how would you know that?"

"I'm assuming that you wouldn't harm an innocent child. Look, Herr Bjorn. You obviously drive a hard bargain. You can take all our money, and if you come with us to Breslau, we'll give you more."

Bjorn guffawed again. "Do you take us for fools?"

Sheftil peeked out from behind Elisha and tugged at his sleeve.

"Grandfather," he said in a loud whisper, "tell them the truth."

Bjorn's ears perked up. "The truth? What's the truth?"

"Nothing, nothing," said Elisha. "The boy didn't mean anything."

"Come out here, you little piece of dirt," said Bjorn. "Stop hiding behind the old man."

Sheftil came out and took two steps forward. He stared defiantly at the Swede.

"I'll tell you the truth," he said. "We're on a secret mission for King Jan Sobieski of Poland."

Bjorn, Sigvard and all the riders burst into raucous laughter.

"You can laugh all you want," said Sheftil. "But it won't be so funny when you're swinging from the end of a rope. My grandfather knows the king for over twenty years. He once saved his life. A few weeks ago, the king came to us in Pulichev and gave my grandfather and uncle an important secret mission. I was right there in the room."

The smile slowly faded from Bjorn's face.

"If anything happens to us," the boy continued, "the king will find out about it, and he'll track you down like dogs and hang your carcasses from the nearest tree."

"I don't believe you, boy," said Bjorn. "And you watch your tongue. Don't forget that you're talking to officers of the Swedish cavalry. Show some respect. Now what's the secret mission?"

"I don't know. The king didn't tell me."

"So how about you, old man," said Bjorn to Elisha. "Is there a secret mission?"

"Yes, there is," said Elisha.

"What is it?"

"You know I can't tell you. Even if you kill me, I am sworn to secrecy by the king."

"You're lying."

Elisha shrugged. "Perhaps. But perhaps not."

"Prove it," Bjorn insisted.

"How should I prove it?" said Elisha. "There's nothing on paper."

Bjorn chewed his knuckles, trying to think through an alcoholic haze.

"Ask them where the king is right now," suggested Sigvard. "We know where he is, because we passed through that town, but how would they know?"

"Good idea, Sigvard. All right, old man. Where is the king now?"

"How should I know?" said Elisha. "My mission has nothing to do with his present location."

Bjorn relaxed. "Nah, you don't know. The whole thing is a lie. A clever lie. But you can't fool me."

"My grandfather doesn't want to say," Sheftil spoke up. "But I'll tell you. The king is in the castle at Lancut."

Bjorn was shocked. "How did you know that?"

"The king told my grandfather where he was going to be. I was in the room, and I heard him."

Bjorn and Sigvard exchanged glances. Then Bjorn shrugged and returned his sword to its scabbard.

"I hope you gentlemen can take a little joke," he said. "You know, of course, that we never meant you any harm."

"Of course," said Elisha.

"We weren't even going to take your money."

"Of course not."

"Well, it's been nice meeting you," he said as he remounted his horse. "Good luck with your secret mission."

"Thank you."

"And give our best regards to the king."

"All right."

"On second thought, give me your word you won't mention our names."

Elisha scratched his chin. "Well, if you insist."

"Let's go, men," said Bjorn. He gave the signal and they rode away.

Rav Amos and Elisha, suddenly weak-kneed, leaned back against the carriage. The Polish driver crossed himself, mumbled something under his breath and climbed back up onto the bench.

"That was very sharp, Sheftil," said Elisha. "How did you remember about the castle in Lancut? It was just a casual remark he threw out — and it was over a month ago!"

"I thought about it a lot," said Sheftil. "I imagined going to Lancut and meeting with the king."

"I see," said Elisha. "Anyway, it looks as if I've lost a bit of my touch. But, Sheftil, my boy, it looks as if you found it."

DO NOT BE AFRAID · 13

CHACHAM TZVI'S FATHER was standing in the parlor when Rav Amos entered the house. His eyes lit up when he caught sight of him, and tears pooled in the corners of his eyes. Without speaking a word, he opened his arms and embraced the younger man, trembling and clinging to him for a long time.

"It's so good to see you, Rav Amos," he said. He smiled ruefully. "It seems I'm not the only one who missed my son's wedding.[35] I'm told that you missed it, too."

"We were delayed on the road," said Rav Amos.

"What can you do?" said the rabbi. "I have to be thankful that at last my wife and I are free and that I've seen my son alive and well and starting a new life as part of the Neumark family. I'll be forever grateful to you, Rav Amos, for everything you did for my son and for us. Your friendship means a lot to him, as it does to me."

"Believe me," said Rav Amos. "I've received far more than I've given. What will you and your wife do now? Will you settle here in Hamburg?"

The rabbi shook his head. "This is not the place for us. But I understand that you're going to live here." He lowered his voice. "And I also understand that we may hear some good news soon."

Rav Amos smiled. "It looks promising, but there's no *mazel tov* yet."

"Take your time. Take your time. But it would be nice if you could break a plate before we leave."

"I'll keep that in mind. So where will you be going?"

"We've decided to go to Eretz Yisrael," said the rabbi.[36] "Everything we had has been destroyed. First Vilna and then Alt-Ofen. I'm too old to start from new. And I don't want to settle here and be a burden to my son and a nuisance to his father-in-law. So we've decided to fulfill a lifelong dream and live in Eretz Yisrael. We'll be poor there, but so is everyone else, so that will make it easier. We don't have children to raise or marry off, so it's just getting by from day to day. You know, I actually look forward to a life of utter simplicity. A piece of bread, a bed, a candle and a Gemara. It sounds wonderful to me."

"It sounds luxurious," said Rav Amos. "I'm happy for you. So when will you be going?"

"We leave the day after tomorrow. We know that we'll probably never see our son and his family again, but we'll keep in touch by letter, and they'll be in our thoughts and memories. It's really the right thing."

The following night, Rav Amos became engaged to a young widow fourteen years his junior named Rivkah Dvosha Katz. Her husband had been robbed and killed on a business trip, and she had been left with a two-year-old boy named Menachem and a pile of debts. Her only family was an elderly father who lived in Lemberg on the other side of the European continent. Chacham Tzvi and his new wife had suggested the match, and the engagement was sealed in their home, a stone's throw from the Ashkenazic synagogue of Altona. Chacham Tzvi's father drank a *lechaim* and danced with Rav Amos, and a day later, he left for Eretz Yisrael.

Rav Amos was euphoric. At the ripe old age of forty, he had not expected to find a wife as young and vibrant as Rivkah Dvosha. She sparkled with life, energy, good humor and a genuine interest in everyone around her. She had agreed to consider him as a possible match because Chacham Tzvi's wife, her good friend, had assured her that he was a man of true greatness in every respect, and she had not been disappointed. When he had first walked into the room, she had seen a tall, imposing, dignified man with flecks of gray at the sides of his black beard, and she had suddenly felt intimidated. But then she had seen the kindness and humility in his eyes, the sad memories and the uncertain hope, and her heart had melted with compassion. Here was a chance for both of them to recapture what they had lost, and they both embraced the gift with gratitude to the Almighty.

Two days after the engagement, Chacham Tzvi and Rav Amos were sitting together in his kitchen late at night. Rav Amos was reminded of another night in Alt-Ofen when they had talked late into the night. But he said nothing, because he knew it would only arouse painful memories.

"My father is convinced you got engaged so quickly," said Chacham Tzvi, "because he asked you to do it before he left for Eretz Yisrael."

Rav Amos chuckled. "He's not entirely wrong. The main reason was that Rivkah Dvosha is clearly the right one for me, as you and your wife also assured me. So why drag it on and give her unnecessary anxiety? I did push it up a day so that your parents could share in my celebration. And there's a third reason. I wanted my entire family, including my sister in Krakow, and Rivkah Dvosha's father in Lemberg to come to the wedding. So we needed as much time as possible to let everyone know and come and go home before deep winter sets in. The letters have already gone out."

"Wonderful. Have you found a place to live yet? I think there is a house available two streets over."

"I haven't looked into it yet. If we don't find anything right away, perhaps we can start in Rivkah Dvosha's apartment. In the meantime, I'm putting my efforts into arranging a learning group for young students. You know, with my income from the fur trade, it looks as if I really won't have to work for a living, and that I can spend my entire time learning. But I need to give a little to others, as well."

"Absolutely. Otherwise your learning will grow stale. Our sages tell us that if we learn in order to teach, we are given the opportunity to do both, learn and teach."[37]

"Did you ever wonder why the Mishnah doesn't mention that if we learn in order to learn we are given the opportunity to learn?"

Chacham Tzvi smiled and nodded. "The question did occur to me. It jumps out at you. I have an idea, but obviously, so do you. So let's hear your explanation first."

"I think that learning Torah is the greatest pleasure in the world, and a person who learns because he enjoys the thrill of absorbing the words of the Almighty into his mind and his heart is fulfilling the mitzvah of learning Torah, and he will be rewarded. But a person who learns in order to teach is doing it for the sake of Heaven, and he deserves a special divine assistance to help him succeed. That is what is meant by being given the opportunity. It means a special divine assistance. A person who learns because he loves it certainly has the freedom of choice to do so. But he has not earned a special divine assistance."

Chacham Tzvi clapped his hands together with delight. "That is a beautiful explanation. I love it, and I believe it is true."

Rav Amos was pleased. "And what is your explanation?"

Chacham Tzvi wagged his finger. "I'll tell you, but not today. This day belongs to your explanation." He cleared his throat. "I need a favor from you, my friend."

"Of course. Whatever you want. It will be my pleasure."

"You know how much I need to be financially independent."

"Yes," said Rav Amos. "I saw how agitated you became in Venice when you thought you might have to take something from Tarantella."

Chacham Tzvi shook his head. "You might think I was overreacting, that it wouldn't have been so terrible to take from someone else in my time of need. But it's not so. You have to understand that I cannot allow myself to be dependent on the generosity of other people. I have a future as a leader and a teacher — and so do you, my friend, don't think otherwise — and the Torah says, 'Do not be afraid of any man.'[38] We'll be faced with making many decisions, and many of them will be unpopular. But we have to do what we believe is the right thing, to make the choices the Almighty wants us to make. There will always be pressures brought on us from people in our congregations and our communities. They'll offer us money, honors and favors, and yes, support for our *yeshivos* and charities, and all in order to gain some control over us."

"You have to take money for charities," said Rav Amos.

"That's right, we have to accept money for *yeshivos* and charities, but we have to realize we're holding smoldering coals in our hands. And we have to be ready to drop them the instant the contributors try to influence our opinions. If we let them, if we allow ourselves to be corrupted in even the most subtle ways, then we're lost, and all our Torah and leadership become tainted."

"I understand what you're saying," said Rav Amos, "but I think this affects you more than it does me."

"Why? Because you think I will hold a more prominent position in the world of Torah than you will? No one can know. And even if it is so, the difference is only a matter of degree, a matter of scale. You'll face your tests, and I'll face mine. And both of us have an equal obligation to remain independent and free of taint, to owe our allegiance only to the Almighty and no one else. But you are a little bit right in a certain sense."

"What do you mean?"

"It's a bigger problem for me than it is for you, because you have your income from the fur trade. You worked hard for that income. You sailed to America, and you risked your life in the lands of the Indians. Sebastian isn't giving you a gift. He's being fair and honorable and giving you what you deserve. As for me, my income is not assured. My father-in-law is a rabbi, and I've not received a very large dowry. Believe me, plenty of people are willing to shower me with money. I've already been approached by a few, but I've turned them all down. Don't be afraid of any man, the Torah tells us. If I take their money, I'll become afraid of them, and I cannot allow that to happen."

"So what are you saying?"

"I need to earn a living without compromising myself. And I've been presented with an opportunity to do so. There's young man here in Altona named Eliyakim Getzel Grunbach. He has an importing business bringing in shoes from Morocco where labor is much cheaper. He is doing very well, and he is looking to expand his business, but he needs capital. He offered me a partnership if I invest my money with him. The returns will be substantial."

"It sound good," said Rav Amos. "But are you sure that your money is secure? Do you know what the risks are? Things can happen in business, you know, unexpected things. Are you prepared to risk losing your investment? And how do you know that this young fellow won't just squander your money and disappear?"

"I've thought about these things," said Chacham Tzvi. "Believe me, I have. Eliyakim Getzel really pressed me for the money, and that made me a little suspicious, so I went to talk with his father, Kalman Grunbach, one of the wealthier merchants in Hamburg. He assured me his son was responsible and reliable, and he said he would sign on to the deal as a guarantor for any mismanagement losses other than ordinary market fluctuations."

"That sounds better."

"Yes, I think it's a good arrangement."

"So what's the favor you want from me?"

"I need your expertise on preparing contracts," said Chacham Tzvi. "You've spent a lot of time learning about contracts, and you understand them well. The Grunbachs are coming by later to draw up the partnership agreement, and I'd like you to review the document and make sure everything is in order."

The partnership papers were signed later that same evening, and Chacham Tzvi's first step in securing his independence was accomplished. The arrangement worked well, and Chacham Tzvi was able to concentrate on his learning and teaching with peace of mind.

As the months flew by, life in Altona assumed a satisfying rhythm for Chacham Tzvi and Rav Amos. Chacham Tzvi's brilliance and charisma quickly won him a broad following. Young men from neighboring towns and cities started coming to Altona to learn under his guidance. Moreover, since his father-in-law, the rabbi of Hamburg and its satellite communities in Altona and Wandsbeck, was old and frail, many of the duties of the rabbinate fell on Chacham Tzvi's capable shoulders. And indeed, as time went on he became the unofficial acting rabbi.[39]

In 1691, two years after Chacham Tzvi's marriage and arrival in Hamburg, one of the leaders of the community, a wealthy man named Moshe Leibushes, led a movement to make his position official and pay him a salary in keeping with the duties he was performing for the community. But there were some in the community who were wary of the rising power of the independent-minded young genius; they were afraid that if his position as the assistant rabbi were made official he would enjoy even greater power over them.

After a period of bitter disputes and recriminations, Moshe Leibushes' movement failed. But he was not to be denied in his burning desire to support and promote Chacham Tzvi's efforts. Shortly after the movement failed, he established a *kloiz* in Altona and appointed Chacham Tzvi as its *rosh yeshivah*. The *kloiz* differed from a *yeshivah* only in the sense that its members included married men as well as unmarried young men and teenaged boys. The salary for the *rosh yeshivah* was a paltry sixty Reichsthalers per year, but Chacham Tzvi was satisfied, especially since he had a stream of income from the Grunbach venture. To Leibushes' surprise, however, he did not relinquish his unofficial role as the rabbi of all of Hamburg.[40]

During this time, the trajectory of Rav Amos' life was also rising, although not as dramatically as that of Chacham Tzvi. His wedding was the highlight of the fall of 1689 in Hamburg. His parents came from Amsterdam, and his brothers and sister from London and Krakow. The entire Dominguez family, Doña Angelica, Sebastian and his wife and Felipe and his wife, came from Amsterdam, as did Carolina Pereira, their sister, and her husband, who lived in the Portuguese community of Hamburg. In addition, Aharon Velvel Leikis, who had accompanied him on his journey to New York, managed to put in an appearance between his latest voyage to the American colonies and a visit to the town of Kuba in the mountains of Azerbaijan.

After the wedding, Rav Amos divided his day between his own learning and the group he had assembled. He also arranged to learn together with Chacham Tzvi for an hour at midnight every day. They started with Mesechte Zevachim in Seder Kadashim, an area not ordinarily part of the normal course of *yeshivah* learning. It was a quiet time, free of all disturbance and interruption, when the learning was wide-ranging, on the highest level and deeply satisfying to both men. In 1691, when Leibushes established the *kloiz* in Altona, Chacham Tzvi invited Rav Amos and his group to become part of the *kloiz*. He could not offer Rav Amos more than the smallest token salary, but Rav Amos didn't need a salary. He had more than enough for his needs.

Within a year after its establishment, the Chacham Tzvi's *kloiz* was a sensation. It became a gathering place for many outstanding rabbis and scholars from Poland and Lithuania who came to learn together under the leadership of Chacham Tzvi. The sounds of ardent Torah learning and heated argumentation in the *kloiz* were undiminished at any hour of the day and night as the august groups filled their minds with Gemara, Rishonim, Halachah, Aggadah, Midrash and even the rules of grammar and eventually returned home as accomplished *talmidei chachamim*.

The years passed, and both Chacham Tzvi and Rav Amos were blessed with children. A daughter was born to Chacham Tzvi in 1691 and another daughter in 1693. In 1690, Rav Amos and Rivkah Dvosha were blessed with a son, whom they named Reuven, and in 1693 with a daughter, whom they named Chanah.

In the meantime, Chacham Tzvi's reputation continued to grow and spread to every corner of the world where Jews lived. Letters presenting *halachic* questions poured in from communities as far away as London, Vilna and Salonika, and he responded to them at great length and in great detail.

Rabbis and dignitaries stopped in Hamburg to pay him their respects. Even ministers and dukes stopped by to meet this world-renowned rabbi who spoke many languages, was conversant in the sciences and had a profound grasp of world economic and political affairs. They often brought him expensive gifts of gold and silver ornaments, and he invariably refused the gifts with grace, sensitivity and diplomacy.

One day, in the summer of 1693, Chacham Tzvi did not arrive in the *kloiz* at his appointed time. The time for his morning session passed without his making an appearance. Another hour passed and then two more, and Rav Amos started to worry. It was certainly unlike Chacham Tzvi to neglect his commitments. If he could not come on time, he always sent notification beforehand so that his disciples should not be kept waiting. And now a good part of the day had already passed with no word from him at all.

Becoming more worried by the minute, Rav Amos left the *kloiz* and went directly to Chacham Tzvi's home. He found Chacham Tzvi sitting in a room by himself, his face dark and morose.[41]

Rav Amos pulled up a chair next to him and waited for Chacham Tzvi to say something. But Chacham Tzvi simply stared at him with sad eyes and said nothing.

"All right," said Rav Amos. "Can you tell me what happened?"

Chacham Tzvi put his hand across his brow, covering his eyes, and hung his head. He took a deep breath and sighed heavily.

"Did someone die?" asked Rav Amos. "Did someone get hurt?"

Chacham Tzvi shook his head. "I'm ruined," he said.

"What do you mean?"

"Grunbach."

"What about Grunbach?"

Chacham Tzvi sighed again. "My investment ..."

Rav Amos got a hollow feeling in the pit of his stomach. "Yes? What about your investment?"

"My money is gone."

"Gone? All of it?"

"All of it. My money is gone."

"But how?"

"Grunbach squandered it, just as you said he might," said Chacham Tzvi. "I sensed there was trouble, so I asked him to give me an accounting."

"So what did he have to say for himself?"

"He didn't. I just found out this morning that he picked himself up and went off to Amsterdam. It's all over. I'm ruined."

"But he must have been doing something right," said Rav Amos. "I mean, he's being giving you a share of the profits for a few years now."

Chacham Tzvi shook his head. "I don't think there ever were any profits. He used my money for who knows what and gave some of it back to me from time to time and told me it was profit." He sighed again and slumped in his chair. "I know I have to break out of this depression and deal with the situation, but right now I'm still in shock."

"It will pass," said Rav Amos. "Just relax and let it flow away. You're strong, one of the strongest people I know. You'll get through this."

"It's not so simple," said Chacham Tzvi. "I'll get through this, I've no doubt about that. We will not die of hunger. But what will happen to me? You know it's not the loss of the money itself that's making me so depressed."

"I know."

"Of course, you do, my friend. You've heard it from me often enough. Look at my situation. I'm married with two small children. My expenses are rising every year, and what income do I have? Sixty Reichsthalers a year as a salary from the *kloiz*? I can't support a family on such a paltry sum. So where does that leave me and my independence? Am I going to have to stick out my hand now and accept the eager generosity of the wealthy and powerful who would love nothing more than to gain control over me?"

"You can't do that."

"No, I can't. But what else should I do? Should I look for a rabbinical position in another city where I can command a decent salary? Should I walk away from my beloved *kloiz*, the apple of my eye, to which I've given my heart and soul? Should I turn my back on my elderly father-in-law who really can't carry the heavy burden of the Three Communities all by himself?"

"You're in a tight spot."

"I certainly am."

"Do you have any money at all left," asked Rav Amos, "money that you haven't invested?"

"A small sum. A really small sum. A sum so small that you can barely see it. I would have to double and triple it every month or so just to be able to cover my basic expenses."

Rav Amos chewed on his lower lip as he thought through the problem.

"Well, all is not lost," he said at last. "Don't forget that Kalman Grunbach, Eliyakim Getzel's father, signed on as a guarantor. He's a very wealthy man. We'll just have to ask him to make good on his commitment."

"Yes, we'll have to do that, I suppose. But who knows what his present financial situation really is? Maybe he invested with his son as well."

"Maybe. But unless he's lost everything, he's obligated to make good on his commitment. Maybe you'll recover part of your investment. That would be better than nothing."

Chacham Tzvi nodded. "Something is definitely better than nothing."

Rav Amos stood up. "You pull out the partnership agreement with Kalman Grunbach's signature, and I'll go pay him a visit."

Kalman Grunbach lived in a mansion. The door was opened by a maid in uniform, who showed Rav Amos into a sitting room and asked him to wait while she announced his arrival. Twenty minutes later, Frau Grunbach made an appearance. She was wearing a richly brocaded gown, and in her hands, she was twisting and turning a lace handkerchief.

"Good afternoon, Rabbi Strasbourg," she said. "It is such an honor to have you cross our threshold. What can we do for you?"

"I'd like to have a few words with your husband."

"May I ask what this concerns?"

Rav Amos arched his eyebrows. "Why would you ask me such a question, Frau Grunbach? Do you screen all your husband's visitors?"

She colored. "A thousand apologies, Rabbi Strasbourg. I did not mean to cause offense. Things are just a little tense right now."

"How so?"

"I know that you're good friends with Chacham Tzvi, who's one of Getzel's investors. You've come about Getzel's troubles, haven't you?"

"I'm afraid I have," said Rav Amos. "Look, I'd rather not discuss your son's affairs with you."

"He's not my son," she said. "He's from my husband's first wife."

"Oh, well, in that case, I should certainly not discuss him with you. Could you tell your husband that I'm here to see him?"

"I'm afraid he can't see you now."

"Why not?"

"He's not well. I shouldn't be telling you this, but I guess you have a right to know. Kalman got into bed today, and he won't eat anything or talk to anybody. He says his stomach is hurting him, he's running a fever and his color is very bad. The doctor was here, and he says his state of mind is making him physically ill. This business with Getzel is making him sick and depressed."

"Can he see me for a just few minutes?"

"He can't," she said. "Believe me, he is not capable of seeing anyone right now. He is seriously ill."

When Rav Amos returned to Chacham Tzvi's house, he found him sitting at his table with the partnership agreement open in front of him.

"Well, what did he say?" said Chacham Tzvi.

Rav Amos repeated the conversation with Frau Grunbach verbatim to the best of his ability, while Chacham Tzvi sat and listened stone-faced.

"I'm not surprised," he said when Rav Amos finished. "Feelings of depression can make you physically ill. I was almost there myself. I'm not going to go after a sick man."

"So you just have to wait a while," said Rav Amos. "This can't go on indefinitely. When he recovers, I'll approach him again, and we'll talk about repayment. With the Almighty's help, you'll get your money back."

Chacham Tzvi shook his head. "The man is sick with worry, and he didn't do anything to deserve it. He signed in good faith. Is it his fault that his son turned out to be a scoundrel?"

"Is it your fault?" said Rav Amos. "You have a right to recover your money. If a person signs as a guarantor he's responsible. He can't say that he thought this and he thought that. He's obligated."

"But the man is sick."

"He'll get better. We'll wait until he recovers, and then we'll demand that he honor his commitment to you."

Chacham Tzvi shook his head. He picked up the partnership agreement, tore it into pieces and handed them to Rav Amos.

"Please do me a favor," he said, "and go back to Grunbach's house right away. Give these to him. They will speed his recovery."[42]

A TIME TO REBUILD · 14

T HE SOLUTION TO CHACHAM TZVI'S problem was not long in coming. When word of his misfortune got out, a number of Hamburg merchants got together and made him an offer. They invited him to invest his remaining minimal capital in their ventures on a deal-by-deal basis and share in the profits.

These ventures generally involved investing in a string of pearls or a diamond necklace. When such a piece of jewelry was offered on the market for a bargain price, the merchants would snap it up and then offer it for sale in more advantageous times and under more acceptable conditions. The profits were usually quite handsome, and the businessmen invited Chacham Tzvi to invest with them and reap the profits.

Chacham Tzvi was very grateful for the offer, but he insisted that he be shown no favoritism in the distribution of profits. He extracted a promise from them that they would give him a percentage of profits which was exactly identical to his percentage in the investment.

As soon as they brought Chacham Tzvi into their enterprise, the merchants began to reap enormous profits. Instead of reselling a pearl necklace within two months for a twenty percent profit, they found themselves reselling it for double or triple the purchase price. It was abundantly clear that the

Almighty was bestowing extraordinary blessings on their enterprise in the merit of the holy Chacham Tzvi.

Chacham Tzvi's investment capital was growing at a shockingly quick pace. At first, he refused to accept his profits, suspecting the merchants of violating their trust and giving him more than he deserved. But eventually, they convinced him that he was only receiving his fair share. He accepted his earnings and thanked the Almighty for His kindness.[43]

Freed of concerns about his financial independence, Chacham Tzvi threw himself into his work with all his talent and energy. He spent most of his time in the *kloiz*, which was his first love. Even though Chacham Tzvi was still in his thirties, with no official rabbinic position other than the head of a small *kloiz*, many of the leading rabbis of Europe sent him their difficult questions, because they knew his responses would be authoritative, erudite, insightful and altogether brilliant. His reputation grew rapidly, and he was soon acclaimed and acknowledged as one of the greatest rabbis of his generation.

He also took upon his shoulders the rabbinic responsibility of improving life for all the Jews of Hamburg, even thought he was not officially their rabbi and was receiving no pay for his efforts, and for correcting injustice wherever he perceived it.

Before Chacham Tzvi's arrival in Hamburg, kosher wine for Kiddush was hard to come by and very expensive when it was available. So he sent people to Italy and France to supervise the production of kosher wine and its importation to Hamburg, so that before too long kosher wine was plentiful and inexpensive.[44] He arranged to have the townspeople keep their *cholent* pots in the baker's ovens on Shabbos, thereby insuring that the people did not do forbidden labors when they tried to keep the *cholent* hot overnight.[45] He organized and streamlined the baking of *matzos* for Pesach under strict supervision, making sure that an adequate supply of *matzos* was available to every Jewish family, regardless of how poor they were.[46] He also established rules for the conduct of business consistent with Halachah and especially with the *ribbis* laws against lending at interest.[47]

He undertook an active involvement in the welfare of the poor. He raised money for impoverished people or other worthy causes. Some of the wealthiest people in Hamburg entrusted large sums to him to distribute to the poor so that the givers and receivers shouldn't know each other's identities.[48]

He also took a special interest in the poor Ashkenazi communities in Eretz Yisrael. At the time, the funds raised in the Sephardic communities of Europe for the Sephardic communities of Eretz Yisrael were reaching their destination. But the situation was unfortunately different as far as the funds raised in the numerous Ashkenazic communities of Europe for the Ashkenazic communities of Eretz Yisrael were concerned. Most of the money was being diverted into the pockets of the fundraisers, and only a small trickle reached Eretz Yisrael, not nearly enough to sustain those communities with their most basic needs. And the small amount of money that did come in was often confiscated by the Turkish government officials.

Chacham Tzvi took the matter under his own control. He turned away the traveling fundraisers and collected the money himself. Then he sent the money to a trustworthy merchant in Livorno, Italy, who sent it on in secret to a trusted rabbi in Chevron. The rabbi then distributed the money privately to the poor in Chevron and Yerushalayim and took receipts from each recipient. He then sent the receipts back to Chacham Tzvi in Hamburg. Chacham Tzvi was thus able to ensure that all the money raised in Hamburg reached its destination.[49]

During this time, Chacham Tzvi's family continued to grow. In 1695, his wife gave birth to their third daughter.

Two years later, his wife bore him his first son. By this time, his father had passed away in Eretz Yisrael,[50] and Chacham Tzvi named his son Yaakov after his father. When the boy was a little older, he asked his father why he signed his name simply Tzvi without mentioning the name of his father Yaakov. Chacham Tzvi answered that the letters that spelled Tzvi — *tzadi, beis, yod* — stand for Tzvi ben Yaakov. And he told the boy that he should sign his name Yavetz – *yod, ayin, beis, tzadi* – which stood for Yaakov ben Tzvi.

The Strasbourg family was not as prolific as the Ashkenazi family. Rav Amos and Rivkah Dvosha did not have any more children during this period of their lives, but they was happy. Little Reuven and Chanah were growing into sturdy children, secure and happy and full of curiosity and zest for life. As for Rivkah Dvosha's son Menachem, Rav Amos went out of his way to accept him as his own, and as a result, the two developed a bond closer and stronger than that of most fathers and sons.

Rav Amos looked at these years as a time to rebuild, both for himself and for Chacham Tzvi. Their lives had fallen apart, and now, they were rebuilding together. Every one of his days was enriched by his friendship and association with Chacham Tzvi. He observed his friend's meteoric rise to the highest pinnacles of the Torah world with deep satisfaction, oblivious to his own steady rise in knowledge, wisdom and stature. The midnight sessions together continued; after they finished Seder Kadashim, they plunged into Seder Taharos and then Seder Zeraim. They also added a twice-weekly session during which Chacham Tzvi, who knew the Zohar and the writings of Arizal practically by heart, introduced Rav Amos to the basic concepts of Kabbalah.

Chacham Tzvi also showed Rav Amos more and more of the rabbis' questions he received and asked his opinion of the responses he formulated.

One day in 1696, Chacham Tzvi showed him a letter that arrived that day.

"This is from Rabbi Shlomo Ayllon," he said, "the rabbi of the Sephardic community of London."

"Ayllon?" said Rav Amos. "The name sounds familiar. Wasn't he involved with a Sabbatean group?"[51]

"I've heard such rumors myself. But even if it's true, it was a long time ago, a youthful indiscretion. I don't think his name has been associated with any Sabbateans for close to twenty years."[52]

"Do you think people can change?"

"Yes, I do. Especially when they're still relatively young. Rabbi Ayllon is a bright and learned man, a respected rabbi. I'm sure the London community did a proper investigation before they invited him to be their rabbi."

Rav Amos shrugged. "You're probably right. So what's his question?"

"It's complicated, but I wanted to show it you for a reason. It involves a case of a man in the London community who died and left his widow in charge of his estate, a large part of which consists of the dowry she brought with her. The man also left four brothers. The oldest has gone to France where he converted to Christianity. The other three are all married, but two of them are married to non-Jewish women and regularly eat non-kosher food. Now, this widow needs to go through the *chalitzah* ceremony in order to marry again. The brothers, however, don't want her to spit at them, so they claim it's the obligation of the oldest to do it. But the oldest is living as a Christian in France. There's also a major dispute between the brothers and the widow over control of the estate. It gets even more complicated, but I won't burden you with all the sordid details."[53]

"So what's your reason for telling me about this case?"

"I just wanted to show you what's going on in the community of London. If this is in any way typical, and from the letter it appears that it isn't so uncommon, then it would seem that the community is disintegrating. I don't know what we can do for them over there in London, but we have to be especially vigilant so that such things should not happen here as well."

"Can I take a look at the letter?"

"Of course. The case has caught your interest, hasn't it?"

Rav Amos scanned the first paragraph of the letter.

"Not really," he said. "I wanted to see how he addresses you."

"Oh."

Rav Amos pursed his lips. "Hmm. He is full of praises for you."

Chacham Tzvi smiled and shook his head. "Don't take those things too seriously. It's just the formalities of these types of letters. If you don't begin with a long and flowery salutation, it's almost like a slap in the face."

"All right, but even if half of it is sincere, it's very complimentary." Rav Amos continued reading. "He seems all right."

"You mean he doesn't sound like a Sabbatean?"

Rav Amos inclined his head. "I suppose that's what I mean."

"So how does a Sabbatean sound?"

Rav Amos threw up his hands. "I give up. I really don't know. I just thought his language would be a little different if he were a Sabbatean, but I guess I was wrong. I don't think I've ever met a Sabbatean."

"Well, I have," said Chacham Tzvi. "When I was learning in Salonika. Believe me, they sound just like you and me. Even when they discuss Kabbalah, it's hard to recognize their true colors."

"What do you mean?"

"Shabbesai Tzvi is dead, and most Sabbateans are not waiting for him to come back to life. So what makes them Sabbateans? It's their approach to Kabbalah and their understanding of the nature of the Almighty. Actually, in a certain way, it has strong resemblances to Christianity."

"Really? Do you think I'm advanced enough in my studies of Kabbalah to recognize the differences?"

"Not yet." Chacham Tzvi shook his head. "You aren't even close. The differences are subtle, but once you know what you're looking for, the evidence is very clear. Right now, you wouldn't be able to pick up on these subtle differences on your own, but you're far enough advanced to understand and recognize the differences once I show them to you."

"So show them to me."

"Right now?"

"Right now."

"Your curiosity is piqued?"

"It certainly is," said Rav Amos.

"All right. We'll do it next time we learn the Zohar. But right now, speaking of former Sabbateans, I want to show you another letter I got recently."

He rummaged among the letters on his table and extracted one.

"Here, let me tell you about it," he said. "It's from the community in Candia, Italy. It involves a man from Salonika who joined the Sabbateans. After a while, he converted to Islam, just as Shabbesai Tzvi did, with some crazy idea that lowering himself he could collect the scattered shells ... I don't want to get into all of that now. Anyway, the man was a Sabbatean and a Muslim, but then he came to his senses and abandoned all that foolishness. He returned to his people in full sincerity, and now he lives in Candia."

"Do they doubt the sincerity of his return?"

"No, he's clearly not a Sabbatean any more. There seems to be no doubt at all about the sincerity of his return. He is by all accounts a fine, upstanding member of the community."

"All right. So everything is wonderful. What's the problem?"

"The problem is," said Chacham Tzvi, "that someone bought him the honor of Chassan Torah this past Simchas Torah, and certain people objected."[54]

"I see," said Rav Amos. "On what basis did they object?"

"No particular basis. They just felt it was inappropriate for a former Muslim to be called up to the Torah for such a high honor."

"But that's not the thrust of the question in the letter."

"No, it's not. The rabbis raise a legitimate *halachic* question."

"So what's the question? Let me guess. They think he may be disqualified, just as a Kohein who converts and returns is disqualified from blessing the people during Birchas Kohanim."

"Exactly. So what do you think?"

"My first inclination is that there is no comparison."

"I agree completely," said Chacham Tzvi. "Let's take out a Gemara Menachos and a Rambam."

The two men plunged into the subject, and soon the table was covered with open volumes. After a good half hour of discussion and arguments, they closed all the volumes and put them away.

"So we're in agreement," said Chacham Tzvi. "The man may be called to be Chassan Torah. Anyway, here's another case of a man who was a Sabbatean and returned in all sincerity. It can and does happen. So even if it was confirmed that someone was a Sabbatean in his youth, I wouldn't disqualify him so quickly from becoming a rabbi if he really turned the page on his past. The Almighty gives people second chances, and so should we."

"My feeling is that we should give them second chances, but we should keep a watchful eye on them. Discreetly, of course."

"I won't argue with that," said Chacham Tzvi. "In fact, we need to be on guard in general. Shabbesai Tzvi has been dead for twenty years, but his particular brand of heretical messianic ideas has survived him. I'm afraid we're far from finished with Sabbatean eruptions. It wouldn't surprise me if it takes decades to repair the damage he and his followers have done."

Deep in the mountains of central Turkey, four men sat on the creaking veranda of an old farmhouse. They smoked water pipes and conversed with each other in low tones. They had gathered in secret. No one knew that these men were associated with one another. No one knew that they had come together for this clandestine meeting. No one knew that they had an interest in the topic of their conversation.

As the sun settled into the treetops, a man came walking down the road. He was in his middle forties, but he walked with the springy step of a man half his age. His intense brown eyes were the most striking feature of his lined and weathered face. His beard was long, wide and black, but turning gray at the edges. He wore a white robe with long gold stripes that glittered in the evening light. A round multi-colored cap covered his closely shaven head.

The other men stood up as the new arrival stepped onto the veranda.

"How is the work going?" he asked.

"It is going well," said one of the men on the veranda, "but it's taking time, more than we expected."

"Do not be concerned about that," said the man in the white robe. "Care is more important than speed. We must avoid suspicion at all costs. Every word must be carefully chosen before it is committed to writing. After your work is done, then my part of the work will begin. We're concerned with eternity here, my friends. If our work takes another few months or even years, it doesn't really matter. It is the end result that matters."

THE CHANGING OF THE GUARD · 15

I t was not the best of times to be traveling in Europe, but Rav Amos was determined to visit his ailing father. The year was 1706, and Europe was engulfed by one of the bloodiest wars in its history, a war that would come to be known as the War of the Spanish Succession, a war in which well over half a million lives were lost, a war that has since been largely forgotten. The issue over which so many people were killed and maimed was the designation of the new Spanish king.

In 1701, Charles II, the king of Spain, died childless. Although he was a descendant of the Spanish branch of the royal Hapsburg family, he was also closely related by blood to the Hapsburgs of Austria and the Bourbons of France. Both of these houses claimed the Spanish throne as their rightful inheritance. The Hapsburgs and most of the rest of Europe were afraid that if a Bourbon ascended the Spanish throne and aligned Spain with France, King Louis XIV would overpower all of Europe and become its undisputed master. Such an eventuality had to be avoided at all costs, and the Dutch were in the forefront of the battle.

Rav Amos boarded a ship in Hamburg soon after Pesach and sailed across the North Sea to Amsterdam in a matter of days. The city was on a war footing when he arrived. Commerce and industry were working at full capacity to equip and provide for the Dutch armies and navy. Young men were going off to the bloodstained battlefields, and a great many of them were not returning. A large French army had moved into the Spanish Netherlands and was approaching Antwerp. And if Antwerp fell, how far behind could Amsterdam be? The older people still remembered when King Louis' armies had reached the outskirts of Amsterdam in 1672 before being repelled. The mood in Amsterdam was hopeful but jittery.

Rav Amos had visited Amsterdam several times since his marriage, but the visits had always been brief. This time, considering his father's advanced age and deteriorating condition, he decided to spend several weeks.

Rabbi Mordechai Strasbourg was one of the assistant rabbis of the Ashkenazic community of Amsterdam, but at eighty-seven years of age, his duties had been drastically reduced. His eyesight was failing, and his feet caused him so much pain that he rarely left his home. His wife, Rebbetzin Yocheved, six years younger and sprightly, tended him day and night.

The arrival of Rav Amos caused a sensation in the Ashkenazic community. His reputation as a great *talmid chacham* had grown in the twenty years since he had left Amsterdam, and people were also aware of his close personal friendship with Chacham Tzvi. They greeted him with respect and adulation and were full of questions about his illustrious friend. His father, however, had only Rav Amos' future on his mind.

"Amos, Amos," his father said to him over breakfast the morning after his arrival. "What do you plan to do?"

"Father, do you realize that I'm fifty-seven years old already? That's the kind of question you ask a man in his twenties."

"So why don't you answer your father's question?" said his mother.

Rav Amos chuckled. "What would you like to know? I live in Altona and teach in the *kloiz*. I learn with Chacham Tzvi. I'm happy there. My family is wonderful. My wife is an angel. My children are a constant blessing to us. Menachem is nineteen years old, Reuven is sixteen, and Chanah is thirteen. I'm already working on finding good matches for them. My life is full and satisfying. What do I plan to do? I plan to pray to the Almighty to grant me long life and let me continue in this way."

"And what about your parents?" said his mother.

"That's true, Mother. That is the one drawback in my life; that I do not get to see my parents and my brothers and sister as often as I'd like. I ask forgiveness from both of you."

"Forgiveness?" said his father. "Pah, you don't need our forgiveness. We are proud of you and everything you've accomplished. It is a great honor for us to have you as our son. And the honor will be even greater when you publish your insight on Choshen Mishpat."

"I don't like to talk about that, Father."

"Why not? I've heard from people who've taken a peek at your papers that it is really something special. And when you're ready you have to come here to Amsterdam to print. The quality of printing in Amsterdam is unrivaled. You take something printed elsewhere, like Berlin or Prague, and you put it side by side with one of the Amsterdam productions, and it isn't even comparable."

Rav Amos laughed. "All right. When I'm ready to print, I'll seriously consider doing it in Amsterdam."

"Good," said his father. "And you should go to Moshe Frankfurt. He runs a very good printing establishment. I've known him for many years, and I can vouch for him. He's a good man, and he does good work."

"You'll remind me when the time comes, Father."

"If I'm still here."

"Oh, Father, please don't talk like that. Of course, you'll be here."

"What makes you so sure? I think that my still being alive today is nothing short of a miracle, and you just can't count on miracles to happen.[55] Amos, listen closely. I wanted to talk to you about an important —"

A sudden fit of coughing interrupted him. After a while, his coughs subsided, but his chest continued to heave as he struggled to catch his breath. Rebbetzin Yocheved poured him a glass of water and held it to his lips, and a little color returned to his face.

Rebbetzin Yocheved watched him for a minute to assure herself that her husband was all right.

"I'm going to leave you men alone now," she said. "I have things to do. Mordechai, don't talk too much. It wears you out. I'm leaving the glass of water by your hand. Take a sip if you feel weak. And Amos, keep an eye on your father. If there's any trouble call me right away."

She gave her husband another anxious look and went off to attend to her other business. As Rav Amos watched her walk away, her shoulders defiant against the specter of death, he couldn't help but think about the sadness of the situation. His parents were so dependent on each other, and they knew full well that any day either one of them could be left old and alone. No one was ever guaranteed a single additional day of life, but old people lived with that thought every day.

"So what are you thinking, Amos?" said his father, his voice still a little shaky.

Rav Amos shook his head. "I was just worrying about my parents."

"Worrying is a waste of time unless you can do something about it," said his father. He thought for a moment. "You know something? I don't know why I thought of this now, but I miss Hurdus. He was a mean bird, but he made me laugh. Wait, I know why I thought of him. It's because he choked on a peanut and coughed himself to death."

Rav Amos shuddered. "So why don't you get yourself another parrot?"

"Nah, I can't do that. When a friend dies you don't just get another one to replace him. You mourn the loss and go on. Anyway, where was I?"

"You wanted to talk to me about something important."

"Oh yes. Something important … something important … something important. Aha! I've got it. Yes, it is important, very important. You know that the Ashkenazic community of Amsterdam doesn't have a rabbi right now. A few assistant rabbis but no chief rabbi."

"I'm aware of it."

"If you give me permission, I'll suggest your name for the position."

Rav Amos smiled. "You're wonderful, Father. But I have to decline."

"Listen to me. We've had some interesting rabbis here in Amsterdam. On both sides of the street. The Sephardim have had theirs, and we've had ours. I remember when Rabbi David Lida came here almost twenty-five years ago. Actually, I think it was in 1682, twenty-four years ago. By the way, did you know that he was the nephew of Rabbi Moshe Rivkes, the author of *Be'er Hagolah*?"

"Yes, I knew it."

"Well, that turned out to be quite a fiasco. He had a major confrontation with the Sephardic rabbi, who accused him of being a Sabbatean. He had to leave Amsterdam under a cloud of suspicion. But then the Vaad Arba Haaratzos, the Council of the Four Lands, came to his defense and cleared his reputation. He returned to Amsterdam, but left after three years." He shook his head sadly. "This Sabbatean business is the curse of our times, and I don't know how quickly it's going to pass."

"Chacham Tzvi feels it's going to plague us for decades."

"Unfortunately, he may be right. Anyway, after Rabbi Lida, we had Rabbi Leib Charif, who died last year. He was our rabbi for a long time, close to twenty years. And now, we're looking for a new rabbi. You're just as qualified as they were. And you're from Amsterdam. The people already know you. Isn't that better than taking someone from far away when you don't even know if he'll be able to get along with the community?"

"I still have to decline, Father. The position is not good for me, and I wouldn't be good for the position."

His father's eyes narrowed. "What do you mean?"

"Don't be alarmed. I think I could handle the *halachic* questions and the teaching and the speaking, but being chief rabbi means carrying the load of the community on your shoulders. It means giving up your own precious time that you could be spending learning and writing and instead getting involved in … in … in everything, community institutions, marital and business disputes, synagogue politics, enforcing rules of behavior, all things that I don't want to do. And because I feel this way, I wouldn't be able to give the community what it needs from a chief rabbi. I see what Chacham Tzvi goes through, the things he must handle and control, and he's not even the official rabbi."

"So look at him. He does everything that's required of him and more, and he can still manage to be the greatest rabbi of his generation."

"You've just answered your own question, Father. I'm not Chacham Tzvi, and I never will be. He is one in a million. As for me, I'm Amos Strasbourg, and I'm trying to make the best of my abilities."

His father sighed. "You are also an extraordinary person, my dear Amos, but I'll grant you that a comparison with Chacham Tzvi is unfair. How about my position? Would you accept my position after I'm gone? Would you consider being one of the assistant rabbis? The position is more suited to you. We have a large and growing community here in Amsterdam, and an assistant rabbi has a lot of responsibility. You have to teach and serve on the courts. I don't have to tell you. You know what I've been doing all these years. And you can also learn and write and publish and enjoy peace of mind, because the burden of the community is carried by the chief rabbi."

Rav Amos looked doubtful. "I'm not sure."

"Why? Don't you want to follow in my footsteps? It would be an honor for me to have you replace me, but don't do it because I want you to do it. Do it because it's good for you. It's a step up from your position in Hamburg."

"I know, Father. But I would have to accept being separated from Chacham Tzvi. I mean why would I want to come to Amsterdam if you're not here any more? What would I have here? Chaim Mendel lives in London. Baruch Ber and Baila Mindel live in Poland. My best and closest friend lives in Germany. I'd much rather stay in Hamburg with Chacham Tzvi."

"All right, Amos. I understand you perfectly. But you never know what the future will bring. Things change all the time. I want to speak to the new rabbi, whoever it will be, and suggest that after I pass away my position should be offered to you. If and when the offer comes, I want you to consider it before you turn it down. That's what I ask of you, Amos. I won't do it unless you allow me to do it. But that's what I would like you to do. I want you to get the offer. I want you to consider it. And I want you to choose what is best. So what do you say, Amos?"

Rav Amos looked at his father's anxious face. "I agree," he said.

"You agree to what?" said Rebbetzin Yocheved as she walked into the room. "What have you men been up to?"

"Nothing major," said Rav Amos. "Father will tell you when I leave."

"Well, I think that's going to be right now. Your friend Sebastian Dominguez is waiting for you in the front room."

Sebastian was standing at the door, waiting for Rav Amos. The two men embraced and then stepped back to take a look at each other. Rav Amos had not changed that much since their last meeting in Pulichev five years before, but Sebastian had changed considerably. His short trimmed beard had gone completely white, and he had thickened around the waist. And there was a different air about him. He no longer had that alienated look of an outsider. He was no longer the former Spanish cavalier trying to fit into a new and different society. At fifty-three years of age, he was beginning to look more and more like a prosperous Amsterdam merchant confident in his status as an insider in the community establishment.

"Come," he said. "My carriage is waiting outside. Let's go take a walk on the Houtgracht. I know you've got canals in Hamburg, but they're not as beautiful as ours."

Rav Amos grabbed his hat and followed him outside.

"Sebastian, you look different," he said as he climbed into the carriage. "There's been a big change in your life. I can tell."

Sebastian sat back against the plush cushions. "There's been a change, yes. But I don't know how big a change it is."

"Are we playing a game?" asked Rav Amos. "Do you want me to guess?"

"Sure. Why not?"

"All right. I enjoy a riddle. Well, let's see. A change. What kind of change could it be? Money. You have plenty of money. More money? That's not such an important change. Your children? You're looking for a young man for your daughter? I wouldn't call that a change. No, somehow your situation has changed. It has something to do with your status. So is it your status with the Dutch authorities or your status in the community? It seems to me that your status in the community would be more important. So … what could it … you've joined the Maamad."

Sebastian laughed. "You're so smart. How did you guess?"

"What else could it be? You've been elevated to the governing board of the Sephardic community. That's definitely important. Congratulations, my friend."

"Thank you."

The carriage pulled up alongside the canal, and they got out.

"Here we are," said Sebastian. "Beautiful day, isn't it?"

"Yes, it is. So I want to hear more about this appointment to the Maamad. I'm assuming Eduardo Colon supported your appointment. After all, he's the head of the Maamad, and he's married to your mother."

"He did better than that," said Sebastian. "He stepped down and suggested I be given his seat. Senhor Colon and my mother are in their seventies, and they're both in good health. They want to take advantage of the time left to them and travel a little. My mother would like to visit her grandchildren in Hamburg, and Senhor Colon has children in Venice and Istanbul. My mother has never been to Istanbul, and she's eager to see it."

"So it works out well for everyone," said Rav Amos. "You said he gave you his seat. Does that mean that you're the head of the Maamad?"

Sebastian laughed. "Not yet, not yet. But I'm next in line."

"That is great. I'm really happy for you, Sebastian. I think you will make an excellent *parnas*,[56] and I think you will find it fulfilling. It's the perfect thing for you. And how's Felipe doing? I hear he's something special."

"That he is. And hardly anyone calls him Felipe anymore. He is Rabbi Pinhas Dominguez. He's one of the important rabbis of the community, and he also serves on the rabbinical court. Who knows? Maybe someday they'll be calling him Chacham Pinhas? Many people wouldn't be surprised."

"Neither would I. Your mother must be very proud."

"She certainly is. So let me catch you up on some of our other friends. Immanuel Almeida is one of the best doctors in the Netherlands. It's hard to get an appointment with him because ministers, dukes and ambassadors are always lined up outside his door."

"Does he spend some time learning Torah?"

"He goes to Felipe's classes, and he has study partners as well. And then there's our dear friend Shamai Cohen."

Rav Amos raised his eyebrows. "Oh, and how is he doing?"

"Quite well, actually. He has a position similar to Felipe's position. He's one of the community rabbis, and he's in the rotation to sit on the rabbinical court. And he hasn't chased anyone out of the *bet midrash* in twenty years."[57]

"People change, you know."

Sebastian shrugged. "They do, and they don't, if you know what I mean."

"People who change for the better always face a struggle, I understand that. And struggles are made to be overcome."

"Hopefully."

"And how's Gonzalo Sanchez doing?"

"That reminds me," said Sebastian. "You owe me a few guilders."

Rav Amos reached into his pocket, but Sebastian stopped him. "I was just joking. Consider those drinks my contribution to the rescue of Chacham Tzvi's parents. So how's Gonzalo? He's Gonzalo. He has his tavern and his friends. He's a little older and a little slower, but he's still one tough cavalier."

"If I don't see him while I'm here, send him my best regards."

"I'll do that. So who else is there? Ah, of course, there's Diego Zuzarte."

"Diego? The one who set you up to be swindled?"[58]

"The same Diego," said Sebastian. "Now there's a man who has really changed. He came to me and begged my forgiveness. He said he would do anything for me, so I gave him a few things to do. And I'm telling you, he's my most loyal employee. He never really was a bad person, just a scoundrel, and he's really turned the page. Believe me."

"All right. I believe you. I just don't understand why you can accept that Diego Zuzarte has changed, but you find it hard to believe that Shamai Cohen has changed."

"Diego was a greedy scoundrel, but he was basically a nice person. He never wanted to hurt anyone, at least not badly. He just thought a little swindling never killed anyone. Now he's got a respectable job, a nice income and a family, so I believe that he has put his silly past behind him. But Shamai was a fanatic, an extremist. He made a terrible mistake, and he was really sorry. I don't think he'd do the same thing again. But I don't trust extremists. They can be very dangerous. Who knows what'll tick them off next?"

"But nothing has ticked him off for twenty years, Sebastian. Twenty years! Maybe the man has really changed."

"Maybe he's changed. I'll grant him that. Or maybe he just hasn't encountered any real provocation in twenty years."

Sebastian stiffened. He put his hand on Rav Amos' arm.

"Stand still," he said through clenched teeth. "Don't turn around. There's someone watching us on the other side of the canal. He's leaning against the last building in the St. Antoniesbreestraat. See if you can look in that direction without turning your head."

Rav Amos turned his head the merest imperceptible fraction of an inch and peered out of the corner of his eye. A dumpy man in a brown waistcoat was leaning against a building. He held a broadsheet in his hands and pretended to be interested in what it contained. But the watcher's real interest was clearly in the two men conversing alongside the canal. Rav Amos turned back to Sebastian.

"What's it all about, Sebastian?"

"I don't know. Remember years ago I mentioned that someone was snooping around Amsterdam?"

"Actually, I do. It was when you came to Pulichev, almost twenty years ago."

"That's right. We never got to the bottom of it, and then it stopped as suddenly as it had started. But these last few months, the snooping has started again. Do you want to help me grab this fellow and find out what he knows?"

Rav Amos grinned. "We're older men now, Sebastian. The time for chasing villains through the forests is over. Maybe Gonzalo can send some of his men."

"Maybe."

"What's he doing now?"

"He's leaving."

"We'll get him next time," said Rav Amos.

Two weeks later, Rav Amos was ready to return home, but travel was too dangerous. The French armies were moving northward, while the British, Dutch, German, Swiss and Scottish forces under the command of the Duke of Marlborough were mobilizing near The Hague southwest of Amsterdam and moving southward. French, Dutch and English fleets prowled the sea lanes. Amsterdam was in a perilous situation, but to leave Amsterdam in any direction would be even more perilous.

During his enforced stay in Amsterdam, Rav Amos spent as much of his time as possible in the Etz Chaim *bet midrash*, and he invited Sebastian to come and learn with him every day. Sebastian came a few times, but he simply didn't have the patience to sit and pore over a Gemara for any appreciable length of time. He needed movement and activity. One hour a day was enough for him. The rest of the time was devoted to raising money for widows and orphans, dealing with community issues that came before the Maamad and a little bit of business.

One day, Sebastian came for Rav Amos in his carriage.

"I have a surprise for you," he said. "Let's go."

"Do you want to give me a hint?"

"No, no hints. No games. And you'll never guess."

They rode through the streets of Amsterdam and into the countryside. They stopped before a country villa.

"Where are we?" asked Rav Amos. "Who owns this place?"

"I don't know who owns it. But I know who's renting it for the moment."

The door opened, and a large black man in a brown coat and a broad brown cape stepped into the sunlight. He wore a tremendous white felt hat adorned with a riot of lavender plumes. He wore a lavender scarf around his neck.

"Rabbi Strasbourg!" he shouted in a loud and deep voice.

Rav Amos' eyes bulged. "Domino? Domino Stuart?"

"That I am," boomed the black man. "I haven't seen you in twenty years, man, and you haven't changed that much."

Rav Amos stared at Domino Stuart. His lips worked, but he could not bring out any words.

"You're struck speechless, Rabbi Strasbourg?" said the black man. "If you want I can speak English the way I used to speak it when we first met. No can home go Africa. New York have stay, make wampum much much fur sell for partners Amsterdam me."

Rav Amos doubled over in laughter. He and Domino embraced, and there were tears in the eyes of both men.

"It is so good to see you," said Rav Amos. "You are really looking well. Thank you for all you've done for us all these years."

"Nothing I do for you can ever repay the debt I owe to you and Senhor Dominguez. You gave me my life and my freedom, and all I've given you is money." He threw back his head and laughed. "And you've given me money, too. How can I forget that? I am a very rich man, Rabbi Strasbourg. I have a mansion in Manhattan and a summer house in Breukelen.[59] And I've invested all my profits wisely so I now own a lot of land in New Jersey. It's pretty empty now, but I believe that someday, it will be full of towns and villages. Maybe not in my lifetime, but it's fine with me if my children and grandchildren reap the fruits of my labor."

"Domino, I can't get over your English," said Rav Amos. "It's amazing."

Domino laughed again. "It's the best that money can buy. I hired a tutor, actually a British duke who was ruined by his gambling debts. He's been coaching me for years. One of these days, I'm going to meet the king of England, and I want to speak properly. After all, the king and I share the same last name."

"Not any more, Domino," said Sebastian. "The Stuarts have been gone for eighteen years."

"Right. I knew that. But I'm keeping the name anyway. I'm used to it. My wife is used to it too. You remember Feather Wind?"

"Of course. The Mahonekett princess."

"That's right," said Domino with unconcealed pleasure. "You should hear her English. She sounds like a British duchess. I'm sorry you can't meet her. She's off on a shopping spree in Rotterdam."

"Well, maybe next time."

"Yes, maybe next time. So Rabbi Strasbourg, Senhor Dominguez tells me that you're marooned in Amsterdam because of the war."

"I'm afraid so."

"That's my good fortune," said Domino. "If you'd left ear-lier, we wouldn't have met. But now that we've met, you can go home."

Rav Amos looked at him. "What do you mean?"

"My sources tell me that the French were defeated two days ago at Ramillies near Antwerp, and that they're retreat-ing. It should be safe to travel in a few days or so."

"Your sources?"

"My sources."

"Are they reliable?"

"If you spend the money, you get reliable sources."

Two days later, Rav Amos boarded a ship in Rotterdam and returned to Hamburg. All the way home, he couldn't stop thinking about his father's suggestion. He knew it was unlikely he would ever see his father alive again and perhaps not even his mother. His father's words, therefore, carried a special weight. They were almost like a deathbed instruction. The pressure would be on him to accept the offer if indeed it came. But he wasn't sure if that was the right thing for him to do.

On the day of his return, Chacham Tzvi came to his home to welcome him back, and Rav Amos wasted no time in unburdening himself to his friend.

"So what do you think I should do?" he said.

Chacham Tzvi stroked his beard. "Your father is a wise man," he said. "He said you should consider the offer at the time it's made. I agree with that. Don't think about it now. Who knows where we'll be in a year or two or three, may your father live and be well for many years to come? When the time comes and you see what the situation is, you'll make your decision. If you want my help, I'll help you. But I have to tell you in advance that I don't want to part ways with you. You're more than my friend. You're my brother. I'll be lost without you."

"And I without you."

"But we both know," said Chacham Tzvi, "that neither of us would be lost. We would just be sad and lonely. We would feel an emptiness, an unfillable void in our lives, but we would not be lost. Life goes on."

Rav Amos pushed the disturbing thoughts away and settled back into the familiar and pleasant routines of his life in Altona.

But things were not going so smoothly for Chacham Tzvi. His fearlessness and incorruptibility had earned him implacable enemies in Altona. The richest merchant in Altona, a man named Ber Kohein, was his worst opponent. Ber was a man of substance. Besides being rich, he also knew how to learn and spent a good part of his day in the *beis midrash*. His home was open to the poor, and he supported Torah generously. Because of his stature, however, he expected respect and obedience from everyone in the community, and he did not hesitate to destroy anyone who incurred his wrath.

He had many ways of expressing his wrath. Because of his great wealth, he wielded enormous influence with the authorities, who feared him and did whatever he wanted. He decided which businessmen should be extended credit to buy merchandise. He decided how much each member should contribute to the community chest. He decided who could hold positions of honor and responsibility in the community. Everything was up to him, and everyone trembled before him and curried his favor. The only person in Altona whom Ber could not intimidate was Chacham Tzvi, who did not hesitate to call him to task for his wrongdoings. Ber seethed inside, but he said nothing. He bided his time.[60]

There was another family of merchants in Altona, the Fursts, who had nothing in their favor but their wealth. They were vulgar people who were less than scrupulous in their observance, and therefore they sought acceptance by arranging marriage connections to prominent Torah families. With a promise of a substantial dowry, they secured for their daughter a young man named Moshe Rothenberg, the son of a respected rabbi in a German city. Moshe was a promising young rabbi, and he bore an illustrious name. He brought respect to the Furst family even after they lost all their money through bad business investments and had to default on their obligations to their son-in-law. Ber sought out the Fursts and enlisted them in his secret plans to undermine Chacham Tzvi.[61]

Late in the fall of 1706, Chacham Tzvi's elderly father-in-law, Rabbi Meshulem Zalman Mirels Neumark, the rabbi of Altona, Hamburg and Wandsbeck, passed away at the age of eighty-two. Right after the funeral, the people acclaimed Chacham Tzvi, who had been the acting rabbi for many years, as their official chief rabbi.

But in Altona there was trouble. The Furst family proposed that Moshe, their son-in-law, should become the rabbi of Altona, and Ber threw his support behind their claim. The people were divided into two camps, those who supported Chacham Tzvi and those who did not dare defy the powerful Ber. The dispute was finally resolved by a compromise. The two rabbis would share the position, each of them serving for half a year. Chacham Tzvi accepted the arrangement in the interest of maintaining the peace. Instead of becoming the rabbi of the Three Communities, as his father-in-law had been, he became the rabbi of the Two-and-a-Half Communities.[62]

THE WIZARD OF SMYRNA · 16

ECHEMIAH CHAYUN RODE DOWN on a camel from the pine-covered hills that towered over the beautiful seaside city of Smyrna, Turkey. His four disciples followed on foot, singing about the prophet Eliahu and the imminent coming of Mashiach. Chayun led his disciples down to the water's edge, where the gentle waves lapped at the golden beach and great flocks of seagulls cawed overhead. He kicked the camel's rump, and it knelt to allow him to dismount.

While his disciples looked on with profound reverence, he took off his sandals and let his toes play in the warm sand. Then he walked into the surf until the water covered his ankles. With his back to his disciples, he threw back his head and lifted his hands to the heavens, and as the receding tide sucked the sand from under his feet, he shouted random verses from Tehillim and Kabbalistic formulations. He lowered his arms, hung his head and remained standing in silence with the waves licking at his legs. Finally, he bent down and washed his hand in the water. Only then did he turn to face his disciples.

"My dear children," he said, "our time draws near. The future of the world is in our hands. We have carried forward the work of our great teacher, the holiest of our holy rabbis, Shabbetai Tzvi, may the memory of the righteous be a blessing. We've battled those terrible forces of evil called the *kelipot*, and we've succeeded in rescuing thousands — no, millions! — of sparks of holiness, the holy *nitzotzot* that these *kelipot* held in their grasp. But our work is not finished. There are still more *nitzotzot* to be rescued before Mashiach can bring our people out of exile. Ay, the Holy Shechinah Itself is in exile, but we will release Her and bring Her back to the place where She belongs."

He looked into the eyes of his four disciples, one by one.

"I'm not telling you anything you do not know already," he said. "I'm not telling you anything that isn't already burned into your hearts and minds, into your very bones and sinews. We are a small group, but together we can move the universe. Our final push starts here in Smyrna. This is where we will reveal our secrets to the world, but we are sworn to secrecy. This is where the thoughts and ideas that we developed through our toil and put down on paper will finally begin to see the light of day. The forces of evil will battle us at every step of the way. They will turn people against us. They will try to humiliate and destroy us."

He drew himself to his full height.

"They will fail!" he shouted and drove his fist into the air. "We will prevail!"

"They will fail!" the disciples repeated. "We will prevail! Long live our great and holy master!"

"We have done excellent work," Chayun continued. "We have concealed our ideas between the lines. Our book will escape the vigilance of our enemies. It will enter the synagogues and the *yeshivot* and the homes of the scholars, and it will inspire thousand and thousands of our people with the ideas of the holy mysteries. Their minds will read the lines, but the words between the lines will speak to their hearts. And in a while — hopefully, a very short while — they will join our movement. And then at last, we will smash the power of the *kelipot*, liberate the last captive sparks of holiness and bring about the final redemption of our people."

He closed his eyes and rubbed his left hand back and forth slowly across his forehead.

"Forty-two years, my children," he said. "Forty-two years have passed since the holiest of the holy rabbis revealed himself to the world. Forty-two long years. But forty-two years is like the blink of an eye in the grand sweep of history. The forces of evil succeeded in slowing down his work, but not in destroying it. We are the successors. This small group will bring his work to a successful conclusion. We are about to enter Smyrna. Do you all know your instructions?"

They all nodded.

"Do you have any reservations about carrying out the deceptions?"

They all shook their heads.

"It's hard to convince people to change," said Chayun. "If we present them with logical arguments, they turn a deaf ear, even if the arguments are perfect. They don't want to hear anything that may lead to change. So we have to lure them with miracles, wonders and all kinds of wizardry. But it's just to get past their defenses. So it's not really a deception. Do you understand?"

They nodded.

"Tell me one by one. Rachamim, do you understand?"

"Yes, holy master."

"Hillel, do you understand?"

"Yes, holy master."

"Moshe, do you understand?"

"Yes, holy master."

"Avraham, do you understand?"

"Yes, holy master."

"Good, excellent," he said. "Now we go to Smyrna. It's been many years since I've been an official rabbi, but it's time for me put on that mantle again. And it's time for my book to become a reality. Then, as a respected rabbi with my book in my hand, I will carry my message to the far corners of the Jewish world. Gentlemen, our campaign begins."

The Jewish community in Smyrna in 1708 had good relations with the Turkish authorities. It had synagogues, schools and a printing press. Its people were prosperous and enjoyed a pleasant and languorous lifestyle. But it was not a great center of Torah learning, and the people were generally unsophisticated. It was the perfect place for Chayun to launch his campaign.

Chayun rented a comfortable house near the synagogue. His disciples slept in the attic and ran the household. They circulated in the city letting people know that a holy mystic had arrived, a man capable of working wonders, a man who conversed regularly with the prophet Eliahu. He would be in Smyrna for only a few weeks, they informed the people. He would see people only between noon and two o'clock in the afternoon, which meant that only a limited number of people would receive his blessing.

Within hours, people were competing for the privilege of being among those who got in to see the mystic, but he refused to see anyone the first day he was in Smyrna. The next day, he and his disciples were up before the roosters. They walked some distance to the seashore and immersed themselves in its night-chilled waters. And as they walked back, Chayun greeted the early risers in the street graciously, allowing them to kiss his hand and bestowing brief blessings on them.

In the synagogue, he shook the rabbi's hand and retired to the rear corner where he stood immobile for two hours and prayed. Afterwards, he spoke to no one but walked back to his rented house with downcast eyes, with two disciples flanking him on each side.

By ten o'clock, the line outside his house had begun to form. His disciple Rachamim, seated at a small table on the veranda, wrote down the exact name and mother's name of each supplicant and handed it to him. Hillel stood at the door, ready to usher the supplicants in and out of the presence of the holy man. Moshe and Avraham made sure the line remained orderly and that no one tried to get ahead of the people already on line.

At twelve o'clock, Hillel opened the door for the first supplicant on line, a burly young man with a black beard. Chayun was sitting in the spacious dining room. His palms were flat on the table, his eyes were closed, and his head was tilted slightly back. The young man waited in silence, transfixed by the sight of a holy man in a holy trance.

Chayun opened his eyes and looked at him.

"Give me the paper, young man," he said.

The young man handed him the paper on which his name was written. Chayun read the paper several times. Then he turned it over and stared at the blank side of the paper.

"What is your problem, young man?"

"My wife and I have seven daughters."

"So you need money to marry them off?"

"That, too. But we would like to have a son."

"You ask a difficult thing," said Chayun. "I examined the combinations of letters in your full name in all their permutations, and I do not discern a formula for a son. But I can write you an amulet. If your wife wears it for three years for at least twelve hours every single day, you will have a son."

"Oh, thank you." The young man grabbed Chayun's hand and covered it with kisses. "Thank you so much."

"When you go out, speak to Avraham. He will give you instructions and tell you how much —"

Loud screams outside the house interrupted him. Chayun grabbed his head and began to tremble.

"It is one of my disciples," he cried out. "Something has happened to one of my disciples."

He pushed past the young man and flung open the door. Avraham was writing on the ground, his face contorted in agony, drool running down his chin. Moshe stood over him with a rock in his hand. Women were screaming, and men were shouting and shoving.

Chayun ran to the side of his fallen disciple. Rachamim and Hillel came running as well.

"What happened here?" Chayun shouted at Moshe, who was still holding the rock in his hand.

Moshe pointed to the ground where the body of a snake lay motionless, its head crushed. Moshe tried to speak, but no words came out.

"The snake bit Avraham," said Rachamim, his voice shaky. "I saw it all happen. Moshe grabbed a rock and smashed its head. But the snake had bitten Avraham already."

Chayun looked at the dead snake. "It's a nose-horned viper, a very deadly snake. Where did it bite Avraham?"

"On the right leg," said Rachamim.

Chayun bent down to examine the leg. People crowded around so that dozens of eyes stared at the two tiny puncture wounds in the leg. Chayun pulled down the trouser leg and covered the wound.

"Avraham," he said, "you may die at any moment. Say Shema Yisrael."

Avraham began to cry, and his eyes rolled in his head. A new paroxysm of fits shook his body. His back arched in pain until only his head and heels touched the ground. A bloodcurdling scream escaped his mouth, then he trembled again and fell to the ground. His head fell to the side, and his chest stopped moving. An unnatural slackness relaxed his tortured body.

"He's dead," breathed Rachamim. "I can't believe it. One minute he is with us, and the next he is gone."

"It is the will of the Almighty," said Chayun. "Cover him."

A woman stepped forward and offered a blanket, and Rachamim spread it over the inert body of his friend.

"We have to call people to help with the funeral," said Rachamim. "We can't just leave him lying here. Maybe we should move him away from the middle of the street." He sighed. "Hillel, come give me a hand."

The people fell back, dismayed by what they had witnessed. Mothers covered the eyes of their children, but it was too late. Everyone in the large crowd had seen the horrible death of the young Avraham.

Word spread quickly through the Jewish quarter, and before long, a bowlegged man carrying a stretcher arrived. He approached Chayun who was standing guard over his fallen disciple.

"I'm here to take the body," said the bowlegged man. "I'll need someone to help me."

Chayun held up his hand. His face was wet with tears.

"Don't touch him yet," he said. "Bring twelve candles in tall glass cups."

"Candles? Here?"

"Yes. Do you have candles?"

"Yes, we do," said the bowlegged man.

"Then bring them," said Chayun. "Twelve of them."

"But why?"

Chayun gave him a sharp look, and the man recoiled in fear.

"Don't ask me why," said Chayun between gritted teeth. "When I say bring candles, you run and bring candles. If you know what's good for you."

The bowlegged man bowed abjectly and backed away. Then he turned and ran off. Two minutes later, he returned with the candles. Chayun placed them all around the body of his dead disciple and lit them. Then he stood back, closed his eyes and prayed, his lips moving but no audible sound emerging. The people were mesmerized by the spectacle of this colorful mystic, this flamboyant holy man who had burst into their lives so dramatically.

Chayun opened his eyes and lifted his hands to the heavens.

"Our Father in the highest Heavens," he cried out, "You know how my disciples and I struggle to defend Your honor. You know how my disciples and I struggle to uplift the spirits of Your people and bring them closer to You. Why does a snake leave its home in the forest and suddenly appear in the streets of Smyrna? Yes, we know the answer. Satan sent him to kill my disciple. And after him, Satan will attack my other disciples. And then he will come after me. Master of the Universe, give me the strength and the power to defeat Satan in this mighty battle. Master of the Universe, let me bring my disciple back to life."

He hung his head and mumbled indiscernible words. Then he inclined his ear as if he were listening to a voice that no one but he could hear.

"Yes, I understand," he said in a somber tone. "I understand, and I am grateful."

With measured steps, he walked over to the body of his disciple. He moved away the candles on the left side of the body and squatted beside it. He placed his left hand above Avraham's heart and his right hand above Avraham's head. His hands began to tremble. The tremors traveled up his arms, and his shoulders began to tremble. The tremors became stronger and spread to his entire body, which was now shaking violently as if a powerful surge of primal energy was surging through it.

With a great visible effort, Chayun drew his hands upward, and as he did, the body under the blanket stirred. The people gasped and shrank back, but their eyes remained riveted on the frightening scene unfolding before them. Chayun drew his trembling hands further upward, and muted moans began to emanate from under the blanket. A great glow of gratitude spread across his face. He grabbed the edge of the blanket and pulled it away.

Avraham lay motionless on his back, his eyes closed, his face deathly pale. But a very slight movement of his chest was discernible, and the barely audible moans continued. Chayun bent down and kissed him on the forehead, and his eyes fluttered open. Disoriented, he looked around and saw that he was surrounded by crowds of people staring down at him. He struggled to get to his feet but fell back panting to the ground.

"Wait, my child," said Chayun. "Stay there on the ground until you recover your strength. You have just been on a journey to a faraway place, and you've returned to us, praise be to Heaven. You must be exhausted."

He turned to the crowd.

"Someone bring him a glass of water," he called out.

A few minutes later, Avraham was back on his feet, although still somewhat unsteady. Chayun asked the people to go home since he would not be seeing any more people that day. Reluctantly, the people trickled away until they were all gone. Chayun patted Avraham on the back.

"Good work," he said. "And you, too, Moshe and Rachamim."

The word of Chayun's raising Avraham from the dead spread quickly through the city. That evening, when Chayun arrived in the synagogue, he was instantly surrounded by people begging for his blessing. But the rabbi of Smyrna was skeptical.

"I hear you brought someone back from the dead today," he told Chayun in front of the crowd. "Are you telling us that you are a miracle worker? Is that what you expect us to believe?"

"One must not always believe what one hears," replied Chayun. "I do not expect you to believe anything."

"The people say they saw it."

Chayun shrugged. "Perhaps they were mistaken. He may just have been temporarily stricken by the snake bite. Who can be sure about these things?"

"He was dead!" shouted a man. "I saw it with my own eyes. I know a dead man when I see one."

"And no one recovers from a viper's bite," added another. "If the venom got into his blood and he lost consciousness, he was as good as dead."

"It was a miracle!" shouted a third man, and a loud chorus took up the cry.

"What do you say?" said the rabbi sharply to Chayun.

Chayun shrugged again. "I am a Kabbalist, and it is against our practice to perform miracles in public. I prayed for the man, and he recovered. Despite what people think, perhaps that is all that happened."

Chayun would not be drawn out any further, and the conversation ended there. But his public denials only helped fuel the excitement and the furor about this holy man and his supernatural powers.

Over the next few weeks, Chayun developed a strong following among the people of Smyrna. They waited on his doorstep and followed him through the streets, kissing his hands and pleading for his blessings.

One day, he called a meeting of the wealthiest of his followers.

"My dear friends," he began, "may the blessings of Heaven shower down upon you until you cry out that you have enough.[63] In these few short weeks, I have come to love you like my own brothers. Now I want you to become my partners in my holy work. I have a manuscript, a Kabbalistic manuscript, that I would like you to help me print here in

Smyrna. I believe this book will draw down the divine illumination and change the world in ways that we cannot even begin to imagine."

One man jumped to his feet. "I will pay for the whole thing," he declared.

"Absolutely not," said another. "Why shouldn't I have a share in it?"

Chayun held up his hands. "Please, my friends, please. Everyone here is entitled to a share. But I need something more from you. Until now, I have lived a hidden life. Over thirty years ago, I was a rabbi for a short while, but my life's work required that I withdraw from public view and think and write, which I have been doing ever since. But now the time has come for me to emerge. I cannot spread the message of my book unless I have a recognized position as a rabbi. I need your help to help me secure such a post."

"I will help you," said an elderly man with wispy white whiskers. "There is an opening in a synagogue in Yerushalayim. My family is prominent in the congregation, and I will suggest that the position be offered to you."

"I am very grateful," said Chayun. "When you receive word that your suggestion has been accepted, I will leave and go to Yerushalayim."

"We will escort you," said the man who had offered to pay for everything. "We will bring you to Yerushalayim with honor and pomp, as befitting a man as holy as you are. And we will hire special camels to carry your holy books."

Chayun was visibly moved. "I don't know what to say," he said. "I am at a complete loss for words. It never occurred to me that my new friends would be even better than brothers to me. You have made me feel very humble. And also very hopeful. At last, my life's work, my book, will see the light of day, and we'll all share in the merit of bring honor to the holy Name of the Almighty."

"May we ask the name of the book?" asked one of the men.

"Of course," said Chayun. "I just wrote it, but the book belongs to all of us. A book is like a child, and we are all the fathers of this book. It is called *Mehemnutha de Kulla*, the belief in everything. It reveals the secrets of everything, even the very nature of the Almighty. It will liberate all of us."

"If it such an important book," said one of the men, "perhaps we shouldn't print it here in Smyrna. Our presses are good enough for our needs, but for a book such as this, perhaps we should go to Venice, Prague, Berlin or even Amsterdam. That's where the finest printing is done. I understand that the type fonts available in Amsterdam are beyond compare."

"My thoughts exactly," said Chayun. "And it is my plan to go there eventually. But in the meantime, it is better to have a hundred copies of a book printed in Smyrna than a single handwritten manuscript."

The men murmured their assent, and the plans were set into motion. The manuscript was brought to the printer and set in movable type, and the printing and binding process began. In the meantime, letters went out to Yerushalayim, and the vacant rabbinical position was secured for Chayun.

When the book was finished, there was a great celebration in Smyrna. Days later, as the rabbi looked on with disapproval, the caravan escorting Chayun set out for Yerushalayim. The caravan moved slowly and deliberately, with a great show of honor and adulation for the holy man bringing his holy book and his holy message to Yerushalayim and then to the entire world.

After they left, the rabbi sat down with a copy of the newly printed book and began to read. At first, the ideas presented in the book seemed innocent enough, but as he read on, he sat forward and the hair on the back of his neck began to tingle. Something was wrong. These ideas were bizarre yet strangely familiar. What was it? Why were all his alarm bells ringing?

Suddenly, he slapped his forehead as he realized what these ideas represented. The rabbi had been to Salonika in his youth, and he had heard the preaching of the Sabbateans. These ideas in the book he was holding in his hands were Sabbatean ideas. He was sure of it. But they were presented in a diabolically clever way. They were couched in terms of classical Kabbalah, but little nuances here and there were changed to insinuate the heretical views of the Sabbateans into the text. And as the book went on, its Sabbatean character became bolder and bolder, even though it was still cleverly concealed. This was a dangerous book, a destructive book. There was no time to waste.

The rabbi sat down and wrote a long report of the events leading up to the publication of this heretical Sabbatean book, and he described the character of the book and its insidious nature. Then he called his oldest son and told him everything that had happened.

"My son," he said, "Are you ready to undertake a secret mission?"

"Wherever you send me, Father, I will go."

The rabbi handed his letter and the book to his son. "I want you to take these to Yerushalayim," he said. "Give them to the rabbis. They'll know what to do. Seek out Rabbi Moshe Chagiz. He is the son of Rabbi Yaakov Chagiz, the leader of the battle against Shabbetai Tzvi. Rabbi Chagiz will appreciate the gravity of the situation perhaps better than the rest, but make sure you show it to all of them."

"I will, Father."

"Hire the fastest horse. I want you to get there before this Sabbatean charlatan and his escort. Avoid them on the road. I do not want Chayun to know that we've discovered his deceptions."

"I will go through the mountains, Father. I will get to Yerushalayim days before they do."

"May the Almighty be with you," said the rabbi, "and speed your way, and may He guard you from all harm."

The rabbi's son arrived in Yerushalayim long before Chayun and his retinue appeared. He brought the letter and the evidence to the Rabbi Moshe Chagiz and the other leading rabbis of Yerushalayim. When Chayun arrived in Yerushalayim, he learned that its rabbis had placed him in *cherem* as a Sabbatean heretic and ordered that his books be confiscated and burned. His supporters immediately melted away and returned to Smyrna in shame.

Chayun took his four disciples, his manuscript, the printed copies that had escaped the flames and the money he had accumulated in Smyrna, and he returned to the mountains of Turkey.

THE HEARTLESS CHICKEN · 17

FOUR WEEKS LATER Rav Amos received the news that his father had passed away. On a frosty day in January of 1709, a messenger arrived at his door with a letter. Even before he opened the letter, Rav Amos knew what it contained. It was an invitation offering him the rabbinical position his father had held for many years.

The letter by signed by Rabbi Aryeh Yehudah Kalischer, who only months before had been appointed chief rabbi of the Ashkenazic community of Amsterdam after the position had been vacant for over a year. Rabbi Kalischer wrote about his respect and esteem for Rabbi Mordechai Strasbourg, whom he had known only briefly. But in that brief time he had come to respect his wide knowledge, his commitment to the community, his piety, his earnestness, his personal integrity, his good humor and the twinkle in his eye.

Rabbi Mordechai Strasbourg had requested, wrote Rabbi Kalischer, that Rav Amos should be considered as his possible successor. He had also insisted that the position should not be offered to Rav Amos unless the selection committee was completely convinced that he deserved the position on his own merits. The committee had deliberated and decided that there was no better candidate for the position than Rav Amos Strasbourg. Therefore, concluded Rabbi Kalischer, the community of Amsterdam would be deeply honored if he would accept the invitation and come to Amsterdam as his illustrious father's successor.

Rav Amos let the letter drop into his lap and sighed. He stared sightlessly at the window as he replayed in his mind his conversation with his father about what he should do if such an invitation ever came. He had promised his father to consider it seriously, and that was what he was obligated to do. But going to Amsterdam was not what he was immediately inclined to do. He would have to do some long and hard thinking before he could clarify his own thoughts beyond the shadow of a doubt, and then he would have to discuss it at length with Rivkah Dvosha.

He was not a young man anymore, and he and Rivkah Dvosha had grown accustomed to the rhythm of their lives in Hamburg. He found his position in the *kloiz* deeply satisfying and his close relationship with Chacham Tzvi precious beyond measure. So what reason could he possibly have for accepting the position? Well, he thought, there were several.

First, there was his widowed mother, now living alone. She needed her son's support. But was this a reason for him to move to Amsterdam? He could just as well have his mother come live with them in Hamburg. Then there was the issue of honoring his father's memory by following in his footsteps. This was definitely something to consider, even though his father had insisted he accept only if he considered it in his best interests.

But what were his best interests? Was it better for him to remain in Hamburg or to go to Amsterdam? Perhaps the position in Amsterdam would offer him a broader scope for his talents. Instead of learning with a small group, he would be teaching many people, perhaps hundreds. And he would be sitting on the rabbinical court and judging cases, something he had hardly ever done. It would certainly be new and challenging. Could he look for new frontiers at sixty years of age? Why not? Traditionally, rabbis are just coming into their prime in their sixties. But would these new opportunities be worth the tradeoff? Were they important enough to uproot his family and move away from his dear friend, a man whom many acknowledged as the *gadol hador*, the greatest of the generation?

Rav Amos sighed again. It would be a difficult decision, but at least, he didn't have to decide within a day or two. It was understood that he could take a reasonable amount of time to make up his mind. His father had not been able to fulfill the duties of the office for many months, so another month or two of vacancy did not really matter.

Two weeks later, Rav Amos received a message from Amsterdam that his mother had passed away in her sleep. At the age of sixty, he had become an orphan, and he felt alone and exposed. He thought of all the times he had spent with his parents, and all the times he had missed out because he was traveling or living somewhere else, time that could never be recovered now that they both were gone. He went into a room, closed the door and wept for a long time.

The day he got up from the Shivah mourning period, he went to Chacham Tzvi's house.

"How are you doing?" said Chacham Tzvi.

"As well as can be expected. There are many regrets."

Chacham Tzvi nodded. "Don't blame yourself. There are always regrets. You were a good son to your parents, and they were very proud of you. You honored them with the life you are leading."

"But we didn't see each other very much these last years."

"That isn't your fault. We're a nation in exile. Not only are we driven from our homeland in Eretz Yisrael, we're also dispersed among the nations. A few thousand here, a few thousand there, a few hundred there, and such great, great distances in between. We live where our destinies lead us, and the separations from family and friends are one of the bitter curses of our exile."

"I received a letter a few weeks ago …. Do you remember our conversation when I came back from Amsterdam?"

"Yes, I do. We spoke about the possibility of your taking over your father's position in Amsterdam." Chacham Tzvi rested his chin in his hand. "Aha, I see. The letter was an invitation."

Rav Amos nodded. "Rabbi Kalischer wrote me a very warm and gracious letter. My father asked that the selection committee should consider me for the position, and it has. The position is mine if I want it."

"So do you want it?"

"I don't know. There are advantages, I suppose."

"A broader role than you have here?"

"Yes. But how can I leave you? You've been such a big part of my life for over twenty years. You're my best friend, my learning partner, my brother. How can I leave you?"

"I feel the same toward you," Chacham Tzvi said quietly. "I don't know what I would do if you left. So why did you come? Do you want my advice?"

"Help me make my decision."

"I have to think this through. It's a very difficult question."

Chacham Tzvi buried his face in his hands and remained silent for fifteen minutes. Finally, he lifted his head and looked at Rav Amos with moist eyes.

"What would you do if I left Hamburg tomorrow?" he asked.

"I'm not sure. I think I'd seriously consider accepting the position in Amsterdam. Is that what you were thinking about for fifteen minutes?"

Chacham Tzvi smiled ruefully. "No, of course not. It wouldn't take me so long to come up with that question. No, my friend, I wasn't thinking about you at all. I was thinking about myself. I was asking myself questions that I've avoided all along. What is my position here in Hamburg? How secure am I? How happy am I here? Is this the best place for me? Is this where I'll be a year from now, five years from now, if the Almighty grants me life and health?"

"What are you saying? Are you thinking of leaving Hamburg?"

"Not right now, I'm not. But I have to face reality. I have enemies here. Quite a few of them. Look at what they did to me in Altona. Half a year my position goes to someone else."

"But you accepted that."

"I know, but what should I have done? And who knows what will happen in the future? My enemies would love nothing more than to drive me out of Hamburg. So how can I know where I'll be a year from now?"

"How about your other question? Are you happy here?"

"Other than my family, which will come with me wherever I go, I'm happy in my beloved *kloiz*, and I'm happy with my beloved friend. If my friend leaves, I'll lose half my happiness. But considering the instability of my situation, I think you should accept the position. Look, in a year I could be in Lemberg or Krakow or Vienna or who knows where? If you're not happy in Amsterdam, you could join me wherever I am. We'll make arrangements. You have your fur trade income, so salary shouldn't pose a problem."

Rav Amos smiled. "And if you're still in Hamburg?"

"There will always be a position open for you at the *kloiz* if you want to come back."

"Thank you. You've helped clarify my thoughts. Now I can talk to my wife, and we can reach a decision."

Chacham Tzvi sighed. "It's a sad, sad situation, but that is life." He brightened. "In the meantime, how would you like to hear a question that came to me the other day?"

Rav Amos sat forward eagerly. "Let's hear it."

"All right. A woman gave a slaughtered chicken to her daughter and told her to remove its entrails. The girl put the chicken on the table and cut it open. The family's cat sat under the table waiting for the scraps that the girl would throw down. The girl opened the chicken and took out its entrails. Suddenly, she realized that there was no heart in the chicken. So the questioner wants to know if the chicken is *treif* because it didn't have a heart."

"Are you serious?" said Rav Amos.

"Absolutely."

"The cat ate it."

"The girl says she never dropped the heart," said Chacham Tzvi. "All she gave the cat was the spleen."

"The girl must have dropped the heart by mistake, and the cat ate it."

Chacham Tzvi chuckled. "You're obviously a rational person. This was a fine healthy chicken running around the barnyard and eating robustly. It most certainly had a heart. Chickens cannot live without hearts. Any rational person can understand that, but I wrote back many proofs from the Zohar and the Maharal to make sure they accept my ruling. Can you imagine what I have to contend with?"[64]

Rav Amos felt more relaxed after his conversation with Chacham Tzvi. He and Rivkah Dvosha considered all the advantages and disadvantages and came to the conclusion that they should make the move.

The new situation did not call for an extremely difficult adjustment for the Strasbourg family. Amsterdam was Rav Amos' hometown, and he had many friends there. The house they moved into was the house in which he had grown up. He had never met Rabbi Kalischer, the new rabbi, but he was acquainted with most of the other rabbis and community officials, both in the Ashkenazic community and in the Sephardic community. The children were grown, and Rav Amos and

Rivkah Dvosha were ready to consider matches for all three of them. Menachem was twenty-two, Reuven was nineteen and Chanah sixteen. Menachem and Reuven joined the *yeshivah*, while Chanah helped her mother arrange the household.

As he had expected, Rav Amos found the responsibilities and duties of his position interesting. And as his father had assured him, he had plenty of free time to work on his own writings. But his separation from Chacham Tzvi was more painful than he had anticipated. Rarely did a few hours go by that his thoughts did not turn to his beloved friend.

A few months after his arrival in Amsterdam, there was knock on the door. It was Sheftil Ringel, the grandson of Elisha Ringel, who was now thirty years old and still as tiny as his grandfather if not tinier.

"You don't recognize me, do you?" said Sheftil.

Rav Amos hesitated.

"If you don't recognize me by my face," said Sheftil, "perhaps you can recognize me by my height, or the lack of it. It's been twenty years."

"Sheftil Ringel! Please come in, come in. Can I get you something?"

Sheftil shook his head. "We're staying in a good inn. It's very comfortable, and the food is good and plentiful."

"So what can I do for you, Sheftil?"

"We need your help."

"We?"

"I'm here with a group. We want to print a Siddur with a new commentary. Three people have put up the funding for it, and I'm managing the project. We gave the job to an old experienced printer in Berlin who does a lot of work for the Jewish community of Prague. He suggested that he take the job to Amsterdam, because there's no better printing anywhere else in the world. And we decided to come along to oversee the production."

"Is this a business venture for you?"

"No, not at all. I'm … uh … well off. My family does well in the spice business. I'm here for personal reasons. The author of the commentary is the son of one of the rabbis in Poznan, and I've known him for years. His name is Rabbi Tzvi Hirsch Chazzan.

"So who is in this group besides me? There's Rabbi Chazzan, the author. Then there are the three sponsors, Moshe Katz, Zalman ben Moshe Raphael and Chaim ben Yisrael.[65] And there's Hans Gunther Wieselthier, the printer."

"And how can I help you on this project?"

"We want to make sure that we're treated fairly," said Sheftil. "That we get the best quality work and that we pay a fair price. I thought that if we come with one of the respected rabbis of the community, we'll get proper treatment."

Rav Amos smiled. "I don't know how much my presence will help, but I'll do whatever you need. Can you tell me something about this Siddur?"

"Of course. It's a special piece of work. Its main feature is a wonderful inspirational commentary on the whole topic of prayer. The commentary, *Ohr Hayashar*, was written by Rabbi Chazzan, but it's really an expanded version of a commentary called *Ohr Tzaddikim* written by Rabbi Meir Poperos, a great Kabbalist who passed away about fifty years ago, in 1662 to be exact. He was thirty-eight."

"I've heard of him," said Rav Amos. "I believe he was born in Prague but went to Eretz Yisrael and learned Kabbalah in Damascus under Rabbi Shmuel Vital, the son of Rabbi Chaim Vital, and Rabbi Yaakov Tzemach."

"That's the one. They say he started learning Kabbalah at the age of thirteen. When did you start learning Kabbalah, Rabbi Strasbourg?"

Rav Amos laughed. "We don't talk about those things."

"I see. The keeper of mystical mysteries."

Rav Amos laughed again. "Which printer are you considering?"

"Herr Wieselthier suggested Moshe Diaz. What do you think?"

"My father spoke highly of Moshe Frankfurt, but I've heard only excellent things about Moshe Diaz as well. If your Herr Wieselthier has a relationship with Moshe Diaz, then by all means go to him."

"We have an appointment tomorrow. Could you come? We'll arrange the hour at your convenience."

"I have no commitments tomorrow. I can come whenever you wish."

"Thank you so much," said Sheftil. "Noon would be perfect."

The group was waiting for him at noon the next day. For a moment, Rav Amos couldn't find Sheftil, because the other men towered over him, especially the printer who was a man of incredibly enormous girth. Finally, Sheftil peeked out from behind the printer's voluminous coat.

Sheftil first introduced Rav Amos to a middle-aged rabbi with a myopic squint.

"Rabbi Strasbourg," said Sheftil, speaking in German. "I'd like you to meet Rabbi Tzvi Hirsch Chazzan of Poznan. I've told you about him."

The two men shook hands.

"And these are the sponsors," said Sheftil. "This is Moshe Katz. This is Zalman ben Moshe Raphael. And this is Chaim ben Yisrael."

Rav Amos shook hands with all of them.

"It's my pleasure to meet all of you," he said. "I look forward to purchasing a copy of the new Siddur."

"We will be honored if you accept a Siddur as our gift," said Moshe Katz. "We arc already honored that you've come here to assist us. We've heard a lot about you in my hometown of Brisk, and of course, the Strasbourg family name is unparalleled."

"That is very kind of you." He turned to the printer and extended his hand. "And you must be Herr Wieselthier."

"I was about to make the introduction," said Sheftil. "You are too quick, Rabbi Strasbourg."

"And too kind," said Wieselthier as he grasped the extended hand.

Rav Amos was struck once again by the sheer size of the man. He looked to be in his high seventies or low eighties but strong as an ox. His broad face was covered by a vast white beard that jutted out to his right and to his left. He was bald on top, but his white hair hung down long and thick behind his head. His blue eyes were almost concealed by the folds of his fleshy cheeks, but they twinkled with kindness and good humor.

"I'm so pleased to meet you, Rabbi Strasbourg," said Wieselthier. "It is the meeting of two great men. You are a great scholar and rabbi, and I am great in a different way." He chuckled at his own witticism. "But seriously, I've heard a lot about you from Herr Ringel and others, and I'm certainly honored. Are you familiar with the printing process?"

"Not really," said Rav Amos. "Just with the end products."

Wieselthier threw back his head and laughed until his belly shook like a bowl of jelly. "Well, I should hope so," he said after he caught his breath. "You wouldn't be much of a rabbi without your books, now would you?"

"Really, Herr Wieselthier," said Rav Amos, "Herr Ringel tells me that you are an expert printer, and I'm looking forward to a very instructive afternoon."

"And you'll have it. If you'd gone yourselves to these printers, you would have received good service, I'm sure of it. But not necessarily the very best. Why? Because you wouldn't know what to demand. But with me as your representative, you'll get the finest product available in the world today."

"I'm sure we will. By the way, Herr Wieselthier, I detect a very slight accent in your German. Are you originally from somewhere else?"

Wieselthier was impressed. "You have a sharp ear, rabbi. I was born and raised in Berlin, and I've lived there all my life, but my mother was Italian. I spoke Italian before I spoke German, and I suppose a little Latin trace crept into my German. But it's so minute, most people don't pick up on it. I'm really impressed. I can still speak a beautiful Italian. *Parlate italiano, rabbino?*"

"*Purtroppo, parlo soltanto alcuni parola, signore.*"

Wieselthier clapped his hands with delight. "*Bello, rabbino, bravissimo.*"

Rav Amos smiled and brushed the compliment aside.

"Rabbi Strasbourg, I've heard that you have many personal writings," said Wieselthier. "Someday, you'll want to publish them and let the world benefit from all your years of learning. When the time comes, if these old bones of mine are still alive and kicking, I'd be honored to help you do it."

"Now you're the one who's being kind, Herr Wieselthier. May you live and be well for a long time, because I'm not quite ready to do it yet."

They spent the rest of the afternoon in the print shop, listening to the thunder of the presses and inhaling the pungent odor of black ink. Rav Amos was completely fascinated by the almost magical process, and he regretted not having toured the presses of Amsterdam earlier.

Rav Amos returned to the printing presses two more times during the stay of the group from Poznan. Each time, Wieselthier went out of his way to show him every little detail of the process and answer all his questions. And when the author presented him with the gift of a finished Siddur, Rav Amos held it in his hands with reverence and a deep appreciation for all the talent, creativity and sheer hard work that had gone into it.

For a long time afterward, Wieselthier's offer reverberated in his head. Until this experience, the stacks of papers closely covered with his serpentine writing kept accumulating in his study with only the vaguest thoughts of bringing them to press. But now the seed had been planted in his mind, and he dreamed of holding his own published writings in his hands. He dreamed of passing them on to his children and future generations who could benefit from all the work he had invested in his learning.

At about this time, things were not going so well for Chacham Tzvi in Hamburg. According to the arrangement with Ber Kohein and his other detractors, he remained the rabbi of Hamburg itself and its Wandsbeck suburb, and in the important suburb of Altona, he shared the rabbinate with Rabbi Moshe Rothenberg, each serving six months of the year. In addition, he sat on the rabbinical court of Altona together with Rabbi Rothenberg.

An incident occurred in which Rabbi Rothenberg took certain steps of which Chacham Tzvi did not approve. Chacham Tzvi expressed his disapproval by refusing from that point on to sit on the rabbinical court together with Rabbi Rothenberg.

Chacham Tzvi's detractors were up in arms over this public rebuke of their choice for the rabbinate, but Chacham Tzvi was not intimidated. They agitated against him and convinced many people that this action could not be tolerated. They appointed a delegation of two people, Yoel Shue and Eliahu Falk, to deliver an ultimatum to Chacham Tzvi. Either he relented and sat on the rabbinical court together with Rabbi Rothenberg or he would be removed from the rabbinate of Altona completely.

Chacham Tzvi, fearless and fiercely protective of his independence and integrity, immediately resigned from the rabbinate of Altona and withdrew to his *kloiz*. The people who had supported the ultimatum were shocked by Chacham Tzvi's abrupt and decisive reaction, and many of them regretted what they had done, especially since people who had failed to honor Chacham Tzvi properly were reported to have suffered divine retribution.

Some people began to insist that they had only sent the delegation to ask him to relent but not to offer him an ultimatum. Such effrontery to a man widely recognized as the *gadol hador* was unconscionable. They insisted that the delegates had done so on their own, and they pleaded with Chacham Tzvi to return to his position as their rabbi. But Chacham Tzvi did not relent, and he never again had any involvement in the community affairs of Altona.[66]

A DELICATE SITUATION · 18

TOWARD THE END OF 1709, Rabbi Aryeh Yehudah Kalisch, the chief rabbi of Amsterdam, passed away. After an appropriate period of community-wide mourning, Rav Amos was asked to serve on a selection committee together with Herschel Pfeiffer and Mattis Green, two leading members of the community. At the initial meeting of the committee, Rav Amos asked to be the first to speak.

"Friends, colleagues," he began, "although I grew up in Amsterdam and spent a good part of my adult life here, I'm fairly new here. As you all know, I was away for twenty years, and most of that time I spent in Hamburg where I could be with my good friend Chacham Tzvi Ashkenazi. I suggest that we offer the position to him. He should be the new chief rabbi of Amsterdam."

These words were greeted by a buzz of excited conversation.

"Rabbi Strasbourg, I am puzzled," said Herschel Pfeiffer. "We all know about your close friendship with Chacham Tzvi, and believe me, it is a great honor for our city that one of our rabbis is among his closest friends. And we understand that you would love nothing better than to have him come here to Amsterdam. But why would he leave his present Hamburg? It is one of the most prestigious positions in the rabbinate. The rabbi of Hamburg is like a king. I mean,

Amsterdam is a wonderful and important community, but why would he leave Hamburg? It would be a real embarrassment for the community of Amsterdam if we made such an offer and he didn't even consider it."

"He'll consider it," said Rav Amos.

"How do you know?" asked Mattis Green. "Why would he consider it? Because of you?"

Rav Amos shook his head. "I don't flatter myself that he would come here just to be together with me. I just think that he is not as happy as he should be with the situation in Hamburg. I think he would seriously consider a change."

"You really think so?"

"I do."

"In my opinion," said Herschel Pfeiffer, "we should make the offer. It would be a real coup for Amsterdam if Chacham Tzvi were to come here. Even the Sephardim would dance in the streets. We should make the offer, and if he turns it down, he turns it down. It's worth the risk."

"He won't turn it down," said Rav Amos.

"I hope you're right, Rabbi Strasbourg," said Mattis Green. "I will agree to make an offer to Chacham Tzvi. But I really hope he won't turn us down. If word got out …"

"There's something you must know," said Rav Amos, "about Chacham Tzvi if you're going to invite him to be chief rabbi of Amsterdam. He belongs to no one but the Almighty. He accepts no gifts or favors from anyone. He expects complete independence to do what he thinks is right, within the guidelines of his responsibilities, of course. He is fearless, and you will not be able to pressure him. If you want him to come here, you have to be ready to give him the complete authority to act according to his understanding of the will of the Almighty. He will leave Amsterdam before he bows to pressure."

"I see," said Mattis Green. "So is that why he would consider leaving Hamburg? Is he having issues with pressure from influential people?"

Rav Amos smiled. "That is a shrewd guess, Reb Mattis. But I really cannot discuss the affairs of another community. So is that condition acceptable to you? Are you willing to give him complete independence?"

"Yes, I'm ready," said Herschel Pfeiffer. "For a rabbi like Chacham Tzvi, I'll forego any influence I might've been able to wield with a different rabbi."

"The same goes for me," said Mattis Green. "Not only that, but I'll defend his independence from anyone who tries to bring pressure on him. For some people, it's all about themselves, and I have to admit that sometimes I also get a flash of such a feeling. But for a great and holy rabbi such as Chacham Tzvi, I'm ready to squash such feelings as soon as they appear."

The letter of invitation went out to Chacham Tzvi. The annual salary mentioned in the letter was the standard five hundred Dutch guilders the community had been paying all its chief rabbis, an admittedly modest sum that was normally supplemented by other streams of income.

In a matter of weeks, the reply arrived. He would be pleased to accept the offer, wrote Chacham Tzvi, but he insisted on an annual salary of a thousand Reichsthalers, which amounted to about two thousand five hundred Dutch guilders. Since he never accepted any gifts or gratuities for himself from members of the community or anyone else, his only source of income would be his salary, and therefore, it had to be substantial enough for the needs of his large family.

"I say we give it to him," Mattis Green commented when he read the letter of reply. "In the long run, we'll probably save money, since we won't have to give him anything for weddings, holidays, selling the *chametz* or anything else.

Actually, when you come to think about it, I think this is quite a bargain."

When Chacham Tzvi and his family arrived in Amsterdam in the summer of 1710, Rabbi Shlomo Ayllon, the chief rabbi of the Sephardic community, came out to greet him even before he reached his house and put down his packages. Afterward, the entire city, Ashkenazim and Sephardim, staged a parade in his honor, replete with musicians and speeches.

Rabbi Ayllon spoke words of welcome that were full of praise and adulation such as can only be addressed to one person in each generation. Rabbi Ayllon, who had served as chief rabbi of the Sephardic community of London for many years before coming to Amsterdam, mentioned that he had sent a complex question to Chacham Tzvi fourteen years before and that the answer he had received was dazzling in its erudition, brilliance and clarity. Many of the other Sephardic rabbis of Amsterdam had also sent questions to Chacham Tzvi from time to time, and they were all thrilled and excited that he would be living among them. It was a moment of high honor for Chacham Tzvi and for the entire Ashkenazic community of Amsterdam.

Many Dutch dignitaries, ministers, ambassadors, generals and noblemen, came to the parade and were amazed by the honor being accorded one rabbi, honor far beyond anything they had ever seen accorded anyone by the Jewish community. The rich Sephardic merchants who were well connected with the government officials explained to them that Chacham Tzvi's breadth of knowledge in Torah, Jewish law, the sciences, philosophy and languages was unparalleled in his generation and that his holiness, integrity and sense of justice were nothing short of legendary.[67]

From that day on, Chacham Tzvi's reputation with the government authorities was firmly established, and throughout his years in Amsterdam, the Dutch magistrates refused to adjudicate any disputes between Ashkenazic Jews. Why do you need us, they would say, when your own rabbi is of such a high caliber and so incorruptible?[68]

On his first night in Amsterdam, the Ashkenazic community hosted a banquet in Chacham Tzvi's honor. The tables were laden with food, including the choicest cuts of meat.

Mattis Green filled a plate and placed it before Chacham Tzvi.

"What is the name of our community *shochet*?" asked Chacham Tzvi.

"Leizer Shochet," said Mattis Green.

"Please ask him to bring me his *chalaf*, his slaughtering knife."

"Right now?"

"Yes."

"Right here?"

"Yes."

"I'm on my way."

Ten minutes later, he came back with an elderly man in tow. Chacham Tzvi shook hands with him, led him into a side room and shut the door. He signaled to Mattis Green to remain during the conversation.

"Please have a seat," he said."Would you like a drink of water?"

"No, I'm fine," said the *shochet*.

"Good," said Chacham Tzvi. "Have you brought the *chalaf*?"

The *shochet* handed an item wrapped in cloth to Chacham Tzvi. It was his slaughtering knife. The blade is supposed to have a sharp edge completely free of any imperfections that can interrupt its smooth passage through the animal's flesh.[69] The *shochet* generally runs his finger lightly along the edge of the blade to check for imperfections.

"How long have you been *shochet*?" Chacham Tzvi asked him.

"Forty years."

"Forty years! That's a long time. So you have a lot of experience."

"Yes, I do," said the *shochet*.

"How are your eyes?"

"They're good."

"And your sense of touch?"

"Good."

Chacham Tzvi took the blade in his hands and studied it. He immediately saw that it was full of imperfections visible to the eye even without running a finger along the edge. He handed the knife back to the *shochet*.

"Here, please check the knife for me, you know, the way you always do."

The *shochet* took the knife and peered at it closely. Then he ran his calloused finger along the edge.

"The blade is fine," he said and handed it to Chacham Tzvi.

"No, no, don't give it back to me just yet. Let's make doubly sure that it's fine. Could you check it for me once again? I just want to be extra careful."

The *shochet* smiled. "I understand. You're the new rabbi, and you want to show everyone that you take your job seriously. Sure, I'll check it for you again. No problem."

He held the knife up in front of his face and then ran his finger very slowly along the edge again.

"The knife is fine, rabbi. I checked it and double-checked it, and it's in perfect condition. I can detect no imperfections."

"I understand," said Chacham Tzvi. He looked up at Mattis Green, shook his head and sighed.

"What's the matter?" said the *shochet*, suddenly alarmed.

"I'm afraid your days as a *shochet* are over, my friend," said Chacham Tzvi. "You've given the community many years of exemplary service, but now, the position will have to be taken by a younger man."

The *shochet* jumped to his feet. "What do you mean? You can't do that!"

"I'm afraid I can."

The *shochet* was livid. "I've been *shochet* here for forty years. It's my livelihood, and my whole family depends on it. You can't just send me away."

"I'm really sorry, but I can't allow the people of Amsterdam to eat non-kosher meat. I don't know how long you've had these problems, but you've been feeding them non-kosher meat. It cannot go on."

"How can you accuse me of such a thing? What do you think I am?"

"I don't think you did it on purpose," said Chacham Tzvi. "But your senses are just not as sharp as they used to be."

"My senses are just fine. You can't do this."

"I'm really sorry." He turned to Mattis Green. "Reb Mattis, please see to it that he has whatever he needs for his livelihood. We don't want to reduce him to poverty."

The *shochet* stormed away in a fury to complain his friends and relatives about the new rabbi's highhanded actions, and Chacham Tzvi had his first set of enemies in Amsterdam.[70]

The second set of problems was not long in coming. A battle had been raging for years in the Ashkenazic community over a dispute between two *chazzanim* each of whom claimed the position of official *chazzan*. One *chazzan* had the support of the simple people, while the other had the support of a group of powerful men who were ready to spend any amount of money and twist any number of arms in order to secure victory for the *chazzan* they were championing. It had become a matter of pride for them, and they were determined to win. The battles between the two sides sometimes resulted in fist fights, and chairs and tables were thrown in the synagogue.

Shortly after Chacham Tzvi was settled in Amsterdam, a man named Shimon Flaks approached him.

"Rabbi, are you aware of the *chazzan* dispute?" he said.

"I heard something about it."

"You have to put a stop to it once and for all, rabbi. Levi is the one who deserves the position."

"I'll look into it."

"That's not good enough," said Flaks. "I need your commitment that you'll secure the position for Levi. I'm not just speaking for myself but for some of the wealthiest and most powerful people in our community."

"Well, all I can tell you is that I'll look into it, and I'll do what I think is fair and just."

"You don't understand me, rabbi." He squinted and gave Chacham Tzvi a sharp look. "Or maybe you do. Maybe you do. All right, this is what I'll do for you. This is the situation. My friends and I will give you twenty thousand guilders. Twenty thousand! And all you have to do is give the position to Levi. Very simple, isn't it? But if you don't do as we demand, then we will become your implacable enemies, and we will not rest until we drive you out of our city."

"Are you finished?" asked Chacham Tzvi.

"Yes, I am. For the moment."

"Then have a good day, and close the door behind you."

Chacham Tzvi's enemies joined forces and tried to undermine his position in Amsterdam. They demanded a commitment from the community council that Chacham Tzvi's contract would not be renewed at the end of his three-year term. But his supporters rallied behind him, and the Sephardic community came out solidly in his support. The support of the Sephardic community, which was larger and wealthier than the Ashkenazic community, was crucial, and in the end, his enemies were isolated. Their businesses suffered, and they eventually went bankrupt and had to leave the city.[71]

The Sephardic community supported Chacham Tzvi so passionately not only because of his towering greatness in every aspect of the Torah; they loved and adored him because of his holiness, his kindness and his unshakable integrity. They also felt a deep connection to him because he had learned in Sephardic *yeshivos* and served as a rabbi in a Sephardic community. In fact, his rabbinic title of Chacham, which was of Sephardic origin, had been bestowed upon him by the Sephardic sages of Istanbul. In a very real sense, therefore, Chacham Tzvi was not only the rabbi of the Ashkenazim of Amsterdam but also of the entire city of Amsterdam.

So in the flush of excitement over his arrival in Amsterdam, Chacham Tzvi enjoyed strong support from both the Ashkenazic and Sephardic communities. But euphoria does not endure for more than a few months, and there was no guarantee that his support would still be as strong a year or even six months later. In the meantime, despite the problems he had encountered, his position was relatively solid.

Chacham Tzvi brought his customary dynamism and high standards to his role as chief rabbi of Amsterdam. The level of kosher supervision rose dramatically, as did many other aspects of community affairs. Chacham Tzvi also established a *yeshivah* similar to the *kloiz* he had established in Hamburg. The house the community had provided for him was too small for his family, since he already had ten children. Therefore, he rented a larger house at his own expense, paying five hundred guilders a year with no reimbursement from the community. He then set aside a large portion of the new house for a *yeshivah* in which *talmidei chachamim* would learn day and night, some of them even sleeping there at night.[72]

The responsibility for the upkeep of the *yeshivah* fell upon his shoulders. He received no rent for the rooms he had given over to the *yeshivah*. As for the costs of housing and feeding the members of the yeshivah, he arranged for that as well. He organized a group of wealthy community activists and inspired them to share the costs. He also joined the group and contributed an equal share from his own pocket.[73]

His contract with the community entitled him to receive a fee from his duties as a rabbinical judge, whether they involved financial disputes and litigations or family matters such as divorces. Chacham Tzvi, of course, refused to take these moneys for his personal use. Instead, he dedicated the money for the use of the community. Outside his room, he put two locked boxes with slots on top. When the boxes were full, a community official would come and empty them. The people coming for financial matters would put their money into one box, the proceeds of which went to the general community fund, and the people who came for family matters would put their money into the second box, which was designated for the *yeshivah*.[74]

Never before had the city had the honor and privilege of being led by a great rabbi widely acclaimed as the *gadol hador*. Never before had the level of Torah learning and observance been so high. Never before had the social machinery of the community run so smoothly. And on top of all that, Chacham Tzvi was still a relatively young fifty-four years old when he became chief rabbi of Amsterdam. The future looked very bright for the Jews of Amsterdam.

One day in the fall of 1710, Rav Amos received an urgent message to meet Sebastian at the offices of the Maamad. Rav Amos hurried over immediately, his heart pounding with worry.

"I see I've frightened you," said Sebastian as soon as he saw his friend. "I should have mentioned in my message that everyone is well. But it's important that you come with me right now. Let's go."

They got into Sebastian's carriage.

"Where are we going?" asked Rav Amos.

"The Toothless Beggar."

"Gonzalo's tavern?"

"You have a good memory," said Sebastian. "We haven't been there in twenty-five years."

"I always remember weird names. Why are we going there?"

"There's someone I want you to meet."

"Who?" said Rav Amos.

"I don't even know myself."

Rav Amos gave him a strange look.

"I'm not trying to be mysterious," said Sebastian. "We'll be there in a few minutes, and everything will become clear. In the meantime, I have something important to ask you. It has nothing to do with where we're going now. I've been meaning to ask you this for a while, but we're both so busy. Is it true that Shamai Cohen has been coming to visit Chacham Tzvi?"

Rav Amos was puzzled. "Is there a problem? Many of the Sephardic rabbis come to him. Even your own brother Felipe — or should I say Rabbi Pinhas? — has been there more than once."

"But I heard that Shamai is coming a lot. Is that true?"

"I can't say for sure," said Rav Amos. "I'm not with Chacham Tzvi all the time. But it's my impression that he has been coming … you know … often. Why do you ask?"

"Some people on the Maamad are a little concerned. It's a delicate situation here in Amsterdam. We have to walk a fine line. We have two separate communities, Sephardic and Ashkenazic, each with its own set of customs and traditions and its own methods of resolving *halachic* questions. For all the years, each community has gone its own way in matters of Jewish observance, and that was perfectly fine. But now we have Chacham Tzvi here, and that complicates matters."

"How so?"

"Because he is so great that he overshadows our own Sephardic rabbis, and even though he is called Chacham, he is an Ashkenaz rabbi through and through. We are a little concerned that our rabbis should not come under his influence to such an extent that they will guide our community by rules and standards that are not traditionally Sephardic."

"I see. And how do you feel about this personally?"

Sebastian shrugged. "It's hard to say. Personally, I'm not very concerned. I don't think these matters are so critical. But maybe that's just my ex-Marrano background. I'm just glad to be free and serve the Almighty. It does not make such a difference to me whether or not we eat rice on Pesach."

"It's not unimportant. Customs preserve our observance."

"I know that, but I just can't get very excited about it. That's just me as a private person. But in my role as head of the Maamad, I have to look at things from a different perspective. Our community is very protective of its Sephardic character, and many people would be upset if it were undermined."

"I'm listening. You were saying something about a fine line."

"Yes, I was," said Sebastian. "We think the world of Chacham Tzvi, and we couldn't be happier and more honored just to have him in our city. We kiss his hand and ask for his blessings. But when it comes to our rabbis, we would like them to look for guidance to our own leading rabbis here and in other cities. Once in a while, I understand. But if Shamai Cohen is going to him all the time with his questions, we are not very happy with that."

"I understand," said Rav Amos.

"Are we wrong?"

"No, I can't say you're wrong. And I think Chacham Tzvi himself would agree with you if you asked him."

"You mean we should ask him not to speak to Shamai Cohen?"

Rav Amos shook his head. "No, of course not. I meant that he would agree with you in principle. If you want to do anything about it, you would have to do it yourself. You know, talk to Shamai Cohen."

Sebastian sighed. "You know Shamai. He's not the easiest person to talk to. He'll insist that he has every right to learn Torah from the greatest rabbi available. He'll get excited, and he'll shout."

"So what do you want from me?"

"I just want confirmation that he's been going there a lot. Has he?"

"I answered the question before," said Rav Amos. "There's nothing more I can add. And why are you so worried about Shamai? He's only one man."

"Well, that's true, but if there's a problem it will start somewhere, and Shamai is a likely starting point."

"Is there some special reason you're concerned about him?"

Sebastian sighed again. "I suppose there is. Shamai had dreams of becoming the new Sephardic chief rabbi of Amsterdam ten years ago, but Rabbi Ayllon was chosen instead. I believe he has harbored resentments since then and that his association with Chacham Tzvi is a way of undermining Rabbi Ayllon as the highest rabbinic authority in the Sephardic community of Amsterdam."

"I never heard about that."

"You were living in Hamburg then. By the time you got here, it was old news. Could be that there's nothing to it. We're just being careful." He looked out the window. "We're here."

They had left the Jewish quarter and entered a neighborhood called the Plantage, or the Plantation. At one time, there had been many vegetable gardens and fruit orchards among the scattered homes and cabins. But the growth of the city had spilled over into this backwater, and it was now a thriving market district whose streets were choked with traffic.

Gonzalo's tavern had recently received a fresh coat of paint and a new sign on the front wall. Gonzalo himself was his usual fierce self. He was about seventy years, and he still bore himself with the carriage of a proud Spanish cavalier. His hair was long, his beard short, pointed and limited to his chin.

"Don Sebastian, Rabbi Strasbourg," he declared, "welcome to my establishment. Our guest is in the back. Come this way."

He led them down a hallway into a storeroom in the back. A man was sitting in a chair in the center of the room. His legs were tied to the legs of the chair. A fat bartender stood guard over him.

"This is the fish we caught, Don Sebastian. He's all yours. If he tries to escape just hit him over the head with that board." He signaled to the bartender, and they both left the room.

Sebastian pulled up two chairs, one for himself and one for Rav Amos. "So what have we here?" he said.

"Please don't hurt me," said the man. "I didn't do anything."

"No one said that you did. What's your name?"

The man's lower lip trembled, and he said nothing.

Sebastian stood up. "If you won't talk to us, we'll go. You can deal with Gonzalo and his men."

The man began to weep. "Why is this happening to me? Why do I deserve this? What did I do?"

"There's no need to cry. No one wants to hurt you. We just want to talk."

The man wiped his eyes. "All right. My name is Duvid'l Goldberg."

"Is that your real name?"

"Yes, I give you my word. My papers are at the inn."

"Where are you from?"

"Prague."

"You're a long way from home."

"I know."

"So do you want to tell us what you were doing?"

"I wasn't hurting anyone. I was just asking questions."

"What kind of questions?"

"Innocent questions."

"Do you have any other business in Amsterdam?"

"No."

"So you're telling me that you came all the way from Prague to ask innocent questions in Amsterdam?"

The man nodded.

"You've been snooping around for a while, haven't you?'

"Not so long. About two weeks."

"That's a long time to snoop, and we find that disturbing. Gonzalo very kindly tracked you down for me and invited you here. So let's begin with your questions. You know, those innocent questions. What kind of questions were you asking?"

"Just questions about the community. Who are the officials? Who are the rabbis? Who are the wealthy and influential people? Where do they live? What are their relationships with each other? Things like that."

"Which community, Sephardic or Ashkenazic?"

"Both."

"Have you gathered a lot of information?" asked Rav Amos.

"Quite a lot."

"How much is quite a lot?"

"Thirty pages."

Rav Amos blinked. "Thirty pages? What could you write on thirty pages?"

"All the personal information of all the people I investigated, their positions, their businesses, their families, things like that."

"Thirty pages," Rav Amos repeated with wonder. "So where are these thirty pages?"

"I sent them back to Prague."

Sebastian and Rav Amos exchanged glances.

"Who sent you?" said Sebastian.

"I don't know."

"Don't be difficult," said Sebastian.

"I'm not being difficult," said the man. "Someone came over to me in Prague and offered me money to do this. He gave me a nice sum right away and promised to pay me the rest when I finished my job. He insisted I send him the material as I gathered it. I could bring the last part with me and deliver it when he gave me the money."

"Who was this man?"

"I don't know. I think he spoke with a Polish accent."

"Was he Jewish?"

"Yes."

"What did he look like?"

The man shrugged. "He looked like anyone else. Dark hair, dark beard. Black coat. A nose. Two eyes."

"Don't be funny," said Sebastian. "This is serious business. I can have you arrested."

"For what?"

"For anything I say. This is Amsterdam. You are on my territory."

"I'm sorry. I really don't know what to tell you. I mean, he didn't have any scars or missing teeth or anything. He was just a man."

"Like you."

"Yes, like me. Just another man. Just like a thousand other men. I can't even see a picture of him in my mind."

"Where did you send the papers?" asked Rav Amos.

"To Prague."

"Where in Prague?"

"An inn. A place where people get messages and packages."

"And where are you supposed to meet this man to give him the rest of your information and get the rest of your money?"

"In Prague."

"Where in Prague?"

"I don't know. He said he'd contact me."

"Did he say why he needed this information?"

The man laughed dryly. "What do you think? Of course not."

Sebastian leaned forward. "Did you send him information about us?"

"The two of you?" said the man.

"That's right. Don't you know who we are?"

The man nodded.

"So did you report on the two of us?"

The man nodded again.

Rav Amos smiled. "Did you say nice things?"

"I never give opinions," said the man. "I just give information."

"What do you do for a living?" said Rav Amos. "I mean, when you're not spying on other people?"

"I'm a peddler."

"What do you say, Sebastian?" said Rav Amos. "Is there anything else you want to ask this gentleman?"

"No, I think we've covered everything," said Sebastian.

He reached down and untied the man's legs.

"As for you, my dear spy," said Sebastian. "You had better be out of Amsterdam by tomorrow morning, and if you ever return, I'll make sure you rot in prison. Trust me, I can do it."

AN APPOINTMENT
IN AMSTERDAM · 19

C HAYUN'S DISCIPLES ARRIVED in Prague long before he
did. They had to prepare the way for their master by
spreading word of his reputation and arranging for an eager
reception. In the meantime, Chayun remained in Venice,
where he had met with some success. After being driven out
of Yerushalayim in 1709, he had returned to Turkey and wandered from place to place. But in 1711, he had shown the rabbis of Venice a manuscript entitled *Raza d'Yichudah,* which
was an excerpt from his larger work entitled *Mehemnutha de
Kulla,* and they had approved its printing. Chayun was convinced that this was the first step in his rehabilitation and
ultimate triumph, and he was elated.

With his newly printed book in hand, Chayun was ready
for his next move. At first, he thought of going straight to
Amsterdam, but someone suggested that he would be better off going to Prague first. If he could get the rabbis of
Prague to endorse his work, he would be better equipped to
continue on to Amsterdam. Chayun considered this plan of
action and decided to pursue it.

When he arrived in Prague, he did not immediately roll
out his customary performances. On the contrary, he rented
a house and stayed out of the public eye. His disciples had

done their work well, and there was considerable interest in this colorful holy man with the reputation for having supernatural powers. But Chayun refused to see anyone. This underscored the authenticity of the man and made the excitement even greater. After all, if he were a charlatan, why would he refuse to see people and take their money?

On his very first day in Prague and every day thereafter, Chayun rose while it was still dark and immersed himself in the chilly waters of the Danube River. Then he went out to the fields and prayed *kavasikin*, greeting the sunrise with his prayers and ululations. Word of the holy man's morning activities spread, and presently, crowds would gather to watch his mysterious movements and listen to his sonorous voice.

After he finished his prayers, he invariably wrapped himself in his *tallis* and pulled it over his head until only a small opening remained. Then he walked back to his house with his head down, looking at nothing but the cobblestones visible through the opening in his *tallis*. In the beginning, people approached him as he returned from the fields and asked for his blessings, but he just continued to mumble Kabbalistic formulations and completely ignored them. A few Sephardim tried to kiss his hand, but he snatched it away.

Once he got home, he locked the door behind him. He disciples stood guard around the house and refused to talk to the people or give them any indication of when they could have audiences with the holy man. He did not even go out for prayers. A few select townspeople were permitted into his house to complete the *minyan*, but they could not approach the holy man, who sat in a remote corner and spoke to no one.

This went on for several weeks, and then he decided to open his doors to the public on a limited basis. But first he went to pay his respects to Rabbi David Oppenheim, the chief rabbi of Prague. He carried a pouch that he held tightly at his side as he set off for the rabbi's home.

Rabbi Oppenheim was still at the synagogue when he appeared on his doorstep, but he was welcomed in by Yosef, the rabbi's son, a young man in his early twenties.

"So you are the famous Kabbalist," said Yosef Oppenheim as he showed him into an opulent sitting room. "Would you mind if I entertained you until my father comes home?"

"I'm not famous," said Chayun, "and I'm not much of a Kabbalist. I'm just a simple Jew trying to serve the Almighty to the best of his ability."

Yosef smiled. "I like that. You see, I have a strong interest in Kabbalah. I have a large collection of Kabbalistic works ... well, actually, it's not my collection. It's my father's library. It was left to him by his famous uncle Shmuel Oppenheim, who the Emperor's banker in Vienna. He was probably the richest Jew in Europe, and when he died he left my father his library. Would you like to see it?"

Chayun sensed that the young man wanted something from him, and he did not want to let the opportunity of establishing a bond with him slip by.

"I certainly would, but it doesn't have to be right now," he said. "Perhaps a different time. According to what I've been taught, a person should focus on where he finds himself rather than on where he would like to be."

"Yes, yes, I understand what you're saying. It's a very deep thought, but it speaks to me. I often find myself torn between where I am and where I will be, and you've given me the answer. Focus on where you are."

"Exactly, and right now I'm here talking with you. That means that right now what is happening between you and me is more important than a visit to the fabulous library. After all, even the holiest books are not alive, and therefore, they do not compare to the holiness of the simplest person."

"Yes, yes, it's so true, so true," said the young man, his word coming out in breathless bursts. "You cannot imagine how exciting this is for me. Do you mind if I ask you some questions?"

"Questions? About what?"

"Just some questions I've been thinking about. They have to do with my studies in Kabbalah."

"But why would you ask me?" said Chayun. "I'm just a simple man with no more than the tiniest bits of knowledge and understanding. Why don't you ask Rabbi Naphtali Kohein, the famous Kabbalist who lives here in Prague?"

"I've tried, believe me," said Yosef, "but my conversations with him are not satisfying. With you I feel a connection. I can sense that you will understand my questions better than I understand them myself."

"I doubt that very much," said Chayun. "But you've been so gracious to me, I cannot refuse you. Ask me what you wish, and I'll do my best to give you answers."

The young man eagerly plunged into his thoughts about the Kabbalah, which only revealed his confusion and lack of understanding. But Chayun was at his charming best. He guided the young man's words into altogether unexpected directions and formulated his words into clever questions that had never crossed his mind. The young man was amazed and delighted at his own cleverness, and he thirstily drank in every word Chayun spoke in response.

The sound of a door closing interrupted their conversation.

"I think my father is home," said the young man. "I'll go and tell him you're here. He heard that you were in Prague, but that you were in seclusion. He will be pleased that you came to him first as soon as you came out of seclusion."

"Well, of course. He is the chief rabbi of Prague, the king. Doesn't the Gemara say that the rabbis are the true kings?[75] Whom should I have visited first if not your father?"

"I'll be right back."

The young man was away for a while, and when he returned he was excited. "I told my father about you and our conversations, and he was pleased. He is eager to meet you. Please come with me."

Rabbi Oppenheim was a middle-aged man of distinguished bearing. He shook Chayun's hand and showed him to a comfortable chair. Yosef remained standing respectfully near the door.

"So what brings you to Prague?" said Rabbi Oppenheim.

"My life's work," said Chayun. "I've stayed away from public view for most of my life and concentrated on my writing, and now I feel the time has come to bring my thoughts to all Jewish people. Much of what I write is what I have learned from others, so I cannot take credit for the brilliance of some of the concepts, but I do know that they will illuminate the world."

"Illuminate the world, eh? That is an ambitious goal."

"It is true," blurted the young man standing at the door. "I've heard just a little bit, and I feel that my life is illuminated."

"Yes, you did mention that, my son," said Rabbi Oppenheim. He turned back to Chayun. "So have you shown any of your work to other rabbis?"

"Oh, yes. Absolutely." He opened his pouch and took out a copy of the book he had printed in Venice and a sheaf of papers. "This is a small part of my work I printed in Venice last year with the approval and encouragement of the rabbis." He handed the rabbi the sheaf of papers. "And these are among my most precious possessions. They are letters of endorsement from the most prominent rabbis of Yerushalayim. Here, please read them."

Rabbi Oppenheim took the letters and read them with reverence.

"This is amazing," he said. "I don't believe I've ever seen such enthusiastic endorsements. They hold you in the highest esteem."

"As I said before," said Chayun, dropping his eyes with humility, "their enthusiasm is not for me personally but for the work itself. It is for the ideas of the great thinkers who came before me whose insights into Kabbalah I have united and compiled. And perhaps just a little bit for the few meager words of clarification and discussion I have added. They believe that my book will advance the study of Kabbalah in a major way, and I thank the Almighty for giving me the privilege of participating in such an important undertaking."

"I am impressed," said Rabbi Oppenheim as he handed back the letters. "Take care of those. And you should also show them to Rabbi Naphtali Kohein." He paused. "My son has asked me to help you. So tell me, is there anything you would like me to do for you?"

"Well, a letter from the illustrious chief rabbi of Prague to add to my august collection of letters would be a wondrous gift."

"It will be my pleasure," said Rabbi Oppenheim. "Leave your book with me for a little while. My son will let you know when the letter is ready."

Satisfied that he had secured this important letter, Chayun settled into the rhythms of his new life in Prague. His goal was still to print his complete book in Amsterdam, where he would gain the fame and wealth that he deserved. But he was patient. When he arrived in Amsterdam with the books he had published in Venice and the books he would publish in Prague, with the support of the rabbis of both cities and with the sheaf of forged letters from Yerushalayim, his conquest would be irresistible.

In the meantime, as he bided his time, he opened his doors to the public and began to grant private audiences. His disciples spread the word that the holy man did not take money from people who came for his blessings but that they could ask to purchase his book before they stated their requests.

This was recommended, since it would cause the holy man to view them with favor. Since there was no specific price for the book, each person could give whatever he chose to give, but of course, the greater the gift the more favor would be gained and the more effective the blessing would be.

He also took his emergence from seclusion a step further by delivering sermons in public that were unlike anything the people had ever heard. Often speaking for an hour or more, he ranged from simple thoughts on the weekly portion to humorous stories and observations to discussions of the deepest mysteries that no one could follow. But follow or not, the crowds were large, and they sat there mesmerized by his charisma and his colorful character

On Shabbos, Chayun conducted lavish feasts replete with the finest wines and foods. Numerous people crowded into his dining room to see the holy man's face aglow with the holiness of the holy day. They strained to hear his voice raised in Kabbalistic song or mellifluously presenting Kabbalistic thoughts on the Torah. On occasion, when the candles burned low and the mood was exalted, he would invite Yosef Oppenheim, a frequent visitor, to sit beside him, and he would share with all the assembled some of the secrets that he claimed the prophet Eliahu had revealed to him personally. And during all this time, with the help of his talented disciples, he performed many of his wonders and miracles.

After he had been in Prague for several months, Chayun received his letter of recommendation from Rabbi David Oppenheim. Rabbi Oppenheim had looked into his book a few times, but he did not have time to review it at length. Nonetheless, he kept it on his desk in the hope that he would find some spare time to familiarize himself more intimately with Chayun's work. But as time dragged on and as his son Yosef pressured him, Rabbi Oppenheim relented and wrote the letter, basing his endorsement on the letters of the rabbis of Yerushalayim. It did not occur to him that they were forgeries.

A few months later, in 1712, Chayun received a letter of recommendation from Rabbi Naphtali Kohein as well. The road to Amsterdam beckoned, but he could not expect to take the city by storm if he came with just a manuscript and a small excerpt. He had to print a few copies and distribute them to the rabbis and the wealthy community leaders. Then he could ask for their financial support to help him publish his book in large quantities, using the best production techniques available, thus ensuring that it would be sold and studied all over the Jewish world. That would be his moment of triumph.

On the recommendation of a local agent who represented a number of printers in different cities, he decided to print his *Mehemnutha de Kulla* in Berlin along with a collection of his sermons entitled *Divrei Nechemiah.* In late 1712, he left Prague and traveled to Berlin, where he rented a house for himself and his disciples.

Well-funded and eager to move on to Amsterdam, Chayun did not waste time putting on mystical performances for the Jewish community of Berlin. At the first opportunity, he visited Rabbi Aharon Binyamin Wolff, the chief rabbi, and showed him his *Raza d'Yichudah,* the excerpt printed in Venice, and his full manuscript. He also showed him the letters from Rabbi Oppenheim and Rabbi Kohein of Prague. Rabbi Wolff was familiar with their correspondence, and he read their letters with interest. Then Chayun presented the sheaf of forged letters purportedly from the rabbis of Yerushalayim. Rabbi Wolff was suitably impressed. He glanced briefly at the manuscript and gave Chayun a letter of recommendation and permission to print his books in Berlin.

The printing establishment the Jewish community of Berlin patronized was just outside the Jewish quarter. A short middle-aged man with hands stained black by ink greeted him at the door.

"You must be Rabbi Chayun," he said. "My name is Moshe Krantz. Rabbi Wolff said that you would be coming by, and he asked me take good care of you. You're in good hands here. My partner will take care of you today. His name is Hans Gunther Wieselthier. He's an old German with a white beard bigger than any I've ever seen on a rabbi, heh heh. But he's strong as an ox." He turned and called out to the back of the shop. "Hans! Come out here. We have a distinguished customer."

Wieselthier came out wearing a leather apron large enough to cover his vast girth. He was wiping his ink-stained hands on a dirty towel.

"Hello, rabbi," he said with a friendly smile. "You don't really want to shake my hand right now. When the ink dries we can shake hands. In the meantime, we can shake hands in spirit."

"Shake hands in spirit," repeated Chayun. "I like that."

"Sometimes I'm tempted to wipe my hands in my beard," said Wieselthier. "Then I'd look thirty years younger. Anyway, rabbi, enough about my hands. What can we do for you?"

"I have two books that I want to print."

Chayun put his manuscripts on the table. They were large and bulky, and Wieselthier eyed them with interest. He lifted the larger one gingerly and riffled through the closely written pages.

"But I don't need too many copies," Chayun added hastily. "You see, it's a little complicated."

Wieselthier smiled at him. "Let me see if I can figure it out. You really want to print your books in Amsterdam. You just need some copies to get you by until then."

Chayun's eyes opened wide. "How did you know that?"

Wieselthier laughed heartily and his eyes twinkled. "You're not the first one to have such plans, rabbi," he said.

"Don't tell my partner Moshe that I said this, but we can't compare to Amsterdam. We do good work here, very good work, but we simply don't have the equipment and the fonts that are available in Amsterdam. Who knows what the future will bring? But right now, Amsterdam is in a class by itself."

Chayun nodded. "That's what I heard, and I want only the best for my book. So you'll do it for me?"

"Of course, rabbi. It will be my pleasure. I love working with Jewish people. They're so sincere and idealistic. I've helped some of them print books in Amsterdam before. It's not easy for someone unfamiliar with the process. The printing presses are very busy there, and it's hard to get personal attention. In fact, I just brought a Jewish client to Amsterdam last year, and three years ago, I helped a group of Jews from Poland print a prayer book in Amsterdam."

"So you're saying I should hire you to come with me to Amsterdam?"

Wieselthier chuckled. "Well, if you're really rich you could do that. I'd have to charge you a lot of money to make a special trip to Amsterdam. But —"

"I'm not rich."

"I didn't think you were, rabbi. But I'm going to be in Amsterdam in July anyway. If you come to Amsterdam about that time, I'll guide you through the process. It's going to take some time anyway to print your copies here in Berlin. It's a long process to set the type for such a large manuscript, and then you'll have to proofread every word to make sure there are no mistakes. By the time your books are ready, it'll be close to when I'll be going to Amsterdam."

"The arrangement sounds good to me," said Chayun. "Let's get started here with the copies I need. And then I'll meet you in Amsterdam."

FIRST CONFRONTATIONS · 20

O N A WARM JUNE DAY IN 1713, Rabbi Shlomo Ayllon was sitting in his office with Sebastian Dominguez. They were discussing a fund-raising campaign for the Sephardic community of Eretz Yisrael. Rabbi Moshe Chagiz, the emissary from Eretz Yisrael, had been in Amsterdam for some time already, laying the groundwork for a major campaign, and now it was time to make it a reality.

"I think the entire campaign will take several months," said Sebastian. "We need to begin with some speeches and talks by the rabbi to warm up the people. Then we have to pay personal visits to all the people of means and secure commitments from them. Then we have to collect the pledged money and hand it over to Rabbi Chagiz. Yes, I would say several months."

Rabbi Ayllon stroked his white beard and nodded. "Yes, I think that's about right. But I'm sure that under your guidance, Senhor Dominguez, the campaign will be a big success."

"You are too kind," said Sebastian. "I'm sure a more capable person could accomplish the task more quickly."

Rabbi Ayllon brushed aside the remark. "You're as capable as they come. And to tell you the truth, I don't mind having Rabbi Chagiz here for a few more months. He is such an interesting person and so full of life. Whenever he walks into the synagogue, he lights up all the faces. Amsterdam will feel empty when he returns to Eretz Yisrael. I will miss him."

"So will all of us," said Sebastian. "And I think Chacham Tzvi will miss him more than anyone else. He and Rabbi Chagiz have become very close, according to what I hear."

"I've heard the same. What have you heard about Chacham Tzvi's situation? Has it changed in any way?"

"Not to my knowledge. His enemies would love nothing more than to drive him out of Amsterdam. In fact, according to my information, the directors of the Ashkenaz community haven't paid his salary in months."

Rabbi Ayllon's eyes opened wide. "Really? Are you sure?"

"Well, I can never be completely sure unless I see the actual records, but my source is extremely reliable."

"Rabbi Strasbourg?"

Sebastian shook his head. "No, Rabbi Strasbourg wouldn't know such a thing, and if he did, he wouldn't talk about it, even to me. No, I have a different source, a very reliable source. It seems that some of the directors on the board are demanding that he return his letter of appointment, which basically means that he should resign. In the meantime, these directors are blocking the release of funds to pay his salary. They insist that when he resigns they'll give him all the accumulated back salary being withheld from him now. But Chacham Tzvi refuses to resign. He sees no justification for such a demand other than his refusal to bow to their wishes. So they're at an impasse. These directors are now insisting that when his three-year term expires, his contract should not be renewed, but Chacham Tzvi insists they cannot do so without justification."

"Terrible situation."

"Yes, it is. And if it wouldn't be for the support of influential men in our own community, the Ashkenazim would have driven him out long ago."

"People like you, Senhor Dominguez."

"Better people than I am, but it is true that I am also among Chacham Tzvi's staunch supporters. We Sephardim have the wealth and the influence in the markets and at the Exchange, and we have the ear of the authorities, so there is a limit to how far Chacham Tzvi's enemies can go in their shameful persecution of their illustrious rabbi."

"It is certainly shameful. But how is the rabbi surviving without his salary? How does he live? How does he feed his children? Are you and others helping him out?"

"Many of us would be glad to help him," said Sebastian. "But as you well know, Chacham Tzvi refuses to take gifts or even loans from anyone. So he has really been reduced to poverty. The rent on his house is paid up for a while, I believe. Other than that, he has a small income from some of his investments he made with the merchants in Hamburg."

"A terrible situation," said Rabbi Ayllon. "Is there anything we can do? Can we bring pressure on the directors to release his salary?"

"It gets complicated," said Sebastian. "There is an understanding between our two communities that we should not meddle in each other's internal affairs. So we can exert a little pressure to stop them from driving out and humiliating such a great and holy rabbi, but we cannot get involved in the payment or non-payment of his salary. That would be stepping over the line."

"I understand. And we cannot give him financial support, because he will not accept it. So where does that put us?"

Sebastian shrugged. "Exactly where we are. Upset but powerless."

"Did you know, Senhor Dominguez, that when I was still the rabbi of the London community — this goes back nearly twenty years — I sent him *halachic* questions? Even back then, I already recognized who Chacham Tzvi was. And now I have to sit by here in Amsterdam and see him being persecuted without being able to do anything. It is difficult for me."

The door opened quietly, and the rabbi's attendant peeked in. He cleared his throat to attract the rabbi's attention.

"There's someone here to see you," he said.

"Who is it?"

"I don't know," said the attendant. "He didn't give me his name. He looks to be from Turkey or Eretz Yisrael. He is not wearing European clothes."

Sebastian stood up. "I think we've concluded our business, rabbi. I won't keep your visitor waiting. We'll talk again in a few days."

Sebastian put on his hat, and with a final deferential nod to the rabbi, he walked out of the room. The attendant remained standing in the doorway, waiting for a signal from the rabbi. The rabbi took a sip from a glass of water on his desk and closed his eyes. He remained lost in thought for a few moments. Then he opened his eyes and nodded. The attendant bowed and backed out of the room.

A minute later, the door opened, and a man with a white beard and large brown eyes that glittered with intensity walked into the room. He wore a robe of gold velvet with light blue trim and multicolored sash, and an Oriental turban sat on his head. He was holding a leather pouch in his hands.

"Hello, Shlomo," said the man. "It's been a long time."

Rabbi Ayllon looked at the man without recognition.

"Age changes people, Shlomo," said the man. "And the passage of time fades the memories. But think a moment, don't you recognize me?"

Rabbi Ayllon shook his head. "I'm afraid I don't," he said with a friendly smile. "If we've met before, why don't you refresh my memory?"

"All right," said the man. "Do you remember Salonika? We were friends back then. We spent many long hours in conversation. I don't know if you're the same person you were then, but I haven't changed, my friend. Oh yes, my ideas and beliefs have matured, and I've become more passionate and determined. But I'm the same person you knew back then …. Aha! I see your memory is returning, my friend."

The smile had vanished from Rabbi Ayllon's face and was replaced by a look of consternation. "Nechemiah? Nechemiah Chayun?"

"One and the same," said Chayun as he settled into a chair. "So how have you been, my dear Shlomo? You've certainly worked your way up in the world, haven't you? Chief rabbi of Amsterdam, no less."

Rabbi Ayllon's face was ashen. "What are you doing here, Nechemiah? What do you want from me?"

"Nothing much, Shlomo. Just a friendly welcome, the kind you can expect from an old friend."

"Look, do you want money? I'll give you money. But I want you to leave Amsterdam right away. No one here knows about Salonika. It was a youthful indiscretion. It's part of the forgotten past, and I want it to stay that way."

"You can call it a youthful indiscretion, Shlomo, but you were one of us. You were steeped in our ideas, and you believed we could change the world and bring the final redemption. You were a good Sabbatean, my friend. Now you may have decided that being a Sabbatean in a hostile world was not an advantage. You wouldn't have become the chief rabbi of London, and you certainly would not have become the chief rabbi of Amsterdam, if your history were known. We both know that, don't we?"

Rabbi Ayllon was silent.

"Don't we?" Chayun repeated.

Rabbi Ayllon nodded, but he said nothing.

Chayun flashed him a brilliant smile. "Cheer up, Shlomo. It's not the end of the world. I didn't come here to ruin your little arrangement. You don't have to worry that I'm going to expose your history."

"So what do you want from me?"

"Just a little cooperation."

"What do you mean?"

"I've spent my life putting together a manuscript," said Chayun. "It's a presentation of some of the most fundamental Kabbalistic principles in very careful language." He opened his pouch, took out a copy of the book he had printed in Berlin and placed it on the table. "Here. This is my gift to you."

Rabbi Ayllon stared at the book but made no move to touch it. "What do you mean by careful language?" he said.

"It's quite simple, Shlomo. The book is based on all the concepts we learned in Salonika. But in certain areas, the language is deliberately vague. Once the ideas, even in this form, spread among the rabbis and the scholars, they will be much more fertile ground for the fuller version of what we believe. Sometimes, the truth has to be given to people in small doses. That is what I dedicated my life to do."

"So what do you want from me?"

"I only printed a limited number of copies of my book in Berlin, because I wanted to do the main printing here in Amsterdam, where the book can be produced with a beauty and clarity beyond compare. So what do I need from you? I need your permission to sell my book in Amsterdam and to raise money to print my book here. That's not so much, is it?"

Rabbi Ayllon stared at him without responding. His face was pasty, and his chest heaved.

"Come, come, Shlomo. If I didn't know better, I would think that you're not so excited to see your old friend."

"I want you to leave, Nechemiah. I don't want anything to do with you."

"You don't always get what you want. That's the way life is. I'm not going anywhere, and you're going to help me. I'm not giving you a choice in the matter. Do you understand me?"

Rabbi Ayllon took a deep breath and nodded.

Chayun smiled. "So let's talk about how we're going to do this. But first, Shlomo, have you really abandoned the ideas of your youth? Are you still one of us in your heart?"

"As I told you before, those times were a youthful indiscretion. I would take them back if I could."

"But you can't, so you have to deal with reality."

"I'm against what you're trying to do, Nechemiah."

"That's unfortunate. But you will help me anyway, won't you?"

Rabbi Ayllon bit his lower lip and nodded.

Chayun laughed. "So your precious position is more important to you than your precious principles. I'm not surprised."

"You don't understand."

"Then why don't you explain it to me?"

"It's for my son," said Rabbi Ayllon. "He's one of the young rabbis in the community. If you told people about what I did forty years ago, it would hurt my son."

"That's very noble of you, Shlomo. And it has nothing to do with risking this comfortable situation you have here?"

"It's mostly about my son."

"All right," said Chayun. "I'll leave it at that. So what's the next step?"

"Do you have any letters of recommendation?"

Chayun pulled his sheaf of letters from the pouch and held them up in front of Rabbi Ayllon's face. "Yes, I do," he said. "So just give me a letter of your own, put in a good word for me here and there, and I'll go to work. My printer from Berlin is coming to Amsterdam in a few days. By the time he gets here, we should be ready to start the process."

"I'm not going to give you a letter."

"Shlomo," said Chayun, his voice full of menace.

"I can't give you a letter. I just can't do it. But I'll turn the book over to a panel of our rabbis. I'll tell them that it seems fine to me but I'd like them to take a closer look at it."

"All right," said Chayun. "I'll accept that."

A few days later, Rabbi Ayllon introduced Nechemiah Chayun to Rabbi Pinhas Felipe Dominguez and Rabbi Shamai Cohen, the two junior rabbis he had selected to review the book. Chayun gave each of them a copy of the book, and he also entrusted his sheaf of letters to them. These two rabbis were familiar with Kabbalah but did not have an intimate knowledge of it.

That evening, Hans Gunther Wieselthier visited Chayun in his rooms.

"I just arrived this morning, rabbi," said the printer. "I'm ready to start the process, that is, if you are. Did you take care of whatever you needed to do?"

"Yes, I did, Herr Wieselthier. I still have to raise the money for the printing, but that should be no problem. I'm good at that. I just have to get the permissions."

"Is there a problem? Is there any reason why they should not give you permission? I mean, you're a well-known rabbi."

"There's no problem. They have to be extra careful. But it's just a formality. I should have the letter of endorsement in my hands within days."

Wieselthier rumbled to his feet. "Good, I'm glad to hear that. Now I have to go and put these old bones of mine to sleep. It's been a hard day."

The books and the letters remained lying on the table in the rabbi's room for two days before Felipe and Shamai could give them the proper attention. In the meantime, other rabbis who wandered into the room from time to time glanced at them and were duly impressed, especially by the letters of the rabbis of Yerushalayim.

Word of their existence reached Rabbi Moshe Chagiz. His interest was piqued, and he came to the room where the books and the letters lay. First, he read the letters. They seemed authentic, but he couldn't be sure. Then he picked up a copy of the book and started to read. After reading a few pages, he sat bolt upright, and the small hairs on the back of his neck began to tingle. As he read more and more, he felt a sinking sensation in the pit of his stomach.

This did not sound right. The differences from the standard Kabbalistic approach were subtle but unmistakable. What did he have here in his hands? Was this simply an innocent variation? Or was this a subtly disguised book of heresies? And who was this author? The title page identified him as Chayun, not an uncommon name. One of his brothers-in-law was Moshe Chayun, married to his father's daughter by an earlier marriage. His father, the celebrated Rabbi Yaakov Chagiz, had died when he was a little child, and he had never had any contact with his father's other children, all of whom were much, much older than he was. In fact, some of them had children who were much older than he was.

Could this Nechemiah Chayun be connected to my family? thought Rabbi Chagiz. Could he be my nephew? Could this Chayun be the same Chayun who had been banned in Yerushalayim a few years earlier? If so, all these letters from the rabbis of Yerushalayim must be forgeries.

For a long time, Rabbi Chagiz stared at the book in his hands, unsure of how to proceed. Finally, he decided to take the book to Chacham Tzvi. He would recognize it for what it was.

It was late at night when Rabbi Chagiz knocked in Chacham Tzvi's door.

"I'm sorry for the late hour," he said as soon as he came in.

"Don't mention it," said Chacham Tzvi. "If it weren't urgent you wouldn't have come. What's on your mind?"

"This," said Rabbi Chagiz, and he handed the book to Chacham Tzvi with a brief explanation of how it came into his possession.

Without another word, Chacham Tzvi sat down near a candle and began to read. He continued to read for an hour without saying a single word or uttering a sound. Finally, he sighed heavily and closed the book.

"It's a piece of Sabbatean chicanery," he said. "There's no doubt about it. And the author is Nechemiah Chayun. I met the man over thirty-five years ago in Sarajevo."

"Sarajevo! I had a brother-in-law there. Moshe Chayun.[76] I never met him, but I know he lived in Sarajevo."

"That's Nechemiah Chayun's father," said Chacham Tzvi. "I met both father and son when I was there. Nechemiah presented himself as a mystical person, but I don't recall him making Sabbatean statements."

"He concealed it, just as in his book," said Rabbi Chagiz. "He wanted to attract people, and admitting he was a Sabbatean wouldn't have been helpful. The man is probably my nephew, although I've never met him before. I believe he's the same Chayun who was banned in Yerushalayim a few years ago. All those letters of his must be forgeries. So what do we do?"

"Go to Rabbi Dominguez and Rabbi Cohen. Tell them what we've discovered. The man must be expelled from Amsterdam and his book banned."

The next day, Rabbi Chagiz sought out Rabbi Dominguez and Rabbi Cohen and told them all about what had transpired the previous night. The three men went together to Rabbi Ayllon, but he was strangely reluctant to get involved. Perhaps it was a mistake, he insisted. There was no reason to be hasty. The three men exchanged suspicious glances. They tried again to persuade him to take decisive action, but his timidity persisted.

After leaving Rabbi Ayllon's house, Rabbi Chagiz suggested they return to Chacham Tzvi and tell him what had transpired. Chacham Tzvi was disturbed by Rabbi Ayllon's reluctance to take a stand against Chayun. There was no question that the book was heretical and that it simply could not be allowed to be printed. There was only one choice.

Right then and there, Chacham Tzvi took the responsibility on his own shoulders and issued a ban against the book, forbidding it from being printed in Amsterdam and anywhere else.[77]

The announcement of Chacham Tzvi's ban caused an immediate uproar in the Sephardic synagogue, and Chayun was asked to leave and never show his face in Amsterdam again. But Chayun was not so easily defeated. He went to see Rabbi Ayllon, but he was told that the rabbi was not feeling well and was unavailable. Chayun was not surprised, nor was he discouraged. Rabbi Ayllon could not hide from him forever. In the morning, he went to see Wieselthier and told him what had happened.

"A ban?" said the old printer. "Why would they ban a rabbi's book? And does this mean that our project is finished?"

"No, it doesn't mean that at all," said Chayun. "It's a temporary misunderstanding, and once I get to speak to Rabbi Ayllon it will be straightened out very quickly. We'll just have to suspend the process for a little while. I can't impose on you to wait here in Amsterdam while —"

"Don't even think of it," said the printer. "I have my own business here that will keep me busy for a while, and if I have to stay here a little longer, it's no problem. Where would I be running? Is there anything very exciting waiting for me back in Berlin? But this business promises to be really exciting. I wouldn't want to miss it."

"Well, I appreciate that, Herr Wieselthier."

"Can I make a suggestion?"

"Sure."

"I'm an old man," said the printer, "and I've learned that it's always good to take the bull by the horns, so to speak."

"What do you mean?"

"I would like to take you to see this rabbi who issued the ban. Make your case that he should retract his ban. I'll tell him that it's hurting my business, and since I'm a Christian, he won't brush me off so fast. He'll also have to treat you more politely than if you went by yourself."

A broad smile spread across Chayun's face. "Herr Wieselthier, I am delighted that you're on my side in this thing. I wouldn't want to have you against me."

Wieselthier chuckled and slapped Chayun on the back. "I'm not on anyone's side. I just want to see this beautiful book come to life. I'm on the side of peace and harmony, that's all. So are we going?"

"Yes. He should be home in about an hour."

"Fine. So while we wait, would you like to share a beer with me, rabbi?"

"I certainly would."

They arrived at Chacham Tzvi's home around noon. His sixteen-year-old son Yaakov opened the door. He instantly recognized Chayun and tried to keep him out, but the mountainous German printer intimidated him into allowing them to enter. He announced their presence to Chacham Tzvi, who was in his office together with Rav Amos, filling him in on the details of the sordid affair. Chacham Tzvi instructed Yaakov to show them in.

Chacham Tzvi was sitting at his desk with Rav Amos standing to his right. Chayun planted himself in front of the desk, while Wieselthier hung back, holding his three-cornered hat in his hands.

"So we meet again, Nechemiah," said Chacham Tzvi. "You look a little older."

"As do the two of you," said Chayun. He leaned across the desk and brandished his fist in the air. "Do you know what you've done to me? You've ruined my life."

Chacham Tzvi sat there imperviously. He did not bother to respond.

"How could you do this to me?" screamed Chayun. "And how could you do it to this gentleman here?"

Chacham Tzvi glanced at Wieselthier for the first time. "And who is this gentleman?" he said.

Wieselthier cleared his throat. "With all due respect, rabbi. My name is Hans Gunther Wieselthier. I'm a printer. I was contracted to print Rabbi Chayun's book. If you ban the book, I will suffer a heavy loss."

"I see," said Chacham Tzvi. "But the book is full of heresies, Herr Wieselthier. Are you suggesting that I lift the ban so that you should not lose business? This book, if it is printed, could cause serious damage to thousands of people. Are you suggesting that I allow that to happen? Would you want that on your conscience?"

"I don't know, rabbi. I'm a simple printer, and all I know is my business. Rabbi Chayun says the book is not heretical, and you say it is. What should I think?"

"I can't tell you what to think, sir. I can only tell you that I have a responsibility to protect the people in my community. If you feel I'm wrong, why don't you bring it up with the other rabbis?"

"Maybe I will."

"Listen here, Chacham Tzvi," said Chayun. "I thought we had made a connection in Sarajevo many years ago. I thought we were friends."

"I'm not responsible for what you thought," said Chacham Tzvi. "You're a Sabbatean, and you are not my friend."

"It's a lie," shouted Chayun. "A slanderous lie. How can you accuse me of something like that? Just because I pray in the fields and live in the world of Kabbalah, you accuse me of being a Sabbatean? Who gives you the right?"

"I read a big part of your book, Nechemiah," said Chacham Tzvi. "It's as clear to me as the midday sun."

"It's your imagination. There nothing Sabbatean in my book."

"Look," Chacham Tzvi, "I'm not going to get into an argument with you. I did what I did, because that's what I think is right. That's all I can say."

"I have a question, Nechemiah," said Rav Amos. "Did you ever marry?"

Chayun bristled. "What does that have to do with anything? So what if I never married? What does that mean? I've devoted my life to my work. Herr Wieselthier, did you ever get married?"

"No, I've had the good luck to remain free all my life," said the old printer.

"What's your point, Strasbourg?" said Chayun.

Rav Amos shrugged. "I just wanted to know."

"Well, you got your answer," snapped Chayun. "Come, Herr Wieselthier, there's nothing more to accomplish here."

Chayun stormed out of Chacham Tzvi's house with Wieselthier trailing close behind.

"Go back to your inn, Herr Wieselthier," said Chayun. "I'm going to see Ayllon, and it has to be by myself."

"Good luck, and let me know what happens," said the printer. "If there's anything I can do to help, please call on me. I didn't like this rabbi, and I didn't care much for his second fiddle. They look like arrogant people to me. Who are they to sit in judgment on your book?"

"My sentiments exactly."[78]

BATTLE LINES ARE DRAWN · 21

CHAYUN KNOCKED ON THE door of Rabbi Ayllon's house. A servant opened the door and told him that the rabbi was ailing and unavailable. Chayun banged on the door with all his might and shouted at the top of his lungs. The servant came running again.

"You tell the rabbi," said Chayun, "that if he doesn't see me right now, I will scream and shout until everyone knows what I have to say."

The servant scurried away. He returned momentarily and ushered Chayun into the rabbi's study.

"What kind of business is this, Shlomo?" he fumed. "You let Chacham Tzvi stab me in the back, and then you lock your door and refuse to see me? What kind of a man are you? Making believe you're sick, of all things. Did you think I'd believe you? And how long did you think you could avoid me?"

Rabbi Ayllon began to tremble. "I wasn't faking," he sputtered. "Your coming here has made me physically ill. I'm running a fever, my stomach is in revolt, and I feel as if my heart is going to give out at any moment."

"Pull yourself together, my friend. You have work to do."

"What do you mean?"

"You have to overturn the ban on my book."

"And why should I do it?"

"Because I'll ruin you if you don't."

"But how am I supposed to do it? Didn't you see the reaction in the synagogue when Chacham Tzvi issued the ban? They adore him. Why, they practically threw you out bodily. What do you think I can do?"

"If you think they adore him so much, why don't you just resign and give him your position? That would solve many problems, wouldn't it? According to what I hear, he's having serious problems with his directors. They're even holding back his salary."

"How do you know that?" said Rabbi Ayllon sharply.

"I know many things, Shlomo. So why don't you just turn over your position to Chacham Tzvi? You don't want to do that, do you?"

Rabbi Ayllon shook his head. "No, I don't. I'm the chief rabbi of Amsterdam. He's not even Sephardic."

"Exactly," said Chayun. "Now you're beginning to make sense. Go convince your people to stand on their own feet. Otherwise, they'll bounce you out as fast as they bounced me out. I promise you that."

"All right."

"I'm going back to my inn. I'll be waiting to hear from you."

Rabbi Ayllon called an emergency meeting in his home for that very night. Sebastian Dominguez, Aharon de Pinto[79] and Benito Carvajal represented the Maamad, Felipe Dominguez, Shamai Cohen and three others represented the rabbinate.

"My dear friends," Rabbi Ayllon began, "we are facing a crisis tonight in our beloved Sephardic community of Amsterdam. You are all aware of what happened with Rabbi Chayun's book, I'm sure."

"I thought it's all over," said Sebastian. "He's been sent away, and good riddance, I say. I don't see a crisis or even a problem."

"Neither do I," said Shamai Cohen. "And why do you call him Rabbi Chayun? He's a Sabbatean."

"Who says he's a Sabbatean?" said Rabbi Ayllon.

"Chacham Tzvi says so," said Shamai. "He knows what he's talking about."

"Oh, he certainly knows what he's talking about," said Rabbi Ayllon. "No one denies his towering greatness. But that is exactly the problem. Here's a man who comes into Amsterdam, a Sephardic man, and he approaches me, the Sephardic rabbi, to approve his book and help him find supporters among the community, the Sephardic community, and I turned the book over for review to two very capable rabbis, Sephardic rabbis, to make a determination of what the community, the Sephardic community, should do about this man and his book. Is there anything I said that wasn't accurate?"

No one spoke.

"I take that as a no. So here is the situation. Is the Sephardic community capable of dealing with its own issues? I would think that the answer is yes. The Sephardic community of Amsterdam is probably the most prominent and illustrious Sephardic community in the whole world. So why is it that Chacham Tzvi, who is the rabbi of the Ashkenazic community, and an Ashkenazic rabbi despite the Sephardic title that he likes to apply to himself, how is it that this great, great Ashkenazic rabbi — I say it again, Ashkenazic rabbi — takes upon himself the right and the privilege of ruling on a question that is a Sephardic question and should be addressed by Sephardic rabbis?"

"All right, rabbi," said Sebastian. "Maybe you have a point, but what's done is done. The man's a Sabbatean, and we're fortunate that he's gone. You can say a word to Chacham Tzvi to be more diplomatic in the future."

"I don't agree," said Aharon de Pinto. "This is a serious business. It seems to me that it threatens to undermine the standing of our community."

"My point exactly," said Rabbi Ayllon. "We have a phenomenal community. The Netherlands took us in because we were the cream of Spanish and Portuguese society. We had wealth and skill, and we helped transform the Netherlands into a world power, economically and militarily. We are the ones who are close to the government. The Ashkenazic community grew up here because of our benevolence and charity. These first Tudescos were poor and bedraggled, and we helped them form a strong community. But we're the older brother here, not they. True, they imported a world-class rabbi from Hamburg — and those ignorant persecutors don't even appreciate him — but it shouldn't change the relationship between our communities. If we let this happen, if we let Chacham Tzvi dictate to us on our internal business, we can forget about the balance of power being in our favor. We'll become the younger brother, and they'll be the older brother. Do you want this to happen?"

A few of them shook their heads. The others sat stone-faced.

"And how about the honor of your rabbi?" continued Rabbi Ayllon. He bit his lips, and his eyes filled with tears. "How about my humiliation? What will people think of me now that ...?"

He broke down and wept openly. Everyone sat still, while the rabbi tried to regain control of himself.[80]

"It's not my personal honor that's important," he said when he could finally speak without weeping. "I'm not important. But my honor as your rabbi, as the representative of the Sephardic community, as its head and its face, yes, in that context my honor is very important. If you humiliate me, you humiliate the entire community. I have been sidelined and humiliated here. I had this book thrust in my face, and I was presented with an ultimatum. I said that we shouldn't be so hasty. What was the rush? We should take our time and look into this matter carefully. Isn't that what I said Rabbi Dominguez?"

"Well, you didn't …"

"Did I say we shouldn't be hasty?"

"Yes."

"There you have it," said Rabbi Ayllon with triumph. "Don't be hasty. A man's life and reputation are at stake. Don't rush to judgment. Think it through carefully. A very reasonable approach, I would say, don't you think so? But no, that wasn't good enough. Chacham Tzvi couldn't wait. He had made up his mind, and he had to have his way immediately. It appears to me that he sees himself as being the rabbi of all of Amsterdam, the Ashkenazim and the Sephardim. But we're not ready for such a capitulation. Our glorious community is not ready to become a satellite of the Ashkenazic community. We have our customs and our traditions and our history, yes, and even our foods, and they're holy to us, they're our sacred heritage. We aren't ready yet to roll over and become Ashkenazim."

"So what are you saying?" said Sebastian. "What do you propose we do?"

"I propose that we counteract Chacham Tzvi's ban in our community. I propose that we recall Rabbi Chayun and give him full honors and support. I propose that we give a ringing endorsement to his book and give full permission and encouragement to have it published right here in Amsterdam."

"But, Rabbi Ayllon!" Felipe protested. "The man is a Sabbatean. The book is full of heresy. How can we do what you're proposing?"

"Look, Rabbi Dominguez, we can't know for sure that he's a Sabbatean unless we make our own investigation. But let's say, for argument's sake, that he's a Sabbatean, and let's even say, for argument's sake, that his book contains heresy. How much damage can it do? What is it anyway? An obscure book about Kabbalistic things that no one understands anyway. And if there's heresy in it, it's oh so subtle. Look at all the rabbis who gave letters of endorsement. Rabbi Oppenheim and Rabbi Kohein of Prague, Rabbi Wolff of Berlin, the rabbis of Venice, and let's not forget all those Yerushalayim rabbis. No one caught on but Chacham Tzvi. Can you imagine how subtle and faint the heresy must be even if it's there? So whom will it affect? Whom will it hurt?" He paused. "Who here thinks this book poses a terrible danger?"

No one spoke up.

"But there is a terrible threat," said Rabbi Ayllon. "There's a terrible threat to the integrity of our community. It's tottering right now, and we have to stabilize it. The only way is to declare our independence in no uncertain terms. Chacham Tzvi may be the greatest rabbi in the world, but our community has its own chief rabbi, it has its own staff of outstanding rabbis, and we are capable of making our own decisions. And unless we ask for outside assistance it should not be offered. And no one has the right to issue rulings for our community except for our own rabbis. Are we all agreed?"

"I agree," said Aharon de Pinto.

Shamai Cohen shifted uncomfortably in his seat. "This is very difficult for me," he said. "I love Chacham Tzvi, as you all know, but there are broader issues here." He sighed. "If I'm forced to take a stance, I have to side with you, Rabbi Ayllon. My first loyalty is to the Sephardic community. The integrity of our community must be protected."

"I'm with Senhor de Pinto and Rabbi Cohen," said Benito Carvajal.

"I'm not comfortable with this," said Sebastian. "It doesn't seem right to me. How can we endorse the book of a man who's probably a Sabbatean?"

"Honestly, Senhor Dominguez," said Aharon de Pinto. "Are you a little concerned about the reaction of your good friend Rabbi Amos Strasbourg?"

"It's crossed my mind," Sebastian admitted. "But I'd like to think that my friendship with Rabbi Strasbourg makes me more sensitive to right and wrong, and this feels wrong to me. Somehow, I feel we can protect the integrity of our community without stooping to endorse a Sabbatean and defy Chacham Tzvi."

"Listen to your own words," said Shamai Cohen. "To defy Chacham Tzvi. Those are the words you said. Why are we in a position of defying or not defying Chacham Tzvi? He's not one of us. I agree with Rabbi Ayllon. We have to make a strong statement, and we have to make it right now."

"I don't understand you, Shamai," said Sebastian. "You were so devoted to Chacham Tzvi that some of us were concerned that you were becoming Ashkenazic. And now you just abandon him when you see opposition mounting against him."

"Senhor Dominguez, I don't agree with you," said Rabbi Ayllon. "Rabbi Cohen is not abandoning a great rabbi whom he admired. He is facing a conflict in his loyalties, and he has decided that his first loyalty is to his own community. Now I'm not advocating a battle with Chacham Tzvi. I'm saying we should take a moderate approach. We should be cool and level-headed and think clearly. We need to say in a calm manner that Rabbi Chayun is our business, and we will deal with him as we see fit. We have to tell Chacham Tzvi very politely that he should not issue rulings for our community unless we ask for his opinion. We will then conduct our own investigation, and when it is over, we will endorse the book, and this whole affair will end."

"I'm not against doing that in a very respectful way," said Sebastian. "But endorsing a Sabbatean and his book? That's going too far."

"We have to make a stand on the issue at hand," said Shamai.

"This is a critical time for our community," said Aharon de Pinto. "We've discussed this long enough. Our rabbi, the one that we've chosen, the Sephardic rabbi who's the face of our community, as he said, has taken a position, and I think we have to decide if we are with our rabbi or against him. I, for one, am with him. How about the rest of you? Benito Carvajal, with the rabbi or against him?"

"With him."

"Shamai Cohen, with the rabbi or against him?"

"With him."

The three rabbis also sided with the chief rabbi.

"That leaves the Dominguez brothers," said Aharon de Pinto. "Sebastian Dominguez, with the rabbi or against him?"

Sebastian felt his heart pounding at his chest. He didn't know what to say.

"Sebastian, with our rabbi or against him?"

"I … this is very difficult …"

"Yes, it is," said Aharon de Pinto. "It's time to make a difficult decision. Are you with our rabbi or against him?"

Sebastian glanced at Felipe and took a deep breath. "With him," he said.

"I'm glad that you're with us," said Aharon de Pinto. "As head of the Maamad, your opinion is very important. So that leaves Rabbi Dominguez, your brother. Rabbi Dominguez, are you with our rabbi or against him?"

"I strongly support our rabbi," said Felipe, "but I strongly oppose this course of action. After the sin of the spies, the Almighty condemned the generation of the Exodus to wander in the Desert for the rest of their lives. But some of them wanted to go and fight for the land anyway to show that they really were loyal to the Almighty. Moshe Rabbeinu told them, 'Why are you disobeying Him? And what you're trying to do won't succeed.'[81] According to Ibn Ezra, Moshe was telling the people that disobeying the Almighty will not bring you favor with Him, even if your intentions are good. If we endorse this Sabbatean charlatan, we will be doing a bad thing for the purpose of protecting the heritage of our community, which is a good thing. It will not be successful. So I am against this course of action."

"Why is it a bad thing?" said Shamai Cohen.

"It's a bad thing, because it's a lie. It suggests that we support this man even though we believe or strongly suspect that he's a Sabbatean. It's a bad thing, because it supports heresy. It suggests we endorse this man's book even though we know in our hearts that it is heretical. And it's a bad thing, because it violates the honor of the Torah by deliberately flaunting a ban issued by the *gadol hador*, regardless of whether he is Sephardic or Ashkenazic. Every way you look at it, it's a bad thing."

"And how about separating yourself from the congregation?" said Shamai. "Is that a good thing? There are five rabbis here, including our chief rabbi, and three members of the Maamad, our leadership council. And we are all agreed that we should do as Rabbi Ayllon said. And you alone stand against it. Is that the right thing to do? Isn't it possible that there is just the slightest bit of arrogance in your attitude?"

Felipe gave Shamai a disdainful look. "The majority may rule, but the minority opinion is still recorded. We do not coerce the person who holds the minority opinion to change his opinion and come over to the side of the majority. Who knows? Maybe some day my opinion will prevail, even if it seems to be in the minority right now."

Rabbi Ayllon tapped on the table. "I think we've reached a resolution, even if Rabbi Dominguez doesn't see eye to eye with the rest of us."

That very night, Rabbi Ayllon sent a message to Chayun at his inn that the Sephardic community would overturn the ban and do its own investigation of his book. A respectful message was sent to Chacham Tzvi, asking him to point out the passages that he found questionable so that the rabbinic committee of investigation appointed by the directorate of the Sephardic community could rule on them. As a further concession, Chacham Tzvi was invited to sit on the committee, but he would only have one vote, just as did everyone else on the commission.

Chacham Tzvi declined the requests and the offers, because he did not recognize the qualifications of Rabbi Ayllon to make an informed and unbiased decision, and he did not want to be exploited to give legitimacy to what he considered was a farce in the making. His refusal to cooperate hardened the antagonism of his opponents in the Sephardic community. It also brought great delight to his enemies in the Ashkenazic community, who saw this controversy as a golden opportunity to bring down Chacham Tzvi and drive him from the city.

The city descended into chaos. Many people in the Sephardic community were outraged at the defiant stance of the leadership against the great and holy Chacham Tzvi, who always spoke with utmost intellectual honesty and rigor. If Chacham Tzvi, one of the leading experts in Kabbalah in the entire generation, declared a book heretical, how could the Sephardic rabbis argue against him?

Many others, however, defended the position of the rabbi and his supporters. Pamphlets had appeared almost overnight explaining the importance of maintaining the integrity and independence of the Sephardic community and its hallowed heritage. The pamphlets were eloquent and played on the fears and pride of the Sephardim, and they were very effective. Although some rabbis and community leaders in the Sephardic community aligned themselves with Chacham Tzvi, the opposition to him was growing.[82]

Rabbi Moshe Chagiz, who had sounded the alarm in the first place, fought valiantly to defend Chacham Tzvi. He stood in the Esnoga, the Portuguese synagogue, surrounded by people shouting angrily at the effrontery of Chacham Tzvi to rule on a Sephardic matter, and he fought with his last ounce of strength to defend and justify Chacham Tzvi's actions.

When two weeks passed and the investigating committee had still not issued a ruling, Chacham Tzvi could wait no longer. It became more and more likely that Chayun's heretical book would not be banned by the Sephardic committee and that it would be printed and published in Amsterdam. This could not be allowed to happen. Chacham Tzvi convened his rabbinical court and placed Chayun in *cherem*, excommunicating him and his writings.

If a fire had raged in Amsterdam before, the pronouncement of the *cherem* fanned the flames even higher. Angry Sephardim threw rocks when Chacham Tzvi and Rabbi Moshe Chagiz passed in the street. They took to staying indoors, because they feared for their lives.

The next day, the committee of investigation issued its report, which had been prepared by Rabbi Ayllon. The report was read publicly in the Esnoga, which was packed wall to wall with Sephardim as well as numerous Ashkenazim. The writings of Chayun, the report stated, had been examined meticulously and found to be free of any trace of heresy. Rabbi Nechemiah Chayun was completely exonerated and the *cherem* issued against him would not be recognized by the Sephardic community. The rabbis of the community hereby issued an enthusiastic endorsement of the book and granted permission for it to be printed in Amsterdam. The following morning, Chayun was received in the Esnoga with pomp and fanfare.

And the battle lines were drawn. Chacham Tzvi's opponents in the Sephardic community aligned themselves with his enemies in the Ashkenazic community to undermine everything he said and did. The battles pitted Sephardim against Sephardim, Sephardim against Ashkenazim and Ashkenazim against Ashkenazim. It pitted brother against brother, neighbor against neighbor and business partners and associates against each other.

And practically every day new incendiary pamphlets appeared. Some of the pamphlets were signed by their authors, but most of them were anonymous pieces of scrap paper printed by disreputable printing shops. The printers could not or would not identify the people who brought in the material for the pamphlets and paid for them. Just nondescript people, they would say. Their money was good, and the work was easy, so why not?

As one day collapsed into the next, the wheels of the glorious community of Amsterdam slowly ground to a halt. The learning in the *yeshivah* was disrupted. Commerce in the Exchange and the marketplaces was ignored. Families and friendships were torn apart. Amsterdam, which had stood for decades as a shining beacon for the Jewish people of Europe, descended into chaos and warfare.

FUEL ON THE FIRE · 22

A S TIME WENT ON, Chacham Tzvi's position went from bad to worse. His support in his own Ashkenazic community steadily eroded as more and more people suffered the consequences of the Sephardic antagonism. Ashkenazic traders who had been doing a brisk business with wealthy Sephardic merchants found that their favorable arrangements and lines of credit had disappeared. Their income dropped drastically, and they were reduced to buying the barest minimum to keep their families alive. This in turn meant a serious loss of business to the Ashkenazic shops and tradesmen they patronized.

The screed of Chacham Tzvi's enemies that had fallen on so many deaf ears previously was now finding receptive audiences. Why, they argued, had their rabbi interfered in the business of the Sephardic community? Didn't he realize that the financial health of the Ashkenazic community depended on good relations with the wealthy Sephardim of Amsterdam?

Chacham Tzvi's following in the Sephardic community also eroded steadily. The Sephardic rabbis and directors, with a few exceptions, had come together to present a united front against Chacham Tzvi, and many of the people who had kissed Chacham Tzvi's hands and asked for his blessings were won over to the side of his antagonists.

The warm welcome extended to Chayun in the Esnoga also had a powerful impact on the people. Chayun was at his best, flamboyant, charismatic and colorful yet humble and self-effacing. He delivered soaring sermons that inspired the people, and he dazzled them with his mystical performances.

Within days, he sold every one of the copies he had brought with him from Berlin, and he also persuaded a few of the wealthier members of the community, with the help of Rabbi Ayllon, to finance the publication of the Amsterdam edition. Within a week after Chayun's rehabilitation, Wieselthier was deeply immersed in the process of printing his book. His instructions were to spare no expense. The people were impressed by the honor and financial support extended to Chayun by the elite of their own community, and they turned away from Chacham Tzvi. Besides, if so many of his own Ashkenazic people had turned against him, why should they continue to support him?

Then there were the cheap sheets and pamphlets published anonymously by both sides of the conflict. New pamphlets appeared every day, but they all followed the same pattern. They reported every bit of gossip and slander that circulated in the streets of Amsterdam in addition to plenty of slanderous assertions about Chacham Tzvi and his supporters that had not been heard anywhere before they appeared in the pamphlets. They also featured eloquent editorials that made impassioned pleas for Chacham Tzvi's removal from office and the restoration of peace in Amsterdam.

The pamphlets that supported Chacham Tzvi followed the same pattern, only they pointed in the other direction. They, too, featured passionate editorials defending their side and attacking the other side. They, too, brought up every bit of gossip and slander they could unearth about Chayun,

Rabbi Ayllon and the leaders of the opposition to Chacham Tzvi and were deliberately designed to fan the flames of hatred smoldering in the hearts of the Sephardim.

In an even more insidious development, prominent individuals in both the Sephardic and Ashkenazic communities began receiving anonymous letters addressed to them personally. The writers of these letters seemed to have a wealth of information about the private lives of these individuals and their personal and business relationships, and therefore, the poisonous falsities and innuendoes that filled these letters had the ring of truth. The letters made outrageously false accusations against Chacham Tzvi and his supporters that could not be substantiated, and they effectively stoked the rage of their recipients. Who was writing these letters? How did he know so much about the people to whom he was writing? No one knew.

As time went on, each side poured so much fuel on the fire that the original cause of the controversy was almost forgotten. The battle became a war between the Sephardim against the Ashkenazim, with a civil war in the Ashkenazic community that was driven by the antagonism of the powerful against their fiercely independent rabbi.

One day, Sebastian visited Rav Amos at home. The two friends had not seen each other since the controversy had begun.

"Are you allowed to come here?" said Rav Amos bitterly. "Aren't you afraid you'll be accused of consorting with the enemy?"

"Look, I'm not responsible for all this," said Sebastian.

"Really? It seems to me that you signed against Chacham Tzvi."

"I didn't have much choice."

"Did you have less choice than Felipe did?" said Rav Amos. "He stood up for his principles. Why couldn't you?"

"Look, I tried to stop this. I said at the meeting that I wasn't comfortable with the proposal and that it didn't seem right to me. But I'm the head of the Maamad. I can't stand against the will of the community. Felipe is just one of the rabbis. He has more freedom than I do."

"Did it ever occur to you, Sebastian, my good friend, that if you had stood up for your principles the will of the community might have been different?"

"You're being sarcastic with me."

"Did it ever occur to you that you should perhaps resign from the Maamad before agreeing to subvert justice?"

Sebastian shook his head. "My position on the Maamad is the crowning achievement of my life. I could not give it up. And besides, if I resigned, the one who replaced me would probably be much more extreme than I am. The best thing is for me to stay on the Maamad and work to keep the actions of the community within the bounds of civility."

"Well, you haven't been successful so far, have you?"

Sebastian studied his fingernails. "You're angry with me, and I can't blame you," he said without looking up, "but are we still friends?"

Rav Amos looked at Sebastian for a long time, then he slowly nodded. "I would like to think we're still friends, but every day this goes on our friendship suffers. If our friendship had not been so deep, who knows if anything would still be left of it?"

"That's why I'm here, my friend. Plenty of friendships and relationships have been destroyed in this fire raging in our beautiful Amsterdam. This used to be such a golden place, such a peaceful, prosperous city. And now look at what it's become. And do you think the Christians in the government are not aware of what's going on in our world?"

"I'm sure they are.

"I know they are," said Sebastian. "And they blame Chacham Tzvi."

"Well, of course they blame Chacham Tzvi," said Rav Amos. "The Sephardim have their ear, and they're pouring all their venom into it. The magistrate used to hold Chacham Tzvi in the highest regard. They refused to hear any litigation between Ashkenazim but instead insisted that they go to Chacham Tzvi. They considered him wise, knowledgeable and incorruptible. Did this opinion change without a little help from your friends?

Sebastian shook his head. "You're right. People have poisoned their minds against Chacham Tzvi."

"Are you one of those people?"

Sebastian flushed. "I find that remark offensive. I would hope you think more highly of me than to suspect me of that."

"You're right," said Rav Amos. "I shouldn't have said that."

"Apology accepted," said Sebastian, his voice trembling with emotion.

He stood up and walked to the window. After a few moments, he recovered his composure and returned to his seat.

"Look at us going at each other like pair of alley cats," he said. "And we're good friends! No matter what, Amos, I will always be your friend. I owe you my life, literally and figuratively. I will always love you with all my heart. But what about all the rest of us here in Amsterdam. How much damage can our beloved city endure? We have to bring this thing to an end."

"I couldn't agree more, but how do we manage that?"

"Let me tell you the reason I'm here," said Sebastian. "I've come to deliver a summons to Chacham Tzvi to appear before a tribunal of the Sephardic community to discuss his past actions and a possible path forward that can restore peace and tranquility to our city."

Rav Amos stared at him. "You must be joking," he said at last.

"I am completely serious."

"By what authority do they issue a summons to Chacham Tzvi?"

"Let's not get legalistic here. If you wish, you can call it an invitation. But I strongly suggest that he come to this tribunal so that we resolve this matter once and for all."

"I can't believe this. He'd never accept this ... this ... invitation, as you call it. They have no right."

"That's why I volunteered to deliver it to you rather than directly to him. I thought we could talk about it and you would see that this is the only reasonable way out of this rotten mess."

"You want me to persuade him to come?"

"Yes. That's about it."

"I refuse," said Rav Amos.

"But why?"

"Because a terrible injustice was done here. A charlatan, a scheming Sabbatean heretic, was embraced just to show defiance against Chacham Tzvi. And what's going to happen at this tribunal? Will this injustice be corrected? Of course not. All that will happen is that Chacham Tzvi will be pressured to retract his *cherem* and accept this evil Chayun as an upstanding rabbi. If you know Chacham Tzvi at all, you know that he'll never do such a thing no matter how much pressure you bring on him. And I certainly won't try to persuade him to do otherwise. Not that it would help if I did."

"But if it really was up to you, what would you do?"

"The same. I would advise him not to back down, not even an inch."

'So where are we headed?" asked Sebastian as he rose to his feet.

"I don't know," said Rav Amos. "I really don't know."

Sebastian extended his hand. "Still friends?"

Rav Amos shook his hand, but his heart wasn't in it.

"Yes," he said. "Still friends."

In November of 1713, a Christian lawyer appeared at the home of Chacham Tzvi and asked to see the rabbi. Chacham Tzvi was sitting in his study and discussing a difficult topic in Gemara with Rav Amos when his son Yaakov announced the Christian lawyer.

"Bring him in," said Chacham Tzvi.

Yaakov turned to leave.

"And, Yaakov," said Chacham Tzvi, "stay in the room while the lawyer is here. You might as well hear this."

"Do you know what he wants?" asked Yaakov.

"I don't know, but it surely another piece of pressure. Tell me, Yaakov. Why do I want you to stay and listen to this? What do I want you to learn?"

"Two things. One, not to bend under pressure."

"Yes. That's what I had in mind. And what is the other?"

"That the Sabbateans will stop at nothing to win."

Chacham Tzvi nodded and smiled. "Yes, you're right. The Sabbateans are dangerous people, and they often masquerade as something they're not. You have to be vigilant against them, Yaakov, because they will continue to plague our people for generations to come." He leaned back and crossed his arms. "Bring in the lawyer."

The lawyer was an extremely tall and lanky Dutchman. He shook hands with Chacham Tzvi and Rav Amos and sat down.

"Rabbi Ashkenazi, I'm so pleased to meet you," he said. "And you, too, Rabbi Strasbourg. I've heard so much about both of you. Here's why I've come .... Oh yes, I should first tell you who I am, shouldn't I?" He chuckled. "My name is Aloysius Alexander Janssen. I'm a licensed advocate here in Amsterdam, and I represent the Portuguese community. I'm here to deliver to you a summons to appear before the directorate of the Portuguese community so that we can bring this whole unfortunate affair to a successful conclusion."[83]

"Thank you," said Chacham Tzvi.

Janssen shook his head in disbelief. "Well, that was easy."

"Then our business is concluded. Good day, sir."

"I will arrange a time convenient for you, rabbi."

"A time for what?"

"A time for your appearance."

"Did I say I was appearing?"

"But you said thank you."

"I thanked you for delivering the summons," said Chacham Tzvi. "Was I required to respond to you?"

"Well, a response would be expected. Will you come?"

"No, I will not."

"I advise you to reconsider."

"Thank you."

"You're thanking me for my advice?"

"Yes."

"You will not reconsider?"

"No."

Janssen shrugged and stood up. "All I can say, rabbi, is that if the Jewish people do not resolve the matter internally, the magistracy of Amsterdam will feel compelled to get involved. The entire city — the entire country — is suffering because of the upheaval in the Jewish community. It cannot be allowed to continue."

"I understand," said Chacham Tzvi. "Believe me, I understand. My son will see you out. Good day, Mijnheer Janssen."

The lawyer bowed politely, put on his hat and followed young Yaakov out of the room.

"What are we going to do?" asked Rav Amos after the door had closed behind Yaakov and the Dutch lawyer. "How will this business ever come to a good conclusion?"

Chacham Tzvi's face was somber. "I don't know, my friend. And I'm not confident that it will. But I do know that I cannot bow to the pressure."

"Would it be so bad to go to Portuguese directorate? Maybe you can reason with them and come up with a face-saving solution. I'm sure they would also like to restore peace to our city."

Chacham Tzvi shook his head. "It wouldn't do any good. It would only do harm. They're not interested in a face-saving solution that removes Chayun and his book. Things have gone too far. They've tasted blood, and they lust for the kill. They want to win on their terms. Otherwise, they won't consider it a victory. They'll pressure me to make some statement that recognizes Chayun as a worthy rabbi even though we all know that he's a venomous snake. And of course, I will refuse. And that will give them even more ammunition against me. They'll say that they tried to negotiate with me but I was unbending and unreasonable. Believe me, my dear Amos, I'm better off not going."

"What if I went in your stead?"

Chacham Tzvi shook his head again. "It would be almost as bad. You and I are seen as one together with Rabbi Moshe Chagiz. Such a courageous man! I really admire him. No, we have to stand firm on our principles, and whatever happens happens. When all is said and done, the Almighty runs the world. Our responsibility is to fulfill His will. And of this I have no doubt whatsoever. He does not want us to come out in favor of Chayun. No, we wait and pray."

Rav Amos sighed and the two men sat together in companionable silence for a long time, each lost in his own thoughts.

"You know," said Rav Amos at last. "I'm reminded of that old woman who spoke to me in the wagon on the way to Budapest. I told you about it."

Rav Amos smiled. "Your midnight intruders? Yes, I remember them. You thought that the old woman was delivering a divine message to you."

"And you said it was probably true."

"I remember. I would say that Chayun certainly turned out to be a midnight intruder. He masqueraded as a genuine rabbi and won the favor of many people, even though he's really a Sabbatean. But he's been unmasked already. So what are you saying? Do you think there are more midnight intruders involved in our troubles here in Amsterdam?"

"Yes, I think there are. Many rumors are being spread by anonymous pamphlets, and I've heard that there are poisonous anonymous letters being delivered to some of the most prominent people in our city."

"Yes, I know all about them. We certainly have some determined enemies who are doing everything they can to destroy us. But midnight intruders, as you explained it to me then, are trusted people who stab you in the back. Do you think all this poison is coming from people we trust? Do you think some of the few supporters left to us are actually midnight intruders? Do you think that your friend Sebastian Dominguez may be behind it?"

"No, I don't think Sebastian would do such a thing," said Rav Amos. "The person — or persons — doing this has a strong mean streak, which Sebastian doesn't have. He is not as strong as he should be, but he's a good person."

"If you say so. In any case, if the thought of the midnight intruders came to you now, we should be especially vigilant — with our friends as well as with our enemies."

A few weeks later, in light of Chacham Tzvi's continued refusal to appear, the Portuguese tribunal issued a *cherem* against Chacham Tzvi and Rabbi Moshe Chagiz. Rav Amos breathed a sigh of relief that they had not included him in the *cherem*, and it occurred to him that he had Sebastian to thank for the omission.

The matter now moved into the Dutch municipal courts. The magistrates obtained several copies of Chayun's book and sent them off to Christian professors in Leiden and Utrecht. A copy was also sent to Willem Surenhuis, a professor of Hebrew and Oriental languages at the Athenaeum Illustre in Amsterdam, who had translated the Mishnah into Latin. In the meantime, until they could form an opinion of Chayun's book, the magistrates ordered that Chacham Tzvi remain in his home for his own protection.

THE DEATHBED CONFESSION · 23

O N A STORMY NIGHT IN January of 1714, Sebastian's black carriage rolled up to Rav Amos' house in the Ashkenazic neighborhood alongside the Herrengracht. Sebastian stepped out into the driving rain and banged on the door. There was no immediate answer, and Sebastian banged again. Finally, there was a stirring inside, and Rav Amos opened the door. He was wearing a robe, and his eyes were bleary with interrupted sleep.

"Sebastian!" he exclaimed. "What are you doing here?"

"Come quickly. There's no time to waste."

"But it's well past midnight. Where are we going?"

"We'll talk on the way. Get dressed. I'll wait for you in the carriage."

When Rav Amos came down minutes later, all the sleep was gone from his eyes, replaced with worry and anxiety.

"What happened, Sebastian? Where are we going?"

"We're going to see a dying man."

Rav Amos sat bolt upright. He could hardly breathe. "Who?" he finally managed to say.

"The German printer," said Sebastian. "Hans Gunther Wieselthier."

Rav Amos was confused. "What are you talking about? Why is he dying? And why are you taking me to see him?"

"He fell off a printing press today," said Sebastian, "and he broke many bones. You can imagine when a man of that size falls the impact must be tremendous. The doctor says he probably has massive internal bleeding, and that there is nothing he can do. The man is dying."

"That's very sad. And how are you involved?"

"It happened in Moshe Diaz's shop, and he asked me to find him a good doctor, which I did. When the doctor said there was nothing to do, I arranged to have him brought back to his inn and made comfortable during his last hours on this earth."

"I see," said Rav Amos. "And how am I involved here?"

"He asked to see you."

"Me? Are you sure?"

"Yes, I'm sure."

"But why?"

"He wouldn't say."

"He said nothing?"

"He said it was matter of life and death."

"Life and death?"

"Yes, life and death," said Sebastian. "Why do you keep repeating everything I say?"

"Because I'm confused," said Rav Amos. "What does he have to do with me? And what is a matter of life and death?"

"We'll find out soon enough."

Wieselthier lay on his bed under a thin blanket. His normally ruddy face was deathly pale. His eyes were open, and he was wide awake. He lay rigidly motionless, as if paralyzed by the fear that any movement would cause him incredible pain.

"Thank you for coming, Rabbi Strasbourg," he said.

"Do you want me to leave?" said Sebastian.

He tried to shake his head but winced with the pain. "No, I want you to stay. Both of you should hear what I have to say. You might as well sit down. It'll take a little while, unless I die first."

Sebastian and Rav Amos pulled up chairs and sat down.

"So where do I begin?" began Wieselthier. "Let me get straight to the point, and then I'll go back and explain. The Jewish community of Amsterdam, both parts of it, is going up in flames, so to speak, and I am responsible for a lot of what's going on."

"You?" said Rav Amos. "What do you have to do with anything?"

"Be patient, rabbi. You met me a few years ago, and I mentioned that you had pages and pages of Torah writings that you might want to publish some day. How did I know such a thing?"

"If I recall correctly," said Rav Amos, "you said you'd heard about it."

"You remember correctly," said Wieselthier. "But how would a Christian printer from Berlin hear such a thing? The question didn't occur to you, because you were pleased. And then I offered to help you publish your writings, and any suspicion you might have had about me was instantly gone. Of course, I never had any intention of doing such a thing. I just wanted to immobilize you with regard to me. And I did. It never occurred to you afterward that I might not be exactly what I said I am."

"Very well, you fooled me," said Rav Amos, "now you've confessed on your deathbed. I hope your conscience is relieved. But what does this have to do with Amsterdam?"

"Everything, rabbi. I know about you because my agents have been gathering information about the Jewish community of Amsterdam for years. I know more about what goes on in Amsterdam than anyone living here. I know what all the important people are doing and how they are connected to each other. And I know the secrets they don't want anyone to know."

"Your agents?" said Sebastian. "Those people snooping around Amsterdam for years and years were your agents?"

"Yes."

"But they've been coming around for over twenty years! Maybe twenty-five, I don't remember exactly. They were all your people?"

"Yes."

"And Duvid'l Goldberg, who showed up about three years ago, he was also your agent?"

"Yes. Of course, he didn't know it. I always worked through layers and layers to protect my identity. Oh, I know that the two of you captured and interrogated him, but what did you find out? Nothing, because he knew nothing. Whatever you say about me, you have to admit that I'm clever."

"But why?" said Sebastian. "Why did you do all this?"

"Because I wanted to destroy the Jewish community of Amsterdam. And I believe I was successful. Now, I'm not saying that none of this would have happened without my manipulations behind the scenes. It probably would have. But I discovered Chayun, and I steered him to Amsterdam. He might have come here anyway, but my people whispered to him that he really ought to go to Amsterdam. And they did it in such a subtle way that he thought it was his own idea. I went to Amsterdam five years ago with the group that printed the prayer book to establish my credentials in the community, as I did with you, Rabbi Strasbourg."

"You're insane," said Rav Amos.

"I may be mad, but I'm not insane. So I manipulated Chayun into bringing me with him to Amsterdam, and everyone was so focused on him that they didn't even see me. Even though I'm as big as a barn, I was practically invisible." Wieselthier stopped to catch his breath. "Could I trouble you for a glass of water? This isn't easy for me."

Sebastian got up and poured him a glass of water from a jug on the table. Wieselthier took the glass and brought it to his lip with trembling fingers. Most of the water spilled over his beard and chest, but some of it found its way into his mouth. A tiny touch of color returned to his cheeks.

"So where was I?" continued Wieselthier. "Ah yes, I came to Amsterdam with Chayun, and I gave him subtle advice and encouragement without him realizing it. And when the battle started I was ready. My people wrote the pamphlets and distributed them. And they wrote all those anonymous letters that were so effective in setting people against each other. All my years of investigation paid off in those letters. I knew everything, all the dirty secrets, and I used every one of them." His eyes gleamed with the memory of what he had done. "I didn't start this fire, but I made sure that it burned with tremendous intensity."

"But why?" said Sebastian. "What did Amsterdam do to you? Why do you hate us so much? I mean to plot and scheme for twenty-five years. You must be out of your mind."

Rav Amos leaned forward and stared at Wieselthier, and a light of recognition appeared in his eyes.

"Ah, I see that Rabbi Strasbourg is beginning to see the light," said Wieselthier with obvious delight. "You recognize me, don't you, Rabbi Strasbourg? As long as I was invisible you couldn't recognize me. But now you do, don't you?"

"Yes, I recognize you," said Rav Amos softly.

"What are you talking about?" said Sebastian. He turned to Rav Amos. "Who is this man? And why did he do all this?"

Rav Amos looked into Sebastian's eyes. "He is Sergio Setubal."

Sebastian was thunderstruck. He jumped to his feet and shrank back.

"Yes, Senhor Dominguez," said Wieselthier. "I am Sergio Setubal. I was once engaged to your mother, may she rest in peace. Thirty years ago, I tried to take revenge against you and your family for a grave injustice your father had committed against me in Spain, but I was not successful. I was exposed in public and humiliated in front of the entire community. I don't have to tell you the story.[84] You know the sordid details as well as I do. But I was clever. I had built a secret tunnel under my house, and I managed to escape. I still had plenty of money in different cities in Europe. So I set out to build a new identity and plan my revenge. But this time the revenge would be not against the Dominguez family but against all the Jews of Amsterdam."

"You are out of your mind," said Sebastian.

Wieselthier smile and winced with pain. "So first of all I needed a disguise. I worked hard to remove any trace of a Spanish accent from the German language I spoke. Rabbi Strasbourg very astutely did detect a faint trace, but I told him that my mother had been Italian, and he accepted that. Then I had to disguise my face and my body. I used to be a slim handsome fellow with a trimmed red beard. But now I'm ridiculously fat, with a bloated red face and an enormous white beard. I don't think my own mother would recognize me. So I concealed my identity, and I schemed and plotted against the Jews of Amsterdam, and I succeeded."

"So you called us here to gloat?" said Rav Amos.

"No, I'm afraid not," said Wieselthier. "I've spent the last thirty years of my life plotting my revenge. I ate it and drank it and dreamed about it, and it gave me tremendous pleasure. But now that I saw the fruits of my labors, I began to have some doubts about what I'd done. Many of those who were hurt and destroyed, including Chacham Tzvi, are good people, and if I were really truthful with myself, I had to admit that they didn't deserve the pain I inflicted on them. And today, when I had my little accident and realized that my life was at its end, and that I would shortly be going to meet my Maker, I felt a remorse for my deeds that I never thought I'd feel."

He stopped to catch his breath. He shuddered with a sudden spasm of coughs, and a trickle of blood appeared on his lips.

"I had thirty years left to me when I fled from Amsterdam," he said. "Thirty years. That's a lot of time. A whole lifetime. I could have enjoyed them. I could have lived out my years in comfort and luxury. I could have traveled all over the world. I could have listened to music and read fine literature and studied art. Perhaps I could have married and raised a family. I was still young enough to do it. But instead, I devoted my time to an obsession with revenge. And in the end, I'm left with nothing. I thought I was successful, but today I realized that I'm a miserable failure."

"I believe you were a secret Catholic when you were in Amsterdam," said Rav Amos. "You should be making your confession to a Catholic priest. What do you want from us? Do you want us to forgive you for the unforgivable crime you've committed against our people?"

"No, rabbi, I don't expect you to do that. I don't even think you have the right to do that. But I want a little bit of redemption. I want to be able to come before my Maker and say that I did something to mitigate the damage I caused. That is why I called you here."

Rav Amos and Sebastian remained silent, waiting for him to continue.

"I'm dying," said Wieselthier. "I could die any minute, and by the morning, I will surely be gone. So I want to give you an important piece of information ..."

"Go on," said Rav Amos.

"Tomorrow morning, the Dutch authorities will arrest Chacham Tzvi and Rabbi Chagiz. They will be brought to trial on charges of sedition and fomenting unrest, and they will be punished."

"How do you know this?" said Rav Amos.

Wieselthier tried to laugh, but the movement was too painful. "It's about time you realized that I know everything. And I have to take a little credit for this arrest. A few well-planted letters turned Chacham Tzvi's admirers against him, and the rest was easy. You, Rabbi Strasbourg, are fortunate that there is no arrest warrant for you. Your friend here kept your name off the Portuguese *cherem*, so the charges do not extend to you. But Chacham Tzvi and Rabbi Chagiz will be arrested. I'm telling you this so that you can take steps to protect —"

A new spasm of coughing wracked his body, and he writhed in pain. A flow of blood appeared at his mouth and stained his white beard crimson. His eyes widened with fright, as if they had perceived a terrible sight. He looked around with wild desperation. His entire body trembled one last time, and then he lay still.

The following morning, Dutch constables appeared at the homes of Chacham Tzvi and Rabbi Chagiz with arrest warrants in hand, but they found no one home. Chacham Tzvi and his entire family and Rabbi Chagiz had fled Amsterdam in the middle of the night.[85]

ENDNOTES

1. Kiddushin 31b.
2. Mishneh Torah, Malveh Veloveh 22:6.
3. Kesubos 91b.
4. Avos 2:15.
5. *Megillas Sefer* p. 21.
6. Ibid.
7. *Megillas Sefer* pp. 21-22.
8. Ibid.
9. Sanhedrin 65b; *She'alos Uteshuvos Chacham Tzvi* 93.
10. *Megillas Sefer* pp. 22-23.
11. *Megillas Sefer* p. 25.
12. Mishlei 12:25.
13. *Megillas Sefer* p. 26.
14. Ibid.
15. Mishlei 13:23.
16. Chagigah 4b.
17. *Megillas Sefer* pp. 23-25.
18. Ibid.
19. *She'alos Uteshuvos Chacham Tzvi* 168.
20. *Megillas Sefer* p. 26.
21. Gittin 62a.
22. *Megillas Sefer* p. 27.
23. Shemos 14:15.
24. Author of *She'alos Uteshuvos Dvar Shmuel.*
25. *Megillas Sefer* p. 35.
26. *Megillas Sefer* p. 27.
27. Bereishis 41:33.
28. Bereishis 41:4-5.
29. Bereishis 41:21-22.

30. *Megillas Sefer* p. 27; the name of the Huungarian noble-man is not mentioned, however.
31. Pesachim 50a.
32. I Shmuel 1:2.
33. II Melachim 2:14.
34. *Megillas Sefer* p. 28.
35. Ibid.
36. Ibid.
37. Avos 4:5.
38. Devarim 1:17.
39. *Megillas Sefer* p. 32.
40. *Megillas Sefer* pp. 38-39.
41. *Megillas Sefer* p. 37.
42. *Megillas Sefer* pp. 29-39.
43. *Megillas Sefer* pp. 38-39.
44. *Megillas Sefer* p. 32.
45. Ibid.
46. Ibid.
47. *Megillas Sefer* p. 33.
48. Ibid.
49. *Megillas Sefer* pp. 33-34.
50. *Megillas Sefer* p. 29.
51. The followers of Shabbesai Tzvi.
52. *Megillas Sefer* p. 51.
53. *She'alos Uteshuvos Chacham Tzvi* 1.
54. *She'alos Uteshuvos Chacham Tzvi* 13.
55. Pesachim 64b.
56. Community director.
57. A reference to an episode in *The Fur Traders*, the previous book in the Strasbourg Saga.
58. A reference to an episode in *Scandal in Amsterdam*, a previous book in the Strasbourg Saga.
59. The original name of Brooklyn.
60. *Megillas Sefer* p. 40.

61. *Megillas Sefer* p. 41.

62. *Megillas Sefer* pp. 41-42.

63. Malachi 3:10; Shabbos 32b.

64. *She'alos Uteshuvos Chacham Tzvi* 74-75.

65. This information is drawn from the title page and Rabbi Kalisch's *haskamah* in the first printing of *Siddur Ohr Hayashar* in Amsterdam in 1709.

66. *Megillas Sefer* pp. 40-44.

67. *Megillas Sefer* p. 45.

68. Ibid.

69. Mishneh Torah, Hilchos Shechitah 1:14.

70. *Megillas Sefer* pp. 46-47.

71. *Megillas Sefer* pp. 47-50.

72. *Megillas Sefer* p. 46.

73. Ibid.

74. Ibid.

75. Gittin 62a.

76. According to the Chida, Moshe Chayun, Nechemiah Chayun's father, was a son-in-law of Rabbi Yaakov Chagiz.

77. *Megillas Sefer* p. 51.

78. According to the secular sources, it is possible that Chacham Tzvi and Chayun knew each other from Sarajevo and that they had a personal confrontation in Amsterdam. Rabbi Yaakov Emden, however, makes no mention of these events in *Megillas Sefer*. Nonetheless, our story does incorporate a fictional adaptation of these events.

79. Aharon de Pinto is a historical character.

80. *Megillas Sefer* pp. 52-53.

81. Bamidbar 14:41.

82. *Megillas Sefer* p. 53.

83. *Megillas Sefer* p. 54.

84. This refers to events described in *Scandal in Amsterdam*, a pervious book in the Strabourg Saga.

85. *Megillas Sefer* p. 54.